The Waterglass War

Jasper Dorgan

Published by New Generation Publishing in 2020

First Edition

ISBN: 978-1-80031-886-1

www.newgeneration-publishing.com

New Generation Publishing

PART ONE

ONE

The feeling that she was being followed began as a fleeting, breezed kiss on the back of her neck, like a feather's lightest touch. It made her shiver.

Georgia pulled her coat collar tighter, shouldered her bag close and shuffled with the other office workers along the crowded early evening streets of Aldwych and the Strand. Clouds of night hung like slate in the London skies, offering a promise of rain and a bad weather prayer that, tonight, the bombers might not come.

It had been another long and tiring day of duty at Bush House and Georgia was too weary and hungry to think beyond walking. But the feather's kiss had woken her from her torpor. She tried to shrug it off as mere imaginings and to convince herself that she was being ridiculous and fanciful, but she knew that it was not a fancy at all. She knew she was being followed.

She queued with the crowd now squeezing along Fleet Street, negotiating the narrowed road and the rubble that spewed the street. Two large craters were cordoned off on one side of the road where fractured gas mains and electricity cables thrust up from their underground tombs like skeletal fingers clutching desperately for air. She used the stillness to glance behind her but could find nothing of alarm. An ambulance siren wailed somewhere along The Mall. The evening smelt of wet clay and gas and smouldering timber. The smell of London at war.

Georgia paced on with the head-down crowd. It was when she glanced into the window of Robinson's Tobacconist and saw those following reflected that she noticed the man. His head erect and hunting while all those about him were slouched. He ducked quickly back into the crowd and was lost in its swell.

But Georgia had recognised him. And in that instant she knew that she was to die.

Horst Blucher had been one of Ernst's hunting band of

brothers. One of the gang of jagd-bruder who had trucked the grasslands of Natal with Ernst at their head, hunting game and danger in tanned knee-high boots and killing anything that flew, fled or bounded before them. Horst was a crack rifle shot with cold eyes and meanness for bones. A man who liked killing, even relished it, and the looming war had been excuse enough to encourage him in the practice and to loosen his already slack morality. Warthog, gazelle, or farm-hand black, it never mattered to Horst. Georgia had seen him bull-whip a native bearer to death for dropping his hunting rifle in a mud bank. Horst was a constant at Ernst's side in all his hunting trips along the Keiskamma Valley and Drakensburg lands of South Africa. Horst had been one of the gang who had crowded around the bed while her husband Ernst had raped her. Horst had pinned her down as if clamping on to a feisty, kicking steer ready for branding. He had whooped and hollered as Ernst took his pleasure. Horst had even fondled some of his own. Georgia could never forget Horst.

Surely she must have imagined him, dreamt him as a returning nightmare, for it was impossible that Horst could be in London. South African Germans could never make it into England in this time of war, let alone be free to walk the London streets. But Georgia had learned to trust her instincts. It *was* Horst. And because her husband Ernst had ordered her dead the faithful Horst would see it done, and take pleasure in doing it.

Georgia entered a small shop to the tinkle of the bell and took a moment to look back down the street through the half-boarded window. Horst was there, drifting with the crowd. He raised his head momentarily and then slid into the shadow of an alley and leaned to the wall, watching the shop.

The shop was a haberdasher. Its shelves were sparse with dull brown wools and duller brown patch-cloths. Two outsize knitting needles stood on a dusty corner counter as an advertisement for Campbell Knitwear. Georgia deftly removed one of the needles and slipped it into her bag. An elderly proprietor emerged from behind a back-room curtain.

"Can I help you, madam?" he said. His hair was white and caramel, swept back. He had only one arm. His cardigan's redundant sleeve was tucked into its pocket.

"I think not," she said, "Sorry to have disturbed you." She made for the door.

"It is good to be disturbed occasionally," said the old man, "It tells me I'm still alive." He chuckled to himself and returned behind the curtain.

Stepping back into the street, Georgia's only plan was to keep among the crowds for as long as possible and to give herself time to think out what to do after that. She had taken barely a dozen paces when her wrist was grasped and pinned at her back, a strong hand gripped her by the throat and she was barged sideways into an alley. She was shove-dragged into its deeper shadows and then thrust hard against the brick wall, choking as the hand at her throat squeezed tighter. Slowly the hand relaxed its grip and she coughed air back into her lungs. Horst was holding a dagger at her throat. He laughed.

"Going to struggle like last time, Gee Gee? It does no good. You know that. But holler like you did then and you die. Slow and messy. Nod to understand."

Georgia nodded curtly. She iced her brain, thinking of options, shaping their outcomes. Trying not to scream.

Horst pressed himself on her. He smelt of tobacco and cabbage.

"Where's the baby? Ernst's baby."

"There is no baby."

Horst snorted and, releasing her wrist, he slapped her hard across the face before wrapping his hand around her throat again.

"Liar," he said. "We know there was a baby. Don't lie, English bitch." He slapped her again. Georgia hardly felt its sting. "There was a baby. Your maid Mizzie told us. After she was persuaded. Only took two of her fingers. Tough little bitch for a darkie. We know you were with child.

3

When you ran."

Georgia stared at him coldly.

"The baby died. On the passage back to England. There was no doctor on the ship, no medicines. It was a packet boat. He died after three days. There is no baby."

Horst studied her. He seemed to sense that she was speaking the truth.

"So it was a boy. And he's dead. That will not please Ernst. And I get to kill you. Now that will please him."

"Kill me and they'll hunt you down," she said. "A German can't hide in England. They will hang you."

Horst laughed. He pressed harder against her, his hand unclasping from her throat to fall to her breast.

"Stupid English. I am not German. I am a Dutchman. Jan van Troost. Working with the Flemish trade office. Here in the very centre of their decadent, rotting Empire. The English will never catch me, they are too stupid. The only one who can tell them is you." He slipped his hand inside her coat and squeezed her breast. His hunting knife glinted beside her eye. "And I don't think you will get the chance. So plenty of time to renew old friendships in the meantime. Eh, Gee Gee?"

Horst was un-buttoning his fly, and then his hand sought under her skirt. He began slavering at her face and neck in urgent, nuzzling gasps. Georgia tried to focus only on the discreet movement of her hand gently opening her bag and reaching inside to search, locate and clutch slowly around the knitting needle. Horst licked at her neck, his fingers burning her crotch. Georgia fisted the needle tight. Horst was tearing at her knickers. He brought his face to hers and grinned.

"Might as well enjoy your dying, bitch."

"I intend to," she said and smiled.

Horst bent to kiss her face while loosening his pants. Georgia let her left hand softly trace Horst's ribs and her fingers brushed lightly over his belly. She focused all the hate, rage and energy she could muster and then thrust her right fist up hard into his chest. An electric wave rippled

4

through her arm as the twelve-inch knitting needle lanced deep and hungry under his ribs and she felt it goring up through flesh and burst into his dark heart.

A look of surprise froze Horst's features and a guttural rasp tore the air from him. He sank slowly to his knees before her, his hand sliding heavy and limp down her sleeve, his mouth opening and closing on no sounds, as he slithered down her body.

Georgia stood panting, her hand shaking in spasm and viscous red with blood. Horst was still on his knees, clutching his guts as if in prayer. He didn't seem to be moving. Georgia shoved him over with her knee. Horst thumped senseless to the cobbles like a dropped sack of coal, the hunting knife clattering from his lifeless hand.

Georgia squatted down against the comforting solid, cold of the alley wall. Her hand was shaking violently and was gloved in blood. She ripped a cigarette from a crumpled pack and rammed it to her lips and lit it with fervent need. She drew in the smoke as if trying to drown in it and felt it burn through her. Her body spasm eased to shudders and she watched the cigarette dancing manically in the hand before her.

She remained there, smoking, until the calm settled and the sound of traffic and London streets crept back into the dark alley. A light rain began to fall. She became aware of an overwhelming feeling of exhilaration and dread sweeping through her. She had killed someone, and with her own hands. It surprised her how thrilling she had found it, how the sense of it thrilled her still, she smelt its echo, tasted its savage sweetness, felt the ripple of death shiver through her.

She leant against the alley wall and silently laughed and sobbed until there were no tears left to shed and the last waves of pleasure and relief had ebbed away into the dark. All that was left was the cold light of recognition that she had killed, and the knowledge that her life had sunk to the very deepest of depths where even the lights of hope and forgiveness could not reach, and never would.

She wiped her bloodied hand off on Horst's shirt, stood up, brushed her clothes and hair back to presentable and strode unsteadily out of the alley to find a policeman.

TWO

Jack Summers read aloud the story about the castle and the forest fairies and watched his daughter Dora drift gently to sleep in Mrs Maynard's lap. Ma Maynard, her fleshy forearms cradling Dora tight to her, drifted in open-mouthed slumber with her.

The small, curtain-partitioned rooms of their temporary home were prematurely dark from the afternoon-drawn blackout curtains and under the cave-like curve of the hut's tin roof the space was comfortingly calm and still. Outside in the street he could hear the rumble of traffic and the sound of big-band music drifting from a neighbour's radio in a nearby hut.

Summers closed the storybook and enjoyed the moment of peaceful relief that always came to him at this time. Getting Dora to sleep early was the only way to keep the night terror of bombs from her, to keep at bay the nightmare that visited her every time the rumble of aircraft drummed in the skies. Dora's three young classmates had been wiped from the world in a bomber raid as if they were just chalked dates on the school blackboard. They visited Dora often, whenever the planes came. Dora had lost her friends and Summers had lost his home in the raid but Dora and Ma Maynard had been safe in the shelter.

They'd been lucky, maybe even blessed. Now they lived together in the council pre-fabs with the other bombed-out families. It was cramped and damp but at least they lived. Once asleep Dora slept like a stone and even the drone of planes would not wake her. But if they came while she was awake she wouldn't sleep. She would be sobbing and clutching him all night through, her small fingers clinging to him like talons.

Mrs Maynard stirred. She pushed an errant strand of grey hair from her eye and checked on Dora.

"Reckon she's deep enough for bed now," she said.

Summers lifted Dora from her lap and took her into the

bed space behind the curtain and laid her down. Dora slept on.

Ma was at the small stove pouring tea when he returned to the room.

"Has Dora been coughing much today?" he asked.

"She's just a little tired and worn out. That's all. There's nothing to worry over, Jack. Young'uns are always sniffling."

Summers picked up his night bag and checked it through one last time. He knew that Dora's bad chest was in part due to the dampness of the hut but their squalid living wasn't going to change while the war raged.

He noticed a crumpled small envelope on the hearth stone by the stove and picked it up. Inside was a small white feather.

Ma snatched it from him and put in the fire door of the stove. She handed him a hot mug of tea.

"When did that arrive?" he asked. He let the enamel heat of the mug burn through his hands.

"This morning. Pinned to the door. I thought I'd burnt it."

It hadn't taken the neighbourhood long to find out about his dishonourable discharge from the army. The feathers had been fluttering through his letterbox or sneaking into his work coat pockets for almost a year. The cold shoulders and sneers for just as long. His factory workmates didn't speak to him, Ma even had to buy his tobacco.

"Must have enough for a pillow by now," said Summers.

"Don't take heed by it, Jack, it's just people being a little crazy. It's the war. Makes fools of everyone. People not in their right minds. You have to just forget it."

Summers gazed at Ma. She had never shunned him like the others, or refused to talk to him. Ma had always believed in him, that he didn't shirk the army because he was a depraved coward. She had known him too long to think otherwise.

"There's no forgetting, Ma, there's only coping."

"You look tired."

"Everyone looks tired."

"Night work again?" she said.

"Yes. A manual needs translating by Friday. Probably a triple shift."

He sipped his tea. Ma had put rum in it. He gulped a mouthful and let it burn on.

"You OK to see Dora to school?" he said, "If it turns into a long shift."

"Do you have to ask?"

Summers knew he didn't. Ma had been looking after him and Dora since before Beth died and after his army discharge. Ma had lost her home alongside theirs. Good friends like Ma were as precious as gold and, in war, rarer than oranges. So he knew he didn't have to ask, but he knew he had to send her a signal. That there was a chance he might be gone for a while longer than just school.

Ma handed him a small parcel of greaseproof paper.

"A sandwich and a couple of chicken oysters. Make sure you eat them. They say there's more raids tonight. Be careful."

"I always am," he said.

Ma gave him a peck on his cheek. "I'm away to sit with Dora. Maybe start that pillow. Just take care, Jack. And don't heed any fools."

Summers waited until the bedroom curtain was closed behind Ma and then propped the envelope containing fifty pounds against the radio. Something to get by for a few days in case he was delayed. His work shift tonight was not at the factory, it was a long cycle ride to his old army station at Camp Bledsoe, the headquarters of the Southern Strategic Command. He was going to rob Colonel Redmond's safe. It would not be without its risks.

THREE

Hildy nestled her shoulder against the warmth of the cow's flank and teased the flow of milk from the burgeoning udder with practiced and gentle hands. The milk spurted into the bucket in rhythmic hissing bursts. Her dog Jip lay at her feet in the straw.

The aroma of dung, grease and cut grass filled the shed and Hildy's breath steamed in the early morning air. The day was beckoning to be fair and hot which meant she would have to get started on cutting Upper Meadow field and hope that her father never found out, and that Davey and Gethyn wouldn't tell him.

As if invading her thoughts she heard Jip make a low growl of warning and, without turning to see, knew it was the two farmhands entering the shed in a slovenly shuffle to take voyeuristic stand in the doorway behind her. They always did. Hildy continued milking, hoping they would go away and knowing that they wouldn't.

"That's a fine squeeze you got going there, Miss Hildy."

She heard the nasal giggle and knew it was Davey. His short, round frame would be jigging with his giggles, his acned nose trailing the usual morning snot snail.

"Anytime you need more practice, miss," joined Gethyn, "I'm willing to offer." There were more giggles. Gethyn was probably rubbing his crotch.

Hildy turned on her stool and faced the two men. They stopped whatever it was they were doing and stood upright against the shed door. They were more boys than men, not much older than Hildy, but they were fox sly, chicken stupid and slug slow. Hildy smiled at them.

"I'd get more practice on a button mushroom than anything you little boys might have," she said. The smile switched off. "Why aren't you up at May field separating Bruno from the herd?"

Davey and Gethyn had come to the farm from Wales. Escaping the threat of working hard coal in treacherous mines they had headed for the English shires and become farmhands. It was the only way to flee the mines and avoid the dangers of call up and fighting. They knew nothing of farming, but they were cheap. That was enough for her father to have taken them on. It was Hildy's lot to have to suffer them. And to boss them. They were a surly and leering crew.

"Well?"

"Bruno don't want to play," Gethyn said. "Can't shift the bugger."

"Don't want to leave his 'arim. Can't blame him now can 'ee." Davey snickered.

They all heard her father's shout crack the morning air like a cannon.

"Here!"

Davey and Gethyn stepped further inside the barn, out of view of the farmhouse. Hildy rose from her stool and headed out into the courtyard.

"Wait here until I come back," she said.

She stood in the cobbled courtyard looking up at her father who was sitting in his usual perch at his bedroom window. He held the farm folder in one hand and his shotgun lay ready across his lap. Her father gazed down at Hildy with his usual stern and hostile gaze. It was a look she had seen all of her life – her father's unwavering disappointment that Hildy had been born a girl, or even born at all. She wondered if he had ever seen her at all, or even if knew her name anymore.

"Where them damn Welsh mules? Supposed to be lifting me to my chair quarter hour since."

"They're up at May field, separating Bruno. I'll send them over."

"And be quick about it. Milking done?"

"Yes."

"Not before time."

Her father consulted the file in his hand, the farm orders of the day.

"Check the corn sacks, them rats will have the lot as soon

as not. Mules can fix the barn roof. I'll watch 'em from here so there'll be no sliding away to fill their guts on my cider. Fencing needs checking and mending up at long field. Got that?"

"Yes."

"And if them bastards from the County come again I want you to bring 'em right here to the courtyard below my window where I can fill their guts with buckshot. You hear!" Her father raised his gun and shook his fist in the air. "Straight here, understand?"

"Yes."

"And I want rabbit for supper. Stew. See to it."

Hildy returned to the cow shed. Davey and Gethyn were grinning like schoolboys in the shadows.

"Get your orders, Miss Hildy?" Gethyn said.

"Not going to smack that nice seat of yours is he, miss?" said Davey.

Hildy ignored them, they were just too pathetic. She had learned to let their suggestive banter slide over her and to deal with them in her own way.

"What's the trouble with Bruno?"

"He just don't want to come," Davey said.

"Or rather he does!" chuckled Gethyn. "Them cows an awful tempt for such a bull as Bruno."

"Tried everything, but he won't budge from them or that field."

"Follow me," Hildy said. "Come Jip."

Bruno was standing massive in May field and snorting the air about him. A small herd of cows grazed in one corner of the field. Hildy stood at the gate and saw the tie-rope still damp from the morning dew. The gate not been opened that morning, Gethyn and Davey must have just called from the fence, too chicken to go to Bruno in the field.

"You haven't even tried, have you?" Hildy said.

"He's dangerous that thing!" Gethyn said, "Stupid, big brute of an animal like that. Can't trust it."

"And all stoked up with the want of cows and that. He was going wild. Snorting and hoofing the ground. I ain't dying for no cow."

"You're not dying for anything, are you boys?"

Gethyn bridled a little.

"Doing important war work us," he said. "You saying we're cowards?"

"Down to your cloven hooves," she said.

For a moment she thought that Gethyn might try to hit her but she knew he wouldn't. Gethyn might be bigger than her, but he was a coward and more than a little afraid of what Hildy might do in return. And Jip was sitting alert and ready to defend her, his teeth part-bared. Gethyn hesitated. Hildy might not be much more than nineteen years old, quite slim and a woman but she had a strength and determination that belied her frame and sex. Hildy knew she passed fair in a frock and was even quite comely in a land-girl way, and she also knew she could hurl a hay bale further than either of these two mules could ever spit. And Jip had sharp teeth. Gethyn returned to a wounded calm.

"Yeah, well, easy for you 'cos you don't have to go in the field and get him. You're so clever and brave, you do it."

Bruno snorted again and shook his huge head so that the sun glinted on his nose ring and flies erupted in small sparking clouds from his back.

Hildy felt her life's frustrations and disappointments bubble through her. She wondered if she would ever get to live her own life, to feel the excitement of it, maybe even to meet a real man. She was stuck on the farm with her angry, crippled father and cowardly farmhand dregs while the dazzle and thrill of the war was happening all about her, even in the skies. It was everywhere but she could not touch it or be part of it. The farm imprisoned her just as the intern camp up the valley imprisoned its German civilians. Hildy felt trapped and useless, that her life was speeding past her and leaving nothing in its wake. Only the drudgery and hard work of the farm and the thunder-threatening cloud of her father's hatred of her, his crushed legs and everything there had ever been or was. Hildy hated herself for hating him so.

13

She missed her mother so much.

Hildy searched in the knick-knacks pocket of her trousers. The pocket where she kept the flotsam and jetsam of possible useful things. Her hand emerged with a piece of string, a pebble with a hole in it, a marble, a small whistle, a compass, a penknife, a large blue handkerchief and a pencil stub. She took the hanky and re-pocketed the rest. Hildy lifted the length of chain from the gate post and strode into the field. Davey and Gethyn hastily closed the gate behind her. Bruno raised his head and watched Hildy advance. The bull adjusted its stance and lowered its head, ready to charge. Hildy waved the blue hanky slowly in long languid sways above her head, as if waving off a liner from the quayside. She began speaking softly as she paced steadily towards the bull.

"Now, Bruno, I'm having a pretty horrid morning with the prospect of a long day of more horrid yet to come and you are being a real pain. I would like to discuss a possible solution with you."

The bull stood before her, its breath steaming in the air, its halter of a neck massive and its hide gleaming. Its large, coal eyes watched the waving rag. It adjusted its stance as if to steady itself before a charge and stared levelly at Hildy. Even from the distance of an arm's reach she could feel Bruno's warm, moist breath on her forehead.

"What I was thinking of was this," Hildy said.

She slowly lifted her non-waving fist and then brought it down fast and hammer-hard onto the bull's nose. Bruno reeled a little, snuffled and stepped back and shook his horns. In his momentary daze Hildy slipped the chain through the nose ring and then began leading the slightly bewildered bull slowly back towards the gate. She handed the chain to an open-mouthed Gethyn.

"Yes," she said, "very wild and dangerous. Now do you think you can get him to the back paddock? On your own?"

"Yes, Miss Hildy."

"Good. Then you can get my father into his chair and then begin on the barn roof."

"That roof's dangerous," Davey said. "Rotten it is."

"Which is why it needs mending. And you're just the brave soldiers to do it. Make sure you take the cartridges out of Father's shotgun. Discreetly."

"Where'll you be then? Not up at Upper Meadow field ploughing? You know what your pa said."

"Over 'is dead body, he said."

"Well we won't tell him then, shall we? Anyway, I'm only grass cutting. Plough it next week. So as far as my father knows I'm mending fences, right?"

"Chapel raised we are, don't take to lying. A mortal sin."

Hildy stared fixedly at them.

"No, you just steal Father's whisky from the cellar, don't you? Hell to pay if he finds out."

Gethyn and Davey were about to protest but thought better of it. They took the chain and began leading Bruno away down the track.

"And don't forget about the gun cartridges," Hildy said.

She worked in the tractor shed repairing the Fordson's linkages and gears. It was late morning before the tractor was ready for its work on the meadow field. She made herself a scarf-wrap of bread and cheese and, along with a bottle of ginger beer, picked up her grandfather's pistol from its secret hide in the barn. It was his gun from the Great War and he had given it to her on her eighth birthday, just before he died. It had been a secret present. She couldn't lift it at first but she had lovingly cleaned it and oiled it and practiced its firing by slow degrees and by the time she was twelve it had felt easy and familiar in her hand. By the time she was fifteen she could hit most things she aimed at. But it was still her secret. She stuck the gun inside her overalls and drove the tractor with Jip at her side up to the meadow field where she had parked the rotor cutter ready for coupling. If her father saw her or found out he would know that she had disobeyed him. Then there would be hell to pay, maybe he'd even blast her with the shotgun, like he had tried to with the representatives of the County Agriculture Committee. Hildy wasn't even sure she wouldn't welcome it; she could see no other escape from the farm.

The meadow field was on a gentle south facing slope surrounded by hedges and trees. It was not a big field but it had a warm, secluded feel and in the summer it was a breath-taking coloured quilt of cornflowers, clovers, larkspurs and fairy toadflax rippling in tall grasses. As she worked the meadow in the hot sun Hildy could understand her father's vehemence against ploughing it up for potatoes. She too loved the meadow. It was the place her mother took her for summer picnics when she was young, just the two of them, feasting on ginger beer and lemon cake, chatting in French and chasing the butterflies among the flowers. But those days were ended and would not be coming back. Now the meadow was needed for the greater good, war potatoes.

The grasses and wildflowers fell scythed under the turning cutter blades and sent clouds of bugs and flitters into the sky. A jack rabbit darted out of the long grass and rested a moment on the swathe of cut grass about fifty yards from the tractor. Hildy stopped the cutters and let the tractor idle. She took her grandfather's pistol, checked and cocked it and stepped down onto the meadow. The rabbit sat still, watching her and Jip and everything about. Hildy had to give it a chance, she knew it would be wrong not to. She shouted out.

"Heyeeah!"

The rabbit stood tall on its back legs for a moment and then bounded hard for the safety of the trees. Hildy swung the gun up easily in her hand, waited for the rabbit's next leap and fired. The rabbit jerked in mid-air as if it had hit a wall and then tumbled sideways back to the grass.

"Go Jip."

The dog bounded away and brought the rabbit back in its soft mouth. Hildy placed the rabbit in a canvas bag. She took a satisfying drink of ginger beer and then carried on cutting the meadow.

FOUR

The police station interview room was large and sparsely furnished and smelt of paraffin and stale cigarettes.

Georgia sat on a lone chair a distance away from a long table behind which Chief Constable Darlow and a Detective Inspector Robbins sat leafing through her statement papers. Two elderly constables stood sentry at the door and side of the room. A little away from the table sat a young man in a smart army officer's uniform. The chief constable had introduced him as Captain Townsend.

The room was quiet while the policemen at the table read the small pile of statement papers. Georgia sat calm with hands loose in her lap and her mind as still and as remote as she could muster. She just wanted to get this over with and to return to her cell for a cigarette.

As if reading her thoughts the young captain stood up and wandered over to her. He offered her a cigarette from his pack. The policemen at the desk continued to read the papers before them. The captain bent low to light Georgia's cigarette.

"You didn't buy the knitting needle in the shop," he whispered, "it was in your bag all the time." He smiled and returned to his seat.

"A most unfortunate business, Mrs Baum," Chief Constable Darlow said, "Most unfortunate."

"My name is Melrose. And miss will do. I no longer consider myself married. No longer Baum. Melrose is my maiden name. Call me by that."

"You are divorced from Mr Ernst Baum?"

Georgia laughed. "Very."

"Do you have the divorce papers?"

"Just the scars."

The two police officers sat back in their chairs and studied Georgia for a moment.

"As you wish, Miss Melrose. But you do not deny that you killed this man, erm…" DI Robbins scanned the papers.

"Jan van Troost?"

"I did not kill Jan van Troost," she said.

Robbins raised his head. "You say you didn't kill him? In your statement..."

"He isn't van Troost, or wasn't. He is Horst Blucher. Or was. I killed Horst Blucher."

"His papers say he is Van Troost."

"And papers never lie, do they?"

The chief constable coughed and sorted more files before him. "So why did you kill this man, this Blucher you say?"

Georgia took a long lungful of smoke and let it escape in a slow drift. "He's a German. Probably a Nazi. Isn't that what we are supposed to be doing in this war, killing Germans?"

"Van Troost was Dutch," Robbins said.

"Well he was Blucher when I knew him in South Africa. And a Nazi supporter. Aren't we supposed to be killing them most of all?"

"Yes, quite," Robbins said. He was a middle-aged man with a pallid face and a beer gut beginning to strain at his high belt. "Blucher. You say he was following you and attacked you in an alley." He cleared his throat, "Er, forcing himself on you. Is that right?"

"Yes."

"Why was he following you?"

"He recognised me and he knew I knew he was a German. A Nazi. He was going to kill me."

Robbins studied her with a fixed gaze.

"You knew he was following you when you went into a shop and saw him back down the street. A haberdasher's shop I believe. Did you buy anything?"

Georgia was aware of Captain Townsend watching her. He crossed his legs slowly. It felt like a signal.

"No," Georgia said. "Just checking my tail. Buying time. Thinking out the options."

"And when you left the shop he followed you?"

"Yes."

"And he forced you into an alley? It must have been frightening for you."

"But not unexpected," Georgia said.

There was a momentary silence. Georgia kept her hands calm in her lap and stared at the air.

"You killed him with a knitting needle," Robbins said, "rather an odd weapon of choice, don't you think?"

"It was the only thing to hand."

"Clinical, the pathologist said. Under the ribs on an upward fifteen-degree penetration path direct to the heart. He was most impressed," Robbins said. "He said van Troost, er Blucher, would have been dead before he hit the ground. Do you always carry a knitting needle in your handbag, Miss Melrose?"

"Of course."

"Why would you do that, I wonder?"

"In case some bastard ever tried to rape me in an alley," she said.

She heard Captain Townsend's stifled laugh. Chief Constable Darlow coughed loudly.

"And after killing him, what did you do then?" asked Darlow.

"I went looking for a policeman."

"That was very calm and calculated," Darlow said, "and strange. Why didn't you just flee? There was nothing to tie you to this man."

"One can't flee in hell, Chief Constable, there is nowhere to flee to. Better to turn and face the fires and take the consequences. And hope it's quick."

"Even at the loss of your liberty and reputation? You are a young, and if I may say, a very attractive woman, your whole life ahead of you. Prison life is not comfortable, even for a woman. Those are heavy consequences."

"Not for me."

"Why is that?"

"I have been raped by my husband, lost my home, had my child ripped dead from me, my life, my marriage, my friends and my self-respect and any faith I might have held in the hope of love and happiness have all been wrenched from me and cast to nothingness, as if they had never been. And I'm living in the middle of a nightmare war. Losing my liberty is nothing. It is almost a relief."

The room fell silent. It was broken by the chief constable.

"Well, Miss Melrose, I know that it has been difficult with the loss of your home in South Africa and, of course, the child. I am sure your story of self-defence will be heard by the court but a murder is still a murder, even in war time. We understand these things and I am sure the courts will come to see it that way. But this is still a serious offence, even in war, you do understand this? I doubt it will mean the noose but, I fear that you face a considerable time in gaol."

"If I'm lucky I may be able to smoke myself to death then," Georgia said.

Robbins laughed.

"You can't die from smoking!" he said.

"Then I'll die trying," she said.

Georgia was taken to an office along the corridor where she read and signed her statement and was measured and weighed and given an extra blanket before being escorted back to her cell. She was surprised to see Captain Townsend sitting on a stool in the corner of the room, a large file open on his knee.

Captain Townsend rose as she entered and beckoned Georgia to a seat on her cell bed, a board chained to the wall.

"That will be all, thank you, Sergeant," Townsend said, "be so good as to close the door on leaving us." The door closed on a heavy clunk and the keys turned. The sergeant's footsteps retreated along the corridor.

Captain Townsend smiled at Georgia and offered her a cigarette. She took it and perched on the hard bed.

"Isn't it rather dangerous being alone with me?" she said, "A desperate criminal with nothing to lose. Aren't you afraid that I might attack you and kill you?"

Townsend looked at her as if studying the thought.

"No," he said.

"Why?"

Townsend reached into the pocket of his tunic and placed a pistol on the top of his file.

"Because you are doubtless many things, Miss Melrose, but being stupid isn't one of them."

A silence drifted in the room. Georgia smoked her cigarette while Townsend glanced at some of the papers in the file. Georgia had no idea what was going on or why the captain was here. She wondered if Ernst had somehow sent him as another assassin or maybe he was from immigration and was going to deport her back to South Africa. After a while Townsend placed the file on the floor and studied Georgia with a calm and easy gaze.

"Can you ride a bicycle?" he asked.

Georgia was taken aback. Smoke caught in her throat and she coughed.

"Bicycle? Yes, yes I think so. What's that got to do with..."

"You speak French?"

"Well, yes. I studied it at Durham University. Before I went to South Africa."

"And German?"

"Some."

"Fluent?"

"I get by,"

"Wo haben sie Deutsch lernen, zu sprechen?"

Georgia stilled on the words. She was used to the written words of German, she worked with them every day at Bush House, but to hear them spoken aloud again, by a man and in the strange, oppressive white tiled cell unsettled her. She feared where things were leading but tried to remain calm.

"Im Sudafrika," she said," Mein mann hatte keine andere sprache im Haus gesprochen. Ich musste lernen, zu essen."

"Your husband doesn't sound like a very pleasant fellow."

"He isn't. He is a bastard."

"You work at Bush House in the Information Section.

Translating communiqués. Interesting work?"

Georgia laughed.

"Mind numbingly dull. Look, why are you..."

"Did you enjoy killing Blucher?"

Georgia was again taken aback by the abruptness of the question and of Townsend's direct stare and piercing green eyes, as if he had been in the alley and seen the attack and knew its impact on her, that he already knew the answer to his question.

"Was it thrilling?" asked Townsend. "To take down your hunter?"

Georgia stubbed her cigarette under her heel and watched its last ash spark on the white tiled floor.

"I killed a Nazi. Lots of people are, aren't they? It's what the war is about."

"But you enjoyed it, didn't you? It was liberating."

"It was certainly more exciting than filing," she said. "What's riding a bicycle got to do with all this? Is this some kind of trick or test?"

"How would you like the chance to get out of here so that you can help us kill more Nazis?"

"I'm under arrest. I did it. I killed the bastard. And yes, I enjoyed doing it. But I'm going to prison. I get no more chances."

"In war anything is possible. And I can make the chance happen. Are you interested?"

Georgia felt her blood ice and then almost as suddenly felt it turn to a burn that glowed its way through her bones. Hope and anxiety and suspicion stirred in her.

"Tell me more."

"I'm recruiting for a special operation section that is looking for people of certain skills and specialised talents to train as agents to fight the Germans. Blowing up bridges and railway lines, co-ordinating local resistance, being a bloody nuisance, that sort of thing."

"And killing Germans,"

"That is one of the perks, yes. Is this of interest to you?"

"But I'm here, in prison. On a murder charge. I can't just

walk out."

Captain Townsend stood and picked up his file.

"There is no can't in special operations, Miss Melrose. We can put doors in the thickest and highest of walls." He banged on the cell door. They heard the footsteps of the sergeant returning.

"Like me to find you a door to the outside. Miss Melrose?"

"With a key?"

"Of course."

Georgia nodded. She half wondered if she was talking in a waking dream.

"Yes, alright." The cell door swung open. Captain Townsend smiled.

"Good. I'll be in touch." He threw his cigarette packet onto the bed. "Try not to kill yourself before then."

Georgia sat on her bed, staring at the door and the white tiled wall. She began to laugh and then to cry and couldn't stop for some minutes.

FIVE

It was three hours hard pedalling to get to Camp Bledsoe. The lanes were dark and deserted but made navigable by the faint lights cast by the bombing raids off to the north-east. Somewhere was getting it hard again tonight.

Jack Summers hid the bike in the undergrowth half a mile from the camp and crept the rest. He sat watching the camp while eating Ma's sandwiches. The camp was low-lit by dim glowing hut lights scattered around the main square, but all was quiet, still and familiar. A couple of sentries smoked in their boxes, another sauntered the distant western wire fence. Beyond the square, he could hear the officers partying in the mess and lights peeped dim at the blackout curtains of the bar. A comforting sound of raucous laughter and singing drifted on the air. Summers had chosen his time. Tonight was Balaklava night, a regimental party, with all of the men and officers remembering the charge of the Fifth at Balaklava and their drinking and partying would last until dawn. Summers checked his watch. It was two hours before the dustbin trucks arrived. He moved off.

Summers knew the route well and had it planned tight. The crawl through the drainage pipes was hard work and the airs were foul but the thought of robbing Colonel Redmond of his safe, his reputation and career kept him moving. He soon found himself at the ventilation shaft and climbed its ladder to the manhole at the back of the cookhouse. It was but a moment to get across to the back of the Admin block and up the stairs to Colonel Redmond's office on the deserted second floor. It took a moment less to pick the office lock.

Summers stood in the colonel's office and cast his thin torch beam around the room. It had been here in this room that Colonel Redmond had charged him and seen him drummed out of the army in dishonour. The embezzling Colonel Redmond who had set his corporal thugs to buggering him in the barrack washroom to keep him quiet.

The Colonel Redmond that then charged him for assault on two corporals when his thugs failed. His subsequent discharge had been all the more brutal and summary. Despite the fires raging inside him Summers had kept quiet. He knew any protests of innocence would be futile. It was the army and superior officers against him, that was just the way it was. It would be his word against Redmond's. Summers had taken it quietly because he knew there was nothing he could do or say to change it. He was cast out of the army, with all the dishonour and demeaning, false rumours following him like a stinking shadow. It had been a tough year back in Civvy Street. The only thing that got him through it all was Ma and Dora, and the planning of revenge.

Jack Summers had learned the thief's trade as best he might, between the factory shifts and long nights in the villains' bars. There were plenty ready to teach. The thieves' guild grew and bloated on the opportunities of war, the curfews and blackouts were a burglar's dream. Jack had learned the trade. Locks and safes and rubber-soled shoes. Needs must in these strange times when all families needed to be fed and daughters needed medicines and decent food. So he learned how to move quickly and quietly about a room, how to thieve and what to steal. Redmond's room he knew by heart. He ignored the large regimental safe in the corner but homed in on the painting of the Balaklava Charge on the opposite wall. It was but a few moments to open Redmond's private safe behind it.

The haul was impressive. Just over eight hundred pounds in notes of various denominations, a couple of regimental silver goblets, a porcelain figurine of a ballet dancer, an orange, a Colt 45 pistol and the defence fortification plans for the whole of the southern coast of England from Kent to Dorset. There was even Redmond's accounts book, with a full list of his dealings and incomes all written out in spidery green ink.

The money was the skimmings of Redmond's many criminal schemes. The payback for supply contracts, soldier's fines, fictitious bar staff and unrecorded deliveries of stores resold on the black market. Redmond was making rich while the world warred and died about him, keeping order and discipline through his two sadistic corporals, Crick and Benson. The money in the safe was enough to buy a modest house. Summers slipped the roll of notes into his pocket and the silver goblets, Colt 45, figurine and orange into his pouch bag. He took out of his pocket a cigarette card of a jackdaw and placed it in the safe and closed the door to a heavy click. He re-hung the picture and checked his watch. There was forty minutes before the garbage truck was due.

Jack settled himself at Redmond's desk and passed the wait studying the defence maps. He soon realised that they were something of a bonus. The money and silver he had expected, Summers had been tracking Redmond's criminal activities for many months and knew of the hidden safe. But the maps were a surprise. The papers were in a thin leather folder and stamped with the highest security code and detailed every minefield, gun emplacement and military depot, troop deployment and camp along the coast. There was also a list of all the troop call and communication codes. It was a set of papers that belonged in the regimental safe at Southern Area Command, certainly not in Redmond's private one.

Summers considered both the luck and the problem of the maps and the accounts book. He knew that if he was caught with the maps he would face charges of treason, if with the accounts book it would be burglary or blackmail. Not to take them would mean that he had no evidence with which to bring down Redmond. The gain of the money and silver would have to suffice, he would leave the rest.

Dawn was still an hour away when the garbage truck drew up outside the cookhouse doors. Summers waited for the driver and his mate to load the bins and take their usual cup of brew in the kitchen. When they were inside, he climbed into the back of the truck and hid himself among the bins. A half hour later the truck was being waved through the camp gate and out onto the Woolwich road. Summers jumped out before the truck made its turn into the depot gates and walked the four miles back to Wandsworth.

SIX

It was night by the time Hildy mounted her bike and headed on the road home and away from Morley Manor. Her early evening class teaching French conversation to the American officers had gone on longer than usual due to their end of lesson antics and banter. Hildy suspected that their high spirits and gentle mischief were a result of an imminent operation and it took all her guile to deflect the many date propositions and offers of a social drink at the well-stocked Morley Manor bar.

Despite the night the road was busy. Trucks and jeeps full of whooping and wolf –whistling Americans roared past her on full beam on their way to the pubs and bars or back to the American airfield camp. Motorbike despatch riders and diesel trucks blared past her. Hildy felt the world and the war passing her by at speed, leaving her to pedal alone in the dark on the five-mile road back to her dismal farm home.

She had been pedalling for some time when she came across an army jeep nose down in a ditch. The front of the jeep was stove-in and a plume of steam drifted idly from under its bonnet. An American Air Force captain sat in the long grass a little way off, grinning sheepishly and holding his arm as if he was afraid it might fall off.

"Goddam English roads!" he said. "You guys never heard of straight roads? Too many goddam trees in this country. 'Scuse the language, miss. I'm afraid my jeep's bought it."

Hildy propped her bike against a tree.

"Are you hurt?"

"Think I goddam broke my arm. And my knee is a bit cronk. But I can probably limp it along."

"It's two miles to the nearest house. I can go get some help. Or go back to Morley Manor."

"Or you could hitch me onto that bike of yours. Ever bike-hitched, miss?"

"Can't say I have."

"Then you're in for a treat. Or at least I am. You'll have to do the pedalling. Help me up."

It took some effort to get the captain up astride the bike and sitting on the saddle. Hildy climbed in front of him and took the handlebars and pedals. The captain let his legs trail beside the back wheel and put his good arm around Hildy's waist.

They set off at a lumbering wobble, Hildy straining against the extra weight, but the ride soon settled to a steady, slow rhythm.

"Perhaps I should introduce myself," the captain said. "Lance T Rockingham at your..."

But any further introduction was cut short by a strange, loud throbbing sound that came from out of the dark skies somewhere in front, above and to the left of them. The sound grew into a growling thunderous rumble.

"What the...." the captain said.

They were instantly engulfed by the sight and sound of a bomber looming out of the dark skies not sixty feet above them. It was gliding on a downward path towards the nearby woods. One of its two engines was on fire, the other was dead and blue-grey smoke and orange sparks plumed from the tail.

"Jesus Christ!" the captain said. The bike toppled sideways under the roaring gale of the bomber and flung the captain and Hildy into the grass. They lay there and watched as the plane seemed to pivot on one wing and then plunge gracefully on to its belly and crash into the fringe of the wood amid the sounds of screaming metal and the salvo of cracks of splitting trees before coming to a ploughed stop. All was still and silent except for the sound of a gentle hissing and black-blue smoke drifting from somewhere near the tail.

Hildy helped the captain to his feet and they made their way cautiously towards the wreck. It was a German Heinkel bomber.

Out of the dark, the sound of a bicycle bell trilled and a

moment later a large, round and elderly policeman emerged pedalling and puffing hard along the road. He parked his bike and joined them beside the smouldering wreck.

"Heinkel 111 that is," the policeman said with some pride. "Must have been on a raid on the docks. Got lost probably. They all dead?"

As if in answer, a man in a flying suit and helmet emerged from under one of the wings. He had a gun in his hand. He pointed it at the watching group.

"Hands up. Or I will shoot you."

"Now then, sonny," said the policeman advancing slowly. "Let's not be foolish."

"Hands up I said!" The policeman immediately stopped and raised his arms. The German pointed the gun at Captain Rockingham. "Hands up, soldier! I will shoot you."

"His arm is broken," Hildy said. "He can't."

The man pulled off his helmet and studied them. He was young with blond hair and a grease-smeared face.

"Then raise the other," he said. "Do it, please. And you, policeman, step back."

"Now look here son."

"Do you want to die?" asked the young man raising his gun. The policeman stepped back, his hands still raised.

Hildy could see another man lying near the back of the plane. He wasn't moving. Another was struggling to get out of the gunner's pod. He had a bloodied head and rolled himself out of the fuselage and then sat in the grass, laughing lightly to himself and coughing hard. Another man emerged from beneath the cockpit. He wore an officer's uniform and he was badly injured. Blood stained his leg and head and his left arm hung limp at his side. In his other hand he carried a gun. He staggered to a rest against a wing and looked about him.

He shouted something to the young man and a heated conversation ensued which was joined by the tail-gunner who was still sat in the grass.

Hildy moved to stand beside Rockingham, offering him support for his bad leg and arm as an excuse to whisper to him.

"The pilot is telling the young man to shoot us, but he refuses. The one in the grass is telling the pilot to shoot himself. There are two others, navigator and gunner, both dead."

"Stop talking and move away please," said the young German. "I tell you I will shoot you if I must."

The pilot shouted at him some more and then raised his gun.

"He has ordered him to shoot us," whispered Hildy. She stepped forward.

"Hat der grosse deutsche Luftwaffe schiessen Frauen und die jetzt verlelzt?" she said. She was aware of the policeman and American captain looking at her in surprise. The young German laughed, shook his head slowly and then seemed to sag in relief.

"No we do not, Fraulein," he said. "But we must follow the orders of our superiors. You speak German. This I did not expect."

"Your English is very good. But your German manners are not."

The young man laughed. He bowed politely. "You are of course, quite right. I think that now we are guests in your country. It is shameful behaviour." He smiled at Hildy, dropped his gun at his feet and then stepped back a few paces with his hands in the air.

The German pilot roared his anger and took a few staggered paces forward. He waved the gun towards Rockingham. The young German pleaded with him to stop but he carried on. The officer shouted in rage, his eyes wild and blood streaming down his cheek from his head wound. He braced his legs and lifted the gun to point at the American. Hildy stepped forward, shoved the captain backwards and away hard into the grass and dived to grab the young man's discarded gun. She tumble-rolled to the soft ground and came up on one knee and brought the gun to sight and fired. The bullet cracked and spat twice in the night. The German pilot's head jerked back as if punched and his body froze. He gazed in a momentary confusion towards Hildy and then fell to his knees, a small black hole in his forehead. Slowly, he toppled forward face-down into the long grass and lay still.

There was a long moment of silence. Hildy stood up and brushed herself down. The captain, policeman and young German looked at her as if not quite believing what they had seen. The German sitting by the plane's tail began to laugh happily.

"Jesus Christ!" said Rockingham, "that was some goddam fine shooting, miss. Jesus fucking Christ!" He limped to the body and stared down at it, testing it for life with his foot. Then he bent down and picked up the officer's gun. He waved the gun towards the young German who still stood with arms raised. "OK, Fritz, let's go find you a nice cell."

Hildy began to feel a little faint and sat down to try and stop herself shaking. She handed her gun up to the policeman who still gazed at her open-mouthed.

"I think you should take them to the police station, don't you?" asked Hildy, "Well, the ones still alive. Or get an ambulance out here or something?"

The policeman seemed to come out of his reverie. "Yes, yes. Of course. Ambulance. Police station."

Moments later a couple of army trucks came along the road looking for the plane that they had seen coming down. They were followed by a jeep and a farmer on his tractor.

Hildy sat smoking a cigarette against a tree, well away from the throng that now swarmed over the wreckage. She was aware of heads turning to watch her every so often, as if they were looking at a freak. The war had come to her very suddenly, exploding out of the night sky and then had gone just as quickly. She had shot and killed a German and was at a loss to order her thoughts or her feelings. It felt like her world had been turned upside down in an instant and she was totally disorientated. She had taken another's life. Her only comfort was a vague notion that he was the enemy and that she had to do it to stop him killing someone else. But the knowledge did not rest lightly in her. It was not the same as shooting rabbits. The feeling scared her. The policeman crouched down and placed a blanket over her shoulders.

"I'm sorry, miss, but you'll have to come down to the station and give a statement. It won't take long and there's bound to be a cup of strong tea in it, might even rustle a bit of rum eh?"

Hildy didn't return home to the farm until after one in the morning. Her father slept open-mouthed and rasping in his chair. He had not saved any of the rabbit stew and bread for her but had emptied the pot. An empty brandy bottle lay on the carpet beside him.

Hildy left him snoring in his chair and went to bed. She cried until sleep took her just before the dawn.

SEVEN

Captain Matthew Townsend entered through the gateless pillars of Regent's Park and saw that Sam Franks was already there. He was sitting on their usual rendezvous bench which backed snug to the north wall and gave a good two-hundred-degree view of the park, lake and gardens before them. It was a spot where they would not be overheard and could not be surprised.

Townsend bought a cup of tea from the vending van just inside the entrance and sauntered in a circuitous route past the empty band stand and the weed-clogged lake. A weak sun tried to warm the day but the chills of early spring kept his heavy overcoat tightly drawn, both for warmth and to hide his uniform of regiment and rank. His meetings with Franks were strictly unofficial and probably treasonable, so there was no sense in leaving anything to chance. He had changed his peaked captain's cap for a nondescript civvy homburg.

When he took his seat at the far end of the bench from Franks they did not acknowledge each other but watched the park before them. Despite the weather the park was busy with hurrying office workers and off-duty strollers. A young couple stood at the lakeside. The man was in a RAF uniform, the woman had her head resting on his shoulder. She seemed to be crying. The ducks quacked raucously for bread. Townsend sipped his tea, Franks ate his paste sandwiches.

"The shoes are a dead giveaway," Franks said. "Too polished for a civilian. Positively screams senior military."

Townsend stared down at his feet stretched before him. His shoes did indeed shine, but then he was army and they had to.

"Meeting brass later and have to look the part," he said. "And I'm hardly senior."

"But high enough to be in the know. Or at least get whiff of it," Franks said.

They lapsed into silence.

Townsend had known Franks since they had worked together in Berlin in the years immediately before the war. Townsend had been a junior lieutenant and Franks had been attached to the embassy in a vague administrative and security role that was never quite defined. During 1938 and the early months of 1939 Townsend had found himself providing secret military escort out of the country for a number of Jewish children left orphaned or adrift by the Nazi internment madness. Franks had been a key organiser of the secret Kindertransport, that emerged after the horrors of Kristallnacht and Townsend had become a transport courier. They had made a good team and despite Franks having a few years on Townsend they had also become good and trusting friends. They had escaped Berlin just weeks before the world erupted into war.

They had gone their separate ways as the war stuttered and then raged about them. Sam Franks was now working for MI9 in the SIS, the secret intelligence service that dealt with overseas diplomatic espionage, while Townsend, after a short but eventful military career in Indochina, had found himself seconded to the less diplomatic Section T, the new Special Operations Executive section operating mainly in Belgium. Despite working for the same side and for the same ends the politics and guiding personalities of both SIS and SOE had created internecine operational frictions between the organisations and a bunker mentality and tribe loyalty was encouraged by both services in their operatives and officers. Clandestine meetings in parks with the enemy within was reason enough for a court martial and instant disgrace. It says much for the friendship and trust between Franks and Townsend that this didn't trouble them too much at all. They just wanted to win the war and knew that working together was better than warring apart.

Townsend watched the seagulls swooping over the rubbled end of Regent's Terrace, the once magnificent white crescent of Georgian terrace housing that had succumbed to a recent bombing raid. A great swathe of one end of the terrace had disappeared as if bitten off by some ravenous giant.

"I hear you might have smelt something fishy in the Prosper network," Franks said. "Raised your concerns with the Department. But it went no further."

"Christ, Sam how did you know that?"

Franks turned and smiled at his friend.

"Intelligence. It's what I do, Matthew. It's called doing my job. Well?"

Townsend lit a cigarette.

"One of our station radio operators came to me. Had some concerns about the piano signature for agent Madeleine, one of our agents sent out to work for Galileo and act as liaison between Prosper and the French Juggler network."

"Piano signature?"

"Each operative has a unique Morse transmission style, like a pianist's fingers on the keyboard or the handwriting in a letter. Difficult to detect in Morse of course, it takes an expert. But it's equally difficult to fake or disguise. My man swears it wasn't Madeleine keying."

"Maybe your man is wrong."

"Evans wrong? More chance that ITMA is funny." Franks laughed dutifully. "No, Evans is one of our best. Probably the best there is. He's never wrong."

"Was that all?" asked Franks, "Just the doubts of Evans?"

"No. I also came across some odd traffic a couple of months back. We had dropped two agents, Celine and Alphonse, on the French Belgian border, they were to tie-up with Juggler to the south. When Alphonse called in he left off his second security code. Some meddling brass hat at Baker Street immediately called him back to tell him his error."

"He did what!" Franks said.

"I know. Unbelievable. Just as unbelievable that Alphonse would miss his secondary code. I recruited him and know him. He would never have missed it. It's too improbable."

"If only it were. How can we allow such brass-hatted idiots to have any part in this war, to have any command? Buffoons and blaggards mostly. They still think war is an honourable cavalry charge! Sometimes I think we don't want to win this war at all. Anything else untoward?"

Townsend hesitated. He watched gulls gliding in the far skies and wondered whether to share his unconfirmed fears. He decided it was better off his chest and shared it with his friend.

"Yes. Or maybe no. I just don't know. Nothing confirmed. Three agents dropped into Belgium two weeks ago seem to have gone off the airwaves. Messages to say they had arrived and then a status report two days later. Then nothing. And no contact report from the resistance groups about them. Nothing, like they vanished into thin air. Their mission was to confirm rumours of downed allied airmen being fed down escape routes run by local Belgians working for the Nazis. But they have disappeared."

"Or in a Nazi prison?" Franks said.

"Or dead."

"Will they talk? If they are in prison I mean?"

Townsend turned to his friend,

"They always talk in the end, Sam, you know that. But the question is why? Why are so many of our agents falling so early in their missions? Hardly seem to land before they're being picked up and swept up."

"It's dangerous and skilled work. Some are bound to fail."

"Yes, I know. But not almost all, including the most skilled and able. It's just not right. It has a smell about it."

"What kind of smell?"

Townsend watched the ducks fighting over bread at the lakeside. Grey clouds were beginning to muster. It would be rain by evening.

"The kind of rotten fish smell, Sam. I think we have one of your rotters in our midst. Selling our agents to the Germans. A traitor. In Beaulieu or Baker Street. It's the only way that the numbers and reason work out."

They were silent for some moments.

"So who have you spoken to?"

"I took my concerns to the fourth floor, got given a cup coffee and lots of reassurance and shown the door."

"There must have been an incident file on the agents."

"No. The following day Alphonse called in and used the security code. Everything all OK. Nothing to report. The missing agents were probably hiding up, or have faulty radios."

"And did you talk of your traitor?"

"No. I had nothing but circumstances. No proof. Just gut instincts. And they were so dismissive of my other concerns about security that I knew it was futile to broach it. So I kept my tongue."

"And of course you had no idea whether you were speaking to the traitor anyway," Franks said.

Townsend turned to his friend. Sam was gazing across the park at nothing, his face a mask.

"So you think there may be a traitor too?" he said. "It's not a crazy idea?"

Sam smiled. "Every barrel has a rotting apple. We have to be on our guard against it rotting the rest. And we have to pluck it out and crush it."

They sat in silence watching the park. Townsend could only imagine what it cost Alphonse to have the code information tortured from him. If he was lucky his reward would have been a quick death by firing squad against a prison wall. There had been so many agents and now another three had disappeared. It seemed like the whole of northern France and Belgium was now at serious risk and the Germans were able to infiltrate and eliminate their agent networks at will. Mechanic, Prosper and Cartwheel could all be blown. Over thirty brave agents. Thirty men and women many of whom he had helped recruit and train. Helped send to their death.

"Why your interest in Prosper?" said Townsend, "Bit off your territory, isn't it?"

"Just keeping a watch on the apple barrel. Need to keep

all our fruit sharp for the winter ahead. Keep the rotters out."

"Do we have rotters?"

Franks laughed. "Of course we do, Matthew. Rife with the blighters. This is the British secret service at a time of war. It's all lies, disguise and deceit. With skulduggery and damned dim-witted brass-hatted foolery aplenty to keep us busy and on our toes. That's why we enjoy it. Rotters? Baker Street is awash with the buggers. Just got to make sure they're our rotters and not the other side's."

"And are they?"

"No. Not all. Like you I strongly suspect we have a true rotter in our midst. Feeding the Germans our agents and secrets. So keep your thoughts to yourself and trust and talk to no one about this."

"Not even you?"

"No."

In the years Townsend had known and worked with Sam Franks he had never learned what it was he actually did, or to whom he reported. He just knew that Franks had a senior and highly influential role in the service, had fingers in many pies and knew everyone in Baker Street and Whitehall who was worth or useful knowing. Townsend also knew that Franks never answered any of his questions for fear he might actually give an answer. In so doing he would not only compromise his personal integrity but he might also put his friend in danger. In war truth always hurts. Better therefore to avoid it altogether.

"How goes the recruiting?" asked Franks. "Still hunting your cats, rats and dogs?"

"Yes, still hunting. Plenty wiping their boots on the menagerie doormat but precious few are suitable."

"Any progress on your invisible pod idea?"

Townsend had often talked to Franks about his theory of effective agent deployment in the field. Small teams of three working together and made up of a cat, the calm killer, a rat, the cunning, dedicated survivor, and a dog, the dependable and tireless goffer and communicator. A fully trained, adaptable, skilful and deadly team. Townsend had also proposed that the teams should be invisible. Unknown to anyone else in the service except each other and their handler. It was the only secure way. Franks had been a good listener and had seen merits in the idea. The brass at Baker Street had not.

"No, it got no further. The menagerie idea got a fair listening. A couple of Commandos brass were interested in the idea and the team balances but the invisibility was definitely a no-go area. No control and oversight by the brass, no accountability, maverick groups going wild. World gone to chaos. Current systems and training more than adequate. No, it went no further."

"Hear about the trouble down at Bledsoe camp?" asked Franks.

The abrupt change of subject momentarily threw Townsend, but he was used to Sam's ways and recovered his thoughts with hardly a jolt.

"Bledsoe? Yes, the grapevine twitched. Regimental safe robbed, wasn't it? And defence plans gone missing. Not under your remit though, is it, Sam? It's strictly military."

Franks smiled. "Always good to keep an interest, Matthew. Keeps the brain ticking. Rather a professional job by all accounts. Stolen from under the noses of a supposedly crack regiment in a fortified and double-sentried garrison camp. Rather impressive don't you think?"

"Have they caught the burglar?"

"No. Nor are they likely to. Military not the best of detectives and I have a notion our burglar is too smart and sharp for them. What about the Heinkel that came down in Hampshire a couple of weeks back? Read the report on that?"

"No, but it's hardly likely to come across my desk, is it? What's so interesting about it? Planes come down every day. Even Heinkels. I have enough to do finding Section T dogs."

"Quite," Franks said. He neatly folded the greased paper that had wrapped his sandwich and placed it in his overcoat pocket. He turned and smiled at Townsend.

"Remember, Matthew, that for something to be invisible, it has to be invisible. To not be seen, by anyone. Like glass crystals in water. Not seen from above, but only by those closest to it, those who put it there. Look after yourself, Matthew."

He rose from the bench and strode away along the lake path. Townsend watched until he lost sight of him among the street traffic.

Townsend idled a while over the last of his cigarette. It was a strange meeting, but then they usually were with Sam. He couldn't shake off the idea that Sam was telling him something without actually telling it. Meetings with Sam always left him rather perplexed and thoughtful.

Sam had known about his talks with the Special Executive Council about his Juggler concerns and also its outcome. As he had Townsend's invisibility ideas. Someone had obviously talked to SIS about them, someone in SOE. Was Sam intimating that there were apples rotting in the barrel and that perhaps the service should not be trusted? For something to be invisible it has to be invisible to everyone. Sam's words stirred in his head and he knew that Sam was warning him that someone in SOE could not be trusted. The only way the invisible pods would happen was if Townsend was to put the glass in the waters himself, and to tell no one else.

Townsend flicked his cigarette stub to the air and checked his watch. He noticed an envelope lying on the seat beside him. It had been left by Sam. Inside were two pieces of paper. One was a cutting from a local newspaper in Hampshire about the downed Heinkel. The story told of a young farm girl who had killed the German pilot at the crash scene. The section about the girl, a Miss Potts, had several phrases underlined in green ink. One was *giving French conversation lessons to American troops*, another was *spoke German with a crewman*. The last underlined section *shot the German pilot officer dead* was accompanied by an exclamation mark in the margin and Sam's added comment *bullet between the eyes from thirty yards and in the dark!*

The second paper was an official looking report extract from Bledsoe Camp command about the break-in and loss of the secret south coast defence plans. Stapled to it was a copy of the army discharge record of an ex-soldier called Jack Summers.

Townsend replaced the papers in the envelope and noticed Sam's small, neat writing in one corner on the reverse of the envelope. Cat, rat or dog?

EIGHT

It was two months before they came for him. Jack Summers had almost begun to believe he had got away with it but he knew the risks he had run had been high. He was working on the Burg Wachter manual at his desk when Davies had poked his head around the door and jerked a thumb over his shoulder.

"Maddison wants you in his office, now." And he was gone.

Summers closed his work file, locked it in its box and took the stairs down to the overseer's office. He entered to find three large, powerfully built soldiers and no Mr Maddison. Before he could turn and make his escape Summers' arms were pinned behind him and a sack was placed over his head.

"You can come quiet or you can come limp, it don't matter to us," said a voice.

"What are you doing? What is this? You just can't..." Summers felt the crack of the fist into his jaw and his world melted to black.

He came to on the floor of a truck with the sack still blackening all sight but he could sense the truck wheels rumbling beneath his chest as he lay face down with his arms still tied behind. He tried to rise but got a boot in his kidney for a reward. A hand grabbed the sack and slammed his face into the truck floor. Black numbness came again.

In a momentary half-wake he heard the soldiers talking. The only phrase he registered was "Camp Bledsoe" and was vaguely aware of the truck being checked in through a sentry gate, the distant bark of parade ground orders and a rumble of army trucks.

He came to in a cell. Two soldiers came for him and dragged him to an interrogation room.

Where are the plans? Who was he working for? Who was he working with? He was a fifth columnist. A nancy-boy queer. A failure. His daughter would go to prison. He

43

was scum. A low-life thief working for the Nazis. Traitors were hung. Where are the plans?

The questions came with blows and kicks but the sack was never removed. The pains were pummelled upon him almost beyond endurance and then a numbness soaked though him so that he no longer felt them. Below his melting greyness and pains Summers kept his mind alive and as intact as he could.

He knew that he was back in Camp Bledsoe, its sounds and sense seared so deep in his being that even in his battered, semi-comatose state its smell and feel could not be doubted. Somehow he had been identified as a suspect in the camp robbery, maybe his past was too chequered and connected to Bledsoe to avoid such a connection. He would be foolish to think that it wouldn't but he was sure that he had left no incriminating evidence. Perhaps this was just a way of finding and beating a convenient scapegoat into submission and admission. It would certainly be the Colonel Redmond way. Redmond had lost a lot of money and the missing plans would be career threatening, Summers would be lucky to emerge alive. His only relieving thought was that Ma would find the money and letter in its envelope in her knitting bag and that she and Dora could afford to move out to a better life in a place where the damp didn't eat young lungs or the rats gnaw cold toes.

And then the questions and beatings stopped and Summers was lying in a dark room on a hard bed. The sack was removed and someone gave him water and a blanket and he slept the sleep of the damned.

Sergeant Meadows marched into Colonel Redmond's office and saluted Captain Townsend who was sitting in the colonel's chair behind a desk of files.

"Summers is now sleeping, sir."

"And?" asked Townsend.

"Nothing, sir. Not a peep. He is certainly a tough one." It was said with some admiration.

"Not a single word?"

"Told me I punched like a girl, sir. That was about it. We didn't take it too heavy, as you ordered. You said not to break anything. He certainly didn't break."

"Thank you, Sergeant. That is good to know. Let him rest and then feed him. Get the MO to look him over and patch him up. I'll see him tomorrow at ten hundred. Can you fix me an overnight bed?"

"The colonel's quarters are free, sir, I'll see 'em ready."

"Thank you. And how is our good Colonel? Enjoying his confinement in the cells, I trust?"

The sergeant laughed. "Kicking up like hell and blue blazes, sir. Says he's got friends in the War Office. Going to have us all shot."

"Well, unless we can find some evidence against him we could all find ourselves against the wall with a last cigarette. Tell the MO to report to me on Summers."

The sergeant saluted. "Sir," and left.

The next morning Summers was in Colonel Redmond's office opposite a smart, young captain sitting behind the familiar desk. The room did not bring back happy memories. It was in this room that Redmond had formally charged him with aggravated assault and gross indecency. Added to which Summers felt like hell and he was having trouble sitting upright on the wooden chair. Every part of him seemed to ache, sting or throb and he was having trouble seeing out of one eye. His vision was watery and his body felt heavy and stolid. At least he wasn't dead. Not yet.

"My name is Townsend," said the young captain, "you know, of course, why you are here."

"No," said Summers.

The captain studied him for a while and then lifted a file from the desk and read from it.

"John Preston Summers, known as Jack, born April 1915. Married Elizabeth Sharples August 1934 and moved to Lille, France in October of that year to work for Girond Engineers. Moved to Lichtenberg, Berlin in 1936 and worked for Heckler Stumm as a leading engineer draughtsman. Fluent French and German. Daughter Dora born 1935. Wife died July 1938 and you and Dora returned to England and you joined the Royal Fusiliers October 1939 stationed at Catterick and then Camp Bledsoe. Dishonourable discharge for aggravated assault and gross indecency in November 1940. Currently a civilian working for Matlock & Peters Engineering."

Captain Townsend let the file fall to the desk. He lit himself a cigarette and leaned back in his chair.

"You were not working at Matlock's on the night of the robbery here at Camp Bledsoe, were you, Jack? We have checked. We also know that you have been learning the thieving trade from ne'er-do-wells in various dens of south and east London for the last year and you applied your new learned skills to rob the safe in this very room and steal its contents, including top secret defence plans. An act for which, I'm afraid, you will hang."

He let the silence in the room grow. Jack Summers said nothing.

"You do not like Colonel Redmond very much, do you?" asked Townsend.

Summers' snort of contempt escaped from him before he could tether it. It scraped over his cut lip as it flew out and he winced at the sting of pain. Townsend offered him a cigarette. Summers took it and drew a careful, deep lungful of smoke.

"No, not much," he said.

"Why?"

"Because he's the worst kind of bastard. That's why."

"But your superior officer."

"There is nothing superior about Redmond except his manner and his greed."

"Why did he have you dishonourably discharged?"

"You've got the file."

Townsend sifted through the papers on the desk and lifted one out. He held it above the wastepaper basket and dropped it in. "You tell me," he said.

Summers collected his thoughts and tried to marshal them. This was an odd interview and something in Townsend's manner exuded in Summers a strange need to want to trust and confide in him, or maybe it was just a vain, desperate hope.

"I was working in the quartermaster office, admin stuff. I discovered that Redmond was embezzling army funds on a massive scale, doing fraudulent deals and dodgy accounts. Pocketing pay for fictitious troops, soldier's made-up fines from pay, selling off NAFFI stores to the black market. I confronted him. He had me arrested, beaten and thrown in the camp cells. There I was visited one night by the colonel's two un-hinged war dogs, Corporals Crick and Benson who thought it might be fun to try and bugger me in my cell. I managed to change their mind. Aggravated, grievous and indecent assault were added to the charge. The trial was a quick kangaroo show, military style. Redmond was judge and jury, his word against mine, and I was out and in disgrace. Redmond did a fine job on me."

Townsend lifted a paper from the desk.

"Benson suffered three fractured ribs, a ruptured knee, a broken arm and severe concussion. Crick a broken ankle, nose and cheek bone and is still recovering from a fractured skull. It took three guards to get you off them. How did your wife die?"

The question almost ambushed Summers. The thoughts of Beth were still warm and raw and as present and persistent in him as his breathing, he still missed her so much. He hated thinking of her death because she burned so bright and alive in him still and was the only warmth of her he had left. He was only thankful that she had been spared his current shame and disgrace. Not that she would have believed it. He maintained what calm he could.

"She was knocked down by a brewery truck in Berlin."

Townsend remained silent, waiting for more.

"She was being chased through the streets by a gang of Hitler Youth. She ran across the street. The truck hit her."

"Why was she being chased?"

"She was a Jew. Apparently that's enough. The Hitler Youth bought the truck driver a drink. They left Beth in the road for the municipal cart. Look, just charge me and get on

47

with it. But you have no evidence against me. It's all circumstantial."

"Shall we have some tea?" asked Townsend. He bellowed his order for tea at the door and moments later the sergeant came in with two cups of tea. He gave one to Summers.

"That's the cool one," he said. "might be easier to sip." He winked at Summers and left the room.

"You are quite right, it is all circumstantial, but I dare say it is still enough and the Army only needs to have a suitable and expendable scapegoat brought to judicial slaughter. Good for morale and paperwork if not for justice. Might as well be you. Quick and clean. I take it you don't want to hang?"

Summers sipped at the tea. The warm liquid seemed to fuel him. He said nothing.

"I want to take that bastard Redmond down as much as you do," Townsend said, "but we can't do it without the evidence that he had the defence plans and some proof of his fraudulent activities. He denies theft and fraud and says the plans were locked in the regimental safe and he has witnesses to that effect. We can get him on misappropriation of secret documents but he will probably muster his brass and Whitehall buddies and get off with a reprimand, maybe even a demotion. And no evidence of embezzlement. It is not enough. Agree?"

"So you want me to help you out by confessing to the theft and giving you the plans that I didn't steal. That's army logic. There's nothing in it for me. No evidence against me. Why should I help the army that beat me and cast me out to disgrace and penury?"

Townsend contemplated Summers for some moments. He reached into his pocket and pulled out a small card and laid it on the desk where Summers could see it. It was the Jackdaw cigarette card.

"I know it was you who robbed the safe, Jack. It was a masterly theft and a brilliantly well-executed plan. Innovative, clever, even brave. Truly, it was. Very impressive. Through the sewers, was it? But the card, I think, was a mistake. You wanted Redmond to know who had done it. Next time be more careful. Make it less personal."

"Next time?"

"The only way out of your current predicament is for you to convince me that it was you who robbed the safe. Give me the evidence that will put Redmond behind bars for a long time."

"And if I don't?"

"Then you will hang."

"And if I do, I will still hang."

"No, you will live to fight again. Working for me."

Summers' mind was spinning with the strangeness of it all, his body ached and he was not sure he was really awake. He was sure he wasn't understanding what was being offered. He sipped his tea for reassurance and time to think.

"What work?" he said.

"Special duties. Working abroad. Blowing things up. Being a nuisance. Killing Jew-hating Nazis. Maybe even a bit of safe robbing. That sort of thing."

"Secret duties?"

"Very. We will train you and support you. To work in a foreign field."

"Sounds dangerous."

Townsend smiled. "Yes, it is rather. But a lot more exciting than Matlock's, don't you think? And certainly more fun than hanging."

"But I'm a civilian now."

"And a thief. And a traitor. And to be out of here all you have to do is give me the evidence to lock Redmond away."

"I couldn't work for you. I can't leave Dora and Ma Maynard. They depend on me. Dora is not well. I have to look after her."

"I'm sure we can arrange suitable help. Maybe even get you out of that ghastly, damp pre-fab you currently live in. It can happen. I work for people of some influence."

"And I wouldn't be charged and locked up?"

"Evidence, Jack. Either you show me some and you walk

or we will just make some up and you hang. Your choice."

"You're just another big bastard like Redmond, aren't you?"

"No, Jack," Townsend smiled, "just a better one."

Jack Summers sat back and felt the pains in his back stab again. Townsend was fixing him in a steady, unwavering gaze. It came down to a sense of trust. Could he trust Townsend and his word, because there was nothing else. No witnesses, no written statements or records, this was just a question of trust.

He placed his teacup on the floor and stood up slowly on unsteady legs. He took a moment to rub some blood back into his arms and legs and then stood before the desk.

"Lift your cup," he said.

Townsend looked intrigued. He lifted his cup calmly from the desk. Summers leaned over and with one arm swept all the file papers off the desk and let them cascade and flutter to the floor. Then he lifted the large leather desk blotter and slid out the defence plans for the south coast that lay under it. He spread the map on the desk. Then he went to the bookshelves on the far wall of the office and removed a plain red book from its bottom shelf near the floor. He threw it onto the desk with the map.

"The map and a copy of Redmond's accounts book. Dates, cash, contacts and transactions. I never stole either of them. They never left this office. You work with poor detectives."

"Can't get the talent these days, Jack. This war is a thief's paradise."

Jack sat down again. Townsend flicked through the book and then leaned back in his chair. There was silence for some time. Townsend was watching Summers. He couldn't help smiling. He offered him a cigarette. By the time they were both lit and enjoying the smoke Townsend was almost laughing.

"I think this will save you from any hangman's rope," he said. "There's enough here to put Redmond away for a good stretch and years of prison food. It'll probably kill the bastard. And it will be deserved. Tell me, Jack, I don't suppose the bicycle we found flung in a hedge a mile or so up the road was yours, by any chance?"

"Probably. It's a long way from Wandsworth and not many buses about after midnight. Why do you want to know?"

"Oh nothing. Just a question I no longer need to ask you."

"What happens now?"

"Go home, Jack, give Dora a cuddle. Let me sort things out here. Be assured Redmond is finished. We may need your witness statement but nothing to concern yourself. Get yourself well and fit. Resign from Matlock's, you will have more important work to do. How much did you lift from Redmond's safe?"

"Enough."

"I bet it was. Might be a gesture of goodwill to return the regimental silver cups though. Post them in a parcel. Military tends to be sentimental about that kind of stuff. Leave the matter of your future accommodation with me, I'll see what can be arranged. We will be in touch. I'll get the sergeant to arrange you a lift home. We know you speak German. How rusty is your French?"

"I can get by."

Townsend collected the papers from the floor and tucked the map and accounts book under his arm. "Might want to brush up on it a bit then. After all, you'll have nothing to do for the next few weeks, will you? Maybe pop down to the library. Language section. Might be useful. There will also be a week of parachute training for you. See you soon, Jack."

Townsend left the room. There was almost a skip in his striding step.

NINE

Hildy was in the barn lying under the tractor trying to tighten the oil sump nut when she saw a big black car take the rise of the farm drive and coast past the door and on down into the courtyard. It took a moment longer for Hildy to realise that it was an official car and probably the men from the County Agricultural Committee come visiting again.

She scrambled out from under the tractor and headed out of the barn and down into the courtyard. She had taken no more than a few strides before she heard her father's gun go off and the sound of stone ricochets and cries of alarm. Hildy quickly appreciated that it wasn't a CAC visit. A military car with a bonnet pennant was parked at an angle to the front entrance and two men were now crouched down behind it in protection against her father's wrath and gunfire.

"Get off my land, you thieves!" bellowed her father from somewhere in his room. "You're trespassing and I have my rights. Get off!"

One of the men cowering behind the car wasn't really cowering at all. He was a uniformed captain and he sat on the running board and seemed highly amused by the events about him. He tipped his cap as Hildy hurried past.

"Your father appears a trifle upset," he said.

Hildy ran into the courtyard waving her arms and shouting.

"Stop this, Father! Now! They are not from the CAC. Put your gun down now."

"They look like them bastards," bellowed her father.

The captain smiled at Hildy.

"You can assure your father, Miss Potts, that we are completely different bastards. And we have come to see you, not him."

Hildy was a little taken aback. She wondered if they had come about the killing of the pilot. Maybe they were going

52

to prosecute her after all. The captain's companion was a tall, broad-shouldered man in a long overcoat.

Hildy called up to her father. "They're not from CAC, they've come to see me about more teaching up at Morley Manor. Now put your gun away."

"Don't need no more teaching time up at the manor, you got plenty of work to do here on the farm. Hear me?"

"Yes, Father." Hildy turned to her visitors. "Probably best if we retreat to the barn."

They sat on the straw bales and the captain, a Captain Townsend, introduced himself and his colleague, Mr Merchant, who nodded perfunctorily.

"Miss," he said.

"Is this about the dead German?" asked Hildy, "because I've told the police everything and they said it was all over and done."

"Brunhilde Evangaline Potts. A rather unusual name," Townsend said, "for a Hampshire lass."

Hildy groaned inwardly. That bloody name.

"I'm Hildy, not Brunhilde," she said. "My father arranged my christening while Mother was still in hospital. He did it to spite her for having a girl. He liked Wagner. And didn't like my mother."

She dropped her hand idly by her side and Jip slipped under it like a nuzzled glove.

"Quite the charmer, your father, isn't he?"

"Having no legs makes you bitter."

"How did he lose them?"

"Driving back from the pub one night he hit a bridge. Spent two years in hospital and came out on wheels."

"And your mother?"

"She died when I was thirteen. Then it was just me and Father and the farm. What do you want to know all this for?"

"Your mother was French? Is that why you can speak it?"

"Yes. We spoke in French all the time. Like a secret thing between us, away from Father. Sitting under the lime trees in the meadow with picnics. Counting butterflies. Reading French stories."

"And your German?"

"Once you have a couple of languages another is not too hard. My father made me read and translate the Wagner operas. Picked it up from there. I only speak it a little."

"There's two men watching us from the cover of brambles by the tool shed," Merchant cut in. He consulted a small notebook he took out of his pocket. "They would be Misters Morgan and Jones I presume?"

Hildy was momentarily at a loss. She wasn't really aware of Gethyn and Davey's surnames but the fact that Merchant and Captain Townsend seemed to and had noted them in a pocketbook raised her suspicions and confusions even more.

"Oh that'll be Davey and Gethyn the farmhands," Hildy said, "They're not good at much else but snooping."

Townsend nodded to Merchant and he sauntered out of the barn and headed towards the car. Hildy noticed that Merchant limped and dragged a leg.

She turned back to Townsend who was lighting a cigarette.

"What is all this about? Are you arresting me?"

Townsend gazed about the barn. The tractor dripped oil into a pan. An old wooden cart lay collapsed on its wheel-less front axle in the corner of the barn like a tired camel sunk onto its front knees. Dull tan straw bales seemed to be melting in all corners and the tin sheet roof was holed and rusted. The barn smelt of damp straw, oil and dung.

"Do you like working on the farm, Hildy?" asked Townsend.

The frustration and anger of the day, the drudge of her life and the intrusion of these unwelcome visitors just seemed to overwhelm Hildy. She also realised that she had straw in her hair and her hands and face were smirched in streaks of oil. She looked Townsend in the eye.

"No," she said, "I absolutely fucking hate it."

Hildy was immediately embarrassed for her outburst.

"I'm sorry. That was very unladylike." She took a cigarette unbidden from Townsend's packet and lit it with the lighter he was quick to offer. She let the smoke kick into her throat.

"No, Captain Townsend, I do not enjoy working on the farm. It is my home, I have lived here all my life but I can't love it, only hate it. Can you understand how awful that is? How it is to feel like that? I used to love it here. When Mother was alive. Our reading in the meadow. Making daisy chains. Picnics in the woods. Planting the wheat. Grooming the horses. But that has all gone. She died and left me. My father despises me, the work hands mock me and a war of excitement and danger and wonder goes on all around me and I am kept from any touch of it, or feel of it, or part of it. I just plough fields and sleep. It is as if the war it isn't happening to me at all. So arrest me and take me away. Your prison has got to be better than this one I'm in right now. You'll be doing me a favour."

Across the yard, Merchant was talking to Davey and Gethyn. It appeared that Merchant had come up at them from behind and taken them by surprise. He had a small book out and was making notes. Gethyn and Davey were shuffling their feet as if eager to be elsewhere.

"I can arrange for you to leave the farm, if you like," Townsend said. "For a short break."

Hildy wasn't sure she heard the words. Her hand ruffled Jip's soft head.

"A break?"

"Yes, like a holiday. For a couple of months or so. Does this idea interest you?"

Hildy laughed. "Of course it does, but it's not going to happen, is it? The farm doesn't run itself. Father would never let me have a holiday."

"Oh, it wouldn't be a holiday like that," Townsend said, "It would be a working break. Only a different kind of work."

"What kind of work?"

Townsend held Hildy's gaze.

"War work, Hildy. We'd like you to join us and maybe

help us fight this war. We will train you. If you pass the training we want you to help us do some more war work. Somewhere abroad, where they speak French and German."

"What kind of work?"

"Dangerous. Exciting. Secret. Maybe deadly."

"Why me?"

"You speak French and German, shoot like Buffalo Bill, mend tractors and you can ride a bike. Why not you?"

Hildy could think of many reasons why it could not be her but none of them really seemed to be true. She was so used to accepting her role as a servile drudge that to think or expect anything else seemed unreal, almost pretentious.

"What if I don't pass the training?"

"Then you'll be back here working again on the farm. Nothing lost but an experience and short respite gained."

Hildy's thoughts and hopes tumbled inside her like hot rocks and she found it difficult to take it all in. Across the yard Gethyn and Davey had made their hurried escape and Merchant now seemed to be taking notes about the farm outbuildings.

"It's your chance to get out of your prison, Hildy," Townsend said, "Even if it's only for a month or two. There's a lot of regrets in life. Don't let this be one of them."

Hildy laughed and shook her head.

"Of course I'd like to give it a go, to get away from here, if only for a month, but I can't. It's just impossible. It wouldn't be right. There would be no one to run the farm and keep the place going. And my father needs looking after and there is no one else but me. Gethyn and Davey can't be trusted and they don't know anything about farming except what I tell them. It's a lovely thought, Captain Townsend but it's one that just can't happen."

Hildy stood up and took the spanner in her hand.

"Now if you don't mind, Captain Townsend I must get on with repairing my tractor. It was nice to meet you and thank you for coming to see me but as you can see I have work to do. So I will have to regret your offer because my life is so full of them right now that one more won't make a difference. Instead I will mend the tractor, plough the top meadow and probably sit under the limes with my cheese lunch and cry my regrets away like I always do. See? Just a silly, sentimental, selfish girl unhappy with her lot. Not recruiting material at all."

"I think you should let me be the judge of that, Hildy. We're looking for people with skills, not for machines."

"Well, it's not going to happen anyway, is it? So there's an end to it."

"What if I could make it happen?" asked Townsend. "Be your fairy godmother. Wave a magic wand and get your father to agree to your going and getting some proper help with the farm while you're gone?"

"Magic me a coach and glass slippers?" said Hildy laughing.

"I was thinking more a staff car and grey coveralls," Townsend said.

Hildy realised, perhaps for the first time in the interview, that Captain Townsend was in deadly earnest and that he may actually have the influence and authority to make such magic happen. The realisation sent a shiver of thrill through her.

"If you can magic that then I will come to your ball," she said.

Townsend grinned. "Then await my call," he said

Hildy did not cry under the limes in the meadow that afternoon but sang French songs on the tractor as she ploughed. Her good mood lasted for several days. Then she woke one morning to find that Gethyn and Davey had left in the night, taking the petty cash tin and several bottles of her father's brandy with them. They had also taken her grandfather's pistol from its hide in the barn. Hildy spent several attempts trying to telephone Captain Townsend and finally managed to speak to him late in the afternoon. She was too upset to make it a long call.

"I'm sorry, Captain Townsend but Gethyn and Davey have left. Fled the farm. You and your man frightened them off and there is no one to run the farm but me. They also took my grandfather's gun. I have to say no to your offer. You must see it's now impossible."

She didn't wait for a response. She slammed the phone down and headed for the meadow with Jip and sat under the lime trees. As much as she wanted to cry, she couldn't, or wouldn't, she was just too angry. Her rage burned through her until the night clouds rolled in.

TEN

Hildy's misery continued. Her father was even more cantankerous and demanding than before, seemingly blaming Hildy for Davey and Gethyn's desertion.

"Them London friends of yours scared them off. Interfering busybodies, always poking about and scheming. Left us in a pretty state. How we going to manage the farm? This'll ruin us this will. You'll have to do more hours. Earn your keep for once."

Hildy worked from pre-dawn to high moon and her world passed in an aching fog of ploughing, milking, fence repairing and a hundred other jobs that needed doing. Most nights she slept for only four hours. The postman Arthur helped her to get her father into his chair in the mornings and the evening routine of cooking her father's meal and keeping the house as clean as she could drifted her into a numbness. Even the news of the Afrika Korps' surrender in North Africa and the spectacular Ruhr dams raid by the RAF failed to lift her gloom. The world and the war were passing her by and she was enslaved in her farm prison, away from all the glamour and excitement of the times, untouched by all.

Arthur handed her the letter one morning after her father had been put in his chair and taken to his breakfast at the kitchen table.

"From London," Arthur said in whisper to Hildy. "And that's the War Office frank. Hope it ain't bad news."

The news was as bad as it was good. The letter was from Captain Townsend informing Hildy that he would be visiting the farm that afternoon; the post had obviously been delayed again as the letter had been sent four days ago. The letter advised Hildy that help had been arranged for the farm and her father and that she was to expect some visitors that day.

Captain Townsend's car pulled into the farm courtyard in the early afternoon and was accompanied by a covered

59

army troop truck. Hildy met the captain and Mr Merchant at the door and ushered them into the large, sparse furnished front room where Mr Potts sat glowering in his chair with a rug over his knees and his shotgun leaned to the wall beside him and within easy reach.

"Good afternoon, Mr Potts," said Townsend.

"If you say so, dare say it is. For some. Others got farms to run. When we're left to run 'em and not being waylaid by interfering Whitehall ponces. What are you doing here? Why should I give you any time of my day?"

"Father, please," Hildy said, "they've just come to talk, to help they said."

"Help? Them? Pah! Their help is trying to send you away like they did them Welsh mules. Not that you'll be missed for all the use you are. But who'll look after me and the farm eh? You ain't going nowhere and that's the last of it."

"What if I took Miss Potts away anyway?" Captain Townsend said, "For war work elsewhere."

Mr Potts reached for his shotgun and laid it in his lap. "You could try it," he said, "but I wouldn't recommend it."

"What if I exchanged Hildy for two experienced, strong farm workers?"

Mr Potts looked up. "More Welsh mules?"

"No, proper farmworkers."

"Not cheap neither, I'll be bound."

"No, these workers will require no wages from you. Just a farmworker's lunch each day."

"But she won't be here to make it, will she?" Potts said nodding perfunctorily towards Hildy. "So that won't happen, will it?"

"No, but part of the deal also includes a live-in house-keeper who will look after you, cook your food and clean your house. She will have her own room which she will share with her granddaughter, who will accompany her."

"They will have the two top rooms off the back stairs," said Merchant, "they are unoccupied. That'll suit them fine. They'll need no wages either. Just shelter from the London

60

bombs."

"What?" said Potts, trying to take it all in. "You just can't march in here and… What workers? And some busybody old maid clattering about the place? And a damn snivel kid? Why would I want all that? And what could you do if I said no anyway? Can't lock me up or shoot me, can you?"

Townsend smiled. "No, Mr Potts, I couldn't have you shot. But I can take your daughter away from this farm for war work if I want to and there will be nothing you can do about it. How long do you think you will last on your own here, eh? A few days at most. But I am a reasonable man. We would like to borrow Miss Potts for important war work, certainly for the next two months, and in return I am offering you a live-in housekeeper and two strong farmworkers for free. Is that not a good deal?"

Potts sat silent and calculating in his chair for some moments.

"Two months?" he said. Townsend nodded. "Free?" Townsend nodded again. "Well, you can have her for all the use she is. When do you want her?"

"Now is as good a time as any, don't you think? After a cup of tea, of course. Perhaps Merchant you will oblige? Thank you. And Miss Potts, you look a little shell-shocked."

"I am," Hildy said. "You want me to go with you now?" Hildy was trying to make sense of it all just as her father had done. She felt the rising excitement ooze through her together with a sudden thought that she had absolutely nothing to wear for a trip to London and wouldn't know what to wear if she did. She knew nothing of fashions, only what she saw in the newspaper advertisements. Or maybe it wasn't even London they'd be heading for.

"Once you've packed a few things and shown the farm's new workers around the place and shown the new housekeeper Mrs Maynard and little Dora their rooms. If you would like to come with us, that is?"

Hildy began to laugh. "What now? Today?"

"Tomorrow morning will suffice, I think. I will arrange

a car to pick you up. Now what about that cup of tea," Townsend said taking off his coat, "and perhaps some cake if you have some?"

"When do I get my workers?" asked Mr Potts.

"Now, if you'd like," said Townsend. He went to the window and beckoned to the truck. Moments later an elderly man in a sergeant's army uniform marched in with two men wearing prisoner of war overalls.

"This is sergeant Harris and these two gentlemen are Walter and Rolf."

"Bloody prisoners of war!" spluttered Potts. "I ain't having no damn Nazis on my farm. Stealing my food, slitting my throat when I sleep. Are you mad?"

"I can assure you that Walter and Rolf will give you no cause for concern or worry. Yes they are German but they are not Nazis. Rolf there," he nodded to a well-built, rotund man in his forties with a bushy grey moustache who bowed a polite nod in return, "has worked on farms all his life and is an expert ploughman and herdsman. Walter," the tall blond, younger man smiled and nodded, "is an expert mechanic and has also worked on farms."

"It is good to see you again, fraulein," Walter said. Hildy realised it was the young German pilot from the Heinkel. "And you too," she blustered. "Are they treating you well?"

"Better than I expected or probably deserve. But it is good, thank you." He smiled and bowed again.

"And as you can hear, Walter speaks excellent English," Townsend said. "Sergeant Harris will bring them here at eight o'clock every morning, stay with them all day and return with them to the camp at seven."

Merchant entered the lounge followed by Mrs Maynard. Dora held on to her skirts and peered round warily at the assembled group.

"Bloody Nazis and interfering old women and their brats, it's too much. It's all wrong. This is a farm not a damn sanctuary for refugees and criminals. You can't do this. I won't allow it." Mr Potts fisted his shotgun and waved it to the room. "This is my house, my farm and I say what goes and what don't. I ain't having no old hag in my kitchens and no brats running around the place. Sergeant there can make me food while he's here. Otherwise she," he pointed the gun at Hildy, "ain't going nowhere, war work or not."

A silence fell on the room. Dora began to snuffle among Ma Maynard's skirts. She bent down to comfort her and then stood up. She smiled and addressed the room with soft words of gentle encouragement.

"Why don't you all go out a have a look around the farm? You can show the German boys and the sergeant here where everything is, Miss Potts. You can take Dora with you, show her the chickens. And I am sure these other gentlemen will wish to accompany you." She fixed Townsend with a knowing stare. "I'll make some tea and rustle some biscuits and keep Mr Potts company awhile until your return. What say you?"

Townsend saw something more in Ma's determined gaze. It was less a suggestion than a command.

"Good idea, Mrs Maynard," Townsend said. "Give us a chance of some air and stretching our legs. Come on, everyone."

Hildy held out a hand to the hesitant Dora. "Come on, Dora. We can go see Ned, our horse," she said, "and see if the chickens have laid some eggs."

Dora accepted the hand. "And see the cows," she said.

"You ain't leaving me with her!" said Mr Potts. "Come back, you hear. I order you to come back."

The room emptied and the door clicked to a close. Mr Potts stared at Mrs Maynard.

"You ain't staying," he said, "neither you nor the kid. Just extra mouths to feed and trouble. You're leaving when the brass go, so don't get used to any other ideas."

"I think we need to talk, Mr Potts," Mrs Maynard said, "civil like."

"Don't need to do anything, especially with freeloaders like you and your brat."

Ma Maynard moved with such speed and agility that Mr Potts had no time to react or speak. Instead he found his throat throttled in a massive and strong grip and was aware of being bodily borne up out of his chair and being held aloft and hard against the wall above the sideboard. His throat was squeezed and he couldn't speak. He flailed an arm but Ma Maynard's free hand slapped him hard against his head with a crack and he was pressed harder into the wall.

In Mr Potts' panic Ma Maynard deftly broke the shotgun one-handed across her thigh and removed the cartridges without being seen. She clicked the barrels home and then stuck the gun into Mr Potts' mouth. Mr Potts immediately ceased all attempts at struggle and froze, staring wide and white-eyed down at the barrel. Ma's iron grip still held him aloft and by the throat.

"Now, Mr Potts, I got a lifetime behind me of lifting coal on the canal barges and I can keep a sack of shit like you up and pinned to this wall all day if need be. Do you believe me?" Mr Potts nodded slowly, trying not to move a muscle. "Good. Now let's get some things clear, Mr Potts. New rules you might say. Rule one, is if you ever call little Dora a brat again I promise you will come to regret it. And you'll do all your regretting with your balls in a jar on the mantle. Do we understand? Good. Rule two, is that you are never to touch this gun again. Agreed?"

After a moment of thought Potts nodded. Ma Maynard removed the gun from his mouth and let him slide down to sit slumped on the sideboard like an unstrung marionette. Potts coughed and spluttered heavy breaths.

"This ain't right," he said, "You're mad! You can't…" He cried out in pain as Ma Maynard slapped him hard against his cheek. He toppled sideways onto the sideboard. Ma Maynard hauled him upright.

"Not fair, Mr Potts?" she said, "Damn right it isn't fair. But there's a war going on, or hadn't you noticed? Fair flew out the window long ago. Just minutes in your company and I can see you're a miserable, snivelling, selfish wretch of an excuse for a man, Mr. Potts and a nasty weasel of a bully to boot. Well I'm here to change you, and change you I will. Me and Dora needs a place to stay away from the damp and bombs and get her some healthy air for her bad chest and this is it. You don't know how lucky you are. Free cook and housekeeper and two strong farmhands. And when your daughter and her friends return you will tell them how lucky you are, won't you?"

Mr Potts was silent. Ma Maynard squeezed her hold at his throat. "Won't you?" Mr Potts nodded. The hold was released. "Good, I'm glad we've come to an understanding."

"It's blackmail," Potts said rubbing his throat.

"With menaces, Mr Potts," said Ma Maynard smiling, "don't forget the menaces. And I will be happy to remind you anytime you like. Rule three, is that you will mind your manners at all times. Ask me nicely and I will get you down from the sideboard. Or would you like to get down yourself?"

"You know I can't."

"As do you, Mr Potts, so start behaving accordingly."

Mr Potts took a while to respond. Mrs Maynard took the shotgun and placed it out of reach on the top of the Welsh dresser.

"Get me down then."

"I'm sorry?"

Mr Potts scowled. "Get me down, please."

"And will there be no problem when the others return? You will let your daughter go?"

"Don't seem I have much choice."

"No, Mr Potts, you don't. And the sooner you start recognising that, the better we will get on and the better your life will be. If not there is always the sideboard."

Ma Maynard lifted Mr Potts from the sideboard without effort and placed him in his chair. She replaced the rug at his knees. "Now, how about I make a nice cup of tea?"

Out on the farm the visit had gone well. Walter and Rolf had been charmed by the farm and its land. It was less mechanised than the farms both had been used to back in Germany but there was much they could do and they were keen to get working.

"Rolf says it is good to smell the cow dung again,"

Walter said, "and to get farm air into our chests!"

Hildy explained to Sergeant Harris and Walter about the farm day book and where the stores and tools were kept. They all rode on the tractor and trailer to see the farm fields and boundaries and Dora was delighted to sit astride Ned for a few steps while the old shire horse pulled the water bucket from the well. Dora also made instant friends with Jip and promised Hildy she would look after him.

Townsend and Merchant found a convenient moment to speak to Hildy alone.

"So, will you come with us?" asked Townsend. "Do a few months training. If things don't work out you can always come back here. But I have to tell you again, if you get through the training, it will be dangerous work you will be engaged in."

"Can't be any more dangerous than facing my father's shotgun. But is it important work?" asked Hildy.

"Vital to us winning this war," Townsend said.

"Then of course I would like to. But I don't think Father will let me. He can be very stubborn."

"Oh, I think he and Mrs Maynard might have come to an amicable arrangement. It might surprise you."

"Here, miss," Merchant said, "we thought you might like this back." He grinned and pulled Hildy's grandfather's gun from his coat pocket and handed it to her. "Our Welsh friends found they had no further use for it."

"You found it!" Hildy held it lovingly, checking it over for damage. "It seems fine. Undamaged. I thought it had gone. For ever. Oh, that is so wonderful! Just to feel it in my hand again. What happened to Gethyn and Davey?"

"Oh, they were given a choice," Merchant said, "ten years detention at His Majesty's pleasure or join the merchant marine aboard the SS Nantwich Bay. Their criminal charge sheet reads like a Dickens novel and runs back all the way to the valleys of their youth. Robbery, ABH, sexual assault, draft dodging, thievery. Even sheep rustling. Faced with a ten stretch they chose a life on the oceans."

"So they will do their bit for the war after all?"

"Yes, Miss Potts, and on the valiant Nantwich Bay they will be doing it in the freezing, northerly gales and cliff-face waves of the arctic Russian convoys. Didn't mention that to Gethyn and Davey, of course. Didn't want to spoil the surprise."

"It'll make men or fish food out of them," Townsend said.

Sergeant Harris took Walter and Rolf in the truck back to the camp with an agreement to return the next day to begin work. The rest gathered back in the front room and were greeted by a jovial Mrs Maynard handing out tea and biscuits and a rather subdued Mr Potts sitting silent in his chair. The shotgun was nowhere to be seen.

"Mr Potts and I have had a lovely chat and everything is arranged," said Mrs Maynard, "isn't that right, Mr Potts?"

Mr Potts grunted. He dunked his biscuit in his tea and didn't look up.

"So, you are happy with the arrangements, Mr Potts?" asked Merchant. "What? I didn't quite catch that."

"Damn it I said yes!" said Potts. Mrs Maynard's cup tinged in its saucer and she shot him a look. "I mean yes," said Potts, "Yes, Ok! How many more times do I have to tell you?"

"I'll fetch your bags from the car, Mrs Maynard," Merchant said, "see you settled to your rooms."

Townsend smiled at Hildy. "I think you have some packing to do, Miss Potts," he said.

Hildy laughed. She turned and bounded up the stairs two at a time.

Ma Maynard steered Townsend to a corner of the room. She spoke in a low whisper while filling Townsend's cup. "This is all for Jack, isn't it, Captain? Me and Dora here."

"Jack was insistent," Townsend said. "He can be very persuasive."

Ma Maynard was silent for some time.

"Is it dangerous work he'll be doing?"

"Maybe."

"And the lass here, Miss Potts, she one of yours too?"

"Maybe."

"Will they be gone long?"

"Maybe."

Ma Maynard reached out and lifted Townsend's cap from his head and then replaced it.

"Just checking there's a human under the hat," she said and wandered over to Merchant to refill his cup from the pot.

"Maybe," said Townsend to no one. He went out into the courtyard and got into the back seat of the staff car. He turned to the figure seated beside him. "There you are, Jack. Your Dora and Mrs Maynard settled away from the bombs and safe. I've kept my promise."

"Germans?" said Jack.

"There is a war on, Jack. We have to be pragmatic. They are just men a long way from home and probably glad to be here rather than there. They're part of the deal. I can assure you that they are harmless here. Or would you want Dora back in her damp tin hut?"

"Who's the girl?"

"Just another part of the deal, Jack. Now sign this." He passed over a paper and fountain pen. Jack studied the paper. It was an official secrets agreement.

"Buying my silence?"

"That's the deal. Take it or leave it."

Jack signed the paper. Townsend took the paper back checked it and gestured for the return of his pen. "Good. I'm glad that's over with. You will now go for a few days' parachute training and then will be going to Beaulieu to complete your training. Now I can give you this."

He passed over a map of Beaulieu estate in Hampshire. There was a circle pencilled around a house in the grounds called The Rings.

"A little test for you, Jack. They will be expecting you at Beaulieu in the next few weeks. There's a Captain Donald Green down there, known as Killer to his friends, of which there are but few. He's in charge of thieves training and he reckons you are an amateur and not worth a candle. I want you to light his wick, Jack. Your personnel file will soon be locked and secure in Killer's office in the Rings house and tightly guarded. When you get down there you will be tasked with burgling your own file. Just thought you'd like to know."

"You're so good to me."

Townsend smiled. "Oh, I doubt that, Jack."

ELEVEN

Merchant looked up from his work among the files and found a slim, tall man in rimless spectacles standing before him. Although he was not wearing a uniform there was a natural authority and presence in the figure that made Merchant stand up and wonder about saluting. His visitor broke into a wide smile.

"So sorry to disturb you. Is Captain Townsend around? Are you Merchant?"

"Yes, er, sir. The captain is in his office. Who may I…"

"Merchant? Wouldn't be the chap who wrote the Mark Three radio paper? Eh?"

Merchant was momentarily taken aback.

"Er, well. I did. Yes. Who are you, sir?"

"Fine work. What weight can the new version save? Fit it in a shoe box? Has the transmitting distance been verified?"

Merchant was saved need for a reply by the appearance of Captain Townsend.

"Sam, what are you doing here?"

"Hope your shoes are buffed, Matthew. You are to come with me. Now. We have an urgent date with the Tailor."

"Now? Tailor?"

"Very much now. We need to be with Lieutenant Colonel Amies in half an hour. It's an order by the way."

Sam explained as they made their way through the corridors and floors of Baker Street. An urgent meeting had been called of the Section T heads with attendance from the Foreign Office and Ministry of War to discuss the action plan for what had become known as the Belgian Problem. The rumour of Belgian Nazi collaborators running an escape line for downed allied airman had now been confirmed by a rear-gunner who had managed to escape and make it back to England through Spain. There was still no news of the three agents sent into the Mons area and the presumption was that they had been captured or killed. The

Belgian Ambassador of the Exiled Belgian Government in London, Emile de Marchinese and the Belgian Foreign Affairs Minister, Paul Henri Spaak, had insisted on meeting with the Head of Section T and to ensure that any proposed action by the British forces was mindful of Belgian sovereignties and the safety of its people.

"Ever met the Tailor?" Sam asked. They were in an alcove a little way along the corridor of the top floor offices of Section T, awaiting their appointed time.

"Me? No not really. A bit lowly in the ranks. And he mixes with kings and generals. Seen him at a few section briefings and from two dozen tables away at the Christmas Ball but no, never spoken. Know of his reputation, of course."

Lieutenant Colonel Hardy Amies, Head of Section T, was known as the Tailor for his selfless determination to always be smartly turned out. Even his uniform seemed to have an elan and cut of cuff and cloth that no others possessed.

"Don't let the Tailor's reputation fool you, Matthew. Amies is no fashion shop mannequin or fop. It is the mistake many have made and lived to regret it. At least some have lived. He is a sharp mind and a steely and ruthless operator so don't be fooled by his dapper appearance or manner. He does not suffer fools or braggarts and likes to hear it straight and true."

"But why am I here?"

"Just to observe and listen. Don't worry, Matthew you'll be in the dark corner. Look upon it as part of your growing education."

Townsend sat in the corner of the room beside a tall bookcase and observed the meeting ebb and flow before him. Sam Franks took a chair in the opposite corner of the room. Colonel Amies was a tall, straight-backed presence at the head of the table who commanded with quiet and calm authority. Townsend's boss, Colonel Forster, of Section T Operations gave a forceful and succinct presentation on the current situation in Belgium and the need to clarify the response with regard to the German-run escape route and the three missing agents. Hillier from the Foreign Office made little contribution other than to warn against reckless action and Beckington of the Ministry of War just made notes. The most animated contributions came from the Belgian representatives. Paul Spaak was a round, balding, jowled man in rimless spectacles who Townsend thought looked a lot like Winston Churchill. Spaak spoke with passion and force and even banged his fist on the table on one occasion. His forcefulness was shared by his colleague Emile de Marchinese who tugged at his bushy moustache and insisted that there could be no British action on Belgian soil that risked the safety of Belgian nationals.

"But we can't just do nothing!" Forster said. "We need to destroy this false escape route. There are British and allied airman's lives at stake."

"And how do you propose to do this?" asked Spaak.

"By assassinating the organisers. We know who they are. Guy Delmain, Henri Latisse and Michel de Fointeau. We simply eliminate them."

"Impossible!" de Marchinese said. "You do not know for sure these are the men. Or that the escape line is a fact. It is all hearsay. The Belgian Government refuses to endorse this action. It demands that it does not and cannot happen!"

"We have the word of our pilot who escaped the line. He gave us names."

"Names in war time mean nothing. How does he know these men were who they said they were? No, we refuse to allow this assassination plan. The Belgian Government says no," said Spaak.

"And what of the agents you sent and are now missing? Do you propose to send in more? For what? To meet the same end? No, it is not to be allowed. Even if it happened the reprisals on our Belgian people would be too terrible to think of. No. It cannot happen," said de Marchinese.

"We can't do nothing!" Forster said.

The meeting's heat cooled to an uncomfortable silence. Eyes turned to Colonel Amies who was gazing at a large portrait of Palmerston on the wall and seemed lost in thought. After several moments he turned back to those gathered around the table and smiled thinly.

"Thank you all for your contributions, gentlemen. I appreciate the delicacies of our situation. We cannot, of course, proceed with any retaliatory action on Belgian soil without the approval and support of its Government. We do not have that and therefore we will not proceed with this action."

"But, Colonel!" said Forster.

Amies raised a silencing hand, his smile still seeking to calm.

"I know this is difficult, Ted but we are bound by such conventions and obligations. I think this meeting is over. Thank you for your attendance. Sam, Captain Townsend, a moment please."

Townsend was startled to hear his name called and even more surprised that Colonel Amies knew it. He waited while the others filed out of the room. The door closed behind them and he was alone with Colonel Amies and Sam.

The colonel went to the sideboard, poured three large whiskies and handed them out. He beckoned them to the easy chairs by the unlit fire.

"So, Captain Townsend, what did you make of that?" asked Amies. He lifted the crease of his trousers and crossed his legs. He was wearing pale blue socks.

Townsend was unsure what he made of it. Sam was watching him with an amused smile playing on his lips, as if he was enjoying his friend's discomfort. Amies was also watching him but with a steady, cool gaze from behind intelligent blue eyes. Townsend took a deep gulp of his whisky.

"I don't think war and politics make for easy bedfellows, sir," he said.

Amies' smile broadened.

"How true," he said, "so what is the solution? Divorce?"

"It rather depends on the couple, sir. Sometimes a trial

separation is the best for some."

"And in this case?"

"We can't do nothing but we can't not do anything. Perhaps we need to separate the two."

"How?"

Townsend took another mouthful of whisky. He saw with some alarm that his glass was now empty and that neither Amies nor Sam had touched their drinks.

"By doing something and not telling anybody we are doing it," he said.

He was conscious of the heavy silence and stillness that had fallen on the room. Amies reached for his glass and drained it off in one gulp and then sat back in his chair.

"Sam tells me you are a clever young man, Captain Townsend. Resourceful too. But are you discreet?"

Townsend could not think of a reply. He was pretty sure he was but it was not something he could attest to. He remained silent.

"Quite right," Amies said, "not a question you can answer yourself. But Sam here vouches for you and that is answer enough for me. Yes, separation is the way forward with our Belgian problem. Show them we are doing nothing while doing something. To act how, I wonder?"

"Invisibly, sir?" offered Townsend.

Amies laughed.

"I see that Sam's estimations were not wide of the mark, Captain Townsend. Quite so. Invisibly. I read your paper on invisible agents. Care to find and unleash some in Belgium?"

"I believe I can."

"Good. Then be about it. I understand that you have some reservations about certain aspects of our department security. You are wise to question but rest assured we are on the case. However, we need to pursue our prey with stealth and care and in the greatest secrecy. So go invisible and be very vigilant, Captain. Our hopes for your success go with you. Sam will finalise the mission details but they will boil down to killing Delmain, Latisse and Fointeau and their Nazi bosses and destroying their treacherous escort escape line. And if you can find our missing three agents that would be the cherry on the cake. Still think you can do it?"

"I know I can try."

"Splendid. Of course we have not had this conversation, no sanction has been given for your action and in the event of disaster we will deny all knowledge and will be only too happy to sacrifice you to whatever dogs are baying loudest and to hang you out to dry alone. You understand this?"

"War is hell, sir."

Amies laughed.

"But such fun don't you think! Come through Sam for anything you need. Good luck, Matthew. Now I have to go to Claridge's for drinks with those ghastly Belgians and play diplomat over glasses of their gut-rot absinthe. War is indeed hell."

Amies shook Townsend by the hand and he was outside the door in the corridor with Sam before he really knew he had left. Sam slapped him on the back.

"Well that all went rather well, didn't it?"

Townsend was distinctly unsure.

PART TWO

TWELVE

The woman a few yards along the roadside also seemed to be waiting for someone. Georgia had been waiting outside Totton station for her car lift to Beaulieu for over forty-five minutes and the other woman had been there just as long. The local bus had been and gone twice. Georgia took in the woman in a practiced casual gaze. She was young, medium height with brown hair and her unfashionable, rather worn coat and skirt suggested rural practicality rather than urban chic. She had a pleasant, open face with a slight cheek flush and, like Georgia, she stood beside a suitcase.

Hildy also took in the woman who waited a little way along the road from her. Her companion was tall, blonde and calmly assured with high cheek bones, good complexion and large brown eyes. She was very beautiful. Her suitcase was new leather and her expensive coat was fur-trimmed at the collar.

Hildy felt a sudden pang of inadequacy ripple within her. The woman was obviously going to Beaulieu and therefore was part of the same recruitment that Hildy had gone through. She was still unsure of what Beaulieu might have in store for her or why she was going there. Captain Townsend had given a vague notion of the training and she knew she was involved in a secret and special programme. The four days in a parachute training school and another two weeks at Henley learning radio Morse had left her in no doubt that the work, whatever it was to be, would be overseas. Looking at the sophisticated, confident woman in the expensive blue coat, Hildy felt suddenly very country bumpkin and was hit by the thought that she would not come up to scratch and would be found out and sent back to work on the farm. It was a depressing thought. She had enjoyed her time jumping with parachutes and learning Morse keys and had even got to meet a few real men and drink a few pints. Even an occasional dance. Her new world and its experiences thrilled her and the idea of going back to her prison farm didn't bear thinking of. She plunged her hand into her coat pocket and sought comfort in the touch of her oddments. There was the little penknife and pencil stub, Bobette's glass eye, the pebble with the hole in it, the dice and small Zip lighter. She let them tumble over her fingers like puppies. Captain Townsend had told her to pack only essentials but Hildy could not leave home without them, they were her friends from home. They might even be useful sometime.

"Are you waiting for a car ride too?" asked Georgia. "To the Beaulieu estate?"

Hildy let the puppies lie. She tried to sound more confident than she felt.

"Yes, I was expecting a pick-up nearly an hour ago. Perhaps it's had an accident. Or roadworks or something."

"Maybe, do you smoke? I'm Georgia by the way. Literally in this case."

Georgia was holding out a cigarette to Hildy who came closer to accept it.

"Hildy," said Hildy. "Thanks"

Smoking had become a guilty new pleasure for Hildy. Like pints of cider and dancing until gone midnight. She took the proffered cigarette and light.

"We could walk it, I suppose," Hildy said. "I think the estate is only about twelve miles from here."

"Not in these shoes," Georgia said. Hildy gazed down at the fashionable heels of the woman's buckled leather shoes. "We'll order a taxi," she saw Hildy's look of alarm, "my treat since I have dressed so inappropriately."

Just then a car sped up the road, skid-turned and came to a halt beside them. A small man in ragged jacket, collarless shirt and moleskin trousers jumped out of the driver's door and greeted them with a wide smile and a stuttered forelock salute.

"Misses Melrose and Potts for the estate?" he said. "Sorry I'm late, ladies but some mix up at the depot. Official car dropped a crank and they called on Benny's Taxis to fill the breach and save the day." He bowed theatrically.

"Benny at your service, ladies. Just stow your cases and we'll be off. Have to go detour because the roads are up at Lyndhurst. Gas main gone. Get you there for teatime. OK, ladies?"

Georgia and Hildy settled in the back seat and watched the Hampshire countryside blur by while Benny sped along the lanes and kept up a continual chatter.

"Roads in Lyndhurst all a mess so have to detour the back ways. Blasted German bombs costing us petrol. But good for navvies eh? I'm in the wrong business. Should get myself a shovel and pair of boots. Where you ladies from then?"

The women sat silent in the back seat. They could see Benny watching them through the rear view mirror.

"So what's ladies like you doing up at Beaulieu then? They say it's some kind of training place. You going there for training? Or maybe you're secretaries. Filing clerks and such."

The women remained silent. Hildy reached into her pocket and withdrew the pencil discreetly. She wrote a note on the back of her travel pass.

"He's got military shoes. A test?" She tapped Georgia's foot with hers and showed her the note. Georgia glanced down at the note and then into the driver's footwell and saw the shine of Benny's black shoes, incongruous against the ragged moleskin trousers and rumpled, worn jacket. She nodded and smiled.

"Yes, I takes lots of ladies up to Beaulieu," continued Benny, "From Scotland, Manchester. Some foreign ladies too. One from the Argentine last week. It's all very mysterious I must say. All that high wire fencing and sentry posts. And strange lights in the woods at night. What do they do up there?"

His passengers remained silent and found disinterest in the passing fields and woods.

"Some round here reckon it's a secret weapons place," Benny went on, "We hear bombs and gunfire and such. So stands to reason. Mind you some say it's a spy school. All them foreigners. What do you do then? Why are you going to Beaulieu?"

"We can't say," Georgia said. "It's supposed to be a secret."

Benny perked up.

"Can't be a secret to me because I'm taking you there ain't I? So tell me, what do you do up there?"

"We really shouldn't say," Georgia said, "it's a bit delicate."

"Don't worry about me, miss. Benny's Taxis is discretion itself. Lips sealed. Like a confessional in here. I mean I'm part of the team like. You know, transport section. Signed the papers and everything."

"We shouldn't."

"Course you can."

"Oh, all right then," Georgia shared a discreet glance with Hildy and winked. "Me and Chantelle here are from Madame Devereux's Escort agency. We have been sent to Beaulieu to entertain some high-ranking officers. There's a party there tonight. We are the after dinner mints and brandy."

Benny was silent for a while. Hildy was giggling inside and trying not to show it. Her travelling companion was certainly daring and her courage was infectious. Hildy decided to press home the pleasure.

"Binky, I mean Major Mann, asked for me and Danielle special like," said Hildy, "A regular at Madame Lily's is Binky. Likes his late-night meat sandwich, if you know what I mean. You gonna be at this party then?"

"Er, no. Not invited."

"Well you are only a taxi driver, aren't you?" Georgia said, "I mean, not a soldier. Why would you be invited?"

"Yes, quite. Are you sure it's Major Mann? Older chap, balding, glasses? Slight limp?"

"That's Binky all right. Never had problems with the limp as I'd noticed! And a gentleman."

"That's right. Always hangs his trousers from a clasp hanger and pays extra for the taxi home," Hildy said. "Broke the mould they did with Binky."

They travelled the rest of the journey in silence, Hildy and Georgia studying the passing scenery through their respective windows with a determination not to make eye contact, or to laugh for fear of giving their game away. Benny studied the road ahead, occupied in his own troubled thoughts.

They pulled up at the outer sentry post behind a courier on his motorcycle who was being checked through the gate by two guards. One of the guards broke away to check Benny's papers and the passes of the two women passengers. They were waved through and followed the motorcycle along the long drive through woods and heathlands where hardy ponies grazed the gorse and grass. They were checked through the inner sentry gates and drove down the long stone driveway towards the main Beaulieu estate. The turreted and tall-chimneyed grandeur of Beaulieu Palace house loomed into view. The driveway bisected well-manicured lawns on which several groups of men and women were reading, or lying on rugs in the sun or gathered in small knots smoking and chatting. At one end of the lawns an impromptu cricket match seemed to be underway with a tennis ball and hockey stick.

The motorcycle courier turned off to the yard at the side of the house while Benny turned off the drive and pulled up outside another gate. He didn't volunteer to help them with their bags.

"Go on up to The Rings," he pointed at a large, red-bricked house of high roofs and many windows that stood at the end of more lawned garden fringed by the woods. "They're expecting you."

They were met at the door of the house by a tall, gaunt woman with a military-drilled straight back, a close-tied bun and a clipboard.

"I take it you are Potts and Melrose," she said. "You're late. I'm Miss Curtis, your mentor. In the office over there. Papers to sign. You've missed supper. Have to do with a cold platter. You're sharing room eight in STS 35. That's

Vineyards. The house half a mile down the track. Clear?"

"Crystal," Georgia said.

Miss Curtis studied them in a slow up and down gaze. She made a few entries on her clipboard and then pointed them to the office. "Papers," she said. "Cold platter in the refractory. Then get to your room, unpack and early night. Breakfast at o-seven thirty. Exercise drills on the south lawn at o-eight hundred."

They watched Miss Curtis stride off down the corridor. Georgia turned to Hildy.

"I don't think this can be a charm school," she said. "do you?"

THIRTEEN

Jack Summers parked the motorcycle behind a wooden shed and took a moment to check his courier pouch. Townsend's despatch sat in its document compartment and in the inner, zipped pocket lay his torch, knotted rope, gloves, cheese roll, burglar tool-pouch, bradle, and Minox Riga miniature camera.

The camera had been loaned from Gustav Stavel, an old acquaintance from the pre-war years. Jack had helped Gustav and his daughter flee the Nazis in 1938 and get safe passage to England. Gustav had been a leading technician with the Minox company and he had escaped with a suitcase of their latest camera supplies and a head full of new technical designs. There were few favours he would not do for Jack. He was even happy to print the film in his home laboratory in Bethnal Green.

The courier motorcycle and uniform had been even easier to arrange. The despatch couriers had favourite cafes and rest depots scattered across London and Jack had just waited outside the biggest of them in Chelsea Docks. This depot had a dormitory, canteen and showers where the hard working despatch riders could rest and recharge before braving the bombs and unlit streets again on untrustworthy machines and at breakneck speeds. Jack had lifted a helmet, jacket, boots and goggles from the change room hangers and, among the lake of motorcycles parked in the rear quad, he found one with the key still in the ignition and its tank near full of petrol. He even found the courier's ID in the jacket pocket. In a despatch rider's full regalia complete with helmet and goggles anyone could look like anyone. Jack slipped into the uniform, gummed a moustache to his upper lip, pulled on the goggles and headed for Beaulieu.

He stood on the gravel of the courtyard at the corner of the house and watched the passengers getting out of the taxi that had followed him up the drive. One of the women looked remarkably like the young woman he had met on the farm. It was not a face easy to forget. Her companion was even more beautiful. A tall and elegant woman in an expensive coat.

Jack hipped his pouch and strode to the front of the house and followed the women up the steps. The foyer was large, polished, bright and busy with noise, soldiers, civilians and clerks. He waited at the reception desk where a corporal with brilliantined hair and razor parting was listening without interest to the murmuring telephone receiver at his ear. He took in Jack with the same indifference. After a few moments the corporal stretched in his chair.

"No," he said into the phone and put it down with a crack. "Well?"

"Despatch for Captain Green," Jack said. He took the letter from his pouch.

The corporal held out a hand. "I'll see Killer gets it," he said.

"Orders, Corporal. By hand to the recipient. Baker Street brass would have my balls otherwise. Yours too like as not. Brass are like that."

The corporal gazed at Jack with ill-disguised contempt. But his expectant hand lowered and turned to a fist that stamped a visitor pass.

"Sign here," he said. Jack signed. The pass was flicked to him. "Up the stairs, second floor, room forty-five." The corporal returned to the paperwork on his desk.

Jack already knew where Captain Donald "Killer" Green's office was located in the Rings house. The Southampton planning office archives had produced much useful information about the layout and construction of the house and of the alterations it had undergone since being requisitioned as one of the Stately 'Omes of England by the Baker Street special forces. Jack had studied the plans and knew the house like his own hand. He just needed to find out where the staff files were locked away.

An orderly met him outside Captain Green's office and, after checking his pass, ushered him in without greeting. The office was large, cluttered with desks and bookcases

86

and several easy chairs and was bright and airy from the two large picture windows that made up one side of the room and looked out onto the lawns. Jack's perfunctory but expert recce located the attic trapdoor in the ceiling in the corner of the room above one of the cluttered desks. Captain Green stood bent over one of the desks, measuring distance on a map before him with a pair of compasses. He looked up as Jack came to attention before him. Captain Green was not a tall man but his natural confidence and authority seemed to add a few inches to his wiry frame. He was in his late thirties, running to baldness and compensating by way of a luxuriant moustache, greying at its tips.

"Yes?" he said.

"Despatch from Baker Street, sir," Jack said handing over the envelope, "from Captain Townsend, sir."

"Aha!" Green said. He was at once attentive and eager. He ripped open the envelope and read the letter quickly. "Aha!" he said again. "Carter!"

A lieutenant came in from the large ante-room adjoining the office. "From that bastard Townsend," Green said. "He's sending down this gutter rat of his he's been on about," he checked the letter again, "a Jack Summers. Says he's a burglar of promise. Hah! I'll give Townsend and Summers promise. He's to rob his own file from the Rings office to prove his worth. Have we got his file, Carter?"

"Yes, sir. It came two days ago. I've filed it with the other burglar possibles."

"Well bring it here. No, bring all four burglar files here."

Jack stood as silent and as inconspicuous as he could and studied the room. It always amazed him how invisible servants can become in the presence of their betters. He took the opportunity to scan and study. The staff filing cabinets were probably in the ante-room office and if there was a safe it could be behind the large picture of the Duke of Wellington that dominated one wall of Green's office, but it seemed too obvious.

Carter came back with files. Green read them off. "Burton, Gilligan, McNulty, ah, Summers."

He opened the file and began reading and scanning the documents. "Doesn't read like any great Raffles to me. Engineer. Dishonourable discharge. Working as a civvy reading manuals. By God he even married a damn Hun." Green tidied the files into a pile. "Still, Townsend might be an arrogant bastard, but he isn't stupid. He's bet me lunch at Paulo's if his man pulls his file without getting caught. Well, we are not going to give his little Hun-loving gutter rat the chance. Paulo's lobster can be on Townsend for once eh Carter?"

He laughed and picked up the four files and took them over to a bookcase. He pulled the bookcase back and it rolled away from the wall on castors. A small safe was hidden in the wall. Jack watched Green pull a book from the top of the case and consult something in its fly leaf before tumbling the numbers, opening the safe, putting the files away, and then closing and locking the safe. Returning to his desk Captain Green seemed surprised to still see Jack in the room.

"What are you still doing here?"

"Reply for Captain Townsend, sir. He said you would give me a Beaulieu pin to prove delivery and receipt. Sir."

Green looked at Jack as if considering a reprimand.

"Worth a lobster, I suppose. Wait there."

Captain Green went into the ante-room, followed by Carter. Jack knew the pins were in a locked drawer of a filing cabinet. He knew because Townsend had told him. As soon as the room was empty Jack leapt lightly onto the corner desk, released the ceiling trapdoor bolts and was instantly back on the floor and at attention awaiting Green's return. He only had moments to spare. Green returned and handed him the small pin.

"Tell Townsend he can stick it in my lobster at Paulo's," he said. "Dismissed."

Jack left the office and headed along the corridor to the end gallery room. There were a few people carrying files or hurrying to meetings but they paid the motorcycle courier no heed. Jack slipped into the small telephone exchange room banked high with switching and relay cabinets and used one as a ladder to reach the ceiling trapdoor into the attic. He was up and through and the trapdoor closed again in a moment.

The attic space of the Rings house was suffused in a dusty, sepia light created by small gaps in the roof and gables. Jack had expected darkness but the dim light was enough to see and navigate by and he did not need his torch to find his way back to the trapdoor of Captain Green's office. He settled himself against a chimney stack, checked his watch and tucked into his cheese roll. He passed the time until full night thinking about Dora and her new farm home and Beth and how much he still missed her and how it burned to want to avenge her death. Perhaps working for Townsend would feed that fire. His thoughts also strayed to Captain Green and Jack was aware of a growing desire to have his gutter rat and hun-lover best the pompous bastard, and to do it in style.

Jack listened at the ceiling boards for almost an hour before he was content that the floor below was vacant and quiet. It was two-thirty in the morning. He screwed the bradle into the trapdoor, lifted it clear and bent down through the hatch to check the lie of the room. It was empty and dark. Jack slid through the hatch and hung a moment while one hand manoeuvred the trapdoor half-back over the hatch. Then he dropped to the desk and slid the trapdoor fully closed.

Jack could not believe the luck he had as the moustached courier. Captain Green had shown him the way as if leading him by the hand. The safe was open and Jack was photographing the files within moments. He copied all four files before replacing them in the safe and wheeling the bookcase back. It really had been too easy. He went into the ante-room and, with aid of his torch, located the staff filing cabinets and picked its simple lock with one of his tools from the pouch. He photographed Captain Green's file, and Carter's and, just for good measure, Major Mann the commandant of Beaulieu station. He returned everything as it was and, after checking the corridor, made his escape silently along the landing to the far window. A sentry patrolled at a leisurely pace along the gravel path below and in the distance the glowing tips of two cigarettes could be seen in the sentry box by the inner gate.

Jack waited for the sentry to pass beneath him and away round the house and then he opened the window and climbed down the wisteria that hugged the wall. He made his way back to the shed and curled up under a tarpaulin in a dark corner and waited for first light. Two hours later he was pushing his motorbike through the Beaulieu woods and then cutting a narrow exit in the wire fence before firing the motorbike up and riding out along the Hampshire roads heading for Bethnal Green and the home of Gustav Stavel.

Despite the early hour Gustav was not surprised to see Jack. Gustav had had too many surprises in his life to find exception in yet another. The old man was slightly stooped and grey and the familiar half-moon spectacles floated above his large, blue-veined nose. Jack handed him the Minox.

"Thanks, Gustav. Returned as promised. With pictures."

"There was no hurry. Or maybe there is," Gustav said, "with life who can tell? You want the pictures?"

"Please."

"Ah, a polite boy. It must be important. You want breakfast? Make it yourself and I will do the pictures. Black coffee, six sugars. Live a little I say. It will be two, maybe three hours."

Gustav ushered Jack into his small shop and to the kitchen at the back. Gustav went into his darkroom while Jack made himself some breakfast of black bread toast and jam. He took the sweetened dark coffee into Gustav who was preparing the trays of chemicals.

"Put it on the bench. Close the door on your way out and don't come in until I tell you."

Jack made himself tea and sat on the old chaise long that served as Gustav's easy chair and bed. Gustav was not a poor man, Jack had got him regular work for various publishers and Gustav's photographic engineering skills were in regular and paid demand, but Gustav preferred to live simply and without extravagance. A picture frame of his daughter, Hetty, sat prominent and alone on the mantle above the range fire. On escaping to England with Gustav, Hetty had joined the WRAF. Gustav did not know where she was and didn't want to know. Jack had offered to try and find out but Gustav would not hear of it.

"Not knowing makes her still alive," Gustav said, "better that than knowing. I can live with not knowing."

Jack woke up with a blanket draped over him. Gustav was sitting at the kitchen table working on a small electric circuit under a large magnifying glass. He looked up on hearing Jack stir.

"Ah, the boy awakes at last! Your pictures are there in the envelope. Hope you are not mixing with bad boys, Jack. Only leads to trouble."

"Sorry, I fell asleep."

"You were tired. Boys need their sleep."

"Thanks, Gustav. I owe you."

"You owe me nothing, Jack. Take what you will and have it gladly. You want lunch?"

Jack checked his watch.

"No, thanks. I must get on."

"I don't think the moustache suits you," Gustav said, "too Prussian for a young boy."

Jack laughed and peeled off his forgotten moustache. Gustav seemed amused.

"If only Prussia was so easily removed eh?" he said.

FOURTEEN

There were twelve of them lined up, eyes front, before Sergeant Evans and two corporals. Hildy glanced along the line of men and women. Her fellow recruits of Beaulieu were all wearing the dark one-piece siren suits favoured by Churchill and which were now adopted throughout the services. It was with some dismay that Hildy noticed that her suit actually seemed to fit her while all the others looked awkward in theirs.

In other parts of the expansive Beaulieu grounds she could see small groups undergoing various training. One group nearby was practising knife fighting, another sat on the grass before a scribble board while a bespectacled, capless major drew electronic diagrams for bombs.

"Eyes front!" barked Sergeant Evans. He was a short, stocky man with enormous shoulders and thin waist and stood a little under five foot six. His hair was a dark, curled bramble, his eyes bright and his voice the sound of crunching gravel. He studied the line before him with a knowing, piercing gaze. Behind him stood two corporals with clipboards, ready to take notes.

"I'm Sergeant Evans and today you are going to begin to learn self-defence. Now you young gentlemen and ladies was all brought up proper and thinking that Queensberry rules is how you play the fisticuffs game. Well forget Queensberry. Nazis don't do Queensberry. They do killing. And so do we."

Evans grinned and gazed along the line. Feet shuffled and the nervousness rippled along the line like a small shudder. Hildy sought her pocket and began playing the objects over her fingers.

"I have done all the boxing booths from Clacton to Blackpool, been in more rings than a jeweller's missus and had near on a hundred pupils like you here at Beaulieu and in all that time no one has landed a punch on me. Not one. Self-defence ain't just about hitting, it's about ducking too.

Now I am a kind and generous old softie so I am going to let you in easy. I am going to let you punch me. Or at least try."

He sauntered down the line and faced a young, blond man.

"Name?"

"Olaf Pederson, sir."

"No sirs, son, sergeant will do. Care to take a swing at me?"

Sergeant Evans leaned forward as if to offer his jaw. The young man laughed nervously.

"I can't just hit you."

"You're Danish right?" Pederson nodded. "Well, King Christian is a cripple of a King who can't sit on a horse without falling off and he leads a country of cowards and capitulators. Cowards like you Pederson who run to England for safety."

"You've no right to say…"

Evans shoved him in the chest. "A lousy Danish coward."

Pederson stepped back and let fly a right fist. Evans seemed to wait for it to arrive and then his head swayed back and away as if it were on a spring. As Pederson's fist went past him Evans ducked and planted his own fist into Pederson's midriff. Pederson gasped a grunt and then doubled up and sank to his knees, wheezing.

"Never get angry, boy," Evans said, "it's all wasted energy."

Evans moved on down the line to face a tall, dark-haired man with a pencil moustache and aquiline nose. He stood nearly a foot taller than Evans.

"You must be our aristo Frenchie."

The man smiled thinly and inclined an acquiescent nod.

"Emile Gustave Francois de Greveney Boudelain, Sergeant. But you can call me Count de Breaville."

"I will call you anything I want, sonny, and it won't be anything royal. Well, no use calling a Frenchie a snivelling coward and rat, is there, Count? I mean that's taken as read.

93

All Frenchies are cowards and quitters. If you want to take France all you have to do is turn up in shiny boots and the French will just roll up and surrender. Care to try a punch?"

"The French aristocracy has learned not to provoke the peasantry, Sergeant, it tends to lead to beheadings."

"Put your arms out straight, Count." Boudelain did so. Evans shuffled up to face him so that his head was in line with the count's hands. He drew a line at his feet with his heel and then toed the line.

"I won't step from this line. Now I'm going to let you have three free punches at me. Are you game?"

"I think you will hurt me. I reluctantly decline."

"I promise you I will not punch you in return," Evans said. "What is there to lose? Three free swings at a peasant and no punch back. You might even connect with one. The first ever. One cock feather in the cap for the French wouldn't you say?"

"I accept," said Boudelain.

Evans grinned. "Good lad. Now make them good."

He proffered his jaw again.

Boudelain skipped sideways and pistoned a short, fast-jabbed fist towards Evans who swayed and let it pass. Almost immediately Boudelain swung his other fist up and Evans swayed backwards from his hips and watched the blow sail upwards into the air above him. The momentum had carried Boudelain forward and he swung another uppercut into Evans' side and then brought his other fist down for Evans's head. Evans dodged and swayed again without ever taking his feet from the line and, as Boudelain's fist came down, he ducked inside it, caught the arm, twisted it and then flipped Boudelain over his back with no more fuss than if he'd been a school satchel. Boudelain cried out and landed on his back in the grass with a thump. He lay there gasping and rubbing his arm

"You bastard! You lied!"

"No I didn't, Mr Boudelain, I told you I wouldn't punch in return and I didn't. And you took four punches not three. Very naughty. Can't trust an aristo. You deserved a little discomfort."

Evans moved onto the next in line – a young woman with grey eyes. She was standing next to Hildy.

"Name?"

"Mila Christophe, Sergeant."

"Ah, our young Greek lady. Nervous?"

"A little."

"Ever been punched?"

"Many times. I have four brothers."

"Like to punch them back?"

"Very much so. That would be nice. They are all dead."

Evans was silent for a moment.

"I'm sorry for your loss, miss. But you still need to throw me a punch. OK? It's an order. From your brothers."

Mila nodded. "I understand, Sergeant."

She adjusted her feet, threw back and arm and let her fist fly. Evans never moved his head or his feet. He simply caught Mila's fist in the air with a fast, rigid hand and held it still. Then he twisted it back upon itself slowly and Mila gasped as she was forced to her knees in fear of the pain. Evans took a knife from his belt and tapped it lightly on Mila's shoulder.

"You're now with your brothers, miss." He released her. "But you'll avenge them yet, eh?"

"It is what I live for, Sergeant," said Mila still on her knees.

Evans offered her a hand up. "Then we'll do our best to make it happen, miss."

Evans stood before Hildy.

"Ever punched anyone, miss?"

"I've punched a bull," Hildy replied.

Evans laughed. Some of the rest of the line grinned with him.

"A bull! You! Why there's hardly anything of you. Floor him did you?"

"No, Sergeant, just confused him a little."

"I bet you did. Fancy a punch at me?"

"What, right now?"

"Yes, now. Your best bull punch," he laughed again.

Hildy reached discreetly into her pocket and let her hand tumble her toys. Her fingers wrapped around Bobette's glass eye.

"All right, Sergeant. But do you mind if I remove my glass eye first as I would hate to damage or lose it."

"You have a glass eye?" Evans smiled, unsure if he was being gulled. "OK, if you must."

Hildy bent over, aware of the rest of the line watching her. She closed her right eye and plucked the glass eye from her pocket and pretended to have taken it from her eye socket. She stood up one-eyed before Evans. She held the glass eye out sideways in her outstretched hand between forefinger and thumb. Evans gazed from her one-eyed face and then turned to stare in fascination at the glass one in her other hand. As he did so, Hildy fisted her left hand and swung it up hard, fast and true into the side of Evans' distracted cheek. Evans had half-turned but was too late to duck the blow. The sound of the crack spat across the ground and Hildy was aware of a stinging pain in her knuckles and wrist. Evans took the punch full force and it sent him staggering backwards into his two corporals before landing him on his backside on the grass. He sat up and looked about, momentarily stunned.

He was quickly back on his feet again. He brushed himself down and was aware of the recruit line in some state of suppressed amusement. Pederson stood with his hands braced at his knees but he was laughing, Even the still prone Frenchie was grinning through the pain of his wrenched arm. Evans was also aware of several of the other nearby groups watching him and his group with amused interest.

Evans came to stand in front of Hildy again. He gazed into a blushing face of young womanhood and into two large, open and perfect, deep-brown eyes. He studied her for some time in silence.

"He giveth his cheek to him that smiteth him," said Evans quietly. "The arrogant shall be diminished."

"I'm sorry, Sergeant?" Hildy said, "I'm sorry, that was

unfair of me. I hope you aren't hurt. Only you said you were…" Hildy was stopped by Evans raising his hand.

"No one's ever hit me let alone put me on the floor, miss. What's your name?"

"Hildy Potts."

Evans consulted one of his corporal's clipboards. He took a pen from the corporal and wrote something in the file.

"Look I'm really sorry, Sergeant. Don't make me leave. Please. I know it was sort of cheating but…" Evans once again held up his hand. He seemed confused by Hildy's pleading.

"You are an instrument of instruction to us all, Miss Potts. We must all learn that we are not above the truth. You hurting, miss?" Hildy was holding her left hand. Her wrist was stinging.

"Seem to have hurt my hand. Sorry. It's nothing. Very silly of me." Evans took her hand. His touch was gentle and expert.

"Nothing to be sorry about, Miss Potts. A little sprain that's all. It was a damn fine punch. But you have got to learn to ride with it. Keep it loose." He turned to the rest of the line.

"Miss Potts here has just taught you what it takes many years to find out. If you are going to get the better of a swine then you have got to be an even bigger, but, and this is the important bit, a smarter swine." He turned back to Hildy. "Not that I think you are a swine, miss. You understand? Thank you, miss. You have taught us all a valuable lesson. Now get off to the MO and have him see to that wrist."

"You're not going to make me leave are you, Sergeant? It's nothing. It hardly hurts at all. Really."

"Leave?" Evans laughed. "Leave she says! You are right in it now, miss, right up to your pretty eyes. Glass or not. Right in it!"

Evans turned to the rest of the line. "Class dismissed early," he barked. "And I reckon you all owe Miss Potts your thanks for the rest reward."

FIFTEEN

Georgia had retired to her room feeling unusually tired and weary from her day of exercises. The PT and the silent killing classes in the morning had been gruelling and physically hard but nothing that she was not able to deal with; she had once trekked and hunted for three sleepless days in the searing heat and scrubs of the South African veldt and had taken that in her stride. The afternoon sessions of bomb making and sabotage had been interesting lectures and she had learned much. The end of the day had been marked by the usual drinks in the crowded Rings bar and a desultory meal of cold meats and colder vegetables in the canteen.

Sitting with her weak, warm tea she had felt suddenly tired, droopingly tired. She wondered if it had all become too much for her and that she was beginning to wilt from within. It had been only two months ago that she was in a prison cell charged with murder, and a year since her baby had died. Her nameless baby. Perhaps it was all catching up with her or had never quite left her. The devil was accounting her many sins and was now picking over her bones with slow, relentless relish.

Hildy was not in the room. There had been much talk of her punching Sergeant Evans that morning and the whole camp seemed abuzz with it. Georgia smiled at the thought of her roommate's new won reputation. She put on her pyjamas, lay on her bed and let such thoughts drift her quickly and easily to sleep.

They came for her a little after midnight. Her mouth was taped, her wrists roped together at her back and a black hood placed over her head before she really even knew it was happening and that it wasn't a dream and that she was being manhandled out of her bed and carried away. She tried to struggle but was kicked for her pains. Her cries of alarm were merely moans against the tape and cut short by a painful flash of light and pain at the side of her head. Three of them were carrying her. Shoulders, waist and feet. She couldn't move. And so she didn't.

It came to her that this was all part of the exercises. Interrogation and resistance. It would be playacting, up to a point. But the blow to the side of her head had been real and painful enough. In a sudden spark of revelation Georgia also realised that her unusual weariness was because she had been drugged, probably in the Rings bar. She tried to think who it might have been, but there had been so many there, wanting to talk or buy her a drink, there always were. It could have been any of them.

She felt the cool of damp airs and smell of fetid basements and heard a heavy door open and then close. She was manhandled onto a wooden chair and her ankles and wrists were manacled to its legs and seat. There was a bright light in the room she could see as a haze through her hood. The hood was jerked from her head and almost instantly a blindfold was tied tight and dark and the tape at her mouth ripped off.

Georgia sat panting in the chair, slightly stooped to ease the strain of the manacles and trying to reach a calmness that was proving elusive. She could hear faint noises in the room, of papers turning, boots squeaking. She smelt dampness and mildew and sweat. She sat still and silent awaiting her fate.

The dump of ice-cold water came out of nowhere and drenched her. It made her gasp and almost shriek as the chair rocked back from the force of the water. A soaked coldness seeped into her, her pyjamas sagged and clung and she knew that her nipples and breasts were showing through the fabric. She tried not to shiver. Georgia waited, her feet and hands getting numb, her head beginning to throb. She waited. She waited a long time. She wondered if she had fallen asleep or was now alone in the room.

"You think this is an exercise, don't you, Frau Ernst Baum?"

The voice was almost a relief, but it was as cold as the water and almost without intonation. It was a man's voice but had no man in it. Intimate but distant. Like a bored machine.

"It crossed my mind," said Georgia.

"Of course it did. You are an intelligent woman. We would expect this."

Georgia heard a faint swish and then a flash of light sparked in her head like a flare and the sound of a piercing crack by her ear. The pain of the slap instantly followed, like flames scorching her cheek.

"But perhaps you did not expect that," said the voice. "That is just to show that we do mean business and I regret to advise you that this is not an exercise. This is for real. How long have you been a spy for Germany, Mrs Baum?"

Georgia tried not to laugh but a half snort escaped her. It was cut short by another lit flare in her head and hot flames scorching her other cheek.

"Certain facts, Miss Melrose," said the voice, "Our British security services have long known of the German plan to infiltrate SOE with their own spies. You are married to a known German Nazi. You arrived on the boat from German South Africa. Remarkably you are found a job at the Ministry of Information, at the heart of communications. You kill, or shall we say assassinate, a South African Dutch trade official in the middle of London and then worm your way into Beaulieu, an SOE training centre. Looks like your German masters' grand plan is coming to pass, wouldn't you say? Your German masters must be very pleased with you. Who are they?"

"Hansel and Gretel," Georgia said.

"Ah, I see," said the voice, "fairy tales. Yes. Most amusing. Who says the Germans have no sense of humour? But you will tell us. I can assure you of that."

Georgia felt herself being lifted in her chair and moved across the room. Two men either side of her. She was tipped forward as if from a great height and she almost screamed but was plunged underwater still shackled to her chair that was being held by the two men. The water froze her head and she felt the drowning panic rise in her. She tried to kick and push out but the manacles would not give and she realised her panic was only shortening her chances of surviving. Her lungs were burning and her sight was whitening at the fringes. Georgia feigned unconsciousness and went limp. The blood in her head began pounding and her chest burned on the cusp of explosion. She and the chair were lifted clear. Georgia gulped and gasped in air and coughed and felt her whole body begin to shiver and spasm.

"Who sent you here? Who is your contact?" asked the voice.

"Bastards," she hissed.

Georgia's shackles were untied quickly and she was hoisted up by her wrist ties until her feet were clear of the floor. She hung suspended from what she presumed was a rope to the roof beam. Her ankles were re-shackled together.

"We will leave you to think, Frau Baum. When we return you will be ready to give us the names of those you have dealt with on your way from Berlin to Beaulieu. Your arms will begin to scream in about half an hour. The pain will be unbearable. You will become unconscious from it. Do want to say anything?"

"Fuck off."

"You know, I think we will. Pleasant nightmares."

The door opened and Georgia heard three sets of footsteps leaving. The door closed and she hung in dark silence. She strained her hearing but could discern no other sound in the room, only her heart beginning to pump harder. Her arms began to burn and she was shivering in spasms. She ground her hips and began to sway slowly. It felt like hot wires cutting into her wrists. Lifting her legs as one she scythe-swept the space about her, feeling for the chair. There was a chance they had left it close. As her arc of swing grew and the pain in her arms began to tear at her bones her foot hit the char. She was fortunate it didn't tip over and she managed to scrape it towards her and eventually to get her feet up onto the seat and to wobble herself to some kind of standing position. The relief from the pain in her arms was almost excruciating, like pins and iced water flooding through her. She stood on the chair and rested her head against her roped hands. It was almost blissful.

Georgia was drifting on her chair for some time, she may even have slept a little, but the faint sound of the door handle being opened wakened her. She quickly but carefully slid off her chair and pushed it away from her. The pain in her arms and shoulders returned like stings of an electric shock. She hung still and pretended to be asleep.

Footsteps sounded softly across the floor as if seeking silence. Georgia heard a sharp tearing sound and then felt the hood being half-lifted and another tape was slapped over her mouth once more and the hood pulled down. She stirred and kicked out but her legs were held by someone standing behind her. She felt a mouth nuzzle against her bared shoulder and nape and a hand reached up under her pyjama top and began kneading her breast. Her feet were wedged between her assailant's clamped thighs and she could feel another hand reaching down into her pyjama bottoms and begin kneading her buttocks. Georgia could feel him harden against her and began to pant slowly as his body stirred against her. She breathed hard with anger and raged hard against her taped mouth but all that came out was a muted, futile groan. She could not see him but she could smell him. A mixture of vanilla, lavender and tobacco. Her attacker wafted unseen but distinctive under her hood. She would remember that smell.

The sound of a distant door bolt opening stopped the assault instantly. Georgia felt his hands pull her trousers and top back to normal and heard his quiet but rapid clothes tucking and then his creeping step across the floor. The door opened and closed on a soft clunk. The room was quiet and still.

Georgia had not been violated but she had been abused. Defenceless and alone she felt the anger rise within her. It was always this way. Always men. Forcing themselves on her, for drinks, for company, for pleasure, treating her as a plaything, a doll. And always finding no reason that it should be any other way or that Georgia had any say in the matter. It was how it was and how it was ever to be. But she had smelt him. Smelt his singular pheromone vanilla and lavender that marked him as her prey. He may have fled the room but he would not escape her vengeance.

The sound of the bolt sliding and the door opening broke the silence. Georgia hung in the dark, feigning unconsciousness and feeling her arms afire and her shoulders splitting bone. Footsteps crossed the room. A chair scraped. The hood was lifted from her but the blindfold remained.

"I thought we un-taped her mouth?"

"Yes, sir. Thought we did. Before we left."

"Has it grown back then, Sergeant?"

"Couldn't say, sir."

"Get her down."

Georgia felt herself being lifted up by two pairs of strong arms. No vanilla or lavender wafted. The rope was untied and she was seated in the chair and once again shackled to its legs. Someone stood behind her, a hand lightly clamping her shoulder so that she knew he was there. The blindfold was removed.

The suddenness and brightness of the light made her recoil almost in pain and it was some moments before she was able to adjust the room to some kind of focus.

A plump, grey-haired major with a bush moustache sat behind a plank board table, his cap, a half-empty bottle of scotch, a couple of cigarette packs, ashtray, several glasses and files of papers were scattered across it. The major was in shirt sleeves, his tunic hooked on the back of the door. Two soldiers leaned against the wall behind him and another was at her back. Georgia tried to let the anger sluice from her and to return to a measured calm that she did not feel.

"Who in SOE recruited you, Frau Baum? This is your final chance to co-operate." The major's toneless voice seemed at odds with his avuncular features.

Georgia said nothing. She stared at her interrogator as if not seeing him. The major leaned back in his chair and sighed heavily.

"Such a waste," he said. He placed his cap on his head and stood up and put his tunic on. "Frau Baum you are hereby formally charged with being a German spy and by the special powers invested in my office you have duly been found guilty of these crimes. I sentence you to be summarily shot as a traitor at dawn tomorrow. There is no appeal."

Georgia hung on to the notion that this was all a test, that it was the final part of the exercise, but something made her doubt herself. Perhaps this was her sins catching up with her at last. The heavenly avenger wielding his cruel irony so that she had become wantonly accused of something she had not done while the self-defensive killing of Horst had been forgiven. Perhaps she was just to be the hapless and helpless victim of incompetent bureaucracy, wrong papers and mistaken identity, such things were hardly unknown in war. She was to be put against a wall and shot because of bad paperwork. The thought grew in her that this may not be an exercise at all. It had all the stupidity to be real. She was surprised how the prospect of her death, up against some damp, dark, ignominious wall in a nameless dungeon, did not trouble her overmuch. At least it would all be over.

"Well, do you have anything to say before the sentence is carried out?"

"Could I have an alarm call?" she said.

The major nodded to the soldier behind her and he unshackled Georgia and lifted her upright. He had to hold Georgia because her legs were numb and she was having trouble standing. And then she was sitting down and the room was engulfed in light from two overhead lamps.

The major took off his tunic and cap and threw then onto the table. He filled two glasses with scotch and handed one to Georgia.

"Well done," he said and smiled. "I expect you could use a drink. Cigarette?" The major's machine voice had gone. He spoke with a soft, west-country burr.

Georgia took the proffered cigarette. A blanket was placed around her shoulders. Her hands shook and she couldn't calm them. The major held the lighter as the cigarette danced about it. It finally caught light and Georgia pulled in a lungful of smoke. Her head felt light and her body ached.

"Take a moment to gather yourself, Miss Melrose. You did rather well. Most ladies don't get past the iced water bucket. Word to the wise however. Never considered a good idea to tell your interrogators to fuck off. Just gets them angrier and more violent. Keep it mundane for lesser pain, eh? It's rather an ordeal I know but we have to go through this. You understand. Test your mettle and all that. Get you used to a little gentle beating, sleep deprivation, darkness and isolation and all that."

"And molestation," said Georgia.

The major looked confused. He laughed lightly.

"We do not do that, Miss Melrose, I assure you. We have our standards. Why would you think we would?"

"Opportunity perhaps," said Georgia. The major laughed again.

"This is England, Miss Melrose, not some lawless Arab bazaar," he said. "Now you will return to your room. Bathe, get some rest. You deserve it. Most commendable. You have no further duties for forty-eight hours. Of course, this interrogation never happened, Miss Melrose and you will tell no one of your ordeal. It's what you signed up for. Understand? You will find a change of clothes next door. Can't have you wandering the estate like a tramp now can we? Visit the MO for a check over, but the bruises will soon pass."

Georgia rose on unsteady legs. She ground out her cigarette under her bare heel and didn't feel it. She staggered from the room, the smell of vanilla and lavender scorching within her.

SIXTEEN

The corporal studied Jack's papers.

"Summers? Expecting you yesterday. Get lost did you?" He pulled a clipboard from the desk and studied it. "You're in Boardmans. ST26. Up the road past Vineyards. Triple chimney pots and you're there. Room 24. You're in with a Frenchie aristo. Emile Boudelain, the count Breaville. So mind your manners and no farting in the bedsheets. Did you come by motorbike? Well, park it round in the stables and get a key chit from the corporal. Stow your kit and report back to The Rings and Captain Green's office at fourteen hundred. Don't be late. Getting Killer angry ain't wise."

Jack parked his bike in the stables and a surly corporal with a bald head and ginger moustache gave him a chit.

"When you want it ooot, give it to a motor pool Rupert… An' saloot him nice, eh?" The corporal took the keys and locked them in a box on the wall.

Jack found Boardmans without trouble. Entering room 24 he was surprised to find it occupied. A tall, thin, dark-haired man with a slim moustache sat legs outstretched on one of the two beds in the room, his feet up on a pillow. He was barefoot and clipping his toenails with a small pair of bone-handled scissors. He looked up as Jack entered.

"Your army boots are murder to the feet!" he said. "They chew them like dogs. Are you Summers?"

"Thought this was a secret camp? Aren't there rules about such careless talk?"

The man laughed and waved a dismissive hand.

"Nothing is secret to Boudelain. I have my spies!" he laughed. "I am an exceptional student. The very best!"

Jack lifted his pack and placed it on the other bed in the room. It was by the room's only window and was freshly laundered and clean.

Boudelain swung his legs off the bed and began pulling on a pair of pale blue socks.

"No, that is my bed. This is your bed. I was just using it

for a moment." He stood up and smoothed the bed linen and wiped the nail clippings onto the floor. He plumped the pillow back to some kind of shape. The impressions of his heels still dimpled the down.

"There," he said, "quite as new. You can put your bags in the cupboard there."

Boudelain placed his small bone scissors in its compartment in a roll-out soft leather pouch that contained a hairbrush, comb, shaver, tweezers and various other oddments for personal grooming. A gold leaf ostrich-plumed family crest adorned the outer flap.

"There may be a war but that is no excuse to be slovenly, eh? We must keep ourselves presentable. Take great care over our appearance. To show a fearless face to our foes. Don't you agree?"

"It's what we're here for, isn't it?" Jack said. "Learning to be someone we are not." He slung his pack into the cupboard.

"Everyone is someone else in Beaulieu," said Boudelain, "It is part of its charm. You are meeting with Captain Green?"

"Do you know everything?" asked Jack.

Boudelain shrugged. "Only that which I must. It is why I am the best spy. Lunch is in the canteen in Ringways. We all meet there. I can introduce you to everyone."

"Maybe," Jack said. While Boudelain bent to lace his shoes Jack took the envelope of files from his knapsack and slid it into his belt and under his tunic and headed off for Ringways House.

Jack was last to arrive. Burton, Gilligan and McNulty were already seated in Captain Green's office and Lieutenant Carter leaned against the desk studying some papers. He looked up as Jack entered.

"Ah, all here at last," he said. He went to the ante-room doorway and nodded and Captain Green strode into the office, leaned to his desk and studied the room without enthusiasm. Jack took a seat at the back of the group, near a bookcase.

"You reckon you are good thieves. Well now you have the chance to prove it. Show us what you're made of. We have files on every one of you locked away in the personnel file safe next door and all you have got to do is to steal your own file. Simple. You have a week to complete the task."

"That is not enough!" said McNulty. He was a round, red-faced man with thinning red hair and fat freckled hands. "A job needs reconnaissance and planning. Just can't go blundering in. Not in a week. We need more time."

Green turned to Carter. "Take a note to Adolf Hitler, Commander German forces Europe, will you Lieutenant. Dear Adolf, please halt all activities until McNulty has made his plans. Yours etcetera."

McNulty bridled in his chair. "That's not what I meant. I just said that these things take time to plan."

"We don't have time, McNulty. Just get on with it." Green looked around at the rest of the faces, "And let's be clear," he said," if you don't steal your file within the week, if you fail, you'll have your bags packed and be sent back to station next day. And you know what that means for some of you. Beaulieu may not be paradise but it's better than Pentonville."

"But we would need to know about any alarms and guards," said Burton, a small, dark-haired man with bright eyes and a brighter smile. "That is what we would check out first. It's not magic we do, it's a craft. It has its methods. It is only fair that we know what we are up against."

"There is no safe alarm but the offices will be guarded and sentries posted. It's what the Germans would do and we won't be any different."

"But we have the day schedule of lessons and lectures and PT as well," said Gilligan, "rather leaves us little time for burgling, eh? We'll be bumping into each other in the small wee hours." He smiled warmly to the rest of the room. Gilligan was tall, well dressed and emanated the sophisticated, languid confidence that marked the gentleman thief. Jack leaned back in his chair and slipped the file from under his tunic. While the room was engaged in banter, he secreted the file between two large volumes entitled Topography of the South West that were suitably big enough to hide the envelope and had a thin and comforting layer of dust that indicated that they were seldom, if ever, referred to. Jack settled his chair back and relaxed. While he had the files on him or in his kit there was always a danger of discovery in a sudden spot inspection. He did not know what the rules were at Beaulieu but he was sure that they would require him to expect the unorthodox.

"You're all excused other duties for the week," Green said, "except morning PT. You've got all day and night to complete your mission. If you're caught you're out, we can't be wasting our time on failures. Yes, it's a tough task and unfair. But this is war and that's how it is. Any questions? What about you, Summers? You going to whine too?"

"No, sir," Jack said. "It's a most interesting challenge. I take it you can assure us that the files are in the personnel file safe next door?"

"Said so didn't I?" said Green. Jack was amused at the hint of fluster in the reply. Carter was finding something of interest at his feet. "Now you've all got your task, so get on with it. We meet back here a week today at o-fourteen hundred. Clear? Good. Dismissed."

The four burglars shared a smoke by the old stable block.

"Impossible," McNulty said, "we're being set up to fail. He'll have guards swarming all over the place."

"I might try to arrange an air raid from the Luftwaffe," said Burton, "sneak in under cover of darkness and bombs."

"It's no skin off my bones," said McNulty, "If you succeed the only reward will be more boot camp and then a midnight drop into bloody France or some such swamp and the prospect of a German firing squad."

"Yeah, I hear the drop rate from here is bad. Agents going missing the other side of the channel as soon as they arrive."

"Where's your patriotic spirit boys?" said Gilligan. He took a short stiletto knife from his shirt sleeve and sharpened the blade against the stones of the stable wall. "You sound quite the fifth columnists they all warned us about. Not spies already, are you, boys? For the other side?"

"Here, what you implying, you fucking…"

"Now, now, boys," said Gilligan. He smiled, checked the glint of his blade and slipped the knife back in its forearm sleeve. He lit a cigarette. "You see, you are far too sensitive and excitable. Why don't you stop whining and just get on with doing what you are supposed to be good at, eh? Save us all a lot of earache. Only a word of warning, boys. Don't try it while I'm on the case, otherwise you are likely to end up with my knife between your ribs. Do we understand one another? Good. Then piss off to back to whatever rock you crawled out from."

Jack and Gilligan watched McNulty and Burton shuffle away, muttering.

"Not going to win the war with that lot," said Gilligan. "Don't say much do you?"

"Nothing to say,"

"If I meet anybody in my night-time prowlings, I think it's going to be you. Now don't you get in my way, will you? I'd hate to have to end our charming friendship."

"Wouldn't dream of it," Jack said. He smiled. "At least not until o-fourteen hundred next Friday."

Jack was going to return to his room but the prospect of having to listen to Boudelain again persuaded him to get some air in a stroll around the grounds. The lawns surrounding Ringways House were pocked with small groups of trainees and instructors with classes in hand-to-hand fighting, map orienteering, field lectures and PT. Along the long tree-lined grass causeway to the main Beaulieu House odd groups of trainees dozed in deck chairs, read newspapers or simply chatted and smoked.

The girl from the farm was sitting under a tree reading a book. Her left hand was bandaged and she propped her book on her knees so she could hold her cigarette with her free hand.

"Would you mind if I joined you?" Jack asked.

She looked up and saw Jack smiling down at her. She put a blade of grass in her page and closed the book.

"Of course," she said.

"My name is Jack. And you are Miss Potts."

"Hildy will do. How did you know my name?"

"I have been here hardly a day but the lady who floored the great Sergeant Evans is the talk of the estate! How's the hand?"

Hildy felt herself blushing. She was unused and uncomfortable with being the centre of such attention. She wasn't sure how to handle it.

"Oh, only a strain. It will be as right as rain in a couple of days. It was really nothing. I didn't expect there to be so much fuss. So I'm trying to avoid it. Hide away with my books."

"And I've come and spoiled it again."

"Oh no! Please. Don't think that. Look, I'm just being silly, that's all. This is all so new to me. It's all rather overpowering."

They sat watching the grounds and the various training sessions about them. The sun shone in a warm, puff-clouded blue sky and above the woodlands a pair of buzzards slow-glided the breezes.

"A strange place and stranger times," Jack said. "It hardly seems real, does it?"

"I know what you mean, like a fairy tale land. Palaces and woods and peacocks."

"Even a French prince," Jack said. "but not necessarily of the charming kind."

"And a most wicked witch over the water," said Hildy, laughing, "I just know I'm going to wake up and find myself back on the farm. All this wonderful excitement and colour gone, back to grey living."

"Is living on the farm grey?"

"It can be. My father is not the easiest of people to get along with. He can make things difficult. I hope he is getting on with the new people who came. A girl and her grandmother. I would hate to think of them putting up with what I had to. It is a worry. Maybe I should give all this up and go back to help Father. The farm won't run itself."

"I don't think there's any need for that, Hildy. The farm was running perfectly fine with Walter and Rolf, and your father seems almost mellow."

Hildy turned to face Jack, not sure she was understanding his words,

"What do you...Who? You know my farm? You have been there?"

Jack laughed. "I'm sorry, Hildy," he patted her softly on the shoulder, "that was very naughty of me. Yes, I have visited your farm. Just four days ago. I went to visit Mrs Maynard and Dora before coming here. To let them know I was OK and checking things were working out for them. Dora is my daughter. Ma Maynard a good neighbour and old and very loyal friend. They are the new guests at your farm. Captain Townsend arranged it all."

Hildy was silent for some time and then laughed. "Captain Townsend! That explains everything. Is my father well?"

"Mrs Maynard has got him tamed and domesticated. He was peeling potatoes at the sink when I called."

"Father! Peeling potatoes? Are you sure you were at my farm?"

"Ma Maynard has worked her usual wonders. Walter is fixing up the old cart and thinks he can make a horse buggy so that your father can get around the farm. They've been drawing up plans for pulleys and lifts. Your father allows Walter to listen to his Wagner records, although I think Walter prefers Al Bowlly."

"Thank you, Jack," she said, "you have taken such a lot off my mind. I can't thank you enough."

"No, really, any thanks are to you and your father. And Captain Townsend of course. Dora is having a high old time on the farm. Clear, clean air, good food and lots of scampering about with that Jip of yours. She says she'll keep looking after him until you get back. There's roses in her cheeks and no growls in her chest. It's me to be thanking you."

"Well that's fine. Will your wife be joining them?"

Hildy knew it was a ghastly error as soon as she said it. She felt the ground rise up to engulf her stupidity. She saw the pained pall pass quickly across Jack's face, like a sun passing behind cloud in a blue sky. Why was she so stupid and gauche? You should never ask such things in war. She felt bereft.

"I'm sorry. I didn't…"

Jack smiled. He reached out and patted Hildy's hand. "Don't worry yourself, Hildy. My wife died a few years ago. It's just me and Dora now. And Ma Maynard of course. Couldn't forget Ma. She held us together, especially through the bad times. Still does. Now it looks like she's sorting your father's life out too."

"Well, it certainly needs sorting. I'm so sorry, I didn't mean to bring up bad memories. I am such an oaf."

"Really, don't worry about it. You weren't to know. And there are plenty other lives that have been lost and broken because of this war. I am nothing special. I am just pleased to have been allowed the time with her that I had, however short. But it's another life now. And it's another world. And I have to live it. But I have to say that castles, peacocks and French counts I did not expect!"

"Yes, it doesn't feel real at all, does it?" Hildy said, "I keep thinking I will wake up and the hens will be calling from the barn and my father shouting at me to get milking."

She gazed about the grounds and lit another cigarette. Her hand still ached but she felt happy in her new fairy tale world, and keen to know and experience its next adventures. It was even an adventure sitting next to Jack, enjoying a smoke and watching the gardens and lawns with dream-like fascination. It surprised how her how easy it was to be beside Jack. All the men in her life had been ogres, fools or knaves. Imprisoned on her farm and in her parochial little rural community she had not had the opportunity to meet a real man, let alone enjoy a smoke and talk with one. But Jack was different. Or so he seemed. His touch at her shoulder and hands had been gentle, reassuring, and she felt their warmth still. All the other men in her life had only ever touched with anger, lust or contempt. Jack's touch was bonding. At the back of her mind Hildy was aware that Jack must be at Beaulieu for some reason. Maybe his talent was as a quiet and gentle killer

Georgia emerged from the woods across the lawn and Hildy gave her a wave. Georgia came over.

"Not interrupting important studies am I?" She sat down without waiting for an answer. "Got a spare?" she asked. "I'm gasping with all this walking."

Jack offered her a cigarette from his pack before Hildy could respond.

"This is Jack," Hildy said. "He's one of Townsend's recruits, like us."

Georgia inclined her head in a theatrical acknowledgement. "Thanks. I'm Georgia. Ah that's better." She drew in a lungful of smoke and blew it to the trees. "God I needed that. I've run out and nowhere seems to sell them here."

Jack tossed his packet to her. "Have these. I have more in my room."

"You are kind. The world suddenly seems a better place!"

"Is everything OK?" asked Hildy. "You look a little tired."

Georgia stared into the trees at nothing. She was aware of her hand shaking and cupped her chin in her hand and rested her elbow on her knee. "Oh, it's nothing. I think I'm just exercised out, that's all. Too much damn PT and not enough gin slings. This place is just so full-on all the time. Like being back in summer term at top school. I had to go for a walk in the woods. Catch some calm. Where did Captain Townsend find you, Jack?"

Jack smiled. "Is this my interrogation?" he said. Hildy noticed Georgia blanche momentarily, but she soon recovered.

"Polite conversation," she said. "nothing more, I

promise."

"I was working in an engineering company reading manuals."

"That doesn't sound very exciting."

"It wasn't."

"Is there much call for manual reading here? Seems a bit sedate for a Townsend recruit."

"The captain obviously felt that I had other hidden virtues."

"Like what?"

Jack leaned back against the tree and thought about it. A flood of images swam before him. Beth laughing. Dora crying. His bombed-out home. The army. Colonel Redmond.

"I think my hatred attracted him," he said. "Hated the army, my life, my situation, my work, my superiors, the war, the Nazis. I have a lot of hate to vent. I think the captain thought he could use it. Aren't you full of hate too? Isn't that why you're here? Why we are all here?"

Hildy watched a group of trainee agents doing PT exercises on the far lawns. From a distance it looked like there were dancing. She thought of her mother and the picnics in the meadow field. Of her father growling from his prison chair and the drudgery of the farm day. The German pilot who had tried to kill her. But she couldn't find hate.

"No, not hate," she said. "It's not that. It's more the absence of something. Living I expect. The feeling of being alive. And someone to share it with. My life has been very dull. All this is exciting and wonderful."

"But dangerous," said Georgia. "Dying is not living and we are all alone doing both. It's the nature of what we have chosen to do. Maybe hate is a useful way to get through it. It's what we're here to learn."

"Well, I still have much to learn then," said Hildy, "but Jack, you have your daughter It can't just be hate for you, can it?"

Jack smiled. "You are quite right, Hildy. I am here for love."

"Love of what?" asked Georgia.

"Oh, king and country, duty and sacrifice, all that kind of thing. Stuff of empire and courage. Love of freedom to hate whomever I choose."

"I don't believe you can love to hate," said Hildy. "You have to love something more than that. Otherwise it's just not love. You must love something more, Georgia, or you wouldn't be here."

Georgia watched the peacocks strutting the far lawns, their feathers glinting like petrol in the sun.

"Love is a far country," she said, "and one as yet un-travelled." She turned to smile at Hildy. "But who knows, with this war anything is possible. But Jack you must have some talent that Captain Townsend saw. Otherwise you wouldn't be here."

"I mix a very good gin sling," said Jack. Georgia laughed.

"A useful recruit indeed!"

"I wish I knew what my talents are supposed to be," said Hildy, "I'm just a farm sparrow among peacocks. They are going to find me out, I know it. And then I'll be back planting spuds."

"This from the girl that laid the legend that is Sergeant Evans out with a left hook that he never saw coming," laughed Georgia, "and, so I've heard, also scored the highest marks in the pistol free shot. I think you may have talents aplenty, Hildy. They certainly won't be sending you home just yet."

"You think so?" said Hildy. The world seemed a suddenly lighter shade. "Really? I was lucky with Sergeant Evans. And everyone on a farm can shoot."

"But they don't get four out of five bulls in a free-standing fifty-yard range," said Georgia, "I got two outers and three in nearby trees. And I thought I was pretty handy with a gun. Do you shoot, Jack?"

Jack smiled. "Only the occasional breeze," he said.

SEVENTEEN

It had been a fruitful day of lectures. Georgia had learned the insignias and uniforms of the German infantry divisions, understood how to become anonymous while walking down a city street and saw an interesting demonstration on how to kill a man with a garrotte or knife. While all very informative and uplifting it was not until the end of the lecture on bomb making that she had found what she had been searching for, or rather sniffing for.

As she filed out of the room with the others she passed the corporal who was holding the door open. The smell of vanilla and lavender was discreet, but as impactful as a punch to the gut. She had been sniffing the Beaulieu airs for it for several days and her sense of discovery was sweet. Georgia looked back to see the corporal staring after her through the heads of the other lecture leavers. The corporal's gaze instantly turned away and back to the room and Georgia knew she had smelt her man.

Georgia learned what she could about Corporal Lancing. She used her guile and charm to discover that Corporal Lancing was one of the weapons instructors, specialising in the De Lisle carbine and the Welrod assassin's pistol. He also doubled-up for support duties on the lecture rota, such as opening doors and helping out in the interrogation basements. He had been at Beaulieu for just over a year and been seconded from the Welsh Fusiliers who were glad to get rid of him, or so the handsome young private in the staff office had confided. The canteen chef told Georgia that Lancing loved his fried mushroom breakfast every morning and got very rowdy if it wasn't available.

"So he's been getting right bloody moody lately because there ain't many mushrooms to be had 'cos of the war. You'd think he'd accept it, but he's an awkward cus and no mistake. If you can find me mushrooms and make him quit riling me every morning, then there's a tin of peaches in it for you."

The plan had come to her quickly. Georgia had walked the woods and grounds around Beaulieu and knew where there were mushrooms to be found. The special ones that the Tsonga peoples used to call the Dreams of Tilo's Maidens. These dreams would be punishment enough for Lancing. Georgia's fury at his cowardly, lascivious assault on her had seethed within her and she knew she could not rest until she had revenge. Had Lancing not been interrupted and had gone further in his assault, Georgia knew that she would have had no hesitation in finding a way of killing him. The short, fumbled assault however was deserving of a lesser sentence, perhaps an assault by Tilo's Maidens would suffice.

Over the next days she took her walks in the estate woods and grounds and collected enough of the psilocybin mushrooms for a single portion. It was no problem to get her trade of peaches from the chef.

The outcome was better than Georgia might have hoped and her delight was only tempered by not being witness to it for herself, but she heard about it at supper that evening in the canteen. She was seated at a long table trying to find some taste in a piece of over grilled fish and floury potatoes. As usual the conversation around the table was full of the day's events and happenings in roars of laughter and whispers of various accents and inflections. The main topic of interest seemed to be the naked corporal.

"I tell you I see it," said Olaf Stuvenson, a Norwegian sailor. "My own eyes. Naked with his rifle. With bayonet. Shouting at ghosts. Trying to kill them. It is very funny."

"Not naked," Boudelain corrected him, "I have it on good authority that he was in his boots."

"And wearing a tin hat," said Lionel Peters from up the table. Peters was a former solicitor now finding his dramas with SOE French section. "Mustn't forget the tin hat. We are talking a man's dignity, after all."

"There's no dignity to be found," said Gregson, a Scot from the Highland regiment. "None at all. The man was charging bollock naked through groups of lectures with his bayonet and rifle and all else akimbo and screaming blue rage at the demons. Right across the lawns. Sent agents scattering to the hills. Shock killed two of the peacocks."

"Who was it?" asked Hildy.

"A chap called Lancing. A corporal instructor," said Peters, "Pressure got to him I suppose."

"But he's an instructor, not an agent. What pressure has he got?" asked Gregson.

"Well," said Stuvenson, "enough to send him running and screaming across the lawns and hold off three commandos beyond the end his bayonet. He was shouting about monsters and his mother and evil clouds. He was quite crazed I think."

"So what happened?" asked Georgia.

"Oh, Sergeant Evans came along and sorted Lancing out," said Peters, "Stood in front of him and told him to drop the rifle. Lancing refused. Called him the evil one and lunged at him with the bayonet. Evans steps inside the lunge, swings a short left hook to the jaw and Lancing is out cold and being ferried to the sanatorium in the back of a jeep. Drama over. Hail Sergeant Evans!"

There was laughter and mock cheers and the raising of beer glasses along the tables.

"Sergeant Evans!"

Georgia lifted her own glass and savoured a long, quiet sip of cool vengeance. The noise of the canteen and the pleasure of the punishment became suddenly overwhelming and she craved some escape and to be alone to enjoy her satisfaction.

She slipped away outside to take a quiet dusk walk of the lawns and to sink into the pleasure of a cigarette. Watching the peacocks pecking at their twilight supper on the edge of the woods she became lost in thought and was unaware that she now had company.

"They roost in trees and nest on the ground," Jack said, "Seems the wrong way round, don't you think? Can hardly be good for survival."

"True, but they are a god-awful eat and that saves them

from the pot. At least from us."

"You've eaten peacock?"

"Well, chewed would be a better description. Meat like rubber. Not as nice as alligator. Or wildebeest."

"You are a travelled bon viveur and adventurer then."

"Needs must in the veldt. One can't be picky."

"How do you kill an alligator?"

"Carefully."

Jack laughed. He offered another smoke and they both settled to a sit on the edge of the lawns, leaning back against a massive oak.

"Would you be so kind as to consider helping me in an adventure?" Jack asked.

"That rather depends. Would it be dangerous?"

"No."

"Deceitful?"

"Isn't that why we are here? Everything is deceitful in Beaulieu. It is what we are supposed to be."

"What does it involve?"

"A simple diversionary act. Nothing too complicated. Just something I have to retrieve."

"And if you don't retrieve it?"

"My Beaulieu bags are packed for me and I'm on my way back to the dismal world of translating manuals."

"Why me?"

"Because I need someone to draw the guard away from Captain Green's office so I can nip in and retrieve something that I have left there. A job of less than a minute. And you are the most beautiful, attractive woman in Beaulieu at the moment and no red-blooded guard could ever resist coming to your aid and assistance if asked nicely. And I think you are a game girl. You kill alligators for pity's sake."

"Flattery aside, what's in it for me?"

"Oh, adventure. Diversion. The thrill of the game. Fun. Usual stuff. Oh, and where poor Corporal Lancing got his mushrooms shall ever remain our shared secret."

Georgia turned to stare at Jack who maintained an

innocent gaze across the lawns.

"Blackmail?" she said.

"I'd rather call it persuasion."

Georgia laughed.

"Then why not. I need some diversion from all these damn lectures."

A plan was quickly established and agreed. Jack had insisted it needed no complexities. Georgia would struggle past the guard with something heavy and awkward and get him to help her down the stairs with it. It was to be done at eight o'clock next morning, while breakfast was underway.

The plan worked as easily as it had been planned. Georgia came down the corridor of Captain Green's office carrying a large, empty urn that they had taken from the kitchen store. Georgia was now set on returning it. She struggled with the awkward load and almost dropped it on the guard's foot.

"Now then, miss," the grinning guard said, "assault and battery that is. Could have you on a charge! And damaging His Majesty's accoutrements 'an all."

Georgia offered her most winning smile. "I am so sorry, sergeant. The thing slipped in my grasp. Have to get it to the kitchen. They need extra brews you see."

"Want a hand, miss? Here let me." The guard picked up the urn and carried it down the stairs, Georgia following and offering her sweetest thanks and kindnesses.

Job done, Georgia headed off for breakfast and had only just sat down when Jack joined her at the table and sat by her side.

"Thank you," he said, "most ably executed. Allow me to return the favour whenever or if ever you might need it."

"And what skill might you have that I would want, I wonder?" Georgia asked, "Assassin maybe? A fighter? Or perhaps an explosives man?"

Jack raised an eyebrow. "Would you want or need any of those skills?"

"Maybe." Georgia shrugged. "You never know. There is a war on,"

"Ah, the rumours are true then. I thought it was rather noisy."

"Well, Jack, what are you?"

Jack spread some marge over his toast and took a slurp of tea,

"A thief, liar and confidence trickster mainly. And a planner of things and a get things done on the quiet chappie. A dirty jobs man."

"Dangerous jobs?"

"Sometimes. But the skill is in avoiding dangers as much as possible."

"How do you do that?"

"Conning someone else into doing them for you is a good start," Jack said.

Georgia's laughter spluttered into her raised mug and sent warm tea spray across the table. She spent a few moments apologising to her neighbours. It took her a few moments longer to realise that Jack was no longer beside her, which was a pity because she was beginning to rather enjoy his company.

EIGHTEEN

Captain Green stood rigid-backed behind his desk oozing a silent rage. Lieutenant Carter sat to his side, gazing at the four would-be burglars seated before him with unconcealed contempt. Four manila files lay in a tidy rank on the desk.

Jack studied his fellow burglars. McNulty sat there looking sullen and staring at his foot, which was encased in a plaster cast. Burton inspected his cuticles and tried to convey his nonchalance for the whole affair. He failed. Gilligan stared ahead at nothing, his face set stern. It was only when he reached up to flick hair from his brow that Jack saw he was handcuffed.

Two powerfully built soldiers stood guard just inside the office door. Jack recognised one of them as the sergeant who had given him tea with Captain Townsend in Redmond's office at camp Bledsoe. The sergeant stared stone-faced ahead and made no acknowledgement.

"Your four files are here, gentlemen," said Captain Green. "Unopened. Un-retrieved. I have just taken them from the safe. The test has been a complete and utter shambles. Total failure. Call yourselves master thieves? One of you caught breaking into the office," Green glared at Burton who continued to study his nails, "one fell off the roof in the middle of the night," McNulty seemed to try and hide his plastered foot under his chair. He winced at the effort. "One tried to escape the guards by pulling a knife and attacking a sergeant before being overpowered." Gilligan stared blankly into a space beyond the walls. "And one of you didn't even bother to try at all. And that's probably the worst failure of the lot." Captain Green fixed Jack with a look of disdain mixed with smug pleasure, "the only positive thing to come out of this whole dismal exercise is that I get a free lobster dinner for knowing that you would all fail. Burglars! Hah, you couldn't nick a purse from a blind granny. Not one of you got your damn file."

"I did," Jack said.

The room turned to look at him. Captain Green snorted. "Townsend's great burglar, eh? You didn't get your file Summers because it's right here before me. Are you blind and stupid as well as incompetent? Look, it's here," Green lifted a file and then slapped it down again on the desk. "Well, you all know the consequences of your failures…"

"And I got all the other files too," said Jack, "if you're interested."

Carter laughed from his chair.

"You really are being rather boring and pathetic now, Summers," he said, "We can all see the files right here, on the captain's desk. Why don't you just admit you couldn't do it, didn't even try as far as we can see. You failed. And miserably."

"No, I didn't."

"Then prove it. Go on. Prove it. Astound us all with your magic."

Jack took a cigarette from his pack, lit it and gazed around the room of faces. He turned to Burton.

"John Henry Burton. Born Bristol 1908 to John and Martha Burton. Robbed his first cash till from Harrison's Newsagents in Keysham aged thirteen. Borstal from 1926 until 1930. Worked as a bookies runner with Benjy Mendes out of Weston Super Mare. Then chauffeur to Fat Eddy in London. Two spells in prison. Released May 1938. Unmarried."

"I was fitted up," Burton said, "no call to bring that up."

Jack turned to McNulty.

"Michael Fraser McNulty. Born Dumfries 1910 to Kenneth and Mary McNulty, local butchers. Ran away from home aged fourteen and worked with the gangs in Glasgow. Safe-blower and part-time lay preacher as cover for a numbers racket which had him two years in Garside prison. Married Nelly Janes 1934, divorced 1936. No children."

He turned to Gilligan.

"Matthew Charles Gilligan. Born Guildford 1912. Adopted at birth by Harold and Susan Gilligan. Expelled from Guildford Grammar for violence, robbed the Epsom post office at knifepoint and spent two years in Shepton

Mallet prison where he learned the burglary trade from Ned Ford. On his release he became a roaming gentleman thief, specialising in hotel robberies and old ladies' jewellery. Is currently on release from a two-year stretch at Pentonville for aggravated burglary. Unmarried."

"You bastard," shouted Gilligan rising from his chair. One of the soldier guards stepped forward quickly and shoved him back to his seat. Jack turned to face Lieutenant Carter.

"Peter Edward Carter, born Preston 20th November 1916 to Sydney and Margery Carter. Educated Manchester Grammar school and Durham University to study law. Left to join up in May 1939. Promoted second-lieutenant Royal Lancashire Regiment 1940, seconded to SOE Administrative Affairs Beaulieu in 1942. Unmarried but engaged to Mildred Hopkins."

Jack turned to face Captain Green. Green had lost his rigidity and he seemed to have sagged a little. He now leaned to his desk as if needing its brace.

"Donald E F Green, Captain Intelligence Corps, SOE. Principal lecturer in safe-blowing, lock-picking, house-breaking and key-making at Beaulieu. Before the war he was a chartered accountant. Captain Green was tutored in the dark burglary arts by Johnny Ramenski, a Scots thief of Polish extraction who has spent nearly thirty years of his life inside. I should know because he taught me too. Do you want me to go on?"

The room was silent. Jack stubbed his cigarette in the ashtray on Green's desk and leaned back in his seat.

"That's all very well," said Carter rising from his chair, "but that's just a memory trick. You just got into personnel files somehow and memorised our details. It's not stealing your file, which was what your mission was. And in that you failed."

"That's correct, Carter. Yes, that's true," Captain Green said. He seemed to reflate behind his desk. "You have not succeeded in the mission. You have failed to steal your file."

"Twenty, eleven, sixteen," Jack said.

"What?" Green said, "what are you blathering about?"

Carter sank slowly back to his chair. He groaned.

"Twenty, eleven, sixteen," Jack repeated. "The combination to your personal safe. It is also the date of Lieutenant Carter's birthday. 20th November 1916. Hardly the most challenging level of security. Of course writing the combination into the flyleaf of the Life of Wellington in the bookcase over there doesn't help. Or rather it does. That is, of course, your personal safe behind that bookcase, not the one in the ante-office and which you assured us was where our files would be kept. Rather unsporting, I thought. Un-British. Un-gentlemanly. Disingenuous verging on outright deceitful. But then we aren't playing by Queensbury anymore, are we?"

Captain Green had sunk to his chair and was looking at Jack with undisguised loathing.

"But you didn't steal your file!" he roared. His fist banged the desk and made the files dance. "They are still here. Look. You failed to steal your file!"

Jack stood up and pulled the envelope from under his tunic. He took a copy of each file out and slowly laid them on the desk.

"Burton. McNulty, Gilligan, Carter, Green. And of course the one I was ordered to steal. Summers. Just for good measure I have added Major Mann, the Commandant's file. Nice to have all the family together, don't you think? I stole the files, Captain Green. I photographed them and I put them back. And all within the almost impossible timescale you set, while your offices were heavily guarded by your very best troops, under your very noses and despite being given deliberately misleading information. I stole them so well, you didn't even know they had been stolen. I believe Paulo's lobster might be on you, after all."

The room was quiet. No one quite seemed to want to break the strange spell that had been cast. Carter leaned forward and picked up the photographs and began comparing them with the manila files. After checking a couple he let the photographs fall to the desk and leaned back in his chair, studying Jack.

"Well? Are you going to tell us how you did it?" asked Carter.

"No," Jack said.

His three fellow burglars were staring at Jack with looks of mixed bewilderment, awe and fury. Jack ignored them. Captain Green stood up so abruptly his chair hit the wall behind him. He was trying to calm his mood and sought release in the sorting of the photographs and files on his desk. He slid the bundle to Carter.

"OK, Summers," Green said, "report for duties and assignments tomorrow o-eight thirty. The rest of you get out of my sight. And remember. You all signed the papers," he fixed the three failed burglars with an icy stare, "so any careless talk or blathering about your time here will be treason and the hangman will be weighing you for the drop and quick. Do I make myself clear?" He took the silence for assent. "Right. Dismissed."

Jack let the others leave first, he didn't want his back to prove a too tempting target for Gilligan's vengeful knife. The sergeant at the door seemed to have enjoyed the drama. He was smiling broadly and he gave Jack a wink as he hefted Gilligan by the collar and escorted him out.

The foyer was crowded with departing would-be burglars, soldiers and administrators. Jack took discreet cover behind an alcove and waited for the crowd to subside. The handcuffed Gilligan was checked out at the desk between two large corporal MPs and taken to a waiting truck. McNulty and Burton waited their turn for discharge back to civvy street.

Beyond the foyer throng, through the window of a small back office, Jack saw Boudelain in happy discussion with a clerk in the despatch offices. Boudelain passed over a small bottle of what looked like brandy to the clerk who hastily slipped it into a draw in his desk. Boudelain sat on the corner of the clerk's desk and there was more discussion and the occasional sound of laughter. The Frenchman had his right hand heavily bandaged. A moment later the clerk picked up some papers from his desk and went out to the ante-office. Boudelain looked around as if checking for observers and then flicked open a file on the desk, scanned a page and made a quick note in a small notebook he took from his breast pocket. The file had been closed and a cigarette lit by the time the clerk returned. The clerk stamped and handed over a green pass to Boudelain. There was more laughter and conversation and then Boudelain left, holding his bandaged hand carefully in front of him.

Jack caught up with him as they made their way across the gavel courtyard to the canteen.

"Been in the wars?"

Boudelain turned to see Jack at this shoulder.

"Ah, this is not a time for your British merriness. No. I have sprained my wrist. Or that oaf corporal in the combat class did. It will be pain for two weeks. It is not fair. Two times now I have been on the list to France, back to my homeland, and I lose it because a fool of a corporal kicks my hand away. It is too much. It is not for joking."

"Were you going to France?"

Boudelain looked around as if wishing not to be overheard.

"I was on the list for going in two days. It was as my dream. To return, to tread on my earth and smell France again. And now I cannot go. All because of a fool corporal. A peasant."

"This has happened to you before?"

"Four months ago I was also on the list. Four days before the mission I am in fever. It is food poisoning. I tell you I think someone is against Boudelain. I am the best spy and I should be in France. Helping to free my county. But I am stopped once again."

"There'll be another chance later. When you heal."

Boudelain laughed and slapped Jack on his back.

"You are right, my friend. There is always another tomorrow, eh? And I will go because I am the best!"

They made their way along the gravel path to the canteen, Jack thinking it odd that Boudelain had slapped his damaged hand to his back, and without any seeming flinch of pain.

NINETEEN

The breakfast conversation was noisy, animated and seemingly good-natured as Hildy slipped into a vacant seat. Only Georgia acknowledged her arrival with a discreet nod and smile. Hildy set about her cold toast and rhubarb jam without much enthusiasm.

But the atmosphere around the table was of slightly forced merriment, where the laughter and repartee seemed to mask something serious that lay beneath. It was not hard for Hildy to guess what that might be. Boudelain was at this usual place at the head of the table, the centre of things as always. Jack and Lionel Peters were at his side and listening while the handsome Dane, Stuvenson recounted some story about parachutes. Among the avid listeners were Gregson and David Metcalfe. The news of agents about to make the jump was supposed to be secret, but somehow Beaulieu always came to know. It was now common knowledge that Gregson and Metcalfe were going to be dropped into France in three nights' time and these were their last hours in Beaulieu before transfer to the waiting station for final briefing and kitting out. As was the way with these things Metcalfe and Gregson kept the pretence of insouciant unconcern and their friends kept the pretence of ignorance.

"I tell you," said Boudelain, "spies have to be normal. There is no other way."

"What's normal then?" said Peters, "A French aristocratic count, I suppose."

Laughter rippled the table.

"But I am French, I can become everyone. But I look normal. Distinguished. And a certain élan to be sure, but normal. I make a good spy. But look." Boudelain gestured down the table towards Georgia, "Melrose cannot be a spy. Look at her. She is too beautiful. To send her to France among the German soldiers. It would be suicide. No, it would be murder. Immoral. She would attract every eye. Like putting a peacock among snakes."

Eyes had turned to Georgia. Hildy noticed the faint flush at Georgia's neck but she gave little other indication of affront. She continued to margarine her toast.

"Well, Emile Gustave Francois de Greveney Boudelain, Count de Beaville, I think you are mistaken," said Georgia. She smiled sweetly. "It is just as easy for the so-called beautiful to become plain as it is for the ignorant peasant to become an aristocrat. The first requires only makeup, the second merely requires opportunity, duplicity and a scant regard for the sanctity of life, especially, as history tells us, one's own family. Give yourself lots of names and you get lots of graces. Anyone can become anyone in war, Emile. Ugly, plain, beautiful, aristocratic, peasant or count, but I hope I will always be a lady and never be mistaken for a peacock, rather than a peahen."

More laughter around the table.

"No fear of that, Miss Melrose!" said Gregson.

"Bravo, well said!" said Peters.

"You have to forgive our dear count," said Metcalfe, "if he gets a little confused. I know he is anxious to get back to his country. To do his bit, count or peasant, it doesn't matter."

"And when he does go, he'll go in better comfort than when he arrived, eh Boudelain?" said Peters.

Boudelain pushed his plate away from him.

"Pah, how can you eat this merde," he said. "It is not even fit for dogs."

"There is a war on. We are an island. Or haven't you heard?" said Gregson.

"Of course I know this, you fool, it is why I am here. It is why my country bleeds. Do you not think I know this?"

The table was silent. Boudelain seemed to sense he had overstepped some line. He smiled and shrugged.

"Forgive me, Gregson. Everyone. I am a Frenchman and all Frenchmen are passionate. About love and beauty and, of course, always about good food."

Laughter and relief greeted the more pleasant change of mood.

"But that does not mean that you cannot eat well, even in a war," he said. He poked at the powdered egg on his plate. "This is just fuel. Like petrol in a car. But at least petrol has taste."

"Maybe you should get one of those pigeons you arrived with," said Peters, "They'd make a tasty casserole, I'd say."

Laughter trickled again, even Boudelain managing a chuckle at the thought. Peters noticed Hildy's confusion at the turn of the conversation.

"Ah, forgive us, Miss Potts. You will not know of the count's tale of derring-do and last moment, seat of the pants escape from the evil clutches of the Nazi war machine."

"Or of his flight from a French airfield in a battered old Breguet," said Gregson, "just ahead of the advancing German army."

"And of the bullets that smashed through his fuselage."

"And being attacked over the channel by two Hurricanes."

"One Hurricane only," said Boudelain, now grinning with evident pleasure at the retelling of his stories. "I have always said only one Hurricane. My broken Breguet had no chance. Like a sparrow against a hawk."

"And crash-landing on the driveway of Lord Chester's estate not ten miles from here, in dear old safe Blighty."

"And what did our brave and lucky count discover in his plane when he climbed out of the wreckage?"

"A crate of pigeons and a crate of brandy!" sang the breakfasters in unison.

"You see, Miss Potts," said Boudelain, "The bullets were everywhere and explosions and everything was chaos. We had to escape from the airfield very fast. Everything smoke and noise and panic. I did not want to be a prisoner of the Germans. I just jumped in the only plane left and took off across the channel. I did not know I was carrying passengers also."

"It all sounds very brave," Hildy said, "what happened to the brandy and pigeons?"

"Ah!" said Boudelain, shrugging a sigh. "the fortunes of

131

war. I gave Lord Chester the pigeons and brandy in payment for his broken driveway. But he is now my great friend. I visit him often and his charming wife, Lady Dorothea. And his kitchen is very fine. He has a French chef." He pushed his plate further away from him and stood up as if he had made a sudden decision. "It is Sunday and all this talk of pigeons has made me hungry. Jack, you have a motorbike, yes? Good. Well, we have cursed PT and then nothing until sabotage in mid-afternoon and I cannot torture my stomach and taste with another canteen lunch. So I will get us half-day passes and you will take me to Lord Chester's and we will have some real food. There is no protest! This we will do. You need some fresh air. And I need some food I can taste."

Hildy joined the others in the light PT exercises on the lawns and then wandered over to the main office to check her pigeonhole for letters. There was one addressed in a hand she did not recognise. Returning to her room, she settled herself at the small desk by the window and read the letter while Georgia sought sleep lying on her bed. Georgia slept lightly and fitfully and long quiets were often broken by a sudden low gasp or slurred moan and her body twitched with the tic of a hand or arm. Hildy was half-aware of Georgia's troubled life and did not envy her the dreams that seemed to menace her in her sleep. Hildy had always slept like a stone and never had a dream that she could remember.

The letter was from Mrs Maynard.

Dear Miss Potts,

Please do not be alarmed, this letter is just to let you know that all is fine at the farm and that your father is well and sends you his regards.

I know that you are doing important war work and that you can't tell us anything or let us know where you are and that is fine. Just keep yourself safe and come back when you can. Dora is doing a grand job in looking after Jip. He sleeps on her bed and I told Dora that's not the farm way but she won't have it and told me that it was her way and Jip is a fine bed warmer and rat chaser so he sleeps on her bed. I doubt you would recognise your father as he has changed so much in his ways and manner. He gets on famously with Rolf and Walter. They made your father a cart from the broken one in the barn and he can now get about the courtyard and fields and he shot two rabbits and we had them for stew on Sunday.

Well, it's just a note to say that we are all fine and hope this gets to you and all is fine with you too. Your father, like any man, doesn't show his feelings, but I know he thinks of you and wishes your safe return. If you happen to see Jack let him know we are all well and that Dora has no more dreams and has learned to ride a horse and walk behind the plough with Rolf and we all send him our love. How this war is changing us all!

I will not expect a reply as I know you might not be able to write but all the best my dear and know we are here and so thankful for the home and roof you have given us and hope you are well and safe and looking forward to coming home once this horrid war is all over.

Yours
Mollie Maynard

Hildy felt a tear welling unbidden in her eye. She felt the tear to be ridiculous and couldn't understand why it came. Perhaps it was the strain and exhaustion of the last few weeks catching up with her, or the just the kindness of Mrs Maynard in getting in touch and seeking to put her mind at rest. Maybe her tear came for the news of her father's changing nature and that she was not there to see and wonder at it. But mostly perhaps because he had only mustered her a regard rather than his love.

Hildy's reveries were interrupted by a knock on the door. She opened it to find Sergeant Evans standing before her. He was not in uniform but dressed in a brown jacket, creased brown trousers and plain brown waistcoat with fob chain. His usual curled bramble of hair had been oiled to a scalp-hugging sheen and he smelt strongly of coal tar soap. He lifted his brown homburg hat carefully from his head and held it by the brim in a knuckle-gnarled hand. He smiled and bowed slightly.

"Miss Potts, forgive the intrusion. I was just passing on my way to the Rings and thought I'd stop by and check on your injury. It mends I trust?"

"Oh, yes. Fine, thank you, Sergeant," Hildy lifted her hand and waved the wrist to the air, "see, fine. Thank you for enquiring. The doctor says I can resume heavy work tomorrow."

"Oh, that is good news. Good indeed. And please, no sergeant if I'm out of uniform. It's Reginald when I'm in civvies, eh!"

"Yes, right." Hildy could think of nothing to say. "Er, Reginald."

"Well, that's fine then. I believe you are free until sabotage this afternoon, are you not?"

"Well, er, yes, I think so. Do you need me for another duty before then?"

Reginald laughed lightly.

"Hardly a duty, Miss Potts, no. Although the call is on us all, don't you think?"

Hildy was finding this conversation a little confusing. She turned to see Georgia, now awake and sitting up on her bed, listening to the scene with evident amusement. Hildy glared at her for help but Georgia continued to smile and shrugged the glare away.

"Yes, quite," Hildy said, turning back to her visitor.

"And have you answered the call?" asked Reginald. "The one we cannot but obey?"

"I'm afraid, Serg... Reginald, I'm not sure what you mean. Are there new duty rosters posted?" Hildy heard Georgia stifle a giggle from her bed.

"Indeed there are, Miss Potts. For this life and that which is to come. Tell me, have you received the call, Miss Potts?"

"Call?"

"Of the Lord, Miss Potts."

All confusion fell from Hildy's mind and her sudden relief of understanding was swiftly replaced by an equally sudden realisation of her awkward situation.

"I am on my way to a meeting of the called, Miss Potts, to partake of thanks and praise for our risen Lord. It is an informal meeting of brothers and sisters thankful for our small mercies and to sing our heart and love to the heaven above us all and the glorious world beyond this veil of war-torn tears. I would consider it a singular honour if you would care to accompany me, Miss Potts? I believe a woman of your qualities will be a boon to us all. A flower among us weeds, eh! There will be paste sandwiches, tea, and apple cordials."

"No gin and bitters?" asked Georgia from the bed.

Reginald leaned in from the doorway and saw Georgia sitting on her bed smoking a cigarette. He had obviously not realised she was there. His hat span in his fist and he laughed lightly.

"The Lord's Exalters do not partake of alcoholic beverages, Miss Melrose," he said. "We do not demand the abstinence in others that we observe in ourselves and recognise that in times of war there are many crutches on which the weak and uncalled seek support. A modest sherry or small glass of wine to aid the grieving widow or broken heart has its place and purpose. But always within limitations of excess or appropriate courtesies. I think there is cake today and Brother Malcolm is going to show us his slides of Jordan. From before the war. Will you come, Miss Potts?"

Hildy stood in a cloud of coal tar fumes and tried to think of a response that was neither hurtful nor disdaining. She stared into Reginald's eager, smiling and hopeful face and still nothing came to her. Perhaps just an hour or so with Reginald was the price she had to pay for flooring him. She was on the point of accepting when she was aware of Georgia at her side.

"Sergeant Evans, er Reginald," Georgia put her arm

around Hildy's shoulders in a seeming act of support. "It is very sweet of you to ask Hildy to your meeting and I am sure, under normal circumstances, she would be only too pleased and honoured to accept your most kind invitation. But I'm afraid she has only just received a letter from home that is causing her some anxieties," Georgia looked down meaningfully to the letter still in Hildy's hand. Hildy immediately clasped it to her bosom, "and she needs time to compose herself and respond with a letter as soon as possible. Finding the right words is always so distressful, don't you find? She is hoping to make the late afternoon postal despatch. So I am sure you will understand that, as much as I'm sure she would love to accompany you to the Lord's Exalters, she will have to decline your kind offer at this difficult time."

Reginald was immediately distraught. His hat stilled in its spin and his face creased into anguish.

"Quite, of course. I am so sorry. I did not think to enquire. Forgive my crass behaviour. What must you think? Please think nothing more of it. I understand. Please accept my apologies for this intrusion into your sorrows, Miss Potts. And I hope that such sorrows that have crossed your path may soon pass. We must have faith in Him to see us through, eh, Miss Potts. Another time maybe." He bowed and replaced his hat. "I wish you well, Miss Potts. Lean on the Lord for your strength and your joys will not be far ahead."

Hildy closed the door and she and Georgia waited in silence, listening to Reginald's receding footsteps down the corridor. They waited until they heard his march crunch on the gravel path before collapsing into laughter.

"Thank you so much!" Hildy said, "I just couldn't think what to say."

"Well, you flowers are not known for your repartee. Our pugilist Sergeant Evans! A Lord Exalter! Who would have thought?"

"It's this place and this war," Hildy said, "everything is upside down and nothing is what it seems or what you

136

expect or what you thought it was."

"It's why we're here," Georgia said, "to learn to assume nothing, to take nothing as read until it is proved and to trust no one but yourself."

"But I trust you, Georgia, don't you trust me? There must be trust otherwise it would all fall apart. We have to trust each other and those who command us. It's the only way we can get the job done. Working together."

"I trust you to floor Reginald," Georgia said, "but would not trust you to resist his brown-suited and scented charms."

Hildy laughed, but thoughts of mistrust disturbed her.

"I'm serious," she said. "I do trust you, don't you trust me?"

Georgia held Hildy's gaze for a long moment and then took her hands in hers.

"Hildy, you are a brave, resourceful, remarkable and determined young woman and you have a warm and tender heart. How could anyone not trust you? But you are also an innocent. You trust too easily, and that is something that we all have to learn to overcome. It is fine here, in Beaulieu, in fair and honest Blighty, but if it ever comes that we are dropped into France then it will be a totally different world and you will have to become a totally different person. You will be a mouse in a snake pit. Everyone you see and meet will be an enemy, wanting to kill you or betray you. Each and every one of them malicious and selfish. War does terrible things to people. It makes them do things they wouldn't ever think they could do. To lie, to betray, to kill. You can trust no one. Not even me."

"But you would never betray anyone," Hildy said.

Georgia released her hold and sat in the chair by the window, staring down at the lawns.

"I'd like to think so," she said, "Wouldn't we all. But who can ever have that certainty? To know how we would act under extreme terror? I'd like to think that I'd have the courage never to betray. But there are drugs and tortures that can make cowards of us all. We can never know what we might face or how we might react." She turned to look up at

137

Hildy and smiled. "Which is why, my dear Hildy, if you hope to survive and to come home again, you must learn to not trust anyone, not even me."

TWENTY

Jack was studying charts of German military uniforms in the Rings library when he was summoned by Boudelain from the doorway.

"Summers, we go now. I get you a fine luncheon. Come let's get the motorbike."

Boudelain was wrapped in an officer's greatcoat, buttoned up to the neck and his leather boots were brilliant with shine. He was eager and garrulous as they made their way to the stables and Jack checked over his motorbike.

"Lady Dorothea has promised lamb cutlets, pommes julienne, asparagus, and cauliflower cheese," enthused Boudelain. "And a thirty-four Merlot. It will be a fine luncheon. Lord Chester keeps a fine cellar."

"Shouldn't I dress for it?" asked Jack. Boudelain studied him. The jacket was rumpled and slightly frayed at the collar, his boots were dull and rough and his shirt had a third day worn comfort. "No. It is fine. Lady Dorothea and Lord Chester do not dine formal. I will tell them you have returned from fighting. Lost your clothes or something. They will understand. Come, we are wasting good dining time!"

Chalfont Hall stood imperious at the end of a long, tree-lined driveway that beckoned through ornate iron gates sculpted in mermaids and dolphins and ended in an arced sweep before the steps of a grand, many-windowed frontage of ancient brick, folly turrets and rampant wisterias.

Jack brought the bike to idle by a large pond of lily-pads and silvered fish and allowed Boudelain to slide off his pillion seat. Jack then parked the bike up on its stand.

A butler appeared on the top steps followed swiftly by three yapping dogs and a small, elderly lady wearing a garden jacket, battered wide-brimmed hat and carrying a small trowel. A twin set of pearl necklaces scarfed her throat.

"Emile! How lovely that you could come again! You

have caught me on my knees among the anemones. We will have such a show this year I think. Stop, Caesar! Penelope, in! Oh, see to them Briggs I'm all garden at the moment. I hope you are hungry, Count? Your hand, are you hurt?"

"It is nothing, a scratch only."

The butler descended the steps and scooped up two of the dogs expertly and shepherded the last back indoors with his foot. He returned dogless a moment later to resume his guard at the door.

Boudelain offered a fond and happy embrace of Lady Dorothea.

"Lady Dorothea, such a pleasure as always. Famished, as I think you English say." He removed his greatcoat and Jack was startled to see that Boudelain was in a neatly pressed and laundered number two dress uniform of a French Air Force Capitaine. He shucked his tie neat and winked at Jack. "We French dress to dine," he said. "It honours the food and respects the hosts."

Boudelain threw his coat over Briggs' ready arm and escorted Lady Dorothea up the steps. Briggs waited for Jack and accepted his motorbike goggles in his free hand. Briggs took the goggles between a gloved forefinger and thumb as if they were mildly toxic. He smiled thinly and Jack followed him up the steps and into the great hall. Briggs opened the door to the drawing room where Boudelain was already inspecting the drinks on the large sideboard. Lady Dorothea left to change for luncheon.

"Help yourselves to a pre-luncheon aperitif, gentlemen, Lord and Lady Chester will join you presently in the dining room." Briggs departed.

Out through the large picture windows the lawns and lands of Chalfont Hall swept past woods, manicured lawns and wildflower pastures and on down to a lake and a river that meandered lazily into a blue, distant haze. Several horses grazed in a far field and a gang of workmen were digging ditches and pathways by a billowing wood of oaks and elms.

"Whisky for the palate," Boudelain handed Jack a full

tumbler.

"They live well, our Lords and Ladies," Jack said. He downed half his whisky. It burned in his throat and glowed his gut. He lifted a small peach from the fruit bowl. "War is indeed hell, eh?"

"Ah, don't tell me you are to play the envious peasant, Summers, it is so bourgeois. So boring. Lord Chester is of a very old and noble family. They have looked after this land ever since the Hanoverians. Ancient stewards. Of course they live well. Who would not who had the chance? They are the backbone and soul of the land, of its people. Like my family in France. Fathers to our people. Old and true blood. It is important that this happens. That we look after it. Bring work to our people. Keep the order of things. It is a noble duty."

"Didn't you have a revolution in France to stop all that? Let the people share the land and the wealth. Égalité and all that?"

The count seemed to stiffen and grow a little taller. "A time of madness. It has only led to chaos and bad socialism. The guillotine killed the best of France and left nothing but ugliness and treachery behind. France was once great in the world. Now we are a cowering and defeated dog. It is too much."

Lord Chester strode into the room. He was an elderly, short, round and ruddy-faced man in crisp tweeds, brogues and green woollen gaiters. He greeted Boudelain with obvious pleasure and energy.

"Emile, dear fellow, so glad you could pop in. Dot's lamb cutlets do the trick, eh?" he laughed. "Got a new pair of Westley Richards Droplocks. Maple stocks. Lovely pieces. You must have a look. Try 'em on a brace, eh? Got them from the Gillie in old Morton's spread for a song. Sorry, running over myself, who's this?"

Boudelain turned to Jack and winked again.

"My chauffeur, Lord Chester, name is Summers."

"Uniform needs a press, I'd say," laughed Lord Chester.

"It is my attempt at English humour. Jack was kind

enough to bring me over here. On his motorbike."

"Motorbike?" said Lord Chester obviously interested. "A good one, I trust?"

"A BSA Y 13," Jack said.

"What, the V-Twin?"

"Yes. A little throaty but it kicks."

"Never ridden a V-Twin," Lord Chester said.

"Help yourself to a run on her," Jack held out his keys.

"Help yourself to another whisky, my boy," grinned Lord Chester. "And pour me one while you're about it. I'll take up your kind offer after luncheon. But we'll keep it from Dorothea, eh? She gets worried about my driving. Doesn't understand these things. Liable to fuss. OK?"

"Of course."

"Good man, now let's demolish a lamb or two. Hear there's roly-poly for pudding too."

Jack was not called on to contribute much to luncheon conversation. From his seat halfway down the long, resplendently opulent dining table, he was at some remove from Lord and Lady Chester and Boudelain who all crowded in convivial chatter at the table's end. Jack was occasionally asked if the lamb was to his liking or made offer of more cauliflower cheese, but for the main he was left to his own diversions. The wine was fine and the food was certainly splendid, Jack could not remember the last time he had tasted lamb. He hesitated over his asparagus until Lady Dorothea offered unwitting instruction on how it was to be eaten. Asparagus was a new experience for Jack. He didn't think much of it and piled on extra potatoes and gravy.

Lady Dorothea twittered and pecked at her food like a nervous bird and it was soon apparent that she was one of those people who are ever happy and busy in the world, but never quite of it. She would proffer a train of thought or comment into a conversation she had neither followed nor heard and then happily float off back to her thoughts again.

Lord Chester and Boudelain were obviously used to her intrusions and would allow Dorothea to finish, let silence

142

momentarily settle, and then resume their conversation as if uninterrupted. Lord Chester might include a rare, "yes, my dear" or a gentle pat of her hand but that was all. Lord Chester and Boudelain talked energetically of guns, managing estates, the dire state of the war, wine and the scandal that was the Beveridge report.

"A licence for idlers and damn slackers!" said Lord Chester. "Welfare. Taking the money out of our pockets and giving it communists. The country has gone mad!"

"Perhaps it is the war," said Boudelain. He waited while Briggs refilled his glass. "The people have lost their feet and confidence and turn to false saviours."

"Mrs Haribold says her chiropodist is now in submarines," said Lady Dorothea. "A lot of bad feet in the Navy, I suppose."

Briggs stepped forward in the silence and retrieved Lady Dorothea's napkin from the floor. "Thank you, Briggs. Are those new shoes?"

"Yes, your Ladyship."

"Squeak a bit, I expect. All new shoes squeak."

"The government is turning this country's people into beggars and layabouts," said Lord Chester, "Learned nothing from the last war, or the peace. Germans pull themselves up from the chaos of defeat through hard work, order and a strong leader. Look at them now! Conquered half the world and getting stronger. What did we do? Give handouts to idlers and cut our army and navy in half to pay for it."

"True," said Boudelain, "but we built our armies in France and it did no good."

"I know, Germans just swept over you like they walked around you in the first war. I'm a patriot, don't get me wrong, but we could learn a lot from the Germans." Lord Chester was becoming more loquacious and strident as the wine took hold. Boudelain seemed at pains to try and restrain his vehemence.

"But in England they did not fly over, eh?" said Boudelain. "The RAF fought well."

"The channel saved us," said Lord Chester. "It won't save us forever. We have the luck of geography on our side."

"Do you remember that holiday in Dorset?" said Lady Dorothea, "the summer it rained? It never rains like that anymore. Mr Jenkins says it's because all the bombs have broken the clouds. I think that is what he said. This war is so horrid. I do miss rain. So does the garden."

"Yes, they'll come soon enough," said Lord Chester stabbing a new potato, "and with better planes, better ships and better tanks than us. It's a disgrace how slack this government has been. We were not ready for war and we have been losing ground ever since. And we have no need to fight them. To sacrifice all our boys again. This isn't our war, it's Europe's. Let them fight it, I say."

Boudelain seemed uncomfortable with the direction of the conversation and tried to regain the patriotic ground.

"But we must make a stand," said Boudelain. He fixed Lord Chester with a stare that Jack thought more a warning than a suggestion, "against the bullies. Don't you agree, Lord Chester?"

Lord Chester seemed to recognise the warning. He gazed at Jack and smiled without warmth.

"Yes, yes of course we must. Stop them. Only thing to do. Just saying they have a march on us, that's all. Talk of them building a new type of fighter plane without propellers. And flying rocket bombs. Go faster than any Spit. We need to be realistic. Don't you agree, Summers?"

Jack contemplated his wine glass and then drained the last of its contents.

"Sometimes, Davids slay Goliaths," he said.

Lord Chester grunted. "Only in myths and fairy tales. You want to risk our lands, lives and liberties on a myth? Far better pull up the drawbridge, sign the peace and let the dogs of war fight it out amongst themselves."

"Foster's Jenny has had her litter," said Lady Dorothea, "Six pups, four bitches. I rather like the tan bitch. She promised us first refusal."

144

Boudelain leaned forward to Jack and spoke softly.

"You have to forgive Lord Chester his anger for war. He lost both his twin sons in the last war. It is hard to lose one's sons."

"Just eighteen," said Lord Chester summoning Briggs to open a third bottle of wine. "That is no age to die. One drowned in mud, the other gangrene from wounds. And for what? But Boudelain here has lost much himself. His family's factories all taken by the government in the last war and turned over to making barbed wire and military trucks. When he got the factories back after the war they were in ruins. Tried to start up again but the bankers wouldn't have it. All Jews of course. Then the money markets crashed. His father never got over it. Losing the factories, his estates ruined. Killed himself. Fine chap, such a waste."

"You knew the count's father?" asked Jack.

Boudelain cut in. "All the old families know each other," he said, "by reputation or marriage or some family connection. It is not unusual. All the noble families. Like your Queen Victoria. Cousins and nephews across Europe. In every castle. Now, Lord Chester has promised to show me his new guns. And he'll need your motorbike keys. Perhaps you can accompany Lady Dorothea on her garden walk?"

Jack was rather surprised that he enjoyed his afternoon stroll in the gardens with Lady Dorothea,

"Call me Dot, dear boy, for heaven's sake, it is so much easier."

He shadowed at Dot's side while she pruned idly among the voluptuous borders of flowers or did some quick pricking-outs in the greenhouses. The aged, cloth-capped and aproned gardener, Henderson, kept at a discreet but attentive distance and would step in when summoned by her Ladyship to clip some overhanging branches or tie back a rampant growth. In between these tasks, he nursed a small but vigorous bonfire beyond the greenhouses and trundled his wheelbarrow of rakings and cuttings to feed it and to rest on his fork while having a smoke.

The air was cool but the sky clear and blue and the stroll and gardens were a wonderful release from the stresses and tensions of Beaulieu. The gardens stretched on either side of the house and were separated by the magnificent manicured lawns that ran from the back of the house to the distant boating lake and river. One garden was given over to flowers, the other vegetables and fruit. Dot chatted and muttered in a world of herself which only occasionally required Jack's response.

"Leaf rust on the raspberries. Have to get Henderson to thin them out. It's the lack of air among the stems you see? I'd like to try apricots. Very partial to apricots. Of course the seasons can be very harsh for apricots. Maybe in the greenhouse. In a pot. Do you have a garden, Mr Summers?"

"No, your Ladyship. I have no house."

"Really? What, none at all?"

"I had one once, but it was bombed."

"Everyone should have a house so that they can have a garden. Don't you think? A garden is so peaceful. So absorbing. It's all the fault of this horrid, horrid war. They wanted me to plough up my flowers and put potatoes in! I told them if they step a foot past the gates, I'd have Chester blast them with his shotguns. I think I shall move this buddleia closer to the south wall. Yes. Over there. Henderson!"

While Henderson and Dot discussed the moving of the buddleia, Jack wandered into the raised herb garden and then into the long, old greenhouse and the huge, leaf- heavy grapevine that filled its entire length like a fat, green caterpillar in a glass tube. Small but plentiful bunches of pale purple fruit hung in its canopy. Jack emerged back into the garden and sat on an old wooden bench under an ornamental cherry tree. Dot and Henderson were still engrossed in lifting the misplaced buddleia and Jack sat in the sun and smoked a leisurely cigarette.

It was a haven of dappled sun and quiet. He savoured the cigarette and listened to the bugs and birds droning and chirruping about him and he could not believe that he was in the middle of war. He wondered how Dora and Ma were faring at the farm and longed to be with them again. From his seat, Jack gazed up at the brick outhouse that once served as a grain store but now seemed to have a dovecote in its rafters. A large pigeon launched itself out of the high gable-end window and flapped its wings hard to get height. The wings sounded like automatic gunfire. The gardens returned to their silence of bugs. Jack was reaching for another cigarette when he heard the noise of a distant engine throbbing. His pulse quickened and he immediately scanned the skies for planes. There were none and he came to realise that the sound was of his own motorbike. Lord Chester was taking it for a spin in the lakeside woods. The garden spell was broken and the press of war enveloped him once more.

Dot appeared around the corner of the herb garden.

"There you are! Thought I'd lost you. I need to check in on the hens."

They made their way past the greenhouses and out into the wide driveway. A couple of outhouses served as chicken coops and the hens scratched among the meadow grasses. Around the corner of one of the houses, Jack was taken aback to see the wreckage of a plane crumpled against one of the walls. The engine and cockpit were scarred and scorched by fire and one wing was broken in half where it had clipped the corner of the wall. The body was crushed to nothing but remnants of the tail were still intact, a couple of letters and numbers still visible on it. The wreckage was so burnt and crumpled that it was impossible to tell what plane it had been.

"Is that the count's plane?" he asked. Dot looked up from her gathering of eggs from the nest boxes.

"What? Oh, yes. That's Emile's plane."

"He wasn't hurt in the accident?"

"Oh, no, Emile is an excellent flyer, or so I'm led to believe. No, he landed it on our driveway and taxied up to the front door! So Emile! He had crates of brandy and pigeons with him would you believe! Chester and Briggs helped him unpack it all."

"I thought he crashed. That's fire damage, isn't it?"

"Oh, no, he didn't crash. He is a good flyer. No, he and Chester crashed it into the wall the next morning. Tried to burn it. That way the disposal people would have to take it away. The plane was broken and not fit to fly anymore and we didn't want it cluttering up our place."

"But it's still here."

"Yes, they keep saying they are coming to get it but they never do. I think they are paying us back for not planting potatoes. Might get the scrap man in. Could even make a couple of bob. What do you think?"

"I think the scrap men all work for the government now," Jack said, "helping make our Spitfires."

"Well, they'll get no potatoes from me."

Jack followed Dot back to the house. Lord Chester and Boudelain were sitting in loungers in the garden room, smoking and cradling balloons of brandy. Boudelain hailed Jack's return.

"Thought Lady Dorothea might have potted you or put you on her bonfire!"

Lord Chester rose and handed Jack his keys.

"Fine ride," he said, "reckon I got her up to fifty through the wood track. Suspension a bit tight but it responds well. I enjoyed it, thank you."

"And thank you for a fine lunch," Jack said, "you have been most kind."

Boudelain rose reluctantly from his chair. "I suppose we had better be getting back to Beaulieu and its savage food and people. We will have to tear ourselves away."

Lord Chester, Boudelain and Lady Dorothea shared fond farewells and promises for another visit and their hosts stood on the top steps to wave them down the driveway.

Jack let the motorbike purr the Hampshire lanes while Boudelain shouted loudly and contentedly in his ear from the pillion.

"I told you I would get you a fine lunch, did I not? The asparagus was too earthy but the lamb was perfection. And a handsome Merlot I think, eh?"

Jack felt Boudelain's thighs clutch him from behind as he weaved and leaned the motorbike through the lanes. Boudelain's bandaged hand was clamped securely on Jack's shoulder. The same bandaged hand that Jack now realised he had seen in the corner of his vision launching the pigeon from its high, old grain barn cote and taking to the bluest of skies amid a rapid gunfire of flapping wings

TWENTY ONE

Hildy jumped down from the truck tailgate and landed in ankle deep grass. Georgia jumped down beside her.

The journey had been long and wearisome and their bones and muscles ached from the truck's heavy suspension and sitting on the hard metal benches crammed tight with soldiers and trainee agents. They had set out before three a.m., woken from their sleep and given ten minutes to dress for outdoors before being herded into the trucks in the dark. The truck's canvas covers had been closed and tied-drawn and the journey had been one of no talking, roaring engines and physical discomfort, with no views out and no idea where they were going or why.

They landed at a deserted, open landscape of hills and a big, grey-clouded sky.

"Looks like Dartmoor," Hildy said. She accepted a cigarette from Georgia and tried to stamp some circulation into her feet.

"Damn cold moor," Georgia said. "I wish I had packed a cushion." She looked at her watch. "Just over four hours of hell transport. That is about right for Dartmoor, isn't it?"

"Unless we were going around in circles."

They stood on a rise of grass moor with granite outcrops behind them and gentle hills sloping down to deep, narrow, tree-lined valleys and on into the distance beyond. Outcrops of harsh stones and rocks erupted from the greenery like flailed mushrooms. Three other trucks were parked in the field with them and more soldiers and agents were collecting beside them, smoking and stamping feet. Two jeeps carrying officers skidded to a halt some distance off. Moments later a few soldiers were organising a brew-up urn from a field stove hauled from the back of one of the trucks.

Hildy saw Jack among one of the other truck groups, and the French count and Peters and Stuvenson. The sight of Jack relieved her of her anxieties, although she could not think why this should be. She was meant to be an agent in training and able to work and to be alone, but the presence of Jack gave her a strange comfort. She counted twenty-four other agents, maybe as many soldiers. One of the officers she recognised from Beaulieu. It was Major Chamberlain from the field craft and survival section. He was a tall, lanky New Zealander who seemed to have a permanent roll-up at his lips and an informal approach to both uniform and military etiquette. Dressed in shorts, bush hat and sheepskin jerkin, he mounted the back of the jeep and gathered everyone to him by way of a forefinger and thumb piercing shriek of a whistle.

"Welcome to France," he said, "or Belgium or whatever goddam country you finally land yourself in. Only you've landed in the wrong place and you've lost all your kit in the jump. You're supposed to be somewhere else and you're miles from your rendezvous and your resistance contact. So you are going to have to walk it."

Chamberlain smiled and gazed down at the gathered agents. "Cold ain't it? Never mind, a long brisk walk will soon warm you up. Only you will not be doing it with any assistance. All money, watches, compasses, knives and other items will be collected by my soldiers and returned to you after this little jaunt. You will be escaping in teams of three. The objective is to present yourselves, as a team, at Winterfold House in Cranleigh, Sussex." Chamberlain stood up and pointed east. "That's about a hundred miles that way." He grinned at the upturned faces. "A stroll in the park. Shouldn't take you more than three days. Of course, you are fugitives in a foreign land, so there can be no contact with the natives. You are on your own and must survive on your own, and your one and only purpose and mission is to make the meeting with a certain Mr Merchant at Winterfold House. All the local forces of order and vigilance have been informed of this exercise and of you, so the police forces, military, and every village and farm nosey parker will be on the look-out for you. You will be issued with ID exercise cards and these you will hand in to Mr Merchant upon completion, or more likely to the policeman who arrests you. This is not an individual challenge, it is a team effort. You all make it as a team or you don't. Stick together, work together, get it done together. No mavericks. Any individual who makes it home alone will have failed. If you get caught you fail the exercise. And you *will* fail because you *will* get caught. Maybe not today but tomorrow. Maybe you might even make it out of Devon and reach the far lands of Wiltshire but you won't get any further because none of you ever do. No one ever has. Any questions?"

"What happens when we fail?" someone asked.

"You will be taken back to Beaulieu with your tail between your legs."

"Do we get breakfast before we go?"

"You have half an hour for a hot brew and to gather your team together and work out an action plan. Then you begin walking. This is a survival, camouflage and cover exercise, like the real thing. Except our boys in blue won't shoot you on sight or hang you from a meat hook. Give them the teams, Harris."

A corporal stepped forward and consulted a clip file.

"Team one, Gunnersby, Sigurson, and Smythe. Team two, Evans, Boudelain, and Forster. Team three, Melrose, Summers, and Potts…"

They wandered away from the crowds and shared cigarettes. Georgia mentioned her shoes and said she wished she'd opted for her walking boots. Hildy went to the tea station at one of the truck's tailgates and brought back three enamel mugs.

"They say it's tea, but I haven't actually seen it move yet. No sugar I'm afraid."

Jack was studying the terrain about them trying to distil some idea that might constitute a workable action plan. He took a mug from Hildy. She was dressed in a trench cost and cloth cap and her hair was awry and her cheeks flushed in the cool, early morning breeze. Not for the first time Jack found himself admiring Hildy. She had an energy and spirt that was almost contagious.

Two soldiers approached the group and frisked them

individually with a full body check. They bagged and tagged the coins and watches and other items but allowed them to keep their cigarettes and lighters before handing out three ID cards.

"Hand them over when you get caught," said one. "Look on it as a tea voucher." The soldiers laughed and moved on.

Team three stood sipping their tea.

"Any thoughts?" asked Jack.

"Hide up on the moor for the day and move by night?" offered Georgia. "Keep off the roads and to the woods. Maybe follow a rail track going east."

"But we'll need a map," Hildy said, "some route plan. Have to steal food along the way. But that increases the risk of capture."

"The prospects aren't good for any of us getting far," Georgia said, "Three ragged civvies wandering the countryside is bound to attract attention and travelling by night will be very slow."

Silence descended. Jack was still studying the terrain.

"Perhaps we don't have to walk," he said, "maybe we could ride."

Hildy and Georgia laughed.

"Nice thought, Jack but not really helpful right now."

"Remember the moments before we stopped here?" Jack said. "Think back."

Hildy could not follow his thoughts.

"Look at the track into this field," Jack continued, "subtly now, don't give our interest away. See the far gate? And the lane leading up to it and from it under the trees? Remember how the truck rode heavy on the brakes as it came over the rise and down the hill of the lane under the trees a little before getting to the gate?"

"Yes, they were braking hard. It was a steep hill. I remember," Georgia said.

"How do you know there were trees?" asked Hildy, "Our truck was covered. We couldn't see anything."

"But didn't you hear the branches brushing the top of the canvas as we came down the hill?"

"Well, maybe. But so what?"

"What about," Jack said, "if we were to wander down the slope here into the valley and then double back up around behind unseen, and up the track and climb into the trees and wait for the last truck to leave. Then simply drop onto its roof and climb inside. Ride all the way home."

Hildy could not think what to say, it seemed too easy, too unlikely.

"You see," Jack said, "the truck will be travelling very slowly up the hill, especially if it's the last in the convoy. No more than walking pace. We can easily drop onto the canvas roof from the trees. Only problem might be getting inside once we're up there. We'd have to work fast."

"Maybe my offiziersmesser will help," Hildy said. She scanned around to make sure no one was looking and then reached under her coat and into her blouse. She pulled out the little multi-blade knife and showed it to the others.

"Where on earth did you hide that?" asked Jack

"In my bra. I knew the soldiers would never look there. I slipped it in back at Beaulieu when we had ten minutes to get ready. I thought it might be handy to have about. We could cut the canvas roof with that and drop through."

"It all seems, well, rather too simple," Georgia said.

Jack smiled. "Simple ideas are the kind that tend to work," he said. "Are we game?"

Georgia and Hildy shared a look. They grinned and nodded assent.

"I'll drop first," said Hildy, "It's my knife and I'm used to riding high hay bales on a moving tractor trailer. I'll make the canvas cut and then you can drop in. Agreed?"

"It'll have to be a lone truck or the one at the back," Georgia said, "otherwise we'll be seen."

Jack grinned. "We'll take that as the game plan then, shall we? The tucks will be heading back to Beaulieu, so we will have to find a time to jump out of the back. Then head across country to Cranleigh. "

Chamberlain whistled the agents to regather. His parting words were brief and to the point.

"Well, what are you all waiting for? Time to take your little stroll in the countryside. Winterfold House, Cranleigh. And it's that way." He pointed east down the slope and into the vague, blue distances beyond. "Cheery bye!"

Eight groups of three began to make their way east. Some heading straight down the slope, others traversing the hill. Team three set off down the slope of the valley and were soon among the trees of the valley floor and lost to sight from the soldiers at the trucks. They waited until the other agent groups had disappeared from their view before turning north up the valley and then west again back up the hillside to the lane leading to the fields where the trucks were still parked. Chestnut and elm trees ranked along the lane, their leafy branches bending low over the lane and the brambles and hedges that grew alongside.

Hildy selected a strong, leafy tree at the start of the incline and climbed up into its branches and looked over at the field.

"They're packing the trucks," she said. "The jeeps look like they're going to be leading. The officers are scanning the landscape with binoculars. They're not looking this way. The trucks are going to be in convoy, I think. First three trucks have soldiers in them. The last truck has the field canteen loaded."

"We'll take the last truck then," Jack said. "Ok? Right, good luck. See you in the truck."

Jack and Georgia selected trees further up the lane while Hildy inched her way along a sturdy, dense-leafed bough that hung over the road and settled to await the trucks. She could feel her heart pounding heavy against her ribs and she tried to calm herself for the task in hand. She took her knife and tucked it into her coat pocket. She missed her pocket playthings but took comfort in the feel of the knife. Laying along the bough giant ants and earwigs marched the twigs and leaves before her and the smell of bark and moss bathed her.

The sound of truck engines revving up in the distance brought Hildy back to alert. She parted a small curtain of foliage to watch and to wait. Moments later the two jeeps carrying the officers sped by under her and she heard a snippet of conversational laughter that was instantly swallowed by the engines' roar. Looking back along the lane she could see the trucks moving into line to the gate and slowly making their way out onto the lane. She took a deep breath and tried to clear her mind of doubts. It was just a children's game she told herself, nothing more. A dare and derring-do. It was what she signed-up for. The worse that could happen is that she could break her back and be in a wheelchair for the rest of her life. Like her father. She would rather die.

The first truck passed underneath her. It was going faster than Jack had suggested and the doubts began to simmer again. But by the time the third truck was under her, the convoy had slowed to almost walking pace. The lead truck was struggling towards the brow of the hill in low gear and the others were slowing up behind.

The last truck came into view and was then underneath her. Hildy lost no time to any more doubts, she swung off her branch and dropped onto the canvas roof. It was a drop of less than five feet but the canvas sagged and bounced and it took Hildy a moment to gain her balance. She fisted the knife and tore a split in the canvas roof. They were approaching the trees where Jack and Georgia were waiting. Hildy could see the back of the lead truck on the brow of the hill about to crest its wave. She grabbed the metal roof bracers and swung herself into the truck and landed heavily on the floor. The field canteen was stacked along one side and its tinny clatter and rattling lids masked any sound Hildy's fall might have made. Two large jerry cans of diesel were strapped to the other side of the truck.

She had no time to take it all in before Georgia's legs appeared through the roof tear. She helped her down and Jack followed within seconds.

They stood in the middle of the truck, swaying against the movements, trying to get their balance and breath and listening for signs of discovery or alarm. Two soldiers talked and laughed in the front cab and the smell of cigarettes and cold tea wafted.

Jack held his finger to his lips. "No sounds," he whispered. He looked around. There was only the canteen and a large canvas sheet rolled up at the back of the truck. A breeze that was almost a wind came from the loose canvas ties and the hole in the roof. It was biting and cold. Georgia was already pulling her coat closer. Jack made his way to the back of the truck and unfurled the canvas sheet. He sat back against the cab's body and beckoned Hildy and Georgia to take a seat beside him. When they had settled, he pulled the canvas sheet about them all.

"Get close and snug and out of the cold," he whispered, "it could be a long trip."

They huddled together and listened to the truck's roar and the talk from the cab.

"Got a fag?"

"Light me one too. This steering is a bastard."

"It's them motor pool slackers. Couldn't fix a pushbike that lot. God I'm hungry."

"Them agent rabbits gonna be a lot hungrier. Looked like a feeble lot. Probably won't make it off the moor let alone out of the county."

"Ginge said that the furthest any of 'em ever got was Taunton."

"I wouldn't mind going a lot further with that blonde one. See her? Wouldn't kick her out of me truck. I'd fuck that one all the way to Salisbury."

Hildy felt rather than saw Georgia colour beside her. She looked at her and smiled thinly.

"Men, they never let you down, do they?" she whispered. "They are always men. Where would we be without them?"

"Walking," Jack said. Georgia laughed.

They rested back against the cab wall. The truck was breezy, noisy and cold but the canvas sheet and their close body heat began to warm them towards a kind of comfort.

Hildy turned to the others, but, despite the cold, they

were asleep, their heads rolling gently against the cab wall.

Hildy could not sleep. She sat breathing in Jack and Georgia's soft sighs of sleep and felt the warmth returning to her limbs under the canvas wrap. The two soldiers in the cab continued to talk in low drones about everything and nothing. Hildy could not quite believe where she was or how far she had come in such a short time. Her recent thoughts of her father had taken her back to the farm but she found that such memories produced no yearnings to return or sadness at having left. She knew she was now a different Hildy Potts. A more confident and hopeful young woman with a life of duty and adventure within her grasp. Here she was even sleeping with a real man, probably the first she had ever really known. The thought made her glow within and she realised with something approaching a desperation that she did not want this new life to end. Or to be apart from Jack and Georgia. Particularly Jack. Except that she knew it would and it must, and probably, end in violence and pain. But she would savour every morsel and taste of it while she could.

The soldiers' conversation began to seep into her abstracted thoughts. They were going to stop for breakfast. A place called Beryl's Café. Hildy slipped out from under the canvas and watched out through a small partition in the truck canopy. They were pulling into a large layby café off the main road. There was a garage attached to the café and the car park was full of trucks, motorbikes and motor cars. The café windows were bright with lights and smoke and steam wafted from several chimneys and kitchen flues.

The truck came to a stop at the far end of the car park and the two soldiers got out of the cab, still chatting and laughing. One, the driver, was wearing a large leather jerkin over his uniform. Hildy had a sudden fear that they would check in the back of the truck and she was on the verge of waking the still sleeping Jack and Georgia when the two soldiers headed off for the café. She saw the driver pocket the truck keys in his jerkin before they disappeared through the café door.

Thoughts careered in Hildy's head as she tried to work out what to do for the best. In the end it was simple. She would go into the café and pick the driver's jerkin of its keys and take the truck. The soldiers would recognise both Jack and Georgia because they were the recognisable kind, but they would not have registered her. Few did.

Hildy slipped out the back of the truck and headed for the garage. A couple of elderly mechanics were busy in an inspection pit under a large truck and they did not see Hildy take the overalls from the peg. She climbed into them, put a little grease on her face and tied her hair up in a slightly soiled red rag. No one batted an eyelid at a female mechanic these days. For good measure she took a wrench off a bench and slipped it into her overall pocket for the look of it.

As Hildy entered the café a wave of warm, steamy air smelling of cigarettes and bacon enveloped her. The place was packed, noisy, hot and raucous. Tables were crowded with soldiers, road workers, truckers and women from nearby factories. No one paid attention to Hildy as she idled her low-profile watch by the coat stand. The smells of the room made her realise how hungry she was. The two soldiers were with a small group around a far table. Hildy saw with some alarm that the driver was no longer wearing his jerkin, but she couldn't believe her luck to find herself standing next to it. It was hanging on the coat rail and it took but a moment to slip the keys and transit papers from its pockets. Hildy left the café as quietly as she had entered and waited a few moments to ensure that her theft had not been seen. No one followed her out. She made for the truck cab, started the engine and pulled away as smoothly and as quietly as she could, She had driven several miles before she realised she had no idea where she was going.

Jack and Georgia woke together as the truck's engine rumbled into life again. They were soon on the move.

"Hildy's gone!" Georgia said. They sat and gazed around the truck space for some moments, rocking gently to the motion of the cab.

"I can't believe she would just leave," Jack said. "I never

had her marked as a quitter."

"Nor me," Georgia said. "Hildy isn't like that. Loyal as a dog. She wouldn't let us down. Anybody down. She wouldn't leave us."

"But she's not here."

"Then something must have happened."

They lapsed into silence.

Jack felt the absence lance him like a knife. He had come to enjoy Hildy's company, to welcome it. With Hildy around, he had even begun to release the ghosts of Beth from his everyday thoughts. He felt they had formed a bond. Leaving him and Georgia like this was a betrayal that he just could not understand or quite believe.

"Well, it puts paid to the mission," Jack said, "we have to do it as a team, or not at all."

"Hildy just wouldn't," Georgia said, "I know her. She just wouldn't."

"I know. I thought the same. We're slowing down," Jack said.

The truck was grinding down through the gears and then came to a stop. They heard the cab door open and footsteps sound on the ground outside.

"Well at least we must have made it past Yeovil," Jack said. He tried to smile but it refused to come.

The canvas awning at the back of the truck was pulled back and the grinning, grease-stained face of Hildy peered through.

"Either of you know the way to Cranleigh?" she asked. "'Cos bugger if I do!"

Jack took over the driving because he knew the general route and the driver's transit papers were in the name of Sergeant Ernest Gordon. If they were stopped he could at least attempt to bluff a pass through. Georgia and Hildy enjoyed a front seat ride in the warm cab and smoked. The roads were not busy, only the occasional convoy of military trucks or heavy lorries transporting tanks and construction equipment making for the coast.

"I'm starving," Hildy said. The smell of the café lingered

in her and her stomach rumbled in protest.

"We have no money and can't afford it or to risk it to go stealing," Jack said, "wouldn't want to get this far and be caught filching food from somewhere."

"Perhaps I can help," Georgia said, "I seem to have contributed very little to our adventure so far." She arched her back in the seat and reached up under her skirts. After a moment of fumbling she pulled out two one-pound notes. "Not a king's ransom," she said, "but enough for a late coffee and a light lunch somewhere, wouldn't you say?"

Jack laughed. "Do you ladies always hide treasure in your underwear?"

"I believe that is the rumour," Georgia said.

They made good time despite a half-hour stop for a soup lunch at a wayside inn and a couple of stops to top up the fuel tank from the jerry cans. The sun was dipping low in the late afternoon sky when they arrived in the large, rambling village of Cranleigh.

Winterfold House was not easy to miss. It was a large, Edwardian, red-brick house set on the side of a hill in large grounds of lawns and trees and a sweeping curved driveway that led up from ornate, solid roadside gates that were guarded by two soldiers.

Jack parked the truck in a layby up the road and they walked the final yards of their journey. The soldiers at the gates watched them approach and took a menaced and primed stance by the barrier.

"We have an appointment with Mr Merchant," Jack said. They handed over their identity cards for inspection. The corporal took them, studied them and gazed back at his visitors with barely concealed disdain.

"Do you now," the soldier said. "Wait here."

He went to a small gatehouse booth while his colleague kept the visitors covered with an idly cradled rifle and an indulgent smile. "Corp is making a phone call. To check like."

It was many minutes before the corporal returned to the barrier.

"He wasn't expecting you," he said, "but he says come up anyway. Room 54. Second floor. Give this chit to the lass on reception. You know you all look like shit, don't you?"

They were frisked and sent on their way up the drive. Ten minutes later they were knocking on the door of office number 54.

Mr Merchant sat behind a large mahogany table covered in small slag tips of papers, files, phones and ink stands. Team three stood before him.

"Reporting as instructed, Mr Merchant," Jack said.

Merchant stared at them, his face a blank mask.

"Well, it is definitely you," he said at last. He looked at this watch. "You were at Dartmoor ten hours ago?"

"And now we're here," Georgia said, "we were promised a cup of tea, I think?"

"And a chance to freshen up," Hildy added, "it's been rather a trying and rough day."

"Yes, why not?" said Merchant. He seemed to melt a little and a smile shadowed his lips. "Why not, eh? Ten hours." He shook his head and almost laughed to himself. "Captain Townsend can't get here until at least eight. We weren't expecting you, well, quite so soon, you see? Weren't really expecting you at all, truth be told. Meantime, you might as well go down to the canteen and get yourself something to eat. Freshen up, like."

They were not summoned back to Townsend's office until just after eight. The office was barely furnished, just a desk and chair and three chairs ranged before it. Townsend sat behind the desk, idling through the three files that lay open upon it. He nodded them to a seat. Merchant stood guard at the door, which he closed, and then locked.

Captain Townsend studied the three trainee agents. They were part-refreshed but the ragged, dirt-stained and weary journey had still left its mark, yet they held themselves erect and alert in their chairs. There may have been internal glows of triumph warming them all but there was little surface evidence of their impressive achievement. No smiles or smirks, just confidence and satisfaction.. He lifted each of the three files before him and dropped them onto the desk.

"Hildy Potts. Georgia Melrose. Jack Summers." He looked up and held the gaze of each of them.

"I have your training assessment reports here from Beaulieu. I am afraid that, with the greatest regret, I have to inform you that you have all failed your training. You will not be returning to Beaulieu. Your things will be collected and brought here and you will return back to the life from whence you came. I'm afraid your party is now over."

TWENTY TWO

Hildy felt like crying but she was determined not to give way to such weakness. She had learned much and experienced more in the last few weeks than she had ever imagined and she knew she had changed. She was stronger, more confident, perhaps more selfish and the thought of returning to the farm angered her. She even considered rising from her seat and seeing if she could land a punch on Captain Townsend like she had Sergeant Evans, but despite its satisfaction the thought was only fleeting and knowingly futile. She had signed the papers and was bound by duty. It was going to be back to the farm and the drudgery of ploughing and milking. Hildy suddenly realised how much she would miss Jack and Georgia and the excitement and fun to her life they had brought, and that she probably would not ever see them again.

Georgia almost laughed. She managed to refrain but could not prevent the cold smile that split her lips. It was a sneering, self-deprecating smile that turned inwardly to illuminate the stupidity and gullibility she felt at, yet again, having being so easily duped. She had almost begun to believe that her sins had been forgiven, if not quite forgotten, and that she had followed the righteous path with commitment and faith towards some form of promised redemption. But it had all been a game, she was just a toy for the devil's diversion and now she was to return to prison. She wished she had a knitting needle up her sleeve. She rose from her chair, not knowing what she was going to do but just wanting to do something.

"Please resume your seat, Miss Melrose or I will be forced to shoot you," said a voice behind her. She had forgotten Merchant. She turned to see him standing still and sentinel by the door, a pistol now held casually but ready in his hand. He smiled and shrugged his apologies. Georgia resumed her seat.

Jack sat silent and expressionless, watching Townsend.

It was several moments before he broke the heavy silence that now seemed to drown the room.

"We didn't fail," he said, "There's something else. Something you haven't told us."

"I'm afraid its official, Jack." Townsend pushed the three files on his desk towards Jack, "read it for yourself."

Jack didn't move.

"No, there's something else. We didn't fail. I stole my file. I saw the other's files. Georgia here withstood interrogation with the highest commendation and was in the top percentile for unarmed combat and silent killing. Hildy is the best pistol shot in Beaulieu and flattened the legend of Sergeant Evans with a single and canny left hook. We didn't fail. You don't just discard people like us, not after all the training. Not even the army is that stupid. And we got here, the three of us, all the way from Dartmoor with nothing and no help and every uniform and nosy parker in the southern counties out looking for us the whole way. And no one has ever done that. Ever. No, we didn't fail. What aren't you telling us?"

Townsend rose from his seat and wandered over to the window. He looked out at the gathering dusk beginning to swallow the lawns and herbaceous borders of the grounds. In the far distant sky two planes were chasing the last of the sun towards the west. He knew he was just playing for time before, inevitably, revealing his secret. The whole idea of sharing the secret was an anathema to him, it struck at the very essence of his being. It was almost unnatural, as if he was betraying himself. Secrets and keeping them had become his life, they had kept him safe and secure and alive. Releasing one felt like discarding a limb. He returned to stand behind the desk and fixed the three agents with a steady gaze and fleeting smile.

"You are quite right, of course, Jack. You are three of the most able and promising agents we have ever had at Beaulieu. Your achievements and skills have been very impressive. Not least in making it here. No one else has ever made it beyond Yeovil. But the truth is, you are still going to fail Beaulieu. And you have failed Beaulieu because I have officially failed you, or at least had Merchant here arrange your failing. All official papers will show that you didn't make it. That you weren't up to the mark, that you failed some element of selection or character profile and were sent packing."

Townsend wandered to the window again and rested on its sill facing the room. He shook out a cigarette and lit it. He threw the pack onto the desk.

"Help yourself," he said. Jack and Georgia lit up, Hildy didn't.

"You have failed officially, but unofficially you haven't. I'm sure I need hardly remind you of the papers you signed and the oaths and allegiances you have sworn. You are still working for SOE, except, now, you aren't. Not officially. You are now working for me."

Townsend waited for questions. None came. The three agents continued to watch him with steady, calculating calm.

"In the last eleven months Beaulieu has sent nineteen agents into the fields of France and Belgium and twelve have been captured, imprisoned or killed within two days of landing. Three of the other seven we have strong suspicions are relaying under German control. Our agents are being swept up as they land. There is no doubt that they have been betrayed. Sold down the river and into the arms of a waiting and deadly enemy. And they are being betrayed by someone in Beaulieu, or someone closely connected to it."

"So why not just close the place down?" asked Jack.

"Because we have no hard proof. Only conjecture and suspicions. And no brass admits to mistakes. Politicians even less so. Closing down Beaulieu could crack open SOE and MI6 and others would rip the carcasses apart with glee. We need to clean this one up for ourselves."

"Who is we?" asked Georgia.

"My concerns are shared by a couple of other senior T section officers and the Head of Section himself. But as I say, we have no proof. Only missing agents."

"I still don't see why that means we had to fail," Hildy said.

"There is still much important work to do in France and Belgium and I need good agents to get a job done. But in order to get them in there and do the job, they need to avoid going through Beaulieu and the wider SOE network. I need the agents to get to where they need to get and to be invisible. That is why you have failed, because I want you to succeed."

"Doing what?" asked Jack.

"You'll be briefed on your particular mission later. Right now you are off the Beaulieu payroll and files and you are now working for me. We will relocate you all to a secret camp and prepare you for the job ahead."

"Who is we?" asked Hildy. "Are we operating under SOE still?"

"We have to keep the need to know group small. Only the trusted. There is me, Merchant here, Colonel Forster, the Head of T Section and several trusted bods in Whitehall. That includes the occupant of number ten. There will be a couple of others to join the support team later and they will be heavily vetted and checked."

"So we are official?" asked Georgia.

"Yes. Unofficially official."

"What does that mean?"

Townsend dropped his cigarette butt to the floor and crushed it under his heel. He smiled at the three faces before him.

"It means that a certain cigar-chewing person and his office in Downing Street has sanctioned and approved our existence and mission but is unable to acknowledge it publicly or politically. It means that if our mission succeeds no one will know about it but us and if it fails no one will come rushing to help us. We will be on our own. We have official blessing, but no official recognition. Every support will be given to us by way of resources and equipment but we cannot be seen to be receiving it. Invisible to all. Like glass in water. And you are to be our first waterglass soldiers. It will be rather fun, don't you think?"

The agents were silent. Merchant appeared at their side holding a tray of glasses and brandy. He placed a full glass before everyone.

"A little something to warm the blood," he said. "And to seal your passing out of Beaulieu. Congratulations."

Georgia laughed. "We are to be congratulated for being sent like mice into the dangers of the snake pit?"

"Yes," Merchant said, "because you will be the first invisible mice. Let us toast success and invisibility."

The glasses were drained.

"What happens now?" asked Hildy.

"You will go to our secret camp," Townsend said, "Merchant has already prepared your quarters."

"Where is it, or aren't we supposed to know?"

"Oh, I don't think there is any harm in any of you knowing," Townsend said, "after all, most of us have already been there."

"Where?" asked Hildy.

"Why, to your charming farm, of course, Miss Potts."

TWENTY THREE

It was the farm, but it was not her farm. Hildy climbed out the staff car and found herself in familiar surroundings, but a remembrance transformed. The stones of the cobbled courtyard were now clean and washed, emerging terracotta once more from the brown, slurry-trod hue they had of memory. The old barn roof had been repaired and new burgundy red tiles patched where gaping holes and sky once leaked. The inside of the barn had been transformed, the walls lime plastered, the floor swept clean and clear back to cobbles and the straw bales ranked neat and high along the back wall. The Fordson tractor stood clean and almost proud in the doorway, looking so fresh it seemed as if had been repainted. The ploughing tack and leather reins shone bronze on their new hanging hooks and a new hen run had been built on the side of the barn and new hens added to the flock. It was all her farm, except it wasn't. It wasn't even her tractor. So much had changed since she had been away, but maybe it was also her that had changed. She wasn't the same Hildy that had left the farm those short months ago.

Even her father wasn't. He sat high on a seat on the cart on the other side of the yard. His scowl replaced by something resembling sheepish, pleasurable surprise. Walter sat beside him grinning and holding the reins of the cart-horse loosely in his hands. He gave Hildy a waved, casual salute.

"Your father is safe up here. We look after him. It is good he gets some air and looks out for the farm, Yes?"

Her father looked almost guilty in his lofted pleasure, a mute grin softening his face. He had nodded to her, a brief, hesitant bob. A rare and begrudged acknowledgement of her existence.

"Yer back then," he said. He seemed unsure what else to say. "Walter and me just come back from high field. Potatoes looking fine. Get out and about a bit now. On the cart. Doing my bit. Dare say we all are. One way or another."

Rolf appeared at the courtyard drive rise, leading a ploughing horse with Sergeant Harris at his side and Dora sitting high and happy on the horse's back. Dora saw the reception party and was hesitant until she saw Jack. She let out a squeal of delight and slid off and down the side of the horse with practiced ease and came running down the courtyard and into Jack's waiting, enveloping arms. Jip followed her all the way until he saw Hildy, He gave a yelp of recognition and bounded over to her. His wet nose nuzzled her hand and his hot, panted breath on her cheek lifted Hildy's heart, but it still didn't feel like coming home. It was just another training camp on the journey to she knew not where.

The following days and weeks fell easily into a routine of hard work. The near derelict tack room and stable block had been repaired and rebuilt and now served as a small operations room with two dormitories of six bed spaces. It was off-limits to all but the agents and guarded and locked by Merchant. Hildy slept in her old room while the other agents bedded down in the new dormitories. There were communal evening meals and breakfasts cooked by Mrs Maynard and served in the large farm-house parlour and a general curfew on anyone leaving the farm to visit the village or walking beyond the farm boundaries. The new arrangements and operations were to be as discreet and invisible as possible but to all local eyes the work of the farm would continue as usual. Merchant went to the village each morning to collect the post and returned with Harris, Walter and Rolf. Any necessary provisions arrived weekly in an SOE van emblazoned with a 'Townsend's Bakery' livery.

After a couple of days of settling in, the agents had been briefed on their mission by Townsend and Merchant. Gathered around a large map and file-strewn table in the operations room, they had listened as Townsend laid out the tasks before them.

"It's quite simple," Townsend had begun, "it is an

important mission of the very highest rank. A mission that might even win us the war. And you are to have the privilege of delivering it."

He let his words sink and settle while he lit and enjoyed the first couple of kicks of a cigarette.

"The invasion of mainland Europe is coming. No need to tell you that, it's common gossip in every pub and street corner and the parlour game of choice. Where? When? Well, wherever it's going to be, we need to make sure that it gets the best reception and red carpet it can get, and that means cleaning up and preparing the ground and bringing order to our comrades and chaos to our enemies."

Townsend stood up and swung a short cane down onto the map with a crack.

"Mons in the Hainault province of Belgium. If the invasion is going to be a success it is vital we gain control of this region, the area between Mons, Lille and Arras, straddling the French and Belgian borders. Inland from the Pas de Calais. The resistance groups in the area are currently in a shambles. They are either compromised or maverick and we need to clean them up and get them working together. Developing a co-ordinated resistance plan that can begin effective sabotage of bridges, railway lines, power stations and communications and so help ease the path of the invasion and see it on its way to Hitler's bunker in Germany. A task that will take all your skills and courage, but one that cannot fail."

Townsend poured himself a large mug of tea and blew across the top of it.

"But that is not all," he said, "we also have another little task, one that requires discretion and ruthless efficiency. An officially sanctioned task but one that cannot officially be recognised or acknowledged. For the past year, we have had reports, rumoured and now confirmed and verified, of an escape line for downed allied aircrew that is operating between Brussels, Mons and Antwerp. It is an escape line that has been infiltrated and taken over by three Belgians working for the Germans and they are delivering the crew into the arms and prison cells of the SS. Your task is to find these three traitors and kill them. Quietly and without leaving any traces. Simple really. Do you have any questions?"

Hildy sat and let the words drift over and through her. The sounds of cows mooing to the sun in a distant field and the faint chug of the tractor somewhere up on High Field wrapped her thoughts. In the kitchen across the courtyard, she could hear Ma Maynard and Dora singing at the washing-up sink. It had sounded so simple and bold. Find these traitors and kill them. Hildy recognised with some alarm that the idea of being an assassin had never quite penetrated or taken root within her. She had vaguely imagined it might be a necessity but really her role was to be a saboteur and messenger. Blowing up inanimate things while hiding behind walls, or sending radio messages from cobwebbed lofts, not killing people in cold blood. She began to fear she might not be able to do it. She returned her attention to the briefing where Mr Merchant was now speaking.

"You'll be undertaking some dedicated training over the next few days and studying plenty of local maps and files. A Mr Evans will be visiting to do one-to-one Morse with you – so he knows and can recognise your piano style. There'll also be briefings on the local ground situation and known German military centres and troop deployments. You will also be getting your cover stories and identities. They are to be as ingrained and as natural to you as your real selves and lives. Briefings will begin tomorrow. Get some rest for now and try to relax. You have a heavy schedule before you and the more you know and learn, the more chances of success."

"And of survival," Townsend said.

"When do we make the drop?" asked Georgia.

"End of the month, in about three weeks. Trusting to good weather. But we'll probably fly you in, not drop. That's all, get some rest now and enjoy Mrs Maynard's excellent dinners while you can."

Hildy wandered out into the courtyard and made her way to the Spring field. She leaned to the fence and watched Bruno guarding his far patch of field, head held high, shoulders hunched and ready to charge. Georgia came to join her at the fence. Hildy was aware of a faint scent of sweet strawberries close at her side.

"He seems ready for battle," Georgia said.

"Yes, our Bruno is always ready. I just wish I was. It all seems so frightening, don't you think? It is so far from this farm and this life now. It all seems so suddenly and dangerously real. I mean actually going into occupied territory, facing enemies and death in all directions and with just your wits to rely on."

"And the odd pistol or two," Georgia said.

"Have you ever killed anyone, Georgia?"

There was a silence.

"Yes," Georgia lit a cigarette and passed it to Hildy. "Once. It was in self-defence. He was trying to kill me."

"But just to kill. To be an assassin. That is so different and so hard to imagine. I just know I won't be able to do it, to pull the trigger."

Hildy was aware of Georgia's hand on hers at the fence rail. Offering comfort.

"I am sure that you will if the time ever came. I think you have an inner strength and courage that very few possess. It will rise up when you need it and surprise you. And I will be there with you to help you if I can."

"Aren't you scared?"

"Down to my little buffed-booties," she laughed. "It would be madness not to be. But I am more scared of not doing it, or at least not trying. In my experience all men are pretty much bastards and doing away with a few of the nastier Nazi-loving ones is an opportunity not given often to us girls, and is not one to be missed. We even have permission to do it."

Georgia's hand remained cradled over Hildy's and she seemed reluctant to move it. Hildy felt a faint discomfort in its gentle press, as if it signalled something more than just comfort.

"Not all men are bastards," she said. "Jack seems like a really decent sort."

Georgia smiled and lifted her hand to light herself a cigarette. "There are some exceptions," she said smiling, "the ones that prove my rule."

***

Jack had remained seated when Georgia and Hildy had left the briefing.

Townsend raised an eyebrow. "Is there something else, Jack?"

Jack waited until the door had closed and only Townsend and Merchant were left in the room.

"I think I know who your Beaulieu traitor might be," he said.

Townsend and Merchant immediately took seats opposite Jack.

"Well?" asked Merchant.

"Our French count," Jack said, "Boudelain."

The silence in the room was sudden and heavy. Far beyond the room Jack could hear a distant clopping of horse hooves on cobbles and the clacking of squabbling chickens.

"What is the foundation for such an accusation?" asked Townsend.

Jack gathered his thoughts and methodically went through the observations and occurrences that had led to his judgement. He reminded them of Boudelain's injuries before both his proposed missions, injuries that seem to have been conveniently temporary and requiring only healing rest. He told them of his visit to Lord Chester and the friendship between the aristocrats and their families that pre-dated the war. Of the close friendship Boudelain seemed to have with the despatchers and administrators at Beaulieu and of gifts of brandy being exchanged. Of the plane that Boudelain supposedly crash-landed on Lord Chester's driveway that wasn't a crash but a proper,

174

controlled landing and a crumpled, burnt plane wreck that was not a Breguet. But mostly it was the witnessing of a pigeon being launched from a bandaged hand in Lord Chester's old grain barn.

Townsend and Merchant sat still and silent, watching the space before them in rapt concentration. Jack could almost hear their thoughts tumbling.

"But why would it be Boudelain?" asked Merchant. "He's a Frenchman, fighting the allied cause. A patriot. One of us. Why would he betray his country, his people, all his friends? On the side of the Nazis? It just doesn't sit tight. Doesn't fit. Why would he do it?"

Jack shrugged. "War does strange things to people. It makes the sane mad, the normal abnormal and explodes all conventions and moralities and beliefs up in the air and lets them land how and as they will. Boudelain is the head of a noble French family and was an important captain of industry and a man of great wealth before the war, a man from a family of substance and distinction. The elite of society. Powerful and rich and blessed. And the French government stepped in and stole it all away from him. Turned his beloved car factories over to the making of munitions. His chateau became a hospital. And they took the Boudelain wealth and name with it. Boudelain has little prospect of getting any of it back after the war. Unless, of course, the Germans win and a deal has been struck with them. Payment in return for services and loyalty. All conjecture, I admit. But it's a persuasive rationale for betrayal. Money, wealth and power always are in my experience."

Townsend stood and refilled his cup and drank the cool coffee down in one.

"Does Boudelain suspect you suspect him?"

"I don't know. We are trained not to show it even if we do, aren't we? But I was sitting below him in the garden when he launched the pigeon. He is more than likely to have seen me there. Smelt my cigarette."

"Then we must move fast," said Townsend. "It's not

damning proof but it is certainly enough to raise concern. Merchant, lock the count down and out. Discreetly and quick."

Merchant left the room, made a call on the hall phone and moments later the sound of a car speeding fast out of the courtyard sent the chickens clattering again.

"OK, Jack. Back to your duties. Say nothing to the others until we know for sure. Blast the man to hell. If it is him, of course. But he's French, so what can you expect eh?"

Later that evening Jack made his way quietly up the back stairs to Dora's room. She lay asleep in the large bed, her hand resting on Jip's back, curled at her side. Jip stirred as Jack entered the room but didn't move away. Jack sat on the bed and stretched himself out beside Dora. She roused from her sleep, saw her father and cuddled in closer to him.

"You come to tell me a story?"

"No, just a cuddle. Haven't seen you all day."

"I was picking mushrooms with Rolf and Sergeant Evans in the top woods," Dora said sleepily, "Do you know they have the same birthday? But Uncle Harry is older."

"Uncle Harry?"

"Oh, Sergeant Harris likes me to call him that. Says the war should stay off the farm. He's going to visit Rolf's village after the war. It's in the mountains. You ski in the winter and all the cows and goats wear bells. Are you going away again?"

Jack took a moment to answer. He had thought of lying but he knew the truth was the only way to face it. You had to grow up fast in war.

"Yes, sometime. Not just yet. But maybe in a few weeks."

"Are you going to be in the war?"

"Yes. But not in the middle of the fighting."

"But you haven't got a uniform or anything."

"I don't need one. I go to war in ordinary clothes. I'm not fighting. I'm watching and telling those in uniform what's going on."

"That's like a sneak. You're not a sneak."

"No, but I am good at hiding and keeping quiet. I mean you didn't hear me come up, did you?"

"Yes, I did. Jip told me."

"Then he's a sneak too."

Dora giggled. "Will you be gone for a long time?"

"Maybe. You have to be strong and help look after Jip and Ma. She's not getting any younger and needs all the help she can get to make the farm run smoothly."

"Ma doesn't need anyone's help doing that. She even has Mr Potts drying the dishes after supper before he gets his nightcap."

"Maybe I'll take Ma with me then. See if she can sort out the war."

Dora snuggled in closer and yawned.

"That'll be nice. Will we stay on the farm after the war's ended?"

"Hildy told me that you and Ma can stay as long as you like. It will be our home."

"Is Hildy going to the war with you?"

"Yes."

"Will she be hiding with you?"

"Most of the time, yes."

"That's good, you can look after each other. I'll look after Jip until she gets back. I like Hildy. She has kind eyes and she can throw a bale of hay onto the cart from the ground. Walter is a little in love with her, I think. She is pretty. Don't you think?"

Jack lay back and thought about it. It felt good to be cradling a sleepy, warm Dora in the dark attic room smelling of hay and apples and thinking of pleasant things. The war could wait while he enjoyed the sensation of calm and comforting happiness. His thoughts turned to Hildy and her large, bright eyes, her smile and the way she looked in overalls and greased face.

"Yes, she is pretty," he said at last, but Dora was fast asleep on his chest and breathing in the deep and clean farm airs. Jack soon joined her.

Merchant did not return for three days. They were all

picnicking in the High Meadow and saw him climbing the hill to them on a stiff leg. Ma and Dora were down at the stream with Rolf and Jip. Walter was taking Mr Potts on a cart ride through the top fields, looking for broken fences.

Townsend rose to meet Merchant halfway up the hill. They were some time in whispered conversation before rejoining Georgia, Jack and Hildy at the picnic blanket.

"It would appear that your suspicions were well founded, Jack," Townsend said. "Our bird seems to have flown."

Georgia and Hildy shared a glance of confusion. Merchant was quick to put them in the picture about Jack's suspicions.

"I returned to Beaulieu to find Boudelain gone," he said. "No one has seen him for four days. He was there for the evening meal then retired early to bed. No one has seen him since. Although Lady Dorothea let slip he visited them early morning three days back, Lord Chester insisting she had imagined it. But she said she remembered hearing the plane and Boudelain was wearing his flying jacket."

"What plane?" asked Jack. "Where did he get a plane?"

Merchant snorted a half-laugh. "As near as we can make it the plane was the same one he arrived in. They kept it hidden and locked in a grain barn on the estate. So said the butler, after a little persuasion. The crumpled plane wreckage you saw was just scrappage taken from the old airfield at Whiteley. So Boudelain just flew off, back to his masters in France."

"He is a traitor?" Hildy said. "The count? But why? What did he do?"

Merchant picked an apple from the blanket and sliced a piece off with a penknife.

"He sent messages to the Nazis by way of carrier pigeons," he said. He bit into the apple and crunched it hard. "Kept them in the loft on Lord Chester's estate. What those messages were, we do not know. But he was friendly with a couple of corporals in despatch and communications and was probably letting his masters know of agent drops and missions. It's the reason so many have failed to come back

178

or make contact. The Nazis were ready and waiting for them. Just swept them up like litter."

A silence hung heavy in the air for some time.

"He betrayed all those agents," Georgia said. "Peters and Metcalfe. And Stuvenson. How could he? He's their ally. His friends. Fighting on the same side."

"Seems Boudelain is fighting his own separate war that has nothing to do with allies and loyalties," Merchant said. "We believe, thanks to Jack's observations, that he was working a deal with the Nazis to get his family lands and factory restored to him. Money and arrogance, the curses of the aristos. Especially French ones. He would prefer to betray his friends and his country rather than his class. Lord Chester is just as bad, but at least we have him. He is with the intelligence boys now, being grilled as his majesty's guest. An ignoble appointment with the hangman's rope or traitor's wall awaits him."

"And Lady Dorothea?"

Merchant shrugged. "All that awaits her is loneliness. Not that she'll notice much difference. She can't be held responsible for Chester, she hardly knows what day it is. Or even that there's a war on. She'll lose the castle, of course. Probably have to move into some local home for retired old ladies."

They sat in silent contemplation, watching Ma and Dora down at the stream fishing for frogs with a small net on a stick. Jip barked excitedly among them.

"So, what does this mean for us?" asked Georgia. "Is it over? Boudelain will know us, have our names and faces broadcast. We won't be invisible anymore."

"Not necessarily," Townsend said. "Don't forget, Boudelain thinks you all failed Beaulieu and across the channel is a big place. He won't be thinking of you, just about keeping himself alive in his viper's nest of new friends. Chances of you running across him are remote. He's probably got himself a safe bolt-hole somewhere with all the comforts and is just waiting it out until the end of the war. So, no reason why he should stop your mission. It's still on."

"And if we do come across Boudelain on our travels?" asked Jack.

Townsend took a cigarette and cupped a hand to light it. He leaned back into the high grasses of the bank and blew a slow jet of smoke into the blue skies.

"Then kill him," he said, "with painful and expert dispatch and with the thanks of us all."

TWENTY FOUR

Townsend had never really been sure of the best way to tell an agent that their dangerous and life-threatening mission was now an immediate reality. In the end the message had to be imparted, the plan confirmed, the times and date set and there really was no point in trying to wrap it all up in wool and blather. Much better to just come out with it and leave the agent to their own thoughts and fears. There was little Townsend could do for them once they were in the air except fear for their safety and the sooner they came to face their fate, the better for all. He was dealing with trained agents and it was not as if the news would be a surprise.

***

Georgia was leaning against the fence rails of the top field watching Dora sitting astride the plough horse and riding in a wide trotted circle while Rolf held the training rope and encouraged her in soft mantras. "Steiff zuruch, hoey kopf, sanfte hande!"

Georgia saw Townsend approaching and could tell from the strain of his casual manner and the file under his arm that something was about to change in her world. She had expected it, but its imminence did force her heart to still on its beat. As Townsend offered her a cigarette and lit it, Georgia took time to gather her calm.

"The mission is on," Townsend said, "you will be leaving on Thursday night. Jack and Miss Potts will follow two nights later."

The news that they were not going together as a team came as something of a surprise, a shock even. The realisation that she would be landing and operating in hostile, enemy territory alone washed over her like a cold wave.

"You'll be flying in. We have marked a field drop a few kilometres south-east of Mons. No French reception committee, can't trust the resistance in the area. But you are to make your way to Mons and contact a Monique Briard, a librarian. Address in the file."

Townsend handed her the large wallet file. The name Felis was written on the cover.

"You'll operate in the field under the name Felis and your call sign is Grace. Full details of your call and security codes are in the file. Also your cover story and papers. You are Agnes Lundorf an administration secretary from Strasbourg visiting Mons to sort your mother's papers. Your mother has just died in Ambrose Pare hospital from pneumonia. Details in the file. Study the file so you know Agnes back to front. Merchant will give you your papers the afternoon of your departure. You go in light. Simple travelling bag with clothes, Welrod, knife and pigeons."

"Pigeons?"

"Two of them. You'll be going in without radio, you need to be travelling light. Radio will come with Hildy and Jack. The pigeons are to let us know you've arrived and are in the safe house with Monique. Two birds have a better chance of reaching us than one. Pack of corn supplied."

"And Agnes Lundorf?"

"Oh, your cover story is solid. Real. Agnes is an administrative secretary in the Home Affairs department at Strasbourg Municipal Offices. Her mother has just died. So has the unfortunate Agnes. Killed in a car crash four days ago on her way to visit her mother in hospital. Car went into a ravine. Local resistance found her and passed on her papers. You are now her. Visit the hospital. You'll be too late, of course. Mother dead and buried weeks before but there is always confusion and communications breakdowns in war. We can use it to advantage to establish you and your story."

They watched Dora and Rolf circle the far meadow is silence. Dora bounced stiff but happy on the trotting horse. Rolf offering his soft mantras of instruction and clicking the horse in encouragement. Georgia could think of nothing because she was thinking of everything. The sudden realisation that her life was about to take a major and frightening turn. Of coming out of a dark sky and landing in a hostile and violent world. Of becoming Agnes, becoming a stranger to herself.

"Frightening, isn't it?" Townsend said.

"Daunting, perhaps," Georgia said. "It seems all so sudden now, doesn't it?"

"It's probably the best way. Just remember your mission objectives and all your training. You are one of the best I've ever had and I have every confidence that you can do it, and do it well. Believe in yourself and all that you have learned at Beaulieu. Make contact with Monique and establish your base. Play the grieving daughter. Trust no one and take no unnecessary chances. Jack and Miss Potts should make contact with you within three days. They will be flying in by Lysander and meeting our only known safe resistance group in the area, led by a Henri Clerque. The times and landing field is in your file. It would be good to meet them there if you can. Otherwise they will find you. Once you team up, your objectives are clear. Destroy the false escape line, kill the leaders and try to get the true resistance groups in the area working together to sabotage the railways, utilities and communications networks before the invasion. Then we'll bring you back home."

"How?"

"Plane, boat or smuggle you into Switzerland. We'll find a way. Now over the next three days study your file and prepare yourself. Merchant will have a new French wardrobe for you and will help you with all the paperwork. Letters to kin, will & testament and so on. Get as much sleep as you can. And learn your cover, Merchant will be testing you on it come Wednesday."

Georgia took the file. It felt heavy and solid in her hand. Down in the meadow Dora was feeding the horse from a corn bag and the surrounding fields rippled in clover, potatoes and barley. Jip chased a Rolf-thrown stick and swifts swooped and darted like spitfires over the distant canopy of elms and oaks. Georgia took a moment to take it all in, to relish it, to breathe its free and summered airs. Then Agent Felis headed to her rooms. She had studying to do.

Merchant cycled behind the jogging Jack and Hildy, encouraging them on. The morning sun was dappling through the top woods and the lane was fringed by tall cow parsley and brambles. Ahead of him, Jack and Miss Potts jogged hard up the stony path incline, breathing hard and their T-shirts dark with sweat.

"Fast sprint to the top of the rise," said Merchant. He tried to pedal harder to keep up with them, but they outran him.

Jack and Hildy lay on their backs on a grass knoll in a patch of sunlight, panting hard. Small whipped-cream clouds drifted lazily across clear blue skies and soft-darting bugs and flies flitted the grasses.

"Are you scared, Jack?" asked Hildy. "You know, about all of this. What's to come."

Jack raised himself on an elbow and gazed at Hildy. The down on her arms and the rose blush of her cheeks made her look impossibly young and innocent.

"Of course I am," Jack said, "only a fool wouldn't be. But we have been well trained. We know what we are going into."

"Yes, I know. And it's good to know I'll be there with you. And Georgia, of course. We are a good team I think. We go well together. We can look out for each other. That sort of makes it less daunting and frightening, don't you think?"

Jack decided that Hildy really did have the most beautiful eyes. Chestnut brown and alive with light.

"Yes, you are right," he said, "together is better than alone. And I couldn't ask for better companions than you and Georgia. Perhaps we will give courage to each other and share the fear. That way we'll get through this and come out the other side."

"Oh, I do hope so," Hildy said, "it suddenly seems very important not to die just yet. Like there is something over on the other side of this. Something precious and exhilarating."

"Like being born anew?" asked Jack.

"Exactly," Hildy said. "No more old Hildy, no more farm drudgery, no more limiting horizons and opportunities. A new life of everything and everywhere and a sloughing off of the old Hildy like a snake skin. It will all be worth it for that. Don't you think?"

"Absolutely," Jack said.

Lying beside Hildy, he realised that he had not thought so much about Beth in recent weeks. She was still very much in his thoughts but she had made fewer appearances of late. Maybe he too was beginning to slough of his old skin. Perhaps the mission in Belgium would help moult the remains of his grief and allow him to begin life anew on the other side. If there was to be another side. Like Hildy, he was beginning to realise that he very much wanted there to be, and not just because of Dora and Ma.

Merchant finally made it to the top of the rise. He dismounted and sat down beside them and tried to rub some blood back into his wounded leg. He pulled three bottles of beer from the bike's basket together with two, large envelope files. He uncapped the bottles on a nearby tree root and passed them out.

"You both go out on Sunday night," he said.

Jack and Hildy immediately sat up.

"You drop by plane into the Belgian French border region south east of Mons. Miss Melrose will already be there, she's going in on Thursday."

"Not all going together?" asked Hildy. Her breathing was still slightly panted and the rosy glow of hard exercise and a cool air still flushed her cheeks.

"Can't fit all three with kit in a Lysander," Merchant said. "So we're splitting you going in. Miss Melrose will be at the landing ground to greet you come Sunday. Here are your briefing files. We'll take a stroll back to the farm and you will spend the next few days learning these files back to front and sideways. It's all in there. Your code names and call signs. Contacts and targets. Maps and papers. Also your

185

cover story and new identity. Learn and digest and know. Your life will depend upon it."

"Sunday?" Jack said. He took a long draught of his beer. "Less than a week away."

"I know it's short notice but needs must. The cover stories happen to fall neatly right now and we can't afford to delay. Jack, your call sign will be Satur. Miss Potts, yours is Lupus. Jack, you are Albert Girond an agricultural mechanic for Fiat. Miss Potts, you are his assistant, Giselle Bernard. You are visiting farms in the Lille and Mons regions on behalf of Fiat Trattori. It's all in the files. Learn it."

"Giselle!" Hildy said. "A lifetime of Hildebrand and now I'm to be a Giselle. Couldn't I be a simple Mavis or Edna for once?" She laughed.

Jack took his file. The name Satur was printed on its front cover in bold, stark type. The file weighed heavy in his hand with the realisation, a pressing portent, that his life was no longer his own and that his new one had suddenly become alarmingly serious, and more dangerously fragile. The life he had known and enjoyed with Dora and Ma would be gone, left behind at the farm, a precious memory only. A squirrel dashed across his view among the trees. A mock of crows cawed in nearby treetops. Jack tucked the file under his arm and began walking back to the farm. He had five days to become his new self and only four nights of cuddle and stories with Dora.

PART THREE

TWENTY FIVE

Georgia perched on the edge of the bench seat and braced herself against the pull of the plane as it the banked and swerved through the dark skies. They were somewhere over Flanders. The silver ribbon of the channel had been glimpsed through breaks in the cloud and now they were inland and heading for a small field in a vast ocean of fields and woods and villages and towns. Searchlights scanned the skies like hunting torches in a mine and the drone of the plane's engine throbbed through her feet and back. Georgia knew that outside in the air the noise of the plane would be no more than a bellicose bee, but inside it sounded as loud as alarm sirens.

Another agent sat opposite Georgia. He was tall, moustached and huddled in a trench coat against the draughts that swept the small cabin. He had only spoken once, to say hello, and was now asleep. Georgia envied him his poise and wondered who he was and where he was going. The only other occupant was the pilot who sat almost touching Georgia. He was nameless but an Australian or Anzac by his accent and he kept up a low conversation with the plane as if it was a moody, reluctant horse.

"Get up there, my matey. Nice and smooth. That's the fella. Now where's that canal. Is that her? Reckon it is. Let's follow her to Beauville. Don't kick now, matey. Keep it easy and watch for them treetops. Don't want leaves up your skirts now do we?"

Georgia felt hollow and chilled. She hadn't eaten before the flight for fear of being air sick. The realisation that she was soon to be entirely alone and in an alien, hostile world that wanted nothing more than to find her and kill her, and to do it painfully, was weighing like molten lead in her gut. What on earth was she doing here? What had she been thinking to agree to this?

"Reckon about five minutes, miss. You all set? I ain't hanging around so get ready."

Outside, Georgia saw the ghostly shapes of hedges and woods in the night's dim light. A small village and larger town loomed on the more distant horizon. They were flying low and quiet, almost gliding over the treetops. Georgia leaned back, closed her eyes and took a deep breath. She was Georgia no more. She was Agnes Lundorf. Agent Felis. Georgia must die so that Agnes can hope to live and survive in this new and hostile world she was about to land in. She had to become and to be, Agnes.

Agnes felt the plane sink lower in its glide. Her guts sank with it.

"We're coming in. Be ready, miss."

Opposite her the other agent was now awake. He offered the faintest of smiles.

"Be lucky," he said.

The plane wheels hit the field with a jolt that shook the plane and then quickly settled to a gentle, bouncing, taxiing glide. The plane stopped momentarily, the other agent opened the door, there was a call of "good luck", a hefting of bags and Agnes was standing in a dark, starlit night in ankle deep grass with her case and bag at her side. She watched the Lysander taxiing a wide turn in the field, gathering speed and then lifting off over distant shades of trees and being swallowed by the night.

Agnes Lundorf was all alone.

Her first act was to squat down and listen. She listened for over ten minutes before she was sure there was nothing untoward to hear. Agnes picked up her case and bag and made her way to the hedgerow. Across several fields to the north-east she could see the rooftops of the village of Sars-le-Bryere and to the north the spire of Eglise Saint Jean Baptiste. Making her way around the fringes of two fields she headed for the Mons road and hid in the tree-lined hedge that ran beside it. She could not move at night with a case for fear of running into a German patrol. She would wait for first light and trust to luck. She took a peck of grain from the pouch in her pocket and fed it to the pigeons cooped tight in their special box in an inner coat pocket. Their soft coos and the pecking of their beaks on her palm were strangely calming. Leaning back to settle against a tree she watched for the first signs of light and listened while the hostile night rustled and creaked about her.

Luck came with the dawn. She hailed an old farmer driving his small truck of pigs to the Mons abattoir. The old farmer was pleased to play the good knight and kept up a happy chatter of nothings on the short drive into Mons.

Agnes sat in the cramped front seat with her case and bag clutched to her lap. They passed the outskirts of a grey-stoned city that was beginning to wake to the new day. Along the Rue de Tieur she saw her first German patrol. A circle of uniforms surrounding two men whose bags were being searched. The officer of the group kicked one of the men to the ground where he lay with his hands clawing the air, beseeching and crying out his innocence, and then the scene was gone, swallowed up by the moving tableau of city streets and passing buildings. The soldiers had looked so smart, so angry and so young.

"Fucking boche bastards," the farmer said. "Their time will come." He spat a brown flume of phlegm out of his window.

He dropped Agnes off outside the abattoir and she made her way towards the Central Square. The streets were beginning to fill with the commute to offices and shops in the central part of the city. The weather was cool but dry and shops and stalls were putting out awnings in anticipation of sun later. The early morning crowds bustled with heads down purpose and seemed to flow around the occasional kerbside knots of German soldiers like river water around rocks. Heavy trucks of soldiers, or staff cars with swastika pennants flying, prowled the city roads.

Agnes kept her head down and her feet walking. Despite the cool of the airs she found herself hot with sweat that she knew to be as much driven by fear as by exertion. She stepped into a tabac and bought some cigarettes and directions to Rue de le Clef.

Number twenty-seven was a narrow-fronted terrace

house of three floors that sat back at the end of an alley leading off the main street. It was a little before seven o'clock. Agnes rapped the knocker as softly as she thought discreet. The door opened almost immediately.

A tall woman in a cornflower patterned cotton bathrobe wrap stood leaning at the half-opened door. Her hair was wrapped in a turban towel and a long cigarette stood smoking among long, fine fingers tipped in red paint. She looked Agnes up and down with a languid eye, took a pull on her cigarette and waited.

"Uncle Henri asked me to call," Agnes said. She tried to remember the rest of the recognition signal. "To bring you news of Mother. I'm Agnes."

"Just Agnes?"

"Little Agnes. With the yellow dress."

The door opened fully and the woman bent down, picked up the case and pulled it into the house.

"Come, you must be hungry," she said.

Coffee had never tasted quite so good. Agnes cradled her third mug and stubbed the second cigarette and felt safe and warm for the first time since leaving the farm. Monique cooked eggs and mushrooms and managed to finish her morning wash and to dress in between briefing talks and inquisitions.

"I have to be at the library in an hour," Monique said. "You get some sleep and meet me for lunch. Midday, at Café D'Accord on the rue de la Coupe. It is a quiet place. We have to change your hair. London has no idea. They think it is still 1920. And the skirt needs to be plainer. Pick something from my wardrobe. No radio?"

"No."

"Good. Germans are monitoring the city and radio transmitting is suicide. I am too alive to die stupidly. How do you contact London?"

"I have two pigeons to let them know I've arrived. I'll send one out now and another tonight."

"But pigeons can't fly in the dark."

"Trained ones can. It's safer than daylight flying over a

hungry land full of guns. But other arrangements have also been made. I will have contact with London in two days."

"I will let Henri know. He has a list of needs. I am trying to get you a position at the library. But there may be other posts. The war is good for secretary posts. Everyone is in need of filers. You can type? Good. Now you have to visit the hospital. For your mother. You need to keep to the story. We will talk about this at lunch. Now get some sleep. Let your pigeon go from the roof. Send Matthew kisses from me."

Georgia scribbled her note of arrival and kisses from Monique and took care to roll and clip the message to the pigeon's leg. She leant against the tall brick chimney and gazed out over the rooftops of Mons. The morning sky was a sepia haze and the horizon still sparked with the lights of camps and villages, like fireflies in a dark forest. Georgia cradled the pigeon in her cupped hands and kissed it on its head.

"Don't let us down, little one. Make it home and with speed." She raised her hands and released the bird to air. The pigeon's wings cracked like gunfire momentarily before lifting away and quiet over the rooftops of Mons. It circled the city as if trying to pick up a scent and then headed into the north-western skies towards home.

Georgia hadn't realised how tired she was. She woke on a strange sofa in a room she didn't recognise and a light was too bright and worn for dawn. It came back to her in a rush. This was Monique's flat and she was in occupied France and she was completely alone. Only she had the feeling that she wasn't alone. That soft feather had stroked her neck again.

As she sat up on the sofa a hand clasped her mouth hard and she saw the glint of a long knife swing up and come to a chill rest at her throat.

"Do not move, pretty one, or you are not pretty no more." The voice was deep and gravelled in her ear. A stubbled face pressed hard at her cheek and Georgia could smell onions, tobacco, dung and absinthe. The hand at her mouth pressed harder.

"You understand?" Georgia nodded.

"Who are you? What you do here?"

"I'm Agnes. Friend of Monique. I am staying here. I have no money."

"Where is Monique?"

"She has gone to work. The library."

"Where are you from, Agnes?"

"I come from Strasbourg. My mother died here, I have come to settle her affairs."

"Now, Agnes, you are lying to me. That is not a good way to start, is it? I think you are a British agent and that you have come to Mons to cause trouble. I expect if I look, I can find a pigeon around here. Maybe we can have it for dinner. Pigeon is very tasty. Especially British messenger pigeons with their fine, strong, meaty breasts. Shall we look, Agnes?"

A deep guttural laugh exploded in her ear and the hand released from her mouth. Georgia stepped out into the middle of the room and turned to face her assailant.

A short, solid, round man of about fifty stood grinning back at her. He wore a greasy flat cap, leather jerkin and farmer's boots and trousers tied with a large, wide buckle belt. A thick stubble darkened his face but bright brown eyes shone through. He wiped his hunting knife on his jerkin and slid it into a pouch in the jerkin's depths.

"You should get Monique to fix her windows. And you sleep too deep. It will get you killed."

"Are you Henri?" The man bowed stiffly from the shoulders.

"Captain of the Mons militia. At your service." He stepped out with a smile. As he approached, Georgia swung her booted foot up hard and fast into Henri's crotch and had the satisfaction of feeling a solid connection. Henri grunted hard and doubled up before falling slowly to his knees. He hit the floorboards with a thud. He crouched, panting against the pain.

"Now that we have introduced ourselves, Henri, we can be friends," Georgia said. "Shall I make us some coffee?"

TWENTY SIX

Hildy stood in a field of ankle high wet grass and watched a plane bank over distant tree silhouettes and disappear into the black of night sky. A shiver of fear flooded over her as she realised that she had no idea where she was or why she should be in the field, nor had any memory of the last hour, maybe even longer. She remembered getting into the plane and crouching on the edge of a hard ledge seat and the feel of the heavy suitcase on her lap. And now she was in a field and had no idea how she had got there. A whispered voice at her shoulder sluiced the fog away as instantly as it had overcome her.

"You OK, Giselle?"

At first she thought that someone else must be with them and her heart fluttered. She turned and saw Jack crouched on the ground checking his bag and pack and realised that she was Giselle. The deadly game had really started. Giselle felt the ice cool her blood and cleanse her head of other thoughts. There was now only survival and the grit to see it through to the end, whatever end that might be. She crouched down beside Jack, checking her case and bag.

"Yes, fine, thanks Albert."

They waited and watched, trying to adjust their eyes to the night. A light flickered in a far hedge. And again.

"That's for us," Jack said. "Let's go."

As they approached the hedge a torch shone bright at them and then was quickly switched off. The flash blinded for a moment and when Giselle found shape and image again she was staring into the face of a smiling Georgia.

"Beginning to think you were planted in that field!" she said.

The three of them embraced in the dark, the release of tension was palpable.

"We have no time for this," said a voice from the hedge, "the German patrols are everywhere. We must go!"

"Allow me to introduce Henri," Georgia said, "and his

men Eric and Fabrice."

The three men emerged from the hide of the hedge. Wary nods of welcome were shared.

"You have better respect for Henri than this Agnes here," Henri said. "She don't treat men well. Kicks the hand of friendship. Come. We go now."

Henri led the way across fields, the three agents following and Eric and Fabrice flanking the rear. A faint rim of dawn light was beginning to chalk the horizons. A tractor with a horse trailer filled with several sheep waited ready in a lane. A compartment at the back of the trailer was opened and the agents ushered in. The space was cramped, dark and smelt of dung and diesel.

"Stay quiet," Henri said. "We ride an hour, maybe half."

They chugged and bounced along in the dark, gears grinding and sheep bleating. Agnes whispered the news of her meeting with Monique and Henri and of her pigeon despatch. It had been agreed with Henri that Albert and Giselle would stay at Henri's farm for the next few days and then seek other options. Agnes would return to Mons as she had an interview for a library assistant job. She would stay with Monique. Albert and Giselle would sleep the day out and be ready for a meeting with other resistance leaders at the farm in the evening, organised by Henri.

"He's not very hopeful," Georgia said, "he says no one trusts anyone and German collaborators are everywhere. He doesn't even trust me."

"Hardly surprising if you kicked him in the balls on introduction," Jack said.

"He deserved it. And he knows it. At least he knows we can fight dirty if we must."

The journey ended with a sudden squeal of brakes and the bleats of alarmed sheep. Eric and Fabrice stood guard at the door to the trailer compartment while Henri ushered the agents across a short yard and into the kitchen of a large farmhouse. An elderly woman in dirty black skirts and tight bunned grey hair stood beside a huge planked table, clutching a loaf of bread and a breadknife, sawing slices onto a wooden bread board. Henri introduced her perfunctorily as his wife, Mathilde. She was even rounder than Henri and she eyed her new guests with unconcealed distrust. A young boy of perhaps twelve years stood by the cauldron pot that hung over a well set and roaring fire. His eyes were wide with excitement at the sight of the new arrivals.

"And I am Gregor," he said grinning, "the garbure is ready. It is rabbit as we have no ham."

"Quiet, Gregor," Henri said. "Go see to the chickens."

Eric and Fabrice came into the kitchen as Gregor left. They sat at the long table and began pouring wine into clay goblets from a wicker-cased flagon the size of small oil drum.

"Sit, eat," Henri said. "We talk, then you sleep. We meet with other groups tonight."

Jack was suddenly aware of how hungry he was. The stew was thick with vegetables, herbs and rabbit and tasted like heaven. The others gorged with him. The wine flowed and the bread soaked up the sauces and the world didn't quite seem so perilous any more.

"You will bring us guns?" asked Henri. "We must have guns. And explosives."

Jack leaned back in his chair and studied his hosts.

"It might be arranged," he said, "if London can be sure they will be used effectively. And by the right people. The region around here is very volatile. Very little order. Lots of bandits. It becomes a matter of trust."

Henri watched Jack for some time. He drew a long hunting knife out of his belt, reached for an apple and began to slice it in his cupped hand.

"You are my guest, Albert, and you are from a country that has never been occupied," he said, "so I forgive you your insult. You do not know what it is to have your life crushed under an invader's boot. An invader who could march in here right now and put us all against my barn wall and shoot us, just because they want to, or because they can, but because they like it and because there is no law or justice

197

anymore to stop them doing otherwise. They take, they kill, they rape, they destroy. They think no more of killing us than they would a fly. Women, children, the old, it does not matter. All are vermin to the Boche. You have to live lightly in times of such lack of care or any chance of justice and retribution. This matter of trust has to be earned, and not by us, but by you."

"London will help, Henri, but it needs assurances. The news of resistance in this area is not one that encourages confidence. It cannot waste its precious guns and explosives on barren land."

Henri leaned forward in his chair and plunged his knife into the planks and left it quivering.

"Trust!" he said. He gestured to the others in the room. "I trust those in this room with my life. I do so every day. As do they in return. Even little Gregor. We do not rest until every Boche is killed or sent back to their midden fatherland and crushed like autumn grapes. Until they starve and lie quivering in the ditches like we do."

"You cannot do this alone, Henri. As just one group. It needs many groups working together to run the Germans out. Can you trust them? Can London?"

Henri shrugged. "Maybe. We know this. There are many groups fighting the Boche hereabouts. Some are led by good men, some not so good. Some by bastards. Collaborators like bad apples are everywhere. The Germans even plant their spies. There can never be trust, only hope of trust."

Georgia lit a cigarette and passed the pack around. Fabrice and Eric took one each and shared more wine.

"London knows of the work you do here, Henri," she said, "It is very impressed. We trust you and your group. That is why we are here. Why we came to you. But you must see that we will need to work with more groups like yours if we are help kick the Germans out. We trust you, but we need more like you."

Henri began tamping and lighting a small pipe. The sweet smelling smoke hung over the table. He smiled at Georgia.

"The beautiful English lady, Agnes, who kicks you in the balls for a greeting, talks of trust!" he laughed. "Ah, the English really are a foreign people."

Georgia reached forward and plucked the knife from the planks. She handed it handle first to Henri.

"You did have this knife to my throat, Henri. Perhaps you should be using it against your enemies rather than your friends. We are here to help. But we must work together, and with other groups you trust. Are there such groups?"

"Maybe three," Henri said. "Perhaps four."

"No more?" asked Jack.

"It is perhaps one hundred patriots. A small army. And they fight well. Bravely. To the death. It will be enough. And more will come when we begin winning."

"And can these groups be trusted?"

Henri looked across at Fabrice and Eric. Fabrice was a tall, prematurely balding man with rimless spectacles and a Ronald Colman moustache. Eric was older, smaller and greyer with silver stubble dusting his jowls like dirty snow.

"Maybe," Fabrice said, "we have put the vermin traps out."

Fabrice explained that they too recognised that the only way they could defeat the Germans and drive them from Belgium was for all the local resistance groups to work together, but like London, they had reservations about some of the groups in the region. The Valenciennes and Namur groups had been infiltrated or betrayed and both groups had been destroyed. Many true patriots had lost their lives and many arrested by the Nazis and shot.

"A dark day for us all," Henri said. "We lost many good friends. But we must carry on. We have to win in the end. But who to trust, eh?"

"So we set a trap, or a number of traps," Fabrice said.

The idea had been simple. They had contacted four groups in the region still operating and told each of them of a top-secret, high-level meeting of all the resistance leaders in the region to discuss a joint attack on a key strategic target of German command.

"But to each leader we gave a different place, date and time," Henri said grinning.

"And we hid and staked out each site," Fabrice said. "To see if the Germans turned up."

"And did they?" asked Jack.

"Only at Tournai," Eric said. "They came in their trucks and waited in the lanes surrounding the barn."

"No others?" asked Hildy.

"No," Henri said, "only at Tournai. The other three groups will meet with us tonight. We go to a place in Binche. The groups from Charleoi, Maubeurge and Wavre will join us there. There we will talk. Make plans. Start killing Germans."

"And what of Tournai?" asked Georgia.

Henri smiled without warmth.

"Christof now knows the trap was sprung. I know Christof and I do not think he is the traitor. But someone in his group can't be trusted. So they are in exile and contempt. Out of contact with the rest of us. It is up to Christof to deal with his Judases."

"And when they discover him?"

"Or her," Fabrice said, "then they will die. A fall in the marble quarries. Shot in the forest. Hung by piano wire. It doesn't matter. The cancer needs to be plucked out and quickly."

"Now you get some rest," Henri said. "It is a long night and drive ahead. Agnes stays with Monique, yes? Good. Your bicycle is in the barn. Mathilde has put some cheese in the basket. A present for Monique. Then you two stay here on the farm. You stay inside and you don't go out. You trust no one but those in this room."

"And Gregor," Mathilde said.

"Of course, Gregor," Henri said. "He is a clever boy. The trap was his idea. He will find a place for your radio. It will be a clever place. Now we have work on the farm. The hide, Mathilde."

Henri, Fabrice and Eric cleared the table and beckoned the three guests to rise from their chairs. Mathilde went to the open range, put on a padded mitten glove, removed the pot from its chain over the fire and pulled the chain. The table rose up on one end from the floor on a hinge to reveal a large, lime walled chamber beneath. A flagon and a wrapped cloth sat on a wooden stool in the corner.

"If the Germans should come, or unwelcome visitors, you hide down here. Air is fine through the floorboards. It is locked from above, a simple bolt but strong. At the moment, you can only be released by someone in the room, but Gregor is working on a release catch to be operated from inside the hole. Maybe soon, eh?"

"Very ingenious," Jack said. His admiration was genuine.

"My Gregor is very clever," Mathilde said. She leaned on the table and pushed it back to the floor without much effort. A bolt at the base of one of the table legs was locked with a kick. "He do all the sums and weight and pulleys in his head. And it is a so small head!"

Hildy didn't think that Gregor's head was that small. She was able to assess it while she walked the farms grounds with him in the afternoon.

Hildy slept for only a couple of hours. Her excitement and fears woke her and wouldn't allow her to return to sleep, so she had left Jack gently snoring in his afternoon cot and set out to explore her new surroundings. As she emerged from the room, she was greeted by Gregor who was reading a book in a window seat and seemed to have been appointed her guard.

"All alone?" asked Hildy.

"Yes, the others are working in the fields. Fabrice is in Mons buying engine grease. My mother is visiting with Madame Veron. She has bad feet. So I am to look after you."

"That's nice of you."

"But I will not be very good because I have not looked after ladies before. Especially English ladies. Have you seen Churchill?"

"No, we are not in the same circle."

"What is your name?"

"Giselle," Hildy was surprised how easy the name came to her lips, without thought or hesitation. Almost naturally. Perhaps the gentle interrogation by Gregor was helping to grow Giselle.

"I expect that is not your real name because you have to be secret. But it is a nice name. Are you to radio London?"

"Yes, as soon as I can."

"I think you need to be secret, yes?"

"Yes."

"And you will have a long aerial. Is that right?"

"A wire perhaps. To carry the signals."

"A long wire?"

"A long wire is best."

"And is the radio big?"

"About the size of a small suitcase. It's in the brown case I brought with me."

"Are you scared of spiders, Giselle?"

Hildy laughed. "No, spiders don't scare me."

"Only some girls don't like spiders. Especially the pretty ones. I have been thinking and looking and I think I have a place for your radio. Very secret. Come."

Hildy followed Gregor across the farm courtyard and into the woods behind the barn. They climbed down a bank of grasses and cowslip and along a narrow track through woods that led to a small clearing of abandoned and decrepit old buildings. Crumbling half-walls of lichen covered stones and collapsed gable ends in a sea of brambles, nettles and ferns. A round tower building, that looked like it might once have been a mill, rose up to three floors and still had some semblance of shape and construction, but the roof had gone and there were gaps in the stonework walls where the forest trees and brambles had sought to regain their lost territory. In the middle of the tower a massive tree had grown tall and sturdy and its branches and canopy rose up and weaved into the forest trees that surrounded the glade. The tree looked like it was wearing an old and oversized stone skirt.

Gregor beckoned Hildy to follow him into the old door archway of the tower. The space was dark, quiet and eerie and curtained in cobwebs. It smelt of mildew and decay. Hildy couldn't help but shudder a little. There was something quite creepy and uncomfortable about the place. She had a strong wish to be back out in the air and light again.

"It is not nice place is it, Giselle?" Gregor said.

"No, not really."

"Good. German soldiers will think so too. Then it is a good place to hide from the Germans, yes?"

Hildy had her doubts. As far as she could tell this was a just an open tower of crumbling stones with a huge tree occupying most of its interior space.

"You can climb?" asked Gregor.

"Yes, but not this tree. There are no branches and the stone tower looks unsafe."

Gregor grinned. He stood by the tree and pulled on a rope that Hildy had not seen. A rope ladder unfurled and dropped down from the canopy above.

"It is not a long climb," Gregor said. He took the ladder in his hands and sped up it and was quickly lost among the leaves above. Hildy followed more sedately, but with little trouble. She emerged onto a section of newly planked floor that was originally the mill's upper third floor. A small wooden table and stool stood in the corner. Gregor pulled up the ladder and wound it back to its simple release pulley.

Looking back down to the ground, all Hildy could see was tree and branches and leaves. It would the same for anyone looking up. Looking out though the gaps in the stone walls she could see most of the woods, indeed almost its full compass. If Germans did come looking she would have plenty of warning.

"The aerial can be lost in the branches and can go high for good signal. And look," Gregor pointed to a large branch that went out though the back of the tower and reached as far as the surrounding trees. "There is an escape to the woods. It is good, yes?"

Hildy considered the hide. She was rather impressed. It was certainly discreet. And Gregor was right, it was eerie enough for any Germans to be less than thorough or enthusiastic if searching. The radio could be stored and hidden here and could only ever be found if its hide was betrayed. There were good views all round, an escape route, and it was far enough away from the farm to keep Henri and his family safe, and near enough to get to quickly. It was a good hide.

"It is fine, Gregor," Hildy said, "but I might get a little wet if it rains!"

Gregor reached up into the leaves above his head and pulled something down. It was a large parasol. He unfurled it and stood under its expansive canopy, grinning. Hildy laughed. It was her first laugh since leaving Beaulieu.

The next day Hildy and Jack, aided by Gregor, set up the radio transmitter in the derelict mill and traced the aerial out through the leaves and branches. Later that afternoon Hildy sent out her first transmission, Jack at her side. Gregor waited on guard in the brambles and ruins below and watched the forest for signs of soldiers. He carried a small jam jar on a wire but did not offer a reason for it.

Hildy clamped the earphones to her head and began tapping her transmission. Her call sign and security codes were accepted.

"What do I report?" she asked Jack.

"All glasses safe in water. Contact with friends made. Plans forming. Shopping list for meat, bread and vegetables soon. Advise best delivery where and when. End. Lupus."

Hildy sent the message and awaited acknowledgement. They both heard Gregor whistling a discordant tune. Jack looked down at him and realised he was giving a warning. Through the distant trees he saw three German soldiers searching the woods and heading towards them.

"Sign off, quickly," he said, "we are about to have company." Hildy signed off and packed the radio away in its case.

Jack and Hildy shrank into the shadows. Jack held his

pistol to hand. Below them, Gregor continued to whistle, but he seemed to be searching among the outer stone ruins for something, his jam jar swinging in his hand.

The Germans called out to him and he stopped still, as if seeing them for the first time. The three soldiers entered the clearing and spread out. A large sergeant barked at Gregor.

"What are you doing here, boy?"

"Nothing," stammered Gregor.

"You're doing something, boy. Do you want my rifle butt in your belly? Answer me."

Gregor held up his jam jar. A large spider sat on its floor.

"I am just hunting for spiders. This is a good place for spiders."

The sergeant looked at Gregor. He seemed to be trying to decide if Gregor was imbecile or imp. His two soldier colleagues wandered among the brambles and old building ruins, rifles to hand, idly searching for something, or someone.

"You alone, boy?" asked the sergeant.

"Yes."

"Seen anyone about this morning? In the woods?"

"No. No one comes here."

The sergeant looked about the ruins and up into the crumbling ruin of the mill tower.

"What is this place?" he asked. One of the other soldiers joined him. He frisked Gregor, pushed him down to sit on a rock and picked up his jam jar. After a moment's study he threw the jar to the rocks where it smashed. He grinned at Gregor.

"Oops," he said.

The third soldier began walking towards the tower.

Gregor turned to the sergeant.

"No one comes here because this is the Devil's Mill," he said. "The villagers won't come near here. They do not dare. But it is good for spiders."

"Why don't the villagers come here?"

"The mill is cursed," Gregor said. "It is an evil place. So it is said."

"Why?" asked the soldier who had thrown the jar. He sat on a lichen covered boulder, rolling a cigarette.

"Many years ago the mill was fine. One of the best in the district," Gregor said, "The miller had a daughter, very pretty. She wanted to marry a cobbler's son but the miller wanted a richer man for his daughter. One night the cobbler's son came to take the daughter away with him but the miller stopped them. There was a fight and the cobbler's son was killed. The daughter went mad with grief and rage and threw herself into the millstream and drowned under the water wheel."

The German soldiers waited to hear more. The one at the base of the tower looked into its dark interior without enthusiasm.

"Well?" asked the sergeant, "What happened to the miller?"

"He tied a rope around his neck and hung himself from the mill sails. His dead body turned on the mill for days before anyone found him. The ghosts of the miller, his daughter and the cobbler's son are supposed to wander the ruins. It is why no one comes here, it is a cursed place. A mill of the Devil. The mill fell to ruins. I expect you have noticed how cold the air here has become. Different from the woods. That is ghost air."

The sergeant gave an involuntary shudder. The soldier at the tower halted in the shadows of the mill tower, and then began backing away, seeking the comfort of sunlight.

"So why aren't you scared?" asked the sergeant.

"If I stay in the sunlight the ghosts can't find me. They only live in the shadows. With the spiders. Some spiders are as big as my head."

"The boy's a fool," said the jam jar soldier. "Come on, there's nothing here."

The sergeant bent down and clutched Gregor by the collar.

"Well there are the ghosts of dead German soldiers wandering the road out there and they don't care whether its shadow or sunlight. They'll eat little boys like you and shit out the bones. You can tell your villager friends that. Sure you haven't seen anyone? No one hiding? Strangers?"

"No, no one comes here. Only spiders."

The sergeant pushed Gregor away. He fell back over a rock and sat in brambles.

"A country of retards," the sergeant said, "let's go."

The soldiers moved off and away into the woods. Gregor waited ten minutes before he gave a signal to drop the ladder.

Jack and Hildy joined Gregor at the base of the tower.

"I didn't know I was sharing my hide with ghosts," Hildy said.

Gregor grinned.

"You are not. There are no ghosts here. Look at the mill. It is a ruin because it was built by a crazy man next to a spring stream. When the waters dropped and the seasons changed the stream died and the mill didn't work and fell into ruin. The Germans are too stupid to see there is no stream. But they will not come back again. Did you send your message?"

"Yes, contact was made with London," Hildy said.

"Then the hide is good?"

"How big are the spiders here, exactly?" Hildy asked.

"As big as you need," Gregor said, still grinning.

TWENTY SEVEN

The barn was warmed by a charcoal stove and low-lit with paraffin lanterns. Jack and Hildy sat on a large hay bale, the four group leaders sat on a semi-circle of bales before them. The air was heavy with cigarette and pipe smoke and dunged straw.

Henri had introduced the attendees perfunctorily. Cesar, a bull of a man with one eye, from Maubeuge, Alphonse, a thin, bespectacled teacher from Wavre, and Jean Mac, a solid-built butcher from Charleroi with forearms like pollarded willow. Cesar had brought a flagon which now circulated the group.

"Whisky," he said, "I make it myself from good Belgian barley."

Fabrice stuck his head around the door.

"OK," he said, "we're secure." Two trusted men from each of the groups stood guard around the barn, ensuring the meeting would not be disturbed.

"So talk," Jean Mac said, "say what you came to say. But know that we do not trust the English. You only help yourselves."

"Give us guns and we might trust again," Cesar said. "Nothing can happen without the guns."

"It is true that we English help ourselves," Jack said, "that cannot be denied. But sometimes by helping others it can help us to help ourselves. Now is such a time. The Nazis must be defeated if England is to survive. If Belgium is to survive. We are not going to win this war alone. Neither are you going to defeat the Germans and drive them from Belgium unless you work with others. With each other, with us."

"We are just a small band of partisans in a small corner of the new Reich," Alphonse said. "Insignificant in the greater order of things. We cannot defeat the enemy because it is too big and powerful and we are too small. We can only kill a few Germans. A small revenge for a great and wicked wrong, but it is all we can do."

"With London's help and our help you could do more, Alphonse," Hildy said. "And with Cesar and Jean Mac and Henri at your side you can do a lot more. Kill more Germans and blow up more railways and bridges and roads and power stations and ammunition dumps than ever before. Enough to make Germany really hurt. Enough to make them run."

Her words were met with ill-disguised distaste, but whether for their content or their narrator, she couldn't tell.

"How many Germans have you killed, English lady, eh?" asked Jean Mac. "Always fine words from the English. Enough of words. We are wasting our time here."

"Why are you here?" asked Alphonse, "I mean here in Mons. Why here?"

"This may be a small corner of the Reich, Alphonse," Jack said, "but it is in a big and important corner when the invasion comes. We are here because if the invasion is to succeed we must lay the path to its success here, in Hainault and across the Brussels, Mons and Arras curtain."

"The invasion is coming? The Pas-de-Calais?" asked Jean Mac.

"I can't tell you," Jack said, "all I can tell you is that we need to be working together to destroy, disrupt and kill the German command structure and capability in this whole region. It is vital that the resistance is ready and working together. All the resistance groups. To lay the pathway towards victory."

The barn was quiet for some time. Jean Mac passed the flagon around. He insisted Hildy took her turn. It felt like a begrudged apology of some kind. The whiskey was raw but sweet. It burned pleasantly in her gut.

"So what do we need to do?" asked Henri.

"We work together as a command team covering the region," Jack said. "We draw up a co-ordinated strategy of resistance across and between the groups. Liaised through Henri here in Mons. We identify the priority infrastructure and operational targets – from power plants to railways. The four groups and London working together. Is this agreed?"

"When will this be?" asked Alphonse.

"We prepare and plan now, we hit easy low risk targets but we keep most of our powder dry, ready for the invasion. Maybe spring next year, or early summer. Now we get our teams prepared and trained and working together. Hitting softer targets. Supply lines, utilities, communications, fuel dumps. Anything to disrupt and annoy, tying up troops and officers in repairs. Then really hit hard when the invasion is about to happen."

"We need guns, explosives, ammunition," Cesar said.

"If we can convince London we are together and have an agreed plan of action, then the weapons will follow. Talk it over with Henri and let Giselle here know the shopping list. Be realistic. We'll arrange it."

There was a sound of commotion outside. The lanterns were instantly snuffed. The barn door opened and Fabrice and another man entered.

"A German patrol truck is up the road. A mile or so. Heading this way."

"We have been betrayed!" Jean Mac said.

"No, we don't think so," the other man said, "it's just a routine patrol. They are not speeding. Probably on their way back to the depot at Valenciennes. Just coincidence."

"I will take the guard team up to the road and make sure they pass by," Fabrice said. "You all need to leave the barn by the back lane. We'll meet back at the trucks in one hour."

Henri led them along a dark, narrow lane between fields and woods. The moon was out and the night was cool and clear. Jean Mac and Cesar began laughing and then softly singing as they stumbled the path. Jean Mac's whisky was having its effect. Even Henri was weaving slightly. They climbed up a short rise on the path and came out on a metalled road, and staggered right into the path of three German soldiers. The Germans were walking along the road, talking and laughing. One was pushing his bike. The tallest soldier unslung his rifle and covered the sudden intruders on their road. A second soldier pulled a pistol from his side holster.

"Halt! Stop or we shoot. Raise your arms."

Henri and the others came to a halt and looked around for escape. There was none.

"Hands up I say!" The German with the pistol was a junior lieutenant. The captives raised their hands. The soldier with the rifle kept it trained on the group while the officer walked slowly around them, studying them.

"What are you doing in that lane, and on this road at this time of night? Breaking curfew. I have every right to shoot you all."

"We have come from a funeral," Henri said, "a dear and old friend. We are late returning home. We took the lane because we did not want to get caught breaking the curfew."

The officer stepped forward and swung his pistol hard into the side of Henri's face. There was sharp crack and Henri stumbled to his knees. He rose unsteadily to his feet, blood flowing fresh from a gash across his cheek.

Jack and Hildy shared a look. They knew that this was not going to end well. Jack moved slightly in front of Hildy, shielding her from the guns.

"Do not lie," the officer said.

"It is not a lie," Jean Mac said. "We are just late. We are a little drunk maybe. We got lost."

Hildy moved toward Henri.

"Stop, lady! What are you doing? Stop or I shoot!"

"This man needs attention," Hildy said. She pulled a handkerchief from her coat pocket and held it up to view. The pistol in her pocket had felt comforting against her knuckles. "Just a handkerchief to help stem the blood. Can I tend to him?"

The officer considered a moment. "If you must. Good cotton is wasted on these peasants. But I am not an unreasonable man."

The officer turned to face Jean Mac. "So you do not lie, eh? You are not a group of saboteurs. Not marquis. You are just lost after a funeral. Sneaking in the night lanes to avoid trouble."

The young officer's stance and tone tensed, a sneer

spread across his clean shaven face.

"You must be stupid if you think that I will be persuaded by such pathetic stories. A country of liars and fools. But I do believe that you will never tell another lie to a German officer. And I can assure you that, in this, I do not lie."

He raised his gun to point it at Jean Mac's head.

The quiet stillness of the night was split by a sharp crack. A second later another crack sounded, almost like an echo. Cesar instinctively ducked to his haunches. Henri and Jean Mac dropped to the road and rolled sideways into a ditch. Looking up, they saw Giselle standing tall and calm in the middle of the road, arm outstretched and with a fisted pistol glinting steady in the moonlight. The German officer lay dead in the road beside her, a small black hole in his forehead, his hand still holding his gun aloft in a crooked elbow as if he was about to shoot the moon. The soldier with the rifle lay face down and still in the road, blood creeping from his mouth and pooling in a halo around his head.

Jean Mac scrambled to his feet and reached out to thank Giselle, but she pushed him aside brusquely, her eyes focused back down the road to where the last soldier was running away beside his bike and trying frantically to find the moment to leap upon it and pedal away to the safety of the dark. The group watched as Giselle raised her pistol in both hands, brace her feet and track the retreating figure with a slow, smooth, steady and measured eye. As the soldier vaulted for his saddle in the gloom, like a hare bounding in a far field, Hildy's pistol cracked again. The soldier jerked, cried out and collapsed onto the bike which went crashing to the road and down into a bramble thicket. The soldier lay still on his back among the brambles as if floating on a gentle sea swell, his bent bicycle frame his raft and his boots pointing to the stars on stiff legs.

Hildy turned back and was aware of Jean Mac, Alphonse, Cesar and Henri staring back at her. Henri had his clothed hand pressed to his cheek, his jaw slack and his eyes wide. The others seemed similarly transfixed. They stood in spellbound silence, unable to quite take in what they had just witnessed.

Jack busied himself taking the guns and ammunition from the dead soldiers in the road.

"Come on!" he hissed, "We can't stand around here all night. There are still Germans about. Get these bodies into the woods. Hide that bike. Get their guns. Take anything that's worth taking. Steal their passes and papers. But let's move, now!"

They set about hiding the bodies. Jean Mac helped Jack lift the officer's body into the woods and into a gulley where they concealed it with ferns and branches.

"Four," said Jack.

Jean Mac seemed confused. "Four?" he said, "What four?"

"You asked how many Germans Giselle had killed. It's now four. These three. And one back in England. Four."

"She kills well," Jean Mac said. "She kills beautifully."

"She also punches bulls in her spare time," Jack said .

TWENTY EIGHT

It was difficult for Georgia to believe that she was sitting in the office of a German General and being gently interviewed for a secretarial pool position, but it was quite impossible for her to believe that her interviewer was a General in the German army.

Helmut Vogel, Generalstabrichter of the Hainault region was a small, round, avuncular man with white hair bushed smooth above his ears, round rimless glasses through which puppy-dog eyes saw delight in all before them and a giggle that would break out on the random discovery of an unexpressed thought. General Vogel had the busy, happy and chatty manner of a rather absent-minded professor of classics. He roamed his office like a child in a toyshop, conducting the interview as a sing-song dialogue with himself interspersed with moments of quiet contemplation or study while he examined an object that he had absently picked up on his rambles from the many shelves and desk tops. Georgia had hardly said anything at all.

"You see they keep on coming in," he said. He looked up from his study of a bronze figurine of a dancing nymph to find no one before him, just a bookcase. He turned around and saw Georgia sitting in the chair. "Ah, there you are! Yes, coming in. All the time. It is the war. So many crimes. So many laws. How to keep up, eh? And it is us lawyers that have to untangle it all! What a dance they lead us, eh! And we must untangle it. Make sense of it, you see? Bring some order to the world. Oh for the world to be quiet for a little, eh?"

"Yes," Georgia said.

General Vogel looked at her as if seeing her for the first time.

"Did Monique send you? You are the one from the library?"

"Yes."

"Ah, Monique! Such a lovely girl. And so clever. Quite

wasted with those old books. I told her she should come and work with me at law. Much more fun. A happy family. We have coffee and cake every morning. We have mountains of files and reports and judgements and it all needs order! And managing. I have twenty helpers in the offices and still the mountain grows! Your mother died?"

Georgia was beginning to drift, she snapped attentive in her chair.

"Yes, at the hospital."

"And you will return to Strasbourg?"

Georgia let a mask of pain cross her face.

"I don't know. I have nothing to go back to in Strasbourg. Not without Mother. And Monique has been so kind."

"Quite so. Kind, yes, indeed. Good. Then you come and work here. With cakes and coffee every morning, eh? Tell Monique this is an order, ha! You have your papers? Good. Any language apart from German?"

"French, a little English. But not the legal language."

"Oh, it is nothing to learn!" he said. "Monique tells me you are very clever, so you will pick it up. You will start tomorrow, nine o'clock. You will join our happy family! Hand your papers to Frau Hagen at the desk outside and she will show you where you sit and how it all works. We will bring that mountain down, eh?"

Georgia found herself outside the general's office. A woman took her papers for registering and other papers were filled and signed. When she left the office three hours later she had her pass, identity card and a job in the heart of the German war machine, if a little in its backwaters. More importantly, she had begun to build a solid cover, and one that would allow her to move about the region with the accreditation of a general and all the necessary official papers. She could hardly believe her good fortune.

Georgia stepped out into the street. It was crowded with civilians lining its pavements. German soldiers were marshalling people into orderly lines and keeping them corralled on the pavements. On the other side of the road the civilian crowds were being similarly marshalled. Other soldiers were lined in guard in the road, rifles held across their chests. The road was cleared of traffic. A pipe-smoking old tradesman on his cart was deemed too slow and he was hauled down from his high seat and onto the cobbles. He was kicked and punched by a couple of soldiers and then thrown roughly into the pavement crowd. His horse and cart were whipped-up and dragged away into a side street.

The crowds were four deep where Georgia stood and she was happy to melt into the back rows and keep her head down. The road was being cleared for some German dignitaries.

Beside Georgia an elderly man in a worn black jacket and dusty homburg swore under his breath and then spat on the pavement at her feet.

"One day this sewage will be swept from our streets and into the gutter," he said.

"Why are we being held here?" asked Georgia. The man turned to Georgia and instinctively removed his hat. He smiled grey teeth and adjusted the tie at his thread-worn collar.

"Enchanted, I'm sure. We are being held to allow some high-ranking German an uninterrupted ride to the Wehrmacht Command offices. We are the dutiful and admiring crowd. Are you ready to wave and throw flowers?"

"So who is coming?"

"The rumour is, that it is the Wehrmacht Militarbefehl-shaber, himself, General Alexander von Falkenhausen. If we are lucky, someone will throw a bomb with the lilies, eh!"

Georgia waited on the roadside, trying to lose herself in the crowds. It was a further quarter of an hour before the sounds of the motorbike outriders drifted up the street like rolling thunder. German soldiers in long coats, helmets and goggles roared up the cobbles on their bikes in a rigid arrowhead formation and sped on by. A staff car with a small red pennant flying from its bonnet glided by, four fresh-faced junior officers settled in the leathered seats enjoying a joke together, before more motorbikes appeared heralding the arrival of two larger staff cars.

Georgia watched the faces of the enemy slide across her gaze. The faces were young and old, fresh and world-worn, stern and carefree. They seemed as aloof and arrogant as any soldier, but the sleek grey uniforms made them look menacing, almost inhuman, like sharks.

The second large staff car glided past. Seated in the back, the slim, tall, balding figure of General Falkenhausen rested back in his seat, an arm laid casual on the open window, his indifferent gaze taking in none of the crowds that lined the street. At his side another officer, a major by the judge of his uniform, sat engaging the general in an earnest conversation.

The tableau was there before Georgia, and then it was gone. Only a moment, a fleeting image frozen in her mind. It was the image of the earnest, excited major sitting beside the general, his black-gloved hands stabbing the air about him, his eyes bright in excitement, his face flushed with passion. It was the excited, earnest and flushed face of Ernst Paul Baum, her husband.

Georgia sat drinking coffee and smoking in a quiet alcove in the Café D'Accord, but her mind and thoughts were anything but quiet. The shock of seeing Ernst had been violent enough, but to see him in the shark grey uniform of a major in the Wehrmacht was savage. But was it really Ernst? The face was only before her for less than three seconds, visible only in moving profile through a crowd of heads. Perhaps it was just an hallucination brought on by the pressure and tensions she was under as an agent in a foreign and hostile world.

"Are you alright, Agnes? You look like you've seen a ghost."

Monique pulled out a chair from under the table and sat down with a heavy sigh.

"You would never think that working in a library could be so hard on the feet." She flicked off a shoe and began rubbing her toes. "Coffee, Bernard! And anything to nibble. Got a cigarette? Is everything alright?"

Georgia handed Monique her cigarette pack and flicked a light for her. She was surprised at how steady her hand was. Maybe it was all just in her head after all. A momentary image short-circuiting in the brain. A malfunction, soon passed. She smiled at Monique as the waiter brought the coffee.

"Fine," Georgia said. "Thanks to you, I now have a post in General Vogel's secretarial section. Typing up summonses and decrees. I have to say, he doesn't seem very much like a general of the mighty all-conquering German army."

"Don't be fooled by his absent-minded uncle ways," Monique said. "Vogel is a hard, ruthless bastard, just like any German. He informed on his own Jewish daughter-in-law. They sent her and her two young sons, his own grandchildren, to Ravensbruck. He also shot two prisoners dead in a locked police cell. He said they were Gypsies and no court's time should be wasted on them. So that is our nice General Vogel."

"He seems to like you."

Monique laughed.

"Keep your lovers cool and your enemies warm," she said. "Vogel likes me because he likes looking at my tits, so I loosen my blouse a little and cross my legs so he can glimpse a stocking top. I speak Latin so he thinks I am clever. And I find him help when he needs it. He doesn't know it, but some of his secretaries are Jews and Romanies. And now he has an English spy. I take my revenge as I can. But Vogel is still a German bastard and will deserve his wall and firing squad when it comes."

"Not until I have made best use of him," Georgia said. "The Germans are fanatical about keeping thorough records and personal files and I am interested in finding a couple of them."

"Well, take care. The Germans are not fools and their spies are everywhere."

Monique took a moment to survey the café. Only one far table was occupied by an elderly couple enjoying coffee and a break from walking the streets. They were reading newspapers. The proprietor was crating empty bottles behind his bar.

Monique leaned forward in whisper. "I do not know your mission," she said, "but I think whatever it is it will work better if our resistance groups are working together, yes?"

Georgia nodded.

"There is a group, in Brussels, Group G. It is a group that began in the university and it has grown. It is a good group, led by true partisans. If there are to be talks, they should be included. I know contacts there. Very trusted. Clever people. I know some of them. I can arrange for you to meet them."

"What's so special about this group?"

"They have over a thousand patriots. But it is their ideas and connections that make them strong. They have good ideas. They are worth talking to."

"I will talk it over with my colleagues," Georgia said.

They smoked and drank coffee and talked the lunchtime through. Georgia had now been in Belgium for just over a month and was beginning to adjust to the new ways and tensions of her life. The ceaseless excitement of it all fired through her like a constant electrical charge, but she was aware of the need to maintain control, calm and vigilance. She had steeled herself to stay alert and aware and she was now reasonably adept at disguising any shock or discomfort a sudden alarm might bring, like walking round a street corner and coming face to face with a patrol of German soldiers, or the sudden sound of nearby gunfire, or a German officer demanding to see her papers while shopping for bread. It was through such control that by the time they had settled the bill and put their coats on, Georgia had almost convinced herself that she had not seen Ernst at all and that it was all a result of letting her guard fall. The tensions had made her see things, imagine things. She shook off the image.

Georgia returned to the flat and settled to sleep the afternoon out. She wanted to be fresh and ready to start her work at the Wehrmacht legal division, and to begin tracking down any files on Guy Delmain, Henri Latisse and Michel Le Fointeau.

TWENTY NINE

It felt uncomfortable to be sitting at the open air café table in the Grand Place square with a folded copy of Le Soir placed at his elbow. The placing of his hat, crown side down, on top of the newspaper, felt ridiculous, almost melodramatic. But those had been the instructions.

The meeting had been arranged by Monique. She felt it was important for Jack and the others to learn about Group G, a resistance group centred on the university at Brussels.

"You should meet with them," Monique had insisted, "they have many good ideas. They are strong. L'Araignee is a good leader. Good to have on your side."

"The spider?" Hildy had said, "meet with the spider?"

Monique had shrugged. "It's a name. And spiders are good hunters, killers and hiders. Some are even scared of them."

"And should we be scared of L'Araignee?" asked Jack.

Monique smiled. "Very," she said.

And now here they all were, sitting at the designated café tables in an open market place in broad daylight with German soldiers patrolling.

A young, slim waitress in owl glasses appeared at his shoulder.

"More coffee, sir?"

"No, I'm fine, thank you."

"Some pastries perhaps?"

"Really, no."

The waitress moved away. Jack lit a cigarette and tried to look nonchalant. At a nearby table Georgia and Hildy sat reading newspapers, smoking, sipping coffee and fending off the eager waitress. Jack hoped he looked as natural as they did, he certainly didn't feel it. The other tables about him were occupied with couples and locals on their late morning coffee breaks or just sitting watching the world drift by.

The Grand Place lived up to its name. The vast cobbled

city square, bounded on all sides by magnificent, ornate buildings, was an impressive place. Cafes, bars, shops and civic buildings lined the square and the open space between them was a huge pedestrianised, cobbled courtyard the size of a parade ground that bustled with market stalls, shoppers and street vendors.

The square was busy with trade and the café tables full of late morning customers. In amongst the crowds, knots of German soldiers, in twos and threes, wandered with their carbines shouldered, checking papers or taking unbidden glasses of wine or pastries from the tables or fruit from the stalls. The crowds were silent about them, letting them through and pass on before resuming their normal Grand Place chatter and lives.

The clock on the tower of the Hotel de Ville struck the half hour. L'Araignee was late. Perhaps he wasn't coming at all.

Jack lit another cigarette and tried to appear as if smoking a cigarette and watching the passing crowds was what he did every day. But the roaming Germans with guns made it difficult.

The waitress returned.

"Are you ready to order more coffee, sir?"

"No," Jack said. The irritation sounded clear in his voice.

"I think you are, sir."

Jack turned to the waitress and saw the muzzle of a pistol poking out from under her lace-trimmed apron.

"Say nothing. Please stand and follow me."

Jack stood. He glanced across to Georgia and Hildy's table. They had risen with him, Hildy with her hand reaching for her coat pocket. Jack was aware of several customers at nearby tables stand and then converge on them. Four men and one woman moved in to surround Georgia and Hildy. Jack realised they had been corralled and ambushed, and it had been done with some finesse.

"Walk to La Brouette, the building to your left. There is a gendarme outside the door. See?"

"And if I don't? Are you going to shoot me?"

The waitress sighed. She pushed her large glasses back on her nose.

"Rather messy, don't you think? No, I shall probably just scream rape and wait for the German soldiers to come. Are your papers all in order? They can be very, well, German about these kind of things."

Jack picked up his hat and walked towards the gendarme. Out of the corner of his eye he could see Hildy and Georgia being ushered along behind him. They were escorted up the steps of an ornate building, the gendarme nodding them through before returning his guardian watch back onto the Grand Place crowds. Jack followed the waitress up the steps and into an opulent wood-panelled foyer and on up another flight of stairs to a small room overlooking the square.

The waitress beckoned Jack, Hildy and Georgia to sit at the table. Three guards from the square took up positions around the walls, hands in the pockets of their coats.

The waitress sat opposite the agents.

"I am L'Araignee," she said. "Yes, I know you thought I would be a man, but I am not. But I look too young, well I am not. Inside I am already old. Deal with it. We do not have time to waste in idle talk, so we will get right to the matter. You are three British agents sent to help the resistance in this area. Yes or no?"

Jack placed his hat on the table. He said nothing. L'Araignee took off her cap and apron, rolled them into a ball and dropped them on the table beside Jack's hat. She was a young woman in her late twenties with long dark hair, alert, intelligent eyes and an aura of supressed, fired energy. Her movements were assured and graceful and she spoke with the calm authority of a natural leader. She obviously commanded respect among her fellow resistance comrades, they obeyed her without question or hesitation.

"Good, it shows you are not stupid," L'Araignee said, "But it does not show that you are not traitors. We have many problems with traitors. Do you speak German?"

"Yes," Jack said.

"You speak it well?"

"Fluently."

"Where did you learn it?"

"In Germany."

"What were you doing in Germany?"

"Working."

"As what?"

"Engineer."

"Why did you leave?"

"My wife died, the war came, take your pick."

"Your wife was German?"

"Yes."

"How did she die?"

"She ran across a road and was hit by a truck."

"That was careless."

"She was being chased."

"By whom?"

"Brown shirts."

"Why?"

"Because she was a Jew."

There was a heavy silence in the room, even the sounds of the market square outside seemed to fade.

L'Araignee turned to Georgia.

"How are we to trust you?"

"How are we to trust you?" countered Georgia, "It works both ways. We don't know you are who you say you are. So far, all we know is that you have abducted us from the street and held us at gunpoint. These are not the acts of friends, but of enemies."

L'Araignee turned to Hildy.

"Have you nothing to say?"

Hildy smiled. One hand played idly with Jack's hat on the table top. There was something about this whole game that simply piqued her. She had come to Belgium to fight the Germans and here she was being ushered off the street at gunpoint by those she had come to help. And now these games. Deep inside, Hildy knew that what L'Araignee and her friends were doing was only right and sensible for her and her resistance group, but that didn't stop it being annoying.

"Well, since we are among friends," Hildy said, "I feel that I must advise you that I have a gun in my pocket and it is pointing directly at your belly. Be assured that I will not miss. I am told a belly shot is one of the worst. A lot of pain and a slow, messy death. I don't think we should try and find out, do you?"

L'Araignee grinned and leaned back in her chair.

"Careful," Hildy said. "You will be hit before a cheek has left your chair. And if I'm as good a shot as people keep telling me I am, then I can probably see off a couple of your wall dogs before they can pull their guns from their pockets. Do you train your people well in the ruthless killing arts at the university?"

"Are you the one they call Marianne?"

"That is not my name."

"No, but it is what other marquis call you. I have heard. My spider web reaches everywhere. You killed three Germans up on the Chemin de Riens. Three expert kills, so it is said. Two forehead kills, one back of the head from sixty metres. At night. The bars and cafes talk of the new Belgian Marianne, The bringer of liberty. A beautiful avenger. You are already made legend."

"And the name of L'Araignee is known and feared," Jack said. "But we would have it as friend. But not at the end of a gun. Why have you brought us here?"

L'Araignee raised her hands in mock surrender and moved her chair further back, but slowly. She kept her eyes fixed on Hildy. Hildy pulled her hand slowly from under the table and laid the pistol gently beside Jack's hat. L'Araignee lowered her hands. She took a cigarette pack out of her dress pocket, lit one and flung the pack to the table. Jack and Georgia lit up. The marquis guards leaning to the walls visibly relaxed.

"We have brought you here to help us kill Germans," L'Araignee said. "Lots of Germans. As many Germans as we can and to run them out of Belgium. To do this we need guns and explosives. London has guns and explosives. You will help us get them."

"Why would London do this?"

L'Araignee looked hard and long at Jack.

"Because if we are to beat the Germans the marquis groups have to work together and we have to focus our limited resources on the targets that matter. Group G is the strongest resistance group in Belgium and we want to work with our friends in the Hainault region. Together we can rid Belgium of Germans. I know Henri Clerque, he is a good man, a strong leader and a brave, true patriot, but he does not have the ideas, the contacts, or the soldiers. Blowing up small bridges and railway lines is fine, but they are of little significance, and soon repaired. We need to make a bigger sabotage impact. We can only do this working together. And with guns and explosives from London. You will get them for us."

"And what does London get in return?" asked Jack.

"Intelligence," L'Araignee said. "Lots of intelligence. Group G has over two thousand people. Many are from the university, but also from industry, business and public service. All are patriots and willing to die for their country, but they have skills and access to intelligence that can change the course of the war. I am just the spider who sits in the middle of the web, gathering it all in. Intelligence that London would give ten thousand guns for and all the explosives we need."

"Like what?" Jack asked.

"Oh, an up to date list of all the German military divisions in Belgium. Their deployment, their leaders, numbers of soldiers. We can tell you what armoury they have, where their guns are placed, where the ammunition, diesel and armoury storage dumps are, their supply routes. Rather useful information if you were, for example, planning to invade the region anytime soon. Wouldn't you think? Of course these are simple matters of information gathering, passive intelligence. It is the active intelligence that will make the real difference. The difference that will make a successful invasion."

"Active intelligence?"

"Group G has over two hundred postal workers in its web. They can read important messages, lose post, delay post, they can warn people they have been denounced or betrayed and give them time to flee. We have administrators and secretaries and engineers and drivers and waiters working throughout the German military machine. We have the finest minds of the university working with us. Drawing up plans of sabotage and disruption. Give us twenty-one detonators and explosives and thirty kilos of fine ground glass and, working with the other groups, we will bring Belgium to a stop. This will show London how their generosity can be rewarded."

"That doesn't seem like a lot to ask for," Jack said, "not very ambitious. You are not going to make much of an impact with twenty-one detonators and few bags of ground glass."

"It is just a demonstration. When we succeed, we will ask for, and get, more, a lot more. And London will be happy to give it. But to start we will place twenty-one bombs at key points in the Belgian power transmission grid and we will put ten kilos of ground glass in three diesel storage plants that handle the fuel for half the German transport divisions in Hinault. Our engineers, professors and mechanics have worked to put this plan together. It will work. When the bombs go off, there will be a complete electricity power cut across Belgium that will take at least four days to repair. When the ground glass is added to the diesel silos, the engines of German trucks, tanks and cars will gradually and literally grind to a halt. It will cause major military disruption and will tie up garage works and fuel supplies for many days. It is not the amount, it is how we use it."

Jack studied L'Araignee's earnest and assured face. She seemed so young and slight to be a major resistance leader, but he could not doubt her determination, or the logic and persuasion of her arguments.

227

"You are happy to work with Henri and the other groups?"

"Of course. Together is better than apart. If Henri is your trusted contact he can liaise with us all. Better to keep the contacts narrow, it is safer, more secure."

"I will speak with Henri. We need to work out a sabotage plan, agreed and understood by all the groups."

"And you will speak with London?"

"I will speak with London," Jack said.

The door burst open and Hildy and Georgia were instantly on their feet, Hildy with pistol to hand. L'Araignee was beside her, a gun ready to hand.

It was one of L'Araignees people. A young woman in a long coat and blue beret came quickly into the room.

"Germans are herding everyone into the square from both north and south and the radial roads are being blocked off. They are gathering everyone into the square. You need to get away, now."

"Follow me," said L'Araignee.

She led the agents up three flights of stairs and took a long step-ladder from a broom cupboard on the top floor and raised it under a trapdoor in the ceiling

"Up into the old bell tower," she said. "Stay there until I can come and get you. If something happens to me and my people make your way across the roofs. Head towards the Saint Elizabeth church tower on the north corner. There are fire escapes behind the buildings that way. Good luck."

They heard the trapdoor shut behind them and the sound of the ladder being folded away and stored. They settled in behind the ornate, gothic columns of the bell tower and looked down into the square, some four floors below them.

Large numbers of German soldiers were herding and driving people at both the northern and southern ends of the square. Tanks and trucks with machine gun mountings were positioned at strategic points to offer coverage of the whole square. More troops and trucks were driving people from the side streets into the square and patrols of soldiers were working through each café, shop and building on the square and getting the people out. More troops with rifles and machine guns were pushing, beating and kicking the people into ranks along the centre of the square, facing the Hotel de Ville. The men, women and children stood in ragged lines, the sound of barking German orders and a murmuring of voices rose up to the listeners in the old bell tower, muttering, moaning, calling in alarm for children, like gulls over waves on a rocky beach.

A black uniformed SS captain stepped out from ranks of soldiers.

"Silence!" he roared. The crowds shuffled to a be-grudging quiet.

The crowds were kept waiting for some time. The wait was ended with a flurry of German soldiers coming out of the Hotel de Ville and lining up along its steps as a guard line. Moments later General Alexander von Falkenhausen stepped out of the huge gothic doors of the building, flanked by five high-ranking Wehrmacht and SS officers.

The group strolled down the steps and out onto the cobbles of the square. Von Falkenhausen studied the crowds before him with seeming disinterest.

"You are gathered here together in the city square to learn and to understand that we will not tolerate any more acts of petty sabotage against our great German nation and its brave solders."

Von Falkenhausen spoke with a clear, high-pitched voice that seemed out of keeping with his smart, shark grey uniform and double ranked chest of medal ribbons. More a civil servant than a military warrior. The voice and words carried easily up to the bell tower.

"In spite of best efforts it is a lesson that you have failed to learn. We are now the law in Belgium and its citizens, all of its citizens, will obey that law. Our law. You have been warned before, but still you persist with your useless resistance. I think the lesson has not been learned. Perhaps it will now."

The general stood aside and a major in a slate grey Wehrmacht uniform stepped forward. He studied the crowd in silence for a few moments, then raised his swagger stick and flicked it to the air. Three soldiers emerged from the back of nearby truck. They brought two young boys into the square, both were held and led by their collars and had their hands tied behind their back. The taller boy's face was bloody and his shirt ripped almost in two. The smaller boy trailed a dead leg and his face was also bloodied. Murmurs of concern and fear rose from the crowd.

"Silence!" boomed the major.

The crowd noises stopped as if switched off. The major looked at the two young men. The younger boy's trouser crotch was dark with a growing stain and urine seeped in a small pool under his left foot. The older boy's nose was bleeding pink with the mix of blood and snot. The major turned to the crowd.

"These young men have been caught putting sand in the fuel tanks of trucks of the German army. They have both confessed. The punishment for such wanton acts of sabotage is death."

"No!" cried someone from the crowd. "Please no!"

A burly, slightly bent, middle-aged man in a soiled jacket and dungarees stepped from the line. He plucked off his hat and crushed it in his fists, which he then held up in plea before him.

"Please, spare my boys!" he stepped forward but two soldiers moved quickly to prevent his progress, their guns ready to take him down. They sought instruction from the major. He nodded and the man was allowed to advance.

"You are the father of these criminals?" asked the major.

"Yes, sir. They are good boys. They are young boys. Philippe is not yet twelve and his brother Jules is but fourteen. Not men, they are just children."

"They are saboteurs."

"Please no. They do not understand what they do. Just children."

"And as you are the father of these saboteurs, you are complicit in their crime. The boys were caught and they will be shot."

"No, no! Please. Not that. Spare the boys. I am guilty. Yes. Shoot me, not them. I implore you."

The major smiled. "Most noble, I am sure. But they must pay for their crimes. But I will be lenient. I will shoot only one of them. Which one shall it be? You can choose. That is your penance for raising saboteurs."

"One? But I cannot. They are my sons. I love them. I cannot do what you ask. Please!" The father had fallen to his knees before the major. The major looked down and stepped away from him and sauntered to position himself behind Jules and Philippe. He pulled a pistol from his flapped holster and raised it casually behind the boys' heads.

"Which is to be, old man? Little Philippe, or big Jules? If you don't tell me, I will shoot them both. Tell me!"

Their father was on his knees rocking and weeping and moaning. A soldier close by stepped up and kicked him in the kidneys. The father grunted.

"You heard the major," barked the soldier. "Which one? Tell him now or they both die."

"I can't," sobbed the father, the soldier kicked him again.

"Jules," the father sobbed.

The major stepped up behind Philippe. The silence was split by a crack and Philippe crumpled as if all his bones had been suddenly plucked from his body. His head hit the cobbles with a dull, hollow thud that echoed up into the old bell tower. Hildy stifled a scream with her fist, her eyes wide with disbelief.

The father cried out in pain. "Philippe, oh my Phillipe!"

"Oh, have I shot the wrong one?" said the major. "How very careless of me. Allow me to make amends." There was another crack and Jules dropped to the cobbles to lie beside his brother. "There, that's put it right, hasn't it? Your wish has been granted and justice is served."

The father rose up unsteadily and stood swaying with grief, gazing at the bodies of his boys lying in the square. He pulled a knife from his belt, threw his head up to the heavens, cried aloud like a pained animal and ran screaming at the major. Before he had run three strides, a volley of rifle shots lifted him into the air and then crashed him back to the ground where he lay, motionless and silent. The echo of the volley ricocheted around the square.

The major holstered his pistol and stepped out to face the now silent and stunned crowd.

"Let this be a lesson to you all," he barked, "The penalty for sabotage is death. Swift and final. The penalty for acts of sabotage that result in the death of a German soldier will be swift and tenfold. For every German soldier that dies, ten people of the city of Mons will be taken and shot. Men or women, old or young. You who have heard this and seen this justice done in the square today – you go tell your families and friends and neighbours how swift and vengeful the law of Germany will be. Go, tell Mons that acts of sabotage have a terrible and exacting consequence. Go and live your lives in lawful peace. You have been warned. Dismissed!"

The major turned on his heel and joined the general and his staff who had been watching from the top of the steps. They all turned and sauntered back through the doors of the Hotel de Ville, distant laughter could be heard from within its dark atrium.

The soldiers formed into ranks and marched from the square. The crowds broke up, many making their way to the three bodies. Two black-frocked priests hurried from out of the throng and knelt beside the bodies, offering last rites. Cloths from café tables were brought to cover the bodies. Several in the crowd were weeping.

The three agents up in the old bell tower had watched it all in silence and tried to find some kind of detachment from it all. They failed.

Hildy sat, collapsed back against a stone column, her eyes moist, her thoughts burning and her body numb. Jack continued to stare down into the square, incredulous and stunned.

"Who the hell was that bastard?" he said.

Georgia turned to them both, her face blanched, strained,

a strange smile fixed. She gave a little laugh.

"That particular bastard," she said, "happens to be my husband

THIRTY

Jack sat is his usual table at the rear and watched the two German soldiers advance towards him through the café, checking the papers of the customers and stealing the occasional glass of wine or pastry off the tables. As usual no one objected.

Hildy sat at the table with him, head down, reading the local newspaper.

"Giselle Barnard," Jack said. Hildy looked up and saw the Germans working their way through the tables towards them.

"Albert Girond," she said and sipped her coffee.

The naming ritual was both a warning signal and comforter. It allowed them both to switch into full agent alertness and to do it together. It was a ritual they had gone through many times since arriving in Belgium. Their papers had been checked and passed so many times that they now had every confidence in them, and their cover story. While this enabled them to face such inconveniences with a wary calm, rather than abject fear, they nonetheless remained primed for possible discovery. It was probably an attitude that helped persuade their many interlocutors of their innocence. The naming game helped Jack and Hildy to be alert to not taking their current freedom for granted.

A young German officer in a pristine grey uniform strode to their table. A surly corporal followed in his wake.

"Papers!"

Jack handed his over. Hildy searched in her bag for hers and then handed them over. The officer studied the documents for a long moment.

"What are you doing in Mons?"

"Working," Jack said, "I am the representative for Fiat Tractors in this area. I am visiting the farms about, trying to sell our new tractor."

"Where are you staying?"

"Here, in a flat above the café." Jack had moved out from

234

Henri's farm after two weeks and set up in Mons. Monique knew the café owner and the flat was a more central and connected location; staying with Henri would only attract unwanted attention and gossip. He met up with Hildy most days to plan and agree tactics and activities. She still lodged with Henri on the farm and sent out her daily reports to London from the old mill.

The officer threw Jack's papers down on the table and turned to Hildy's documents.

"You work together?" asked the officer.

"Yes," Hildy said. "we visit the farms."

"You are the secretary?"

"No, I am the engineer."

The officer smiled.

"Engineer? Is that so? A woman engineer. That is very unusual. I think it is a cover, yes?"

"Cover?"

"You are lovers perhaps. The engineer story is to deceive, is it not? You are an adulterer maybe? A jezebel slut? Admit it!"

"No, I am an engineer. For Fiat. I travel here to visit the farms about."

"Yes, yes. I heard. Selling the new Fiat tractor. So, what is this new Fiat tractor, engineer? Why don't you tell me all about it, engineer lady, eh?"

Hildy held the officer with a calm, detached stare. She reached for a cigarette,

"I am sure it is too boring for an important and busy man like you, Lieutenant."

The officer smiled.

"I can assure you, I am all agog to hear about the wonderful new Fiat tractor," he said, "Please. Oblige me."

Hildy lit her cigarette. She resumed her detached stare.

"We are here to introduce the new tractor. The model Fiat 400 Baghetto tractor is a new upgrade of the old 35 HP model that we introduced back in 1938. The new model is a 25 HP version with a multiple tow coupling, improved suspension and comes with an innovative multi-fuel operating option. Diesel, kerosene, or petrol. The new tractor can run on any of these. It's not as big or as unwieldly as the old tractor models but its power and fuel versatility makes it an ideal tractor for working the smaller fields in the farms here about and in these troubled economic times. Just the right kind of tractor for the smaller farms and hard up farmers in this region. I show the farmers how to use and operate the tractor. I am the engineer. My colleague, Monsieur Girond here, will be happy to arrange attractive terms if you are thinking of buying one."

The officer studied Hildy for a while.

"Show me your hands," he said. Hildy held out both her hands for inspection. The officer held them lightly in his gloved hands as if they might be infectious. He turned them over slowly and studied them. Hildy was aware of the unkempt nails and minor grazes and bruises that marked her farmyard hands. Perhaps for once they were to be a blessing. The officer released her hands.

"Peasant hands," he snorted and then tossed her papers to the table. "If I ever bought a tractor it would be German, not a fucking Italian pile of junk," he said. He strode on to the next table.

"Impressive tractor knowledge," Jack said when the Germans had finally left the café.

"I read the brochures, not much else to do at the farm. He's right though, they are junk. Ah, there's Monique."

Monique was advancing towards them through the tables. She was carrying two large boxes and was met by Gerome, the café owner. Who took the boxes away to the cellar.

Monique sat down and reached for a cigarette.

"Saw you had company," she said, "trouble?"

"No, just routine checks. You brought gifts?"

"Candles, for Gerome, and there is kerosene in the back yard for his generator. We have been playing Father Christmas all over Mons. Cafes, hospitals, clinics, bars. The group gets twenty percent of all candle sales and thirty percent for kerosene."

"It's on for tonight then?" asked Hildy.

Monique looked at the café clock.

"We'll know in an hour," she said.

"How is Agnes?" asked Jack.

"She is on edge, but managing. She is keeping a low profile and getting her head down in work and keeping her eye out for danger. It has been a shock though. But I think hiding in plain sight is good. Her major is unlikely to visit the back rooms of the legal office, he is too busy murdering children in the street. Agnes copes."

Jack, Hildy and Georgia had remained up in the bell tower for many hours after the square had been cleared and took a long time to return to some kind of calm. They hadn't quite believed what they had seen, couldn't accept it as real. The casual, insouciant manner of its execution, and against no more than children. It was a barbarism and brutality that defied understanding but it brought home the urgency of their mission. They had talked until the night crept in and the air cooled, and their guts warmed on a rage of murder and revenge, and a fear that all was under threat of being lost. The risks had now become even greater, their situation the more perilous.

"We just have to deal with it," Jack said. "We now know why we are here. Seeing that in the square suddenly makes it all so very real and very immediate. It was like an electric shock."

"It takes some getting used to," Hildy said. "I know it's what we were trained for but that doesn't make it any less awful. We were sent over to get the resistance groups working together. I had put the idea of the rest of the mission out of my mind. But it hits home hard now. We are an execution squad. It doesn't feel comfortable. But after today, I know it has to be done."

"It has come as a shock to us all," Jack said. "It just shows that if we are to beat these bastards we have to be as ruthless and savage as they are. We have no choice, even if we don't like it."

"I am now the weak link," Georgia said. She held up a

hand as the other began to protest, "We must be realistic," she said. "This changes how the team can operate. How I can operate. I need to keep out of the limelight, to move backstage into the shadows. We can't afford to have Ernst discover me. Not until I am ready."

"Ready?" asked Jack, "Ready for what?"

"Why, to kill him, of course," Georgia said.

By the time they rose and made their way across the dark rooftops towards the church spire they had agreed a plan of action. News of her husband's presence need not be shared with London, at least not yet. The mission would carry on. Jack and Hildy would concentrate on co-ordinating the local groups while Georgia would use her newfound job to locate the whereabouts of the three Belgian traitors. Jack and Hildy would split up, Jack coming to Mons, Hildy staying at the farm. It was agreed that the less time they spent together, the safer it would be for all. Georgia would have to work alone and detach herself from the other two. She would liaise with the others through Monique.

They had found the fire exit and climbed down to the street. They stood at the foot of the ladder in a close huddle, checking for danger. Georgia reached out and took each of their hands in hers. She kissed Jack on the cheek and Hildy on her forehead.

"It's been an honour. Really an honour. Be lucky and blessed," she said. She turned on her heel and strode away into the night. Jack and Hildy had not seen her since.

Monique leaned forward on the table and spoke in low tones.

"Agnes has found the files on Guy Delmain, Henri Latuse and Michel Le Fointeau. Delmain and Latisse are in the Mons area. Le Fointeau is in hospital in Brussels. Broken shoulder from a motor accident."

Monique glanced around the café and then slipped a note across the table to Hildy.

"Delmain and Latisse are currently active. These are their last known addresses. Agnes says they seem to move around a lot. They report to Colonel Hauptman in the

Wehrmacht. Are they traitors?"

Jack explained the nature of their interest. Monique was silent for some time.

"You are sure they are doing this? Bringing allied airmen to the Germans?"

"As certain as we can be."

Monique lapsed to thoughtful silence again.

"Then they are traitors to the resistance also. It rings bells. Many in the marquis will now not help downed airmen because too many who have done so in the past have been betrayed. Have disappeared. They say the wings on the badges of allied pilots are of gathering angels, not eagles. They bring death. What do you plan to do?"

"Find them and kill them," Jack said, "and anyone else working with them and the Germans. To cleanse the escape line of traitors."

Monique was silent for some time.

"I will see to Le Fointeau," she said. "It is time I got my hands dirty and out of books."

"How can you do this?" asked Jack, "He is in the hospital."

Monique smiled. "I will talk with a spider," she said, "there are many nurses and doctors wrapped in her web. Leave Michel to us. I will let Agnes know when it is done. But how will you kill the other two?"

Jack leaned back in his chair and drained the last of his cold coffee.

"I was wondering about maybe becoming a downed airman," he said. "Our friends have returned."

The German officer and sergeant had entered the café once more, moving among the tables checking papers.

"Persistent buggers, aren't they," Jack said.

The officer arrived at their table.

"Selling tractors is hard work I see," he said. He turned to Monique, "and this is another engineer no doubt. Papers."

Monique held out her papers, the officer snatched them and studied them.

"You live in Mons?"

"All my life."

"Doing what?"

"I work in the library. I am the assistant manager."

"These are friends of yours?"

"No. I have not met them until tonight."

"Why are you meeting them?"

"They wanted a list of all the farms about. They are selling farm equipment or tractors or something like that. Hoped the library might be able to help."

"And could you?"

"As I was just telling them, the library has such lists. They will come in to the library tomorrow and copy it."

"And how much will it cost them?"

"Just shoe leather and time. The library is a free public service."

"Pah! This is a peasant country." The officer threw Monique's papers across the table, "infested by feudal serfs."

The café air buzzed and then crackled and all the lights went out. The café was in darkness and outside the lights of the square and its buildings were also off.

"What is this?" the officer said. His voice was anxious and alarmed. It rose in pitch. "Is it a raid?" he called out into the dark. "Is there a generator here? What about candles? Get them! Someone bring light now! That is an order!"

There was a flash of a match and moments later two waiters entered with lit candles in bottles like a religious processional. They placed a candle on each of the tables.

The officer was conscious that his pistol had appeared in his hand and was searching the mirk about him with frantic sweeps. He regained a degree of calm and returned the pistol to its holster.

"Sergeant, check with the patrols. Find out what is happening." The soldier left the café.

"It's a power blackout," Monique said. "That's what happened. The power grid is down. Probably someone pulled the wrong lever, pressed the wrong button."

"We Germans do not press wrong buttons," the officer

said, "Germans do not do this. It is the work of the resistance and their saboteurs. They will pay a terrible price for this."

The sergeant beckoned from the café entrance. The officer gazed at the three expressionless, candlelit faces before him

"This is what we will do," he said. He leant down and swept his arm across the table. The candle, bottles, glasses and pastries went crashing the floor. "Just like that," he said, "Like corn before the scythe. No need for tractors when we have machine-guns. It is how all peasant races fall. To a superior race and superior weapons."

He turned on his heel and strode from the café.

Jerome appeared with another candle and placed it on their table.

"Excitable sort, our young officer," Gerome said. He began sweeping up the crockery shards and mopping the table, "and positively no manners at all. It appears the demonstration was a success."

He handed out three new glasses and filled them with a blood red wine. He raised his own glass.

"To the power of darkness," he said, "may it shine its light in London and keep the Germans busy for a few days."

"Two at most," Monique said. "Or at least that's what the bods tell me. But enough to make our point, eh?"

"We will let London know," Jack said. "Give Giselle your list and we will deliver it."

THIRTY ONE

Jerome handed Gregor the small glass of brandy and gave him an encouraging punch on the shoulder.

"For courage," said Jerome. Gregor tipped the drink back in one. He coughed lightly and his eyes watered, but he didn't gag. He grinned.

"Another when you return," said Jerome. "Now remember, I found him in my cellar asleep. He says he is an English airmen. I sent you to find someone in the marquis, Ravel the grocer sent you on to the Bar Andre to find Guy Delmain. OK? That's all you need to say. Bring him back here, to the cellar."

"What if he won't come?"

"He will come, trust me. Now go. Do your work for Belgium, eh?"

Gregor left the café.

Jack slid his thumb knife into the small sheath strapped to his inner forearm and shucked the shirt and jacket over his head. The trousers were too big, the tied-rope belt too tight and the shirt smelt of oil and sweat. He wondered whose it was. The ensemble had come from Monique, the boots from Jerome.

Jack stood before Jerome.

"What do you think? Shot down airmen and on the run enough?"

"Forgive me," said Jerome, "But not quite."

Jack didn't see or expect the right fist that slammed into the side of his face. A crack of pain exploded in his cheek and he reeled back, blood already oozing from his nose...

"What the hell…"

"You escaped from a crashing plane two days ago," said Jerome, "you need to look like you did. Delmain may be a traitor but he is no fool. Here take this cloth and hold it to your nose. The blood will stop by the time Delmain is here."

They didn't have to wait long. Jack heard Gregor's eager, urgent voice in the side alley, he was encouraging someone along in his wake. Jerome sat on a crate on the far side of the cellar, a pistol held on Jack, who cowered in a corner. Jerome gave him an encouraging smile.

Gregor came into the cellar followed by a lean, middle-aged man with hunched shoulders, heavy jowl stubble and a scarlet red bandana loosely knotted at the neck. His movements were wary and his pale eyes darted the room. They rested on Jack, crouching in his cellar corner, and studied him for a while.

"I found him asleep in here this morning," said Jerome, "didn't know what to do so sent the boy to Ravel. Says he's an English airman. But my English is poor and his French is nothing. You can't trust anything anymore. He could be a spy."

Delmain nodded slowly. He broke into a grin.

"You are quite right, Jerome, trust is of the past. You were right to call me. Have you checked him for papers?"

"Yes, he has none. Just the clothes. I think he stole them from a tinker. He smells bad. I can't have him here. I have a café to run. I can't get mixed up in all this. You understand? "

"Quite so, Jerome, I understand. It is most sensible. Why make trouble eh? It is for the best. I can take him off your hands. I know someone who might help. Find a safe house for him. Then we can see whether he is friend or foe, eh? You did right. What any true Belgian would do." He patted Jerome reassuringly on the shoulder and turned to face Jack.

"What is your name?" asked Delmain in English.

"Pilot Officer Dalton,"

"When were you shot down? What was your flight and mission?"

"The plane crashed three nights ago. I've been on the run since then."

"What squadron? What mission?"

Jack gazed into Delmain's pale, eager eyes. They seemed to burn with a lustful pleasure of his discovery. Like a snake before a wounded and downed bird.

"Pilot Officer Henry Dalton, 8122397," he said.

Delmain laughed.

"Well he is no fool," he said. "You did right Jerome. I will take him now." Delmain made a show of pulling a pistol from the inside of his jacket, checking the chamber and then summoning Jack to stand.

"You did well Jerome. And you too boy. But now it is silence. He wasn't here. You weren't here and all mouths are shut, yes? Understand? Good."

He gestured his gun towards the cellar door. "After you Dalton. You follow my instructions exactly or I will shoot you in the back and leave you in the street for the rats, do you understand?"

Jack walked ahead of Delmain, obeying the whispered directions from behind.

"Along the street. Walk slow Dalton, like it is every day. Turn right into Rue Fontaine. Here. Remember I have a gun in my jacket. Now past the butchers and turn left into Rue St. Denis."

Jack fixed his gaze ahead and hoped that Hildy was tracking them. He was unaware that they were being followed, which he took for a good sign, Beaulieu taught its agents well.

"Wait"

Delmain paused to light a cigarette and check the street scene around and behind them. Satisfied, he urged Jack on. They walked the streets, often doubling back on themselves, but eventually Jack was stopped outside a funeral parlour. A tall man in a clerk's suit and bow tie rose from his lean at the wall as they approached. Delmain greeted him with false pleasure.

"Henri, we have another recruit for the pigeon club. He claims to have flown far. How is the rest of the coop?"

Henri looked Jack up and down without seeming interest or warmth. His eyes were dark and his skin blotched with the scars of bad youthful acne. Jack realised, with heart pounding, that he was now standing before Henri Latisse, the third member of the treacherous escape line.

"They are up in the flat. Fed and safe. Francois is with

them, standing guard. They are keen to be off. Who is this?"

Delmain scanned up and down the street.

"Not here," he said, "inside."

Jack was ushered into a dim lit and dank alleyway beside the parlour and in through a side door and up a flight of stairs into a sparsely furnished room over the parlour. There was a large mattress on the floor, two stools and low table carrying the debris of recent bread and cheese meals. Two men in soiled and torn greatcoats and farmer's boots sat on the floor against a wall. They looked unkempt and tired and watched Jack with wary suspicion.

"We have another of your downed RAF boys," said Delmain cheerily. " You can stay with Donald and Baxter here. Until we can sort out your escape. Things to arrange. You understand. Says his name is Dalton. Another pilot. Is that right Dalton?"

"Yes," said Jack

"And you were shot down on a mission. Where did you say?"

Jack gazed at Delmain and then fixed his gaze on Donald and Baxter. He could only see distrust, fear and fatigue in their eyes.

"Pilot Officer Henry Dalton, 8122397" he said. And said nothing more.

Delmain laughed.

"You English are so stubborn, so suspicious, eh? I leave you all together here. You must have lots to talk about, Get to know each other, eh? Then we bring food and we get you back to England. You are safe here. Francois will be downstairs. You will not be disturbed until we return"

Jack was left with Baxter and Donald. All he could do was to distrust them as much as they distrusted him. It was what any downed pilot on the run would do. Tales of German spies pretending to be downed airman were rife in every airfield bar across Britain.

Jack took his time to study the room, looking for what he knew would be there. The street window curtains were part drawn and the natural light was subdued, almost dim.

The mattress on the floor was stained and bedraggled and the room contained little else apart from a low, small table, a couple of stools and an empty open shelf unit. Paint peeled from the walls and the bare-board floor smelt damp and musty. Then he saw it, above the frame of the door, a small electrical junction unit, no bigger than a matchbox. The wires were new. Jack knew it wasn't a junction box. It was a listening microphone.

"On the run two days, eh?" It was Baxter. "Pretty tough I imagine."

Jack said nothing. Baxter was a thick-set, curly-haired man with a thin moustache and a crooked nose.

"I'm from Bristol," said Baxter. "What I'd give to be there now. Where are you from?"

"London," said Jack.

"I know London," said Donald. He was a small man with a flyweight's shoulders and compact build. "Lived there all me life. Borough of Reigate. Know it?"

Jack said nothing. Baxter and Donald shared a look.

"John and I have been arguing," said Baxter, "Not much else to do here. I say Ascot but he says Doncaster. Where do they run the Gold Cup? Do you know?"

Jack stood up to make sure that they were watching him. He put a theatrical finger to his lips. He stepped over to the door and gently lifted up the small box with its wires to show to the others. He cupped a hand to his ear and then replaced the box back on top the door. He retraced his steps and sat down.

"Gold Cup's in Cheltenham, isn't it? Never been there myself. Dropped the kite in on Staverton airfield a few times though. Know it? Just by Cheltenham. Always get a warm welcome from Big Sal at the canteen there."

Baxter smiled and nodded to Donald. Big Sal was well known in the flying fraternity. Jack silently thanked Merchant for his background briefing. Small snippets make for truer truths. Jack had never met Big Sal but he knew she must be quite a girl.

"Big Sal," Baxter said, "now there's a girl worth your

sugar ration eh?"

Baxter gave Jack a nod and thumbs up.

The three fugitives fell to making small talk and inconsequential banter. The best last meal. Favourite holiday destination. Greatest England fast bowler. Best night club in London. Anything as long as it was nothing. It was a waiting game.

***

Hildy watched the alleyway and front of the funeral parlour from the shadows and hide of the doorway of an abandoned shop. The shop had been a jewellers, but was now just empty shelves and racks. She had seen Jack with Delmain and the other man that she came to recognise with something of a shock, was Latisse. They had stopped and talked briefly outside the parlour then they had disappeared into the alley, moments later she had seen movement at the front window curtains on the first floor. A while later Delmain and Latisse had emerged back onto the street and shared a smoke and long talk before another man came from the parlour and they all disappeared back inside.

Hildy considered the options ahead of her. Two of the escape-line traitors were now in the parlour along the street, together with a least one other who was working with them. There may be others, but Hildy had seen no one else and knew that any more were likely to be too much of a crowd for this type of chaperone work. Jack was inside and would presumably be taken on somewhere by Delmain or Latisse and handed on to the Wehrmacht, or even the SS. She might try to follow and intercept them somehow but there were at least three of them that might provide escort for Jack, and there was only one of her. Jack might even be shackled in some way. It would be smart for Delmain and the others to take Jack out together and then split apart. Any tracker couldn't follow all three. They would probably leave by car which would make following them almost impossible. The mission was to kill Delmain and Latisse and if was to be done, it had best to be done now.

Hildy reached into her coat pocket, checked her pistol and the six cartridges in its magazine, which she clipped to the long gun-barrel and nestled it in her coat pocket. She was a farm girl no more. She was a trained assassin. Her targets no more than bounding field rabbits.

The street appeared quiet. Hildy sauntered across the road, her heart pounding and her ears alert to every sound. She tried to appear casual and normal, just walking between appointments, nothing out of the ordinary. Standing before the funeral parlour window she looked in at the display of wreaths and tombstones. An ash wood coffin was open in display on a far wall, black and scarlet ribbon hung like cobwebs in the window bay.

The alley to the side of the parlour was blind, a far wall marking its end with various bins and boxes littering its base. A thin, young man in a worker's jacket and flat cap leaned casual to the alley wall, just inside from the street. He was the man she had seen speaking earlier with Delmain and Latisse and was now assigned guard watch duties in the alley. He watched Hildy with a leery grin.

Hildy walked into the alley and was past the man before he really knew it. He sprang from his lean at the wall and grabbed Hildy's arm.

"Hold on there, missy. Where are you going eh? This is private property. Can't just wander in."

"Albert died," said Hildy. She sought distraction and confusion in her voice. "I must bury him. He needs to be buried. My Albert. You see? I must speak with the undertaker. It was so sudden. He went. In a moment. No time to makes plans. I have to see hm." She wandered the alley absently, looking for the door, talking to herself.

The man tried to pull her away.

"You don't see no one without an appointment. Anyway the parlour's closed for the day. Undertaker gone to Valenciennes. For a wedding. Yeah, that's right, a wedding. So be off with you. Come back tomorrow,"

Hildy pulled out of his grasp and moved into the alley.

"No, no, my Albert has to be buried. Today. Don't you see?" She moved confused among the rubbish and wood and metal that littered the alley. "Has to be today, you see?" She idly picked up a short metal bar and seemed surprised it was in her hand

The man followed her.

"Yeah very sad. Poor Albert. But he's not getting buried today. The undertaker is away, I told you, now get out and go back home or I'll be happy to persuade you." The man pulled a long bladed knife from inside his jacket. "Understand? "

Hildy pulled the pistol from her coat pocket and pointed it at the man's head. She was still and calm, all her feigned distractions gone.

"How many upstairs?" she asked.

The man looked at the gun and then at Hildy. The colour and menace seemed to drain instantly from him.

"Don't know what you mean," he said.

"There's Delmain, Latisse and you. Anyone else?"

"Fuck you," said the man. He pulled back his arm to throw his knife. It never got past half-cock. Hildy swung the metal bar hard and fast into the man's head and he instantly crumpled to his knees, the knife falling from his grasp to clatter on the cobbles

Hildy dragged the comatose body to the base of the wall and hid it behind the bins and rubbish. She slid his knife into her skirt belt, flung the metal bar to the rubbish pile. Pocketing the gun, she re-buttoned her coat and entered the side door.

She crept up the stairs and listened at the door.

"We will move you individually," Delmain said. "It is safer that way. Too many tramps together will raise suspicion and we need to keep you safe and away from the SS. You understand?"

"How far are we going?" Jack asked

"No more than half-an hour away. We walk slow and easy. It is a safe house where we can feed you and you can sleep. Then we will get you out of Mons, by truck. Maybe tonight. Make for Antwerp. Then passage across to England. It is good, no?"

"When do we leave?"

"We begin now. All is ready. I will take you and Latisse can stay with Baxter and Donald. Then I come back for them. OK?"

Hildy knew it was time to act. They would miss their alley guard and find him knocked out. They would summon help from their German masters and Jack would be whisked away. She opened the door to a peeked crack and saw Jack and two other men seated against a far wall, Latisse and Delmain stood with their backs to door. She took the Welrod from her coat, checked the magazine and safety and moved silently into the room. She brought the Welrod up to the head of the nearest traitor, it was Latisse.

Phht.

Before Latisse's limp body had hit the floorboards Hildy had swung the Welrod to a heavy press against Delmain's cheek.

"Move one muscle and you die," she said. Delmain froze, his yellow eyes wide in confusion and alarm.

Jack sprang from his seat on the floor and began checking Latisse for papers and weapons.

"Pleased to see you! I knew you wouldn't be far away," said Jack smiling. "Just hoped you wouldn't be too late. What about Francois in the alley?"

"Unconscious, but I don't know for how long."

"Baxter, find something to tie Delmain. Then we'd better think of moving out. They are bound to have made arrangements and rendezvous."

Baxter and Donald were standing mute and confused. They stared at Hildy in half wonder, half terror. They sought to collect their thoughts and say something, but they couldn't.

"You were being taken to the Nazis," Jack explained, "our friends here are working for the Germans, pretending to be resistance helping downed airman escape back to England. But they just feed them to their Nazi friends. We have been sent out here to stop them."

"You are mistaken," said Delmain. He was scanning the room, his face pale and panicked, searching for escape or understanding. "This is all wrong. I am no traitor. I work to help the resistance. To help Belgium. A patriot. To help you. This is madness!"

Donald looked at Latisse lying dead, his coat and shirt ripped open, and his papers now being pocketed by Dalton.

"So who are you?" Donald said. "Who is this man? What about him?" he pointed at the body of Latisse.

Jack stood and pocketed Latisse's pistol. He checked over a few of the papers he had retrieved from his pockets.

"We are soldiers," Jack said, "of sorts. The secret kind. Working behind the lines. Hidden soldiers wearing civilian uniforms. Like glass soldiers in water. Take Delmain's neck tie and bind his hands."

Baxter did as he was bid.

"These two gentlemen," said Hildy, "and the one downstairs, are members of a group of Belgian traitors working for the Germans. They were going to feed you both down the escape line to the SS."

Jack passed a small card over to Baxter.

"A German identity pass. In the name of Latisse. The body at your feet."

"What are we going to do with the other one?" Baxter asked.

"We're going to kill him," said Jack. "Unless he talks,"

***

From a window of a first floor office Georgia looked down on the various comings and goings of the undertaker's alley with growing confusion and concern. She had seen Jack and the two traitors enter the parlour and could see shadows of movement in the flat above the parlour. She had tried to imagine the scene and activities playing out in hidden, dumb show before her and to identify and locate the characters. She thought she had it about figured, but the arrival of Hildy on the scene and to watch her cross the street and enter the alley and out of view, only sought to confuse her mind further. She also saw that little Gregor had obviously been following Hildy and was now hiding in a doorway watch further down the street.

Georgia had learned from Monique of Jack's plan to become downed airman bait. Furtive searches of the legal office files had revealed the undertaker's parlour as the likely venue for the pick-up as it seemed to be the traitor's safe-house of choice in previous betrayals. That the exchange deception was going to be taking place had been secreted to her by someone in the legal office leaving a note in her coat pocket. Georgia had no idea who her mystery messenger was and she was content to not try and find out, inept or ignorant investigation was likely to imperil both detective and suspect. Better to leave still waters calm.

The card had noted the date and address and was signed "friend". It might well have been a hoax of course, or bait of its own to get her exposed, but the picture of a spider web drawn in a corner of the card and the name Albert hanging in thread from it convinced her of its authenticity. Georgia had checked the street of the rendezvous point and found the abandoned first floor office opposite the parlour. On the appointed day she had called in sick, checked and pocketed her Welrod and taken up vigil at the upper office window.

Georgia reasoned that as long as all remained contained in the parlour there was little call or need for her intervention. She was contemplating the possible scenarios when a tall man came into view, striding purposefully down the street. The figure wore a long, dark coat and sported a wide-brimmed homburg. The man came to a stop outside the undertaker's parlour and stood before the window. He used the mirror of the parlour window to adjust and straighten his tie. Then he removed his hat, swept a hand-comb through his hair, replaced the hat and tugged its brim to shape.

In the fleeting seconds between the hat's removal and replacement Georgia found herself looking at the unmistakeably aquiline and aristocratic features of Emile Gustave Francois de Greveney Boudelain, the Count of Breaville.

Boudelain stood at the entrance to the alley and seemed to be calling to someone. Moments later he disappeared into the alley only to emerge to view again pulling and pushing someone ahead of him. It was the man that Georgia had seen talking with Delmain earlier. He sought lean by a wall and seemed groggy and confused and held his hand to his head. Delmain was shaking and slapping him back to some kind of consciousness and sense and the talk seemed urgent and forceful. Boudelain reached inside his long coat and pulled out a Mauser automatic pistol. He checked its mag and safety. He reached into another pocket and pulled out a smaller Sauer pistol and forced it into the hands of his still groggy ally and pushed him into the alley and out of view.

***

Jack dragged Latisse's body to the corner of the room. Hildy was helping Baxter tie Delmain's hands behind his back.

"You're making a huge mistake," said Delmain, "I am no traitor. This is madness. I am a true patriot."

"Where were you going to take us?" said Jack. "Who is your contact?"

"To a safe house. The contact I cannot say. I do not know. We do not work with names it is too dangerous. But to a safe house. Untie me I am not a criminal. This is all wrong."

"You are working with the Wehrmacht. We know this. Who do you report to? Tell me"

"This is madness! I am loyal Belgian. I do not work for the Germans."

Jack grabbed Delmain by his collar.

"Tell me! Who gives you your orders? Who do you report to?"

"Well, Jack, I suppose you could say he reports to me."

The voice oozed with a calm, iced confidence. It froze

the room. It was quiet, but it commanded all the eyes in the room to turn towards it.

Boudelain stood by the door holding a semi-automatic Mauser at arms-length pointing at Jack. By his side, a still slightly woozy, Francois held a pistol on Hildy

Boudelain smiled and stepped a few paces into the room. He scanned the room with casual expertise, never seeming to take his eyes from Jack and Hildy.

"I can see you have had quite a party. Untie Delmain," he said. Hildy hesitated.

"You either untie him or you die Miss Potts, the choice is entirely yours."

Hildy freed Delmain from his bonds. Delmain immediately stepped to Boudelain's side rubbing his wrists.

"They jumped me," he said, "they know about the escape line. I didn't tell them. They knew already. Someone has talked."

"Shut up you fool," Boudelain.said, "Get their guns. Check them over. All of you back against the wall. Hands up high.

Delmain and Francois herded the four prisoners to a line against a wall. Their guns were taken and thrown on the table top.

"You know, I just knew I would see you again, Jack," Boudelain said. "I just had that feeling, you know? Something about your Beaulieu failure always had the whiff of deceit. A subterfuge. One gets a nose for it. And Miss Potts. I knew you didn't fail. You were both too good. So Townsend is running his own team now is he? Sent you here to chase me down eh?"

The line at the wall was silent.

Boudelain laughed. "Of course they did. I must be a terrible embarrassment for all the Wardour Street brass hats. Led them a pretty dance haven't I? And now they will have their revenge. Well, that hasn't quite worked out either, has it?"

"What do we do with them?" asked Delmain. "Kill them?"

"Of course, But not yet. We need to get them to Rue sur Ville and Major von Staffel. He will deal with them. We will send the girl first. Tie her hands and take her. Tell von Staffel I sent you. Get him to bring troops and a truck back to pick up the rest of them. Francois and I will keep them here. But don't be long. If the girl gives any trouble just kill her. Don't take risks, she fights bulls. Now go! And come back quickly!"

***

The possible scene in the parlour flat was now too complicated for Georgia to fathom with any degree of clarity or confidence. She left her office hide and moved down to the street and managed to come up behind Gregor in his doorway without discovery. Gregor turned in fright as she touched his shoulder but quickly regained his calm and courage. He told Georgia what he knew, which was little. He had just followed Giselle because he thought she might need help.

Georgia told Gregor what she believed was happening inside the undertaker's parlour flat and who they were.

"Now if any one comes out of the flat and alleyway I want you to follow them, OK Gregor? Find out where they go and then come back here and tell me. Got that?"

Gregor nodded, his eyes wide with fear and fortitude. "I can do this, yes."

"But no heroics, Gregor promise me. We just need to know where they go. Understand?"

"Yes, so what do we do now?"

"We can only wait and see them play their hand."

It was only a few minutes of waiting. Hiding in their doorway they saw Hildy emerge from out of the alley with Delmain close behind her, they seemed almost co-joined. Hildy was walking slowly and Georgia could see her hands were bound behind her and Delmain was holding a gun to her back.

"They are taking Giselle!" whispered Gregor with alarm.

"They have her!"

"Follow them, Gregor. But carefully. Find out where they are taking her and come back to tell me. This is very important, Gregor. Have courage. Giselle relies on you." She kissed him on the top of his head. He smelt of straw. "Now go!"

She watched Gregor cross the road and saunter along the opposite kerb, his hands deep in his pockets, keeping watchful distance on his prey. They all disappeared from view around a distant corner.

Georgia checked the Welrod in her coat, took a last check along the street and entered the alley.

***

Jack knelt on the floor, hands clasped to the back of his head. Baxter and Donald knelt with him. Jack was calculating his chances of getting the thumb knife from his arm sheath and hurling it at Boudelain, before either he or Francois could get a shot off. He knew the chances were slim to nil. He would just have to play this one by events, and hope that chance, any chance, might show itself.

His mind turned to Hildy and he felt his guts ice at the thought of what would now happen to her. Death would be the least of it, there would be plenty of tortuous persuasion before that final release. Jack's head burned at the thought of Hildy in pain. Of how he had allowed her to be taken without a fight. Hildy with those cow eyes and shy smile, The resourceful, kind, clever and braver than a bull Hildy. His Hildy. He wondered if it was love, or just guilt that was overwhelming him. All he knew was that Hildy had been taken and he wanted her back with him at his side, and that he was going to do whatever it took, whatever it needed, to make that happen.

Boudelain, was still crowing with arrogant triumph over his besting of all at SOE and Beaulieu.

"I just flew out," Boudelain said. "It was so easy. The fools even supplied the petrol. The whole of SOE is a security nightmare. So casual and amateur. Gubbins, Mann, Green, they're all incompetent donkeys. Empire soldiers of the last war. I was there in Beaulieu for nearly two years and they never suspected me once. I told you, I am a great spy. The best."

Jack and the other remained silent.

Boudelain smiled.

"You won't be silent for long my friends," he said, "Von Staffel and his doctors have ways of loosening tongues. They are masters at it. They will be here soon and we can all take a nice ride to Rue sur Ville. The cells there are not very pleasant I'm afraid, but you will not be in them long. Yes, I knew you were not failed. You were too good. They could not fail the great burglar and the sharp shooter. And what about that other one? The beautiful one. The peahen with the long legs and siren curves. What happened to her, eh?"

"I didn't go very far Boudelain, Right behind you, actually."

Phht

Boudelain cried out in pain as his hand exploded and his gun fell to the floor. Francois turned to face the voice and found himself looking into the barrel of Georgia's Welrod pistol. It was his very last sight.

Phht.

Francois crumpled to the floor at Boudelain's feet. Georgia brought her pistol to a pressed rest against Boudelain's pale and throbbing temple.

"Move Count, and you join the other dead rat on the floor."

Boudelain was panting against the pain in his hand and straining hard not to show it. He studied his mangled, bloodied hand with an almost detached disbelief. He tried to stand tall and bring his shattered hand rest against his chest, as if to comfort it. He cradled it with his other hand for support. He began to sweat with the pain and fear.

"I was right. I knew it. I knew you never failed," he said. "I knew it."

Jack and the others had risen to their feet. Jack retrieved Francois' gun and Baxter and Donald dragged his body to the corner to join Latisse. Jack tossed the gun to Donald.

"Keep a watch at the widow." Jack turned to Georgia, "Never have I been more pleased to see you!" Jack said. He kissed Georgia's cheek. "They've taken Hildy,"

"I know, I saw her leave with Delmain. Gregor is following them. He will come back and tell us where they've taken her. What do we do with this bastard?"

"He's a traitor. We have our orders. Kill him."

"You cannot kill me." said Boudelain, "It would be murder. Plain murder. The English do not execute. I am just a soldier doing my duty. I am wounded. It is against the rules of war." Boudelain winced against his pain. Blood was running down his arm and darkening the elbow of his coat.

"What rules would they be, Count? Rules of loyalty and justice?"

"I am just a soldier doing my duty. A soldier under orders. War rules. It is the way of war."

"By betraying Belgium and the Allies and all those agents at Beaulieu?" Jack said, "Weren't they soldiers too? Some even your friends? Don't hide behind duty and blame orders, Boudelain. We all have to make our choices, one way or another. And we live and die by them. You chose wrong. You're just another pathetic, self-serving thug on the make for whom the war is a convenient path to power and riches."

"And why not? Why should I have loyalty to a Belgium that stole my family's estates and made them into factories for wire and hospitals for cripples. All for this stupid war. So why shouldn't I fight to get my name and my lands back. Belgium does not want me, it treats me like a common peasant, but I am the Count de Breaville and cannot be treated so. Germany sees my injustice and respects my name. They will restore my family to its rightful position, return my lands. I did what is right."

"And what about Pederson, Peters, Stuvenson, Gregson and all the others? Was what you did to them right?"

Boudelain shrugged. "Fortunes of war. In war some people die, and some people live. Nothing more."

"We need to be moving," Georgia said. "We'll have a truck of soldiers on our doorstep soon."

"You have to take me with you," Boudelain said. "To kill me would be murder. The English do not execute. They believe in justice. You know I am right."

"No, Boudelain," Jack said, "that justice is dead. Now, like you, we only believe in the fortunes of war. War rules. It changes us all. I will live, so you must die. There is nothing more."

Jack raised his gun and shot Boudelain in the chest.

Phht.

Boudelain rocked back, his eyes wide with alarm and disbelief. He staggered, tried to raise his hand and then fell back and hit the floor like a felled tree. Jack stood over his body and shot him again in the head. An execution of his orders and of his duty. A traitor's execution. He almost felt elation in its end, like a burden lifted and chains unloosed. And in that moment he knew he wasn't going to die. Not yet. He checked Boudelain's pockets and took the papers and wallet and stuffed them into his coat.

"I'll take Baxter and Donald to Jerome," said Jack, "You wait across the road somewhere and wait for Gregor. Then we'll meet up at the café tonight. It would be good to get Monique there too. Let's go."

Georgia sheltered in Gregor's doorway down the street and comforted herself with a calming cigarette. She watched Jack and the others walking briskly away down the street and disappear from view. It had begun to rain a light drizzle and the street was quiet, an occasional bicycle passed and a couple of pedestrians carrying bags or pushing prams, but that was all.

It was several minutes before she heard the sound of the truck coming along the street and saw it come to a skidded stop outside the funeral parlour. It was a German troop truck. Six soldiers and an officer jumped down from the truck and headed into the alley. Georgia could see Delmain sitting in the front passenger seat of the cab. The driver got out of his side of cab and strolled into the alley for a piss and a cigarette.

Georgia moved out of her hide and walked on the blind side of the truck. As she came alongside the cab window she looked in. Delmain sat idling chewing a toothpick and staring up the road at nothing. He turned, un-picked and straightened at the sight of the young, attractive woman in his window. He grinned.

Georgia smiled warmly. Up in the flat she could hear raised voices. The smoking soldier disappeared from view into the alley. She lifted the Welrod to a rest on the cab window

"A present from London" Georgia said. Delmain's features froze, his face instantly paled. He was about to cry out. He was given no chance.

Phht.

Delmain slumped sideways silently across the seat. Georgia needed to make sure.

Phht.

Georgia pocketed the pistol, turned her collar up to the lightly falling rain and strolled on her way up the street.

THIRTY TWO

Captain Townsend watched the stream of visitors and clerks flow in and out and around the suite of offices. From his seat in the corridor it looked like a busy insect hive of comings and goings, of files and briefcases, reports and tea trays and clusters of whispering groups and earnest, striding clerks. All were in uniform of one kind or another, even the women secretaries.

The clock on the far wall showed it was now past midnight, but the hive still buzzed. Sam Franks sat beside him glancing through a magazine, seemingly unconcerned at the lateness of the hour, or of their lightly steaming uniforms. The rain had been torrential in the short walk from Wardour Street and Townsend felt like he had walked through a lake. He dripped onto the plush, green carpet, a growing damp shadow of a darker green pooling at his feet.

A bright-smiling and attractive young Wren seemed to operate as organiser and gatekeeper of the hive and Townsend was as much taken by her calm energy and efficiency in all that confronted her as he was by her other charms. During a brief lull in her traffic control and organising duties she had managed to find two large towels for Townsend and Sam.

"Sorry about this wait." she said. "The Colonel is anxious to clear all his decks before meeting you. Colonel Foster will be joining us as well and he's stuck in Whitehall, but should be here imminently. I'll make sure there is a good fire in the Colonel's grate. That will soon dry you out. Oh dear, here's Major Anderson coming. I have to fend him off. The Colonel is not in the mood tonight for his problems. Excuse me gentlemen,"

They watched the Wren warmly greet a surly looking Major with a handle-bar moustache and expertly guide and turn him mid-stream and escort him away down a side corridor. She emerged moments later, Major-less, and then disappeared into Colonel Amies' office.

"Now that's the way to win a war," said Sam, "with grace, guile and efficiency"

"And a little beauty and nice smile helps too," said Townsend. Sam raised an eyebrow.

"Potent weapons of war to be sure," he said. "Are your wounds deep?"

Townsend laughed.

"I can think of worse ways to die."

It was a half past midnight before the corridors had reduced to just a trickle of insect clerks. The Wren appeared at Colonel Amies' office door and called them in.

Colonel Amies welcomed them and indicated the leather chairs by a large fire. Colonel Foster was already seated and nodded them a warm welcome.

"Robbins said you were drenched so she had me make up a roarer for you. Soon dry you out. Dare say Robbins can rustle up some brandy."

Even as he said it Wren Robbins appeared at his shoulder with a tray of glasses and brandy bottle. She placed it on the table and poured four glasses."

"Don't forget yourself, Robbins. A perk for working so late. Any of those Belgian butter biscuits left, or did General Harris filch the lot?"

Amies sat in a leather chair and stretched his legs before him. Tonight his socks were of a canary yellow. Townsend rather envied a pair.

"So, Matthew, you have some news of our Belgian adventure, eh?"

Townsend was taken aback by being called by his name but tried not to show either his shock or pleasure at the compliment. He was aware of Wren Robbins sitting at a desk by the door, watching him.

"Well Colonel, it is rather delicate. Need to know and all that."

"Oh, you mean Robbins! Don't worry about Robby. Trust her like my third hand. She's fully cleared. Knows all my secrets, poor lass. Carry on. Everyone in this room is cleared. How are our glasses in water?"

"We had contact earlier tonight. Agent Felis reported that two of the Belgian traitors are now dead. Delmain and Latisse. The third is being dealt with by Group G. They report that Le Fointeau was killed in a Brussels hospital. Induced heart attack. Delmain and Latisse are confirmed kills. We are waiting for final confirmation on Le Fointeau."

"All tidy?" Amies asked. "And quiet? No incriminating crumbs?"

"Clean and clear," Townsend said, "as far as we know. There is more. Count Boudelain appeared on the scene. He was working for his masters in Brussels and happened in on Mons and the false escape line."

"That bastard!" spat Colonel Foster. He realised Robbins was in the room. "Sorry, Robby, forgot myself."

"That is quite alright Colonel. I understand the war is full of them,"

"But to think of him striding around Mons in his jackboots and toasting his Nazi masters in schnapps just boils the blood."

"Well allow me to cool it Colonel," said Townsend. "Boudelain was also killed. By agent Satur. It is a confirmed kill."

"That's the ticket!" said Colonel Foster. He slapped his chair arm in pleasure and spilt his brandy. "Good show and damn good riddance, eh!"

"Fill the glasses Robby!" Amies said. "Well, that is some good news I can share with Winston tomorrow at Chartwell. He was interested to know how the Belgian operation was going, This will cheer him. He was delighted with the Brussels blackout business. He said I asked them to set Europe alight, but a blackout will serve as well for now. He said anything you need just put your request in through me and Sam. How are the drops going?"

"We've made three drops in the last two months. Henri Clerque is working with Group G out of Brussels and they now have eight groups co-ordinated in the network. All groups now have guns, explosives, detonators, mines and grenades. They are ready. We have coded them as the

Spider network."

"And they are clear on their targets?"

"Yes, our agents have devised a co-ordinated sabotage strategy for the groups. All cleared by T Section here in London. Individual targets. Power stations, rail junctions, telephone exchanges, ammunition dumps and roads and bridges. They will make quite a chaos and mess when the call comes."

"Well, hopefully it won't be long," said Forster. "But excellent groundwork by your team Townsend. Damn good show!"

Sam Franks leaned forward in his chair and grinned at Matthew.

"Captain Townsend is probably too modest to say, Colonel," he said, "but his team has also rescued two of our downed pilots from the treacherous escape line. Pilot Officer Donald and Pilot Sergeant Baxter, are on their way by truck to Antwerp even as we enjoy this fine brandy."

Colonel Forster slapped the arm of his chair again.

"Bloody good show!"

"Felis is not the usual contact is she?" Amies asked.

Townsend was almost taken aback by Amies' sudden change of tack. Not for the first time he was aware that behind the casual air and canary socks, Amies' mind was stiletto sharp and on point. He didn't miss anything.

"No sir, it's usually Lupus, Agent Giselle. Not known why she wasn't on the radio."

"Trouble?" asked Amies.

"Nothing to report, sir. Giselle may be ill. Felis didn't report any problem,"

"Do we know it was Felis on the keys?"

"Yes sir, Evans confirmed it was the hand of Felis, Agent Agnes. He trained her and knows her piano style. All the security codes and sign-ins were right. It was Felis."

"Well, that is some good news to end the day. Well done, Matthew," said Amies. "Bound to have stirred up the hornets in Mons though. What are the plans for your three agents? Got an exit strategy?"

"Get them to lie low and we'll find a way to get them out. The Spider network is now equipped and primed. I will send in replacement agents to keep regional plans on track and ticking over."

"The Germans are going to be hunting them with a vengeance," Forster said. "They can't lose four top collaborators like that without it causing alarm. Need to balance the books and then some. Save face. They'll be out hunting in force and with rage. Pity the citizens of Mons, they'll be in for a rough time."

"Good work, Matthew," Amies said. "Get a report to the usual T Section group and I'll make sure Number 10 and Command are in the know. Sure you'll be requested to attend a few meetings over the next few weeks, so get yourself rested and prepared. A new uniform might not come amiss either. Who is your tailor?"

"Er, I don't have one sir,"

"God man! Everyone should have a tailor!"

Amies walked over to his bureau. Robbins had already pulled a card from its drawers. Amies handed the card to Townsend.

"Grieves and Clarke. Ask for Melton and say H sent you. Old cutters and set in their ways but top quality and they don't squint on the thread work. Resist any over indulgence on back venting though. Melton's one blind spot. Now go get some sleep, and well done."

Townsend and Franks were escorted down the now deserted corridor by Wren Robbins.

"It was good of the Colonel to offer me his tailor, but I really am quite happy with my current uniform. It just needs a clean and press that's all."

Robbins smiled.

"I think you'd look very smart in a new uniform. Especially one from Grieves and Clarke."

"But I don't think my bank manager would share your view. I'm only a lowly Captain after all"

Robbins now laughed. Her smile could light tin mines.

"Oh, I am sure you are more than that, Captain

Townsend. But you didn't think the Colonel expected you to buy a new uniform did you? He, of course, will be paying. It is all on his account. It is his way of thanking you. Job well done and all that. Others give out medals and commendations, Colonel Amies gives suits. Or tailored uniforms."

Robbins waved them off from the top of the stairs. Matthew and Sam found themselves on the street. The rain had passed and the smell of wet tar and gas hung in the airs. Townsend was surprised to find that, despite it being nearly two o'clock in the morning, he wasn't feeling very tired at all. Maybe it was the elation of having some success with the Belgian operation, maybe it was even the prospect of a new tailored uniform. He had never had anything tailored in his life before. Or maybe it was the thought of Wren Robbins' smile and the chance that when he had his new uniform he might meet with her and her smile again and show both of them the town.

"Is there a problem with Lupus?" asked Sam. "Strange to break the routine, don't you think? Something amiss?"

Townsend returned his thoughts to duty.

"Perhaps," he said. "But I'm thinking of illness rather than anything more sinister. The contact was certainly Felis and it was all clear and correct. I will keep it in mind and hand, but I don't have any evidence or reason to believe there is anything of a problem yet."

"What kind of problem?"

"Well, she could be ill, or wounded, or, of course, dead."

"Or taken."

"I am sure Satur or Felis would have said. It would jeopardise too many others not to say."

"I know a bar around the corner that stays open until dawn" said Sam. "I think we deserve a drink don't you?"

THIRTY THREE

Jack stared at the building plans spread over the candle-lit table and tried to focus his thoughts. Jerome refilled his wine glass and carried on around the room, filling the glasses of Georgia, Henri, Monique, Gregor and Monsieur Courdan, the public works buildings engineer. Boxes of ammunition, grenades, fuses and rifles from a recent drop piled against the walls of the attic room. They had been gathered just before dawn and now awaited the opportunity for distribution to various groups and safe stores over the coming days. It was the third drop collected in a fortnight and Jerome's large attic now housed an arsenal of boxes of grenades, pistols, detonators and fuses and Georgia was checking then off against the inventory.

A fidgeting but resolute Courdan perched on one of the boxes and tried to hide his nervousness, but he was sweating in the close airs and heat of the attic room. He was a large, pudding of a man with small rimless glasses and sparse, wayward dark hair that coiled his crown like flatworms. He gulped down his third glass of wine and tried to keep his bravery intact. When the call had come from Monique he had responded like a true patriot, a very nervous one, but true. As the Second Deputy Chief Engineer of Public Works in Mons, Phillipe Courdan had ready access to the archives and plans for all the public buildings in the city, including the old police station on Rue sur Ville. He may have been forced to work with the Germans, but he had never worked for them. Stealing the building plans under the watch of the Germans had not been without its dangers or fears, but Courdan had, somehow, come though.

"I can see no way," said Henri. He lit his small pipe. "The place is guarded front and back, night and day. Busy all the time. And that is before you face the cells in the cellars. Do we have the cellar plans Courdan?"

Courdan searched the papers in his brief case and began pulling some out. He scanned them briefly.

"There are six cells in the cellar floor and two more up on the third floor, to the back of the building. The cells are iron grill with Folger and Adam deadlocks and lock bolts. The two third-floor cells are half wooden door and iron bar construction with high level deadlock and deadbolt security."

"And each cell is guarded by at least one soldier, day and night," said Monique.

"It would help if we knew where she was being held," said Jack. He downed his wine and reached for a cigarette.

"Giselle is being held in one of the upper cells," said Gregor. All eyes turned to him, he seemed to shrink a little. "I think,"

"It is not the time to think, Gregor," said Henri, "it is the time to know. To be sure. Why do you think Giselle is in the upper cells?"

Gregor collected his thoughts.

"When I followed the man and Giselle to Rue sur Ville I waited outside on the street with the German drivers and sentries. Listening and watching. They gave me cigarettes. One, a sergeant I think, was a driver and he told the others that he had been chosen to drive the prisoner truck to the station in the morning. A special prisoner. After some time the man who was with Giselle came out again and he was talking with M Dufour of the railway. He was angry with Dufour and told him he needed a secure train for the morning to take a precious package to Brussels. Dufour asked what the package was and the man said they had a precious caged bird up there they and were going to make it sing. Not down there, you see? In the cellars, but up there. So I think that Giselle is held in the upper cells. On the third floor."

His words fell into a room of thoughtful silence.

"Good work, Gregor," said Jack "Excellent. Brave too. Jerome, fill his glass."

Jerome obliged and winked at Gregor as he held out his glass.

"I told you my Gregor is a clever boy," said a beaming

Henri. He also took another glass in celebration.

Georgia inspected a grenade. It felt so light and insignificant in her hand, but she had seen its destructive powers. It was almost a thing of beauty. A treacherous beauty. She slipped a couple into her coat pocket and carried on with her inventory.

"That would seem to tie in with what I heard at the office," she said. "One of the secretaries was talking about a special train for a prisoner to go to Brussels. Mid-morning tomorrow. Top priority."

"Then it has to be done tonight," Jack said. "Or never."

He continued to stare at the building plans, hoping for inspiration, for a key.

"Courdan, tell me about the roof."

Courdan studied his papers.

"Terracotta interlock tiles over a waxed sheet membrane and wooden tile battens supported by roof beams."

"Flying attic?"

"No, the space was divided into storage rooms off a long landing back in the twenties. Not big enough for offices or accommodation. Stairs down to the fourth floor at the western end."

"Size of the storage rooms?"

"Four metres by three metres"

"The length of the landing?"

"Forty metres. The width of the building. Less the stairs of course.

"Of course. And what colour are the storage rooms?"

Courdan was momentarily taken aback. "Colour. Ah yes. I am not sure but I think they may be bamboo tan. There was a store of this paint the Germans requisitioned when they took over the building. I saw the invoices."

Jack laughed. He slapped Courdan on the back.

"I was joking about the colours Phillipe! But you knew!"

Courdan seemed to relax. He smiled warily and accepted another glass of wine from Jerome.

"I am happy to be of help," he said, "For Belgium and Liberation!" he drained his glass in one. It was quickly refilled.

"How do I get to the roof of the old police station?"

"Ah yes," Courdan said, "I looked at the plans and options when Monique called. I have studied and I think the only way is to go in through number twenty-four Rue Sur Ville, it is a private house at the other end of the street and the owners are away in Marseilles. It will be discreet. You can get up to the roof through the attic window and balcony. It is a short pull up onto the roof. Then you can make your way along the street rooftops to the old police station. There are eight rooves and a few parapet walls and chimneys, but the pathway is clear."

"They will have guards up there," Monique said.

"Yes," Courdan said, "but my boy says there is only one posted at a time and only over the police station, It is a small machine gun post on the roof. The guards are old men. It is cold up there and they sleep a lot."

"Your boy?"

"Alain and his friends like to find things out," Courdan said. "Most German soldiers are fathers away from home, they like to boast to children, like to talk. Some are not monsters. Alain and his friends just listen. And watch. And then tell me what they know. What they find out. Everyone fights in this war the way they can. I tell Alain to stay in the house but he is a young boy with a young boy's spirit and lust for adventure and he wants to help. So he plays in the streets and he listens and watches. What they find out, they tell to me and I tell it all to the Spider."

"Phillipe, you are a brave and true patriot!" Jack said,

Courdan flushed and tried to shrug off the compliment.

"I just do what is right. For Belgium. Many are like me and Alain also. And Gregor here too. Many little spiders. We work and fight to free our land of the Boche. However we can. In our small way. Whatever it might cost."

"Right," Jack said. "I go in through the roof. I go in alone and I go in tonight. Henri, I need a good pair of gloves, ten meters of three gauge rope, a small but powerful torch, pencil beam if you can, pliers, lever spike, rubber soled

270

shoes, size forty two, and a small flask of brandy and a knapsack to put them in. You can do this?"

Henri looked at Monique. She nodded.

"We can do this," said Henri, "but, Albert, I say as a friend, brandy is not good for climbing and heights. I would forget the brandy."

"It's not for me Henri, it's for Giselle,"

"Ah, yes I see, for sure. What about a pistol?"

"No, I have my commando knife. If it gets to a gunfight then I am already lost. The noise will bring every guard down on me and all hope of getting Giselle out will be gone. No, I need to do this silently. Just the knife."

Henri knocked his pipe on the crate and began filling it again.

"You know, Albert, that you cannot leave Giselle in there. You have to stop her talking. She knows too much, knows too many. If you can't get her out. There is no other way. You know this?"

"She is trained Henri, she won't talk."

"Ah, my friend, I know this," Henri said, "I have known Giselle but a few weeks, but I know that she is brave and strong and a great fighter. But even a lioness can be made to talk with the drugs. She will talk without knowing she is. You know this."

Jack shared a look with Georgia. Her face was pale and expressionless, but she nodded her understanding.

"I will make sure," Jack said, "one way or another. I will leave at midnight."

"I will come too," Henri said, "I can help you. I climb like a cat. I can guard the roof."

"Not this time, Henri. This is a one man job. I can't be worried about you as well as the Germans. But thanks. I couldn't wish to have a better man with me, but not this time. I do this alone."

***

Gregor was posted as guard on the street corner outside

271

number twenty-four Rue sur Ville, He could see all the streets about from this vantage point. He had a hat to wave at any sign of danger.

It took Jack no more than a minute to pick the lock of the front door of number twenty-four and he left Monique on guard in the hallway while he and Henri made their way up to the fourth floor and out onto the under-eave balcony. A crescent moon offered a subdued light behind grey, scudding clouds. It was dark enough to offer protection with just enough light to make out necessary hazards. Jack checked his knapsack and then climbed onto the balcony rail. Henri stood stiff to take Jack's weight on his shoulder. He grimaced under a sharp pain as Jack stepped onto him and pushed off and onto the roof.

The breezes blew chill on the roof and Jack laid low to get used to the light and to check the path ahead. The rooves of the Rue sur Ville stretched out in a rippling sea of terracotta tar with reefs of low parapet walls. The street looked a long way down. A couple of trucks drove past and several German soldiers stood in groups, smoking and laughing around a street brazier. Three staff cars waited parked on the street outside the old police station.

Jack moved slowly over the tiles, keeping as low and quiet as he could. The rubber shoes supplied by Monique gripped well. He rolled over two low parapet walls and then squatted behind a chimney stack and studied the way ahead. From the positioning of the brazier in the street below he could judge that he was two rooves away from the old police station. Ahead, in the dim light, he could make out the dark silhouette of the roof-top guard post. It was a nest of sandbags at the roof's edge just above a balcony. A machine gun on a tripod pointed to the heavens and he could just about make out the top of a helmet in the nest. He watched and listened for some minutes. Behind the distant sounds of the soldiers in the street and motorbikes, he heard the faint sound of low, rhythmic snores.

Jack moved quickly across the roof spaces and up to the ridge tiles and parapet wall of the old police station, whose storage rooms should be just below his feet. He counted the tiles down from the ridge and in from the wall, until the measure that Courdan had suggested was reached. Listening for the continuing snores, Jack set about levering up a roof tile. The first one took some time as Jack took care not to make any noise, but he soon discovered that the tiles levered up with surprising ease. He stacked them by the parapet wall and soon had opened up a large enough area of roof to be able to climb through. He cut the roofing sheet with his knife and exposed the roof battens beneath. Shining his torch into the darkness below he saw a small store room lined with boxes and shelves. The snoring was still sawing softly in the night airs. Jack trusted to luck and boldness and stamped hard down on the battens. Two snapped with a dull crack. Jack held his breath and listened. The snores sawed on, the chatter from the soldiers did not alter. Jack levered the battens back until they broke and soft stamped a couple more to break them and leave the hole large enough to drop though. He tied the rope around a chimney stack and dropped it down into the hole. He slid down into the dark.

The storage room was packed tight with boxes. Jack took a few moments to stack some as an escape climb ladder under the roof hole. Listening at the storeroom door and, hearing nothing, he made his way out.

A dim ceiling light offered the faintest illumination of an empty landing, but Jack could hear muffled voices on the floor below. Moving to the stairs, he crept down enough steps to be able to crouch low and reconnoitre the floor below. It was a dimly lit landing with two iron-barred cells occupying most of the area. Two doors either side of the cells led to office and guardroom spaces. There was a stove and kettle in the nearest of the rooms. A white-haired, overweight German guard sat reading a newspaper in a chair tilted back against the wall between the two cells. An unseen German guard was in the kitchen space and talking with the other guard about the roster times and the price of bread.

Jack waited several minutes. The guard in the kitchen

emerged onto the floor and made his way to the room at the far end of the landing. He was carrying a pillow and coffee mug and seemed to be settling for a sleep. He told the seated guard to stay alert and wake him in two hours and then went into the far room and closed the door. The remaining guard continued to read his paper on his slowly rocking chair. Within minutes the chair had come to rest on all four legs, the paper had been lowered and gentle snores sounded.

Jack moved quietly and quickly along the landing. The first cell was empty. The second held Hildy. She sat slumped on the floor in the corner of the cell, her back wedged at an awkward angle against the far wall. Her hair was ragged and her face was cut and bruised. One eye had almost disappeared under a small purple ball of bruise and her lips and nose had bled heavily. Her bloodied blouse was ripped, her skirt torn and she was barefoot. She appeared to be asleep or perhaps unconscious. She looked like a ragged and beaten doll cast to the corner rubbish. Jack could see small black spots spread along one leg. It took him a moment to realise that they were cigarette burns. He could feel his rage fire though him but he knew he had to keep his calm. All that mattered now was getting Hildy out.

The sound of a chair creaking to the side of him snatched his attention. The fat guard was waking from his doze and taking in the shaping vision of Jack as if not quite believing he was seeing him. It took a moment more for the guard to find focus and then recognition. The guard fumbled for his pistol holder, but Jack was quicker. He closed in on the chair, smothered any chance of the guard's cry of alarm with a firm, clamped hand over his mouth and, with a measured calm, slid his knife to his other hand and thrust it hard and deep under the guard's ribs. The guard grunted, wheezed and seemed to deflate on his chair. Jack held him and his chair up from crashing to the floor and made sure he was dead before settling the body back to rest in the chair. He pocketed the guard's pistol and searched the pockets for the keys and then tilted the chair and guard back to a rest against the wall and placed the newspaper over his face.

Jack opened the cell door and tried to wake Hildy, She groaned and moaned a little but did not open her eyes. At least she was still alive. Jack guessed she had been drugged. He picked her up and slung her over his shoulder. He was surprised how light she was, but knew it was probably due to the floods of adrenalin and anger that were coursing through him at that moment. He closed and locked the cell door and threw the keys inside. It was a tight and heavy squeeze up the stairs but he was soon at the base of the boxes and looking up into the hole in the roof and seeing clouds and stars. He tried to rouse Hildy again, but she was still out of it. Taking the rope he tied it under Hildy's arms and breasts and knotted it. He climbed up his box steps and checked the roof. The guard nest still snored and he could see the soldier's helmet against the top sandbag. Down in the street all was quiet. A light, gentle rain had begun to fall and the roof tiles sheened dark with slippery menace.

Jack braced his legs and feet and hauled Hildy up through the hole, pulling, hand under hand, until her shoulders were through. Lifting her under the shoulders, Jack pulled Hildy up and out and on top of him. He was breathing hard and he could feel his heart pounding. He lay with Hildy's face and hair on his neck and her weight pressing him hard into the tiles. She groaned. Jack lay a moment to catch his strength and let the light falling rain refresh his face. He rolled Hildy off him gently, undid the ropes and lifted her onto his shoulder once again. He had to get her off the roof and safe. He had got not more than ten paces before her heard the voice of the guard call out to him from behind. He turned to see the roof guard standing unsteadily on the tiles, trying to find a balance against the slope and pointing a pistol at him. He was a large man in a grey greatcoat and grey walrus moustache.

"Stop now or I shoot. Both of you," said the guard. "You are my prisoners. Put the lady down. Now. Do it or I shoot you both. Or I shoot you and the lady goes over the side and into the street. Do it. Now"

"OK, I will put her down. Slowly. Alright?"

"No tricks. Or I will shoot. You are my prisoners. Both of you. I will get promotion for this. Maybe a medal."

Jack began to ease Hildy from his shoulder. The guard waved his pistol in irritation.

"Quickly please. No tricks. Then raise your hands."

"You said carefully, I am doing what you asked,"

The guard reached into his pocket and pulled out a whistle.

"Let us have some company up here on the roof, shall we?" The guard laughed. He put the whistle to his lips and then spluttered. The faintest of wheezed whistle sounded, like the last air escaping from a shrivelled wet balloon. A hand appeared and spread over the guard's mouth and nose and his eyes stared wide in confusion and alarm. As the guard sank slowly and silently to his knees Henri Clerque seemed to emerge from out of the back of the guard's coat. Henri gently cradled the dead guard down to a peaceful lie on the roof tiles, withdrew his knife from the guard's back and wiped it on his coat. He looked up and grinned at Jack.

"I told you I climb like a cat. I kill like one too. Giselle is alive?"

"Just about."

"That is good. Come, we get her off this roof and away from here."

There was a commotion down in the street. Soldiers were running and quick marching into the building and others jumping into trucks. Orders were being barked and motorbikes revving and a general alarm seemed to be gathering pace and noise.

"I think they know Giselle has escaped. We had better move fast, eh? Let us carry her between us. Monique has got a .truck waiting. We soon be far away from here. And we can enjoy that brandy, eh?"

THIRTY FOUR

Hildy took care in sliding off the bed. She didn't want to re-open the cuts on her back and legs again, nor did she want to wake Jack, who slept beside her on the large farm bed. Hildy managed to find and stand unsteadily on the floor and felt the burn of blood tear through her limbs. Her head floated around a throbbing ache and her jaw still felt like she was chewing on a sharp rock. At least the swelling at her eye had subsided, leaving a pool of purpling, tender pain on the side of her face. The heavy poultice on her left leg was stiff and she had to move slowly to avoid the stabs of knives at every step. She wondered who had dressed her. The skirt and blouse she had been wearing had been replaced with a pair of working trousers and a man's shirt and moth eaten pullover. She guessed her dresser was Mathilde and her wardrobe was borrowed from Henri.

Jack slept on. He was in his clothes, his overcoat a blanket. Hildy watched his chest slowly falling and rising, one booted foot on the floor, one arm thrown over his head as if trying to scratch his ear. He looked like he had slept as he had fallen. Hildy resisted the urge to kiss his cheek, she did not want to wake him. She took an overcoat off the door peg and wrapped it tight to her against the dawn chill. She made her way slowly down the farm stairs to the kitchen where Gregor slept, hugging his knees in an armchair by the still smouldering embers of the range. Hildy put a log on the range and crept out into the yard.

She had woken early from a night of strange and harrowing dreams, and could not get back to sleep. She was surprised, and happy, to find a fully clothed Jack snoring quietly beside her and it had taken some moments for her to remember and understand where she was. The smells of the farm dawn and the forlorn lowing of the cows in the barn had drawn her out of her troubled rest. She fed the yard chickens from the grain bucket and set about getting the three cows ready for milking. The low milking stool and the old electric motor suction pump proved something of a challenge but she managed to get everything, plugged in, switched on, attached and working and by stretching her leg our straight and leaning against the cow's flank she was able to perch with a degree of pain-free comfort and to get milk flowing into the bucket.

Hildy could almost feel she was back on her own farm. The thought of the faraway fields and woods and of Jip and of the top meadow in flower was almost overwhelming. She wondered if she would ever see them again. Even if she was lucky enough to do so, she knew she would not see them with the same innocent and naïve eye of her youth. She had been through too much, seen too much and lived too many times to ever hope to see her home farm in such simple beauty again. It had been a just a few short months, but the farm of her youth seemed a lifetime ago. Perhaps if she wasn't to make it back it wouldn't be too great a loss, she would still have the purity of its memory. This new Hildy and this new life of hers might not last very much longer, but they certainly felt exciting, vital and alive, more alive than she had ever hoped to dream. And this new life had Jack in it. She could ask for little more.

"You should be resting."

Hildy turned to see Jack standing in the doorway of the barn. He was still half asleep and his hair awry and uncombed.

"The cows needed milking. And I've rested enough. What day is it?"

"God knows. Monday maybe? You have been out for two days. Where's Gregor?"

"Asleep in the kitchen. Leave him, he's had a busy time. He must be tired. And I don't mind. It is good for my rehabilitation and recovery. Takes my mind off things."

Jack pulled an upturned bucket to a seat beside her and sat down.

"You farmers keep such mad hours. It's still night for god's sake! So how does this thing work then?"

Hildy went through the basics of cow milking. She

allowed Jack to try milking the second cow.

"Hey, look!" said Jack, "Its working. The milk's flowing. I did it!"

"The cow's doing it," laughed Hildy, "you're just holding the bucket."

"Bucket holding is pretty vital to whole process I would have thought. No café au lait without the bucket holder. How are you feeling?" Jack took two cigarettes from his pack and lit them. He passed one to Hildy.

"I'm fine, Jack, really. I am walking and the aches are fading. Really I'm OK"

They smoked in the barn and watched the bucket gradually fill with milk.

"They were going to take me to Brussels in the morning," said Hildy, "To the Gestapo headquarters. Is that why you came for me? To stop me from talking? Maybe to kill me? It would have been right. There was no other choice. But you needn't have risked it you know. I had already decided to kill myself, you see? I had worked it out. Not to talk or give anyone away. I could never do that. Never live with myself if I did that. But we know they have drugs. I was going to tie my blouse and hang myself from the roof beam before I had the chance to betray anyone. I had decided that. But they came and wouldn't leave me alone and tied me down and I could do nothing after the needles. "

Hildy shivered at the memory. She stroked the black scorches on her leg as if to try and wipe them away.

Jack turned to look at Hildy. She was bruised, cut and bedraggled but he thought he had never seen her quite as lovely as she was then. He reached out and took her hand and just held it for the connection it gave.

"Yes. If I couldn't have saved you, I would have killed you," he said. " Quick and clean. We both know that it would have been for the best. But if I couldn't have saved you then I wouldn't be able to save myself either. So I would die with you. I would make our deaths quick and hope that all the stories of an afterlife are true. Then you can take the time to teach me how to milk goats."

Hildy laughed.

"But, you see, I knew I could save you," Jack, said "So I chose to do just that. The after life's goat's cheese lessons can wait a little longer."

"I am here, only thanks to you" said Hildy, "You know I can never ever thank you enough for what you did, don't you? I know I'm only here and alive and milking these cows because of you. Henri told me all about it. What you did. You were incredibly brave. And such a true friend. I can never, ever repay you."

"Henri is a good man and a fine friend, but he is a damn blabbermouth. It was him as well. And Monique and Gregor. It wasn't just me."

"You killed the prison guard and carried me out over the rooves. Was I much trouble?"

"You were out of it. Drugged."

"Was I very heavy?"

"As a bull."

Hildy laughed and then immediately winced as her lip cracked in pain.

"I need to contact London," she said.

"Already done. You've been out of it so I radioed in. Report has gone in and all received. They are looking to bring us out. Back to England. In the next few days."

"And Georgia?"

"Georgia too. We need to co-ordinate a plan. London will be sending a couple of agents to replace us. It's getting too hot for us."

"London is right." They turned to see Monique standing in the barn doorway. She came in and leaned against the cow's flank. She took a cigarette from Jack.

"What a lovely cow," she patted its flank fondly, "It is good to see you up and about Giselle, but I must warn you, you have to stay inside. Both of you. I have come from Mons and the Germans are all over the city looking for the three British agents. Now they are in the villages and countryside also. I have never seen them in such anger.

They have posted big rewards for news of you. Patrols everywhere. That new Major has got everyone jumping and kicking down doors. They have shot six members of the resistance in the Grand Square. It is very dangerous. They are going crazy in search for you. You must stay here. Keep hidden. Gregor will bring you food. I will talk with L'Araignee and Henri. We will find a way to get you out. Then you will need to tell London, but until then you must stay hidden here."

But that afternoon Jack and Gregor had crept out to the old mill for Jack to make his call and report to London. The plan was for London to have a plane drop in to a landing strip in a field near Peronnes lex-Binche in four night's time. Jack packed away the radio and returned to the farmhouse.

The aromas of Mathilde's cooking stew and baking bread had been wafting the farm house airs all day and by the time Jack, Henri and Gregor had returned from milking and feeding the animals they were ravenous. Hildy, Fabrice and Monique joined them and the evening meal turned into a council of war.

"The Germans are intensifying their searches," said Monique. "It is not good to be caught out on the streets, so people are bolting themselves in their houses. The fear of betrayal and accusations means no one trusts anyone. The city is crazy. They know about Giselle and they say there are two other British agents. They talk of the Belgian Marianne and victory. The air is potent with revolution and uprising. The Germans are crazy for revenge and they hunt for the Marianne to make an example of her. They know one of the agents is you, Albert. You were with Giselle in the café. You were seen. The Germans try to beat it out of Jerome but he said nothing. He is badly hurt. The doctor says he may lose an eye."

"It will not be long before they come looking for me," said Henri. "Someone will talk. It is the way in war. Not everyone resists. Neighbours can become betrayers. Not everyone is strong. Survival breeds many cowards. It is the way of war."

They drank wine and ate the stew, wiping their plates with fresh baked bread and returning to the pot for more.

"I spoke with one of Jean Mac's women," said Fabrice, "she says Jean Mac and Cesar are planning to take some of the pressure off Mons. Wants us to help, for you to get in touch."

"What are they talking about?" said Henri.

"Setting up some sabotage hits in and around Charleroi and Tournai. Maybe the rail depot and power plant. Draw off troops from Mons. Take the pressure off a little. Diversion and scattering."

"It would be good for you to be away from the farm for a while, Henri, just for few days." said Monique. "They know you are here. And they must come for you sometime. If they take you it will endanger the resistance in the whole region. You must stay safe."

"I could not leave the farm, my family. The animals. I could not leave Albert and Giselle. It is impossible. It is cowardly."

"Go, Henri" Jack said, "it is a good idea to get you, Gregor and Mathilde away from here. Just for a few days until things quieten down. London is sending a plane for Giselle and me in four nights. We can lie low here until then. We are trained to it. You and the others have already done far too much for us, now it is time to look after yourselves. So go, Giselle and I will be fine here. Nothing cowardly about it. Don't talk so. You are too important to be taken by the Germans."

"But Giselle needs looking after," Mathilde said.

"I'm fine, Mathilde," Hildy said, "Really. Jack is right. He usually is. The Germans are bound to come here eventually. They may be monsters but they are not stupid. Someone will talk somewhere, or they will chance upon something and chase and close the trail. They will find their way here eventually and you can't be here when they do. We just need to hide out for a couple more days. The sabotage plan is a good one. It will take the minds and attention of the Germans away from Mons and this farm."

"I am not going to leave you," Gregor said, "You can't make me. You need me to help run the farm. Feed the chickens and milking. I won't leave. I refuse to leave."

"You must come with us," Mathilde said, "tell him Henri, tell your boy."

"Don't you see?" Gregor said, "We can't just abandon the farm. It will look too strange. The Germans will know something is not right. But if I am here they will not be suspicious. Papa and you are often away and I stay here to do the farm chores. I have to be here. I can make sure they do not find Giselle and Albert. They will not harm me, I am too young. So I stay."

Henri looked long at his son. He poured two glasses of wine and passed one to Gregor.

"He is no boy, Mathilde, he is a young man. And he is my son." He lifted his glass to Gregor and his son responded. They drank the win off in one. Henri wiped his mouth on the back of his hand and ripped another wedge of bread to his plate.

"Gregor is right, Mathilde," he said, "If the Germans come they are going to think it odd if the farm is deserted and all the family have gone. It will mark us as resistance as if we were caught with a grenade in our hand. I can be gone to market, you can be visiting friends, but we would have left someone here. We wouldn't abandon the farm. Gregor is a brave young man and a sensible one. He will not do anything stupid. Is that right son?"

"Yes, papa,"

"Then it is settled," said Henri. "I will go to Cesar. He has a cave in the hills. Very secret, very comfortable. We can use it as our operations base. Mathilde can go to visit with Veronique and help her look after her old mother. She is bedridden and help is always welcome. We will keep in touch through Monique. Albert, Giselle, I will see you off to London in four nights. If I can. We will leave the farm early tomorrow. In the meantime, Fabrice open more wine."

Jack and Hildy lay on the old iron-framed bed. Through

the large bedroom window they watched the stars trace slow arcs across a cloudless night sky illuminated to an almost ghostly light by a gibbous moon. Despite their well-fed and wined fatigue, sleep eluded them both.

"It feels like this terrible, wonderful fairy tale is almost coming to an end," said Hildy, "all the evil princes dead, the land coming alive again, the quest ended. I don't know whether I feel glad or sad. It's all been so overwhelming, so horrible, so wonderful, so life changing. It is going to be hard to return to real life. It is almost over."

Jack raised himself onto his elbow.

"Talk like that again and I will push off this bed and throw you down the stairs, wounds or not," he said. "Even if you so much as think like that again. It is not over. It won't be over for us until we land back in England, and that is still a dangerously long way off. It is far from over. That kind of talk drops your guard, makes you lax and only brings trouble. Or even worse. It's not over for Henri and Gregor and Monique and all the others and it won't be until the Germans are dead, defeated and gone and the war finished. You are Giselle and you must be Giselle until will we are finally back in England. So stay focused."

"Your bedside manner needs a lot of work," said Hildy. "Can't a girl in pain dream a little? Even in the privacy of night?"

"No," said Jack lying back to the pillow, pulling his coat tighter for warmth, "not even a little. Dreams only get you dead. And I didn't carry you across half the rooftops of Mons in the rain for you die on me now."

"You must think of Dora and Ma and home, how else can you get through this awful nightmare?"

"By just thinking about you," said Jack. "and only you. And Georgia. And bastard Germans. And our mission. That's how,"

Hildy sat up against the headboard and tried to ease the ache in her shoulder and leg. She lit two cigarettes and handed one to Jack. But Jack was finally asleep.

She smoked both cigarettes watching the stars until the

faint eerie glows of the pre-dawn light crept at the window's corner. Jack was right. This nightmare fairy tale could not end for her yet. Getting back to Hildy Potts was still far away. She had to be the fairy tale Giselle for a while yet. The idea did not disappoint her half as much as she thought it should. Living in the nightmare fairy tale had its compensations. Prince Charming was still around. He slept on the bed beside her. She rather hoped he would never leave

THIRTY FIVE

"They're there again," Hildy said. Jack joined her at the window. "Over by the large ash trees, just down the farm lane. See?"

A young girl in an oversize, heavy coat and blue beret stood in the bushes by the side of the lane. A younger boy in a cap and jacket stood close beside her. The girl was perhaps eleven or twelve, the boy maybe nine or ten. They stood in silence watching the lane and the farm house. A light drizzle dripped in the trees and the air was chill under grey skies.

"Just local kids," Jack said. "Nothing to get concerned about. Where's Gregor?"

"He's over at the Chavelle's place trying to barter some fuel oil. Back soon."

It had been two days since Henri and Mathilde had left the farm and Jack and Hildy had been on heightened watch. It was wearying work. They slept and watched in rota and ate frugally on corn fritters, wine and eggs. Hildy was dozing in the chair by the range and Jack was watching by the kitchen window when Gregor came in through the back door. He was slightly out of breath from cycling and had a large knapsack on his back.

"I didn't see you coming," Jack said. Gregor grinned and began unloading the knapsack. He was wet from the rain and towelled his head with an old jumper.

"I have a secret, hidden track through the woods. It leads me to the back of the house. Some supplies from our good neighbours." He unpacked bread, cheeses, a pie and cold sausage and laid them on the table. "Hungry?"

Hildy rose and stretched her back.

"Ravenous," she said, "I expect our little guards are hungry too."

"Guards?" Gregor asked.

"A couple of kids have been hiding in the trees along the lane. Been there all morning."

Gregor strode out into the yard. He put his fingers in his mouth and whistled. The two children emerged from their hide and scampered across to Gregor and after a long, whispered conversation Gregor ushered them into the kitchen.

"This is Yvette and Georges," Gregor said, "they are sentinels. They have news of German searches."

Yvette stood dripping rain and warming herself by the range. She seemed older than her young years. She watched Giselle and Albert through wary, intelligent eyes of the deepest brown. She was tall, quiet and exuded a confidence she probably did not feel, Georges was younger, maybe ten. He stood open mouthed, watching Giselle as if not quite believing she was real.

Jack ladled two glasses of hot toddy that warmed on a pot hanging over the range, Yvette and Georges took them eagerly, cupping their hands on the warmth. "Sentinels?" Jack said.

Gregor shrugged. "They are my friends and classmates and their brothers and sisters. We children have an army too. They have been watching the roads and the Germans and reporting. All over. To give early warning where it is needed"

"And is it needed here?" Hildy asked.

Gregor nodded encouragement to Yvette,

"The Germans are now working their way through the villages outside Mons," Yvette said. "Around the compass. They have done north and most of east, now they are working west. House by house, farm by farm. They will be searching in the south tomorrow. The Germans could be here by tomorrow. We came to tell Gregor. To warn him."

"Thank you," Hildy said. "You are both very brave."

Georges continued to cradle and sip his toddy and stare at Hildy, his eyes bright with wonder.

"You are the Marianne?" he said. "My father says you are an angel, sent to protect us, Giselle, the Belgian Marianne. You killed the German soldiers with spit fire. You escaped their prison and flew away over the rooftops."

Yvette shook Georges gently by the shoulder. "Don't be so rude," she said, "I am sorry but my brother is a little in awe and his brains have been left in his socks. Do not worry, we will not betray you. We only come to tell Gregor. To warn. Now we must go."

Gregor spoke with his two sentinels outside in the yard before Yvette and Georges ran off down the lane. Gregor returned to the kitchen.

"I must contact London," Hildy said. "before the Germans come,"

"OK," Gregor said, "I will accompany you. But we do it now I think. There is no time to waste."

"What else did Yvette report?" Jack asked

"She says the Germans have guard patrols on every road, day and night. It will be impossible to move anywhere for a few days. They are getting angrier. They have executed three saboteurs outside the town hall. They threaten more."

"We have to try to get out," Jack said, "I cannot live on other people's lives, it's too much. We will run, get away from here, and take our chances."

"Then we will all have risked and given our lives for nothing," Gregor said, "We do not do all this for you Albert, or you Giselle, but for our Belgian Marianne. The spirit of our nation's fight and which has now appeared amongst us. It unifies us all. Fighting alongside us. You are both willing to die for your country or you would not be here. It is no different for us. We die for our country and our people, just like you. But also for our freedom. The Germans cannot be allowed to take you or the spirit of Marianne will die with you. We must keep the Marianne flame burning, for everyone. We must hide you until you can escape to England and then Marianne can return to us when we need her again."

"But they'll find us here," Hildy said, "Then they will kill you and Henri and the others too."

"They will not find you in the hole," Gregor said.

All eyes turned to the floor under the kitchen table.

"With food and water you can stay there for many hours.

Maybe two days. The Germans will not find you there. I will be around. It will be fine."

***

They came in the late morning. Gregor had been watching from the front yard while feeding the chickens and pigs. High up in the tall tree on the far ridge he saw a sentinel red flag waving from a small arm. He lifted and waved his cap as sign of message received and scattered the last of the corn to the yard before heading for the kitchen.

"They are coming," he said.

They lifted the table and packed the hole with the prepared food, water and blankets. A small flagon of brandy was added to beat the chill. Watching the lane from the window they saw a German convoy approaching slowly, the fumes of diesel shimmering the surrounding woods and scattering the birds to the clouds. A convoy of two troop trucks and an open half-track in the lead carrying the officers and a mounted machine gun. The officer standing tall in the half track was scanning the road and woods about through field binoculars. It was the major from the square. It was Georgia's husband.

Jack and Hildy climbed into the hole. It was deep enough for them to sit on the floor with the trap door of thick floorboards half a metre or so above their heads. Hildy settled on the blankets and tried to appear confident.

"Almost cosy," she said.

"It will not be for long," said Gregor. "And you will be able to hear everything going on in the kitchen. Now you must stay quiet."

Jack and Hildy sat as Gregor closed the trap door and the light in the hole dimmed to a pre-dawn haze as the large kitchen table covered them. They heard the dull clunk of the locking bolt being kicked secure.

The air was musty but plentiful and there was enough light seeping through the floorboards to enable them to see each other's silhouettes with reasonable clarity. Jack settled to a seat beside Hildy on the blanket. He took his pistol, checked the chamber and laid it on the floor beside them. He put his arm around Hildy and kissed her gently on the forehead.

"Nothing to do now but wait," he said.

"Jack, I want you to promise me something," Hildy said. Jack was silent. It was a silence of foreboding.

"If we are discovered, I want you to promise me that you will finish the job you were going to do at Rue Sur Ville. Don't let them take me. I couldn't face that again. I couldn't let everyone down. Better to finish it. Quickly, Here in this hole. Do you promise?"

"We won't be discovered. It won't happen."

"Promise, I mean it Jack. If you have any friendship for me, any love for me, you'd do it. Say it."

Jack pulled Hildy tighter to him. The night on the Rue sur Ville was here again. The choices equally stark and real. He knew he would have killed Hildy that night if they had been discovered. He would have shot her with the guard's pistol, and killed himself with his second bullet. Nothing had changed. Except that he now knew for certain that he did not want to live without Hildy in his world. And that now he would take the third bullet, not the second. The second he would reserve for the major.

"Promise," he said.

The distant roar of diesel engines became a deafening, vibrating rumble that seemed to pour like tar into the hole. Chickens clucked and scattered in alarm and the yard was full of the sounds of shouting soldiers and boots and outhouse doors being kicked open.

Down in their hole Jack and Hildy heard the farmhouse door break open to kicks and the floor above them thundered and drummed with running boots and sharp orders. They heard the major.

"You, boy, where is the farmer? Henri Clerque. Be quick boy."

"He is not here, sir,"

"Are you their son, Gregor is it?"

"Yes, sir."

"Where is your father?"

"He is gone over the market in Vanciennes. To sell some chickens."

"And they left you here alone?"

Heavy boots sounded down the stairs.

"No one upstairs, Herr Major."

"Yard and outhouses clear," said another voice.

"Corporal, find me a half-decent bottle of wine and get some coffee on the go. We will have to wait and make ourselves comfortable here for a while. It's been a log day. Tell the men they can brew-up, but no wine. I will shoot anyone who disobeys. Doze if they want but keep look-outs posted. Hide the trucks in the barn and keep the front yard clear. If Clerque returns I don't want him to see his farm full of soldiers. I don't want him scared away. Go."

Jack and Hildy traced the shadows of the major's footsteps as he wandered the kitchen. He kicked out a chair and they heard the thud of his boots coming to heeled rest on the kitchen table above them and the creak of the chair as the major rocked back. Jack could see the boots of a soldier standing look-out by the window. Another couple of soldiers were making coffee at the range or searching the back pantry for food and wine. The smell of cigarettes, sweat and damp cloth seeped into the hole.

"Come, stand in front of me, boy. How big is this farm, boy?" asked the major,

"Seventy acres, sir" said Gregor.

"That is not a farm, boy that is a cow pat. I have over a hundred thousand acres of land. That is a real farm. You can ride from dawn to dusk and not leave my land. What say you to that boy?"

"It must be very lonely, sir" Gregor said, "a long way from neighbours. And for checking the herds."

"The boy is a simpleton!" Laughter sounded from the other soldiers in the room. "But what can you expect, eh? A peasant boy in a peasant country."

"But the wine is passable, herr major." There was more

laughter and the sounds of glasses being filled.

"When does your father return, boy?"

"I don't know, sir. Maybe not until tonight. He is at the market, then has supplies to find"

"You mean he is in the bars and brothels. Feeding his bestial needs. Abandoning his honour and his family. Anything to keep away from this shit hole of a farm,"

The dutiful laughter rolled.

"You would tell me if you had seen any strangers about here, wouldn't you boy? You wouldn't be so stupid as to lie to me. You know what I do with liars. Don't you?"

"Yes, sir"

"Well?"

"I haven't seen any strangers sir,"

There was the sound of a sharp crack and of Gregor toppling onto the floor. Hildy felt the floor vibrate to the fall and saw Gregor's hand shadow across the floorboards for a moment and then was gone as he staggered back to his feet again.

"Don't lie to me boy. There are more strangers here about than you can count. Wars breed strangers like a corpse breeds maggots. So don't lie, boy"

"Truly, sir, I have seen no one. I have to look after the cows and the farm. I have to do my chores all day and do not leave the farm. I have seen no one until you arrived."

"Well, we need to see Clerque and we can't wait here for ever. Is that your bicycle in the yard? Good. Then you can cycle to the market and tell your father that if he is not back at this farm by dusk tonight I will burn his farm down. You understand?

"But, sir…"

Another crack sounded followed by a toppled fall. One of the soldiers added a kick that made Gregor gasp and then groan.

"There are no buts boy. Bring your father here or I burn the place down, slaughter his cows and treat my men to a feast. Go!"

Jack and Hildy heard the door being opened.

"It will take me three hours to get to market and bring my father back." Gregor said, "If I can find him. Maybe four. The roads are bad. I will bring him back. You won't burn the farm will you? I will be back. I promise."

"Dusk," said the major. "or whoosh!"

THIRTY SIX

By early afternoon the air in the hole was becoming stale and dusty and making breathing uncomfortable. Hildy's leg was cramping badly. It took many silent, cautious minutes for her to be able to move herself to a more comfortable position among the blankets. Jack massaged her calf and foot while they listened to the soldiers above them. Both were tired and fought the urge to simply lie back and let blissful sleep take them away from the here and now, but they knew it would mean death. Snores or dreaming grunts or night terrors would mean their discovery, and their end.

Major Baum kept up a steady stream of instructions and orders to his men and the floorboards drummed with hurrying boots and heel-clicked salutes. From the overheard orders and talk and the theatre of shadows played out above them Jack and Hildy knew that the truck and a number of troops had been sent on to the next farm, leaving a smaller contingent waiting for Henri Clerque's return. Jack estimated that there were a ten soldiers left on the farm, four in the kitchen, a couple on watch duty and a handful in the barn, probably sleeping or brewing up.

Jack was beginning to droop against the hole's damp walls when a soldier broke though the hubbub of the room.

"Herr Major! Someone is coming. Along the lane. It is a woman, on a bicycle. And what a woman, eh!"

Boot steps strode across the room.

"Give me those glasses," There was silence for a long moment

"It can't be," said the major, "not here. It simply can't be." There was further silence.

"It damn well is!" said the major. His voice became animated and urgent, almost excited. "Sergeant, tell the men in the barn to stay hidden until I say. You two at the windows, clear out upstairs and stay there. Franz, stay with me in and keep your pistol to hand. You never can tell."

"Is she dangerous, Herr major?" asked the sergeant.

"I'll say, Franz. That woman is my wife."

Jack and Hildy involuntarily jerked upright in the hole. They shared a look of alarm. "Georgia?" mouthed Hildy. Jack shrugged, and pulled his pistol to a grip in his hand.

"Stay back, Franz," said the major, "you can leave me to affect the introductions. My wife and I have a lot to catch up on."

***

Georgia had stood in a hide of trees and brambles watching the coming and goings at Henri's farm. She had seen Ernst pass by, standing in his sleek grey major's uniform like a triumphant Caesar, followed by his truck of troops. She had watched the soldiers search the farm and Gregor departing on his bicycle and a truck of troops head off to search other neighbouring farms. There had been no sign of Jack or Hildy, so they had either escaped or were hiding in Gregor's hole.

It was time to move, to get this thing done. Georgia checked her pockets and despatch bag, smoothed her hair and coat to presentable, retrieved her bicycle from the hedge and cycled slowly along the lane towards Henri's farm. She calculated that there were about ten soldiers remaining at the farm and as she broached the brow of the slight hill she saw a glimpse of soldier scurrying to hide himself away in the barn.

Georgia took her time and cycled slowly. She gorged on the moment and the pleasure of the fresh air and sunlight and the smell of the woods that were sweetly pungent after the recent rain. A pleasure made all the more intense and evocative and precious because she knew it was to be her last.

She rode as steadily as she could towards the farm yard and rested the bicycle against the large water butt. Mounting the steps to the front door she knocked and tried to exude a calmness she did not feel. The door was wrenched open and Ernst stood tall and defiant before her.

Georgia affected surprise

"Ernst! What are… Is it you?....It can't be. Is it…"

Ernst grinned.

"Well, well, my little GeeGee. Here is a turn up, eh?"

Ernst grabbed Georgia by the arm and pulled her into the room and kicked the door shut behind her. A sergeant stood leaning to the wall by the range, grinning. Another soldier was on a stool slicing mud off his boots with a long hunting knife.

"Gentleman, allow me to introduce my wife," Ernst said, "you are still my wife aren't you Georgia? A wife who deserted her husband. Stole his child. A beautiful bitch. An English bitch no less and that I once thought loved me, worshipped the ground at my feet. A treacherous English bitch. And here you are. In Belgium. An English spy. Walked right into my den. And we weren't even hunting you. Providence, eh? Or is it divine retribution? You were always a one for divinities, weren't you, Georgia? I don't think your Gods will save you now. I am going to take great pleasure in having you shot. Maybe even hang you."

"You have it all wrong Ernst, I am no English spy. I am working for the Germans. Just like you. For General Vogel. I work in the legal department. A legal secretary. Look…"

Georgia reached into her bag and was immediately stopped by the two soldiers pulling threatening rifles to bear. Georgia sought Ernst's OK. He nodded curtly. Georgia pulled out her card and passed it to Ernst, who snatched it, studied it and then flung it on the nearby sideboard.

"Why are you working for us, for Germany? You are English."

"Why not? Germany is going to win this was and I have no love of England. I haven't seen England since I was sixteen and England is the past. England died long ago. Germany is my future. I did not know that you were here, in Belgium. With the Germans. It is such a shock to see you. It is wonderful to see you again Ernst. I thought you might be dead."

"And I thought you had run away to England. With my baby. Yet here you are. What happened?"

"Our baby died, Ernst. I became ill. I wasn't thinking. Everything was collapsing on me. You remember that time. I had to get some space to breathe. My mind was all storm. I didn't know what I was doing. I became ill. I just ran. I don't know where to or how. On the boat. There was nothing that could be done. I was on a packet boat and they put me in a hospital in Italy. But the baby died and I was all alone. When the war broke out I was working for the German attaché in Rome. Now I work for General Vogel."

"Why have you changed your name? You are a spy. Your papers are false. Who is this Agnes Lundorf?"

"She was on the packet boat. We were cabin companions. She died of the fever and I took her name and papers when we landed in Rome. It is not easy to have an English name in Rome in thirty-nine. I had no wish to be English or to return there. The war makes names of little consequence or importance. So I became Agnes Lundorf and worked for the German attaché. I was reborn. A chance to start anew, It was easier that way. Georgia died many years ago. I am Agnes."

"What are you doing here, at his farm?"

"I've come to serve papers on Henri Clerque. It is my work with General Vogel. Clerque is summoned to appear at Rue Sue Ville. I have the papers"

She rummaged in her despatch bag and handed the major Clerque's papers. The major read them studiously and then handed them back. He stood watching his wife, weighing up the truths and doubts of this unexpected ghost from his former life.

"Clear the room, sergeant. Find somewhere else to perch. I wish to talk with my wife. Alone. We are not to be disturbed. Do you understand?"

"Yes, Herr major," the sergeant grinned and gathered up his boots and wine and gestured to the other soldier to follow him.

"Leave me the brandy," the major said.

Doors closed. Georgia and Ernst were alone. The major took two glasses down from the dresser and filled one with brandy. He drank it off in one.

"You ran away, GeeGee. From Me. Your husband."

"I didn't know what I was doing, Ernst. You have to understand that. Everything was so mixed up and confusing. You must remember that time? It was all such chaos and confusion and the war coming and the farm in trouble and the workers unhappy. I didn't understand what was happening, where I was going. And then that night Ernst, you were so angry, so savage. You hurt me so Ernst. It was brutal. You raped me. And in front of all the others. How could you do that?"

"You were out of control. You had to be taught the lessons of obedience."

"But I never disobeyed you Ernst. I was only ever true to you. Loyal to you."

"You took the blacks side against mine, stirred up unrest on the farm. Disobeyed my expressed wishes and commands. That couldn't be tolerated. You had to understand, to relearn to obey. You had to pay penance for your crimes. I did it because I loved you. You were becoming weak. I couldn't stand seeing you falling apart. Something had to be done. To save us. To save the farm."

Georgia tried not to look for the floorboards under the kitchen table, or to imagine Jack and Hildy crouched in the hole beneath. Perhaps they were not there, but had made their escape earlier. She couldn't be sure, so she moved over to the sideboard at the far wall. She poured two glasses of brandy.

"It was a hurtful love, Ernst, And in front of all your men like that. It was shattering."

The major grabbed Georgia's arm and pulled her to him.

"You were so beautiful GeeGee, I couldn't bear the thought of losing you. My love was all consuming. A hunter's love, driven by the chase and the thrill of the kill. I had to have you. It was in my blood, my passion. I was animal. Driven mad by desire."

"And now?" Georgia asked.

The major grunted. He downed the glass in one, and poured himself another.

"The years have passed. New passions arise. Like this war. Now, there is a mistress to really boil my animal blood. One who never let me down. Doesn't betray me. Or stopped loving me in return."

Georgia drank some brandy and felt its kick in her guts, warming her courage.

"I never stopped loving you, Ernst," she said. "Not ever,"

Ernst grinned. He pulled Georgia's head back by her hair. Her breasts pressed on him, her neck arched to his cradling hand.

"Lying bitch!" he said.

Georgia cupped her hand behind his head and pulled him down hard onto her kiss.

"A lying bitch in heat," she whispered.

Ernst pressed back, his lips locked on hers and his hand reaching up under her shirt, kneading her breast. Georgia began to unfasten his belt and buttons. Ernst laughed,

"Meet your dog, bitch," he said "Now tell me how much you love me."

Georgia reached into her coat pocket, felt the comforting swell of the grenade and then took Ernst's hand in hers.

"I love you Ernst," she said. "Always have. Always will. Here is my ring. A token of my undying love."

She slipped the ring onto Ernst's finger and gripped his hand in hers. She clamped her legs around Ernst and then enwrapped him with a bear's unyielding hug.

Ernst stopped nuzzling at her neck and looked down at his finger. The ring was thin and dull lustred, it looked like a ring pull.

"What ring is this?" he said.

Georgia looked up into his eyes,

"It's an eternity ring Ernst. It means we will always be together. For eternity. Perhaps we will see Phillipe and Jules there. You can say hello."

The light dawned on Ernst even as Georgia tightened her grip on him. His eyes widened in horror and he had trouble catching his breath for any words. Ernst tried to break free to beat her off but she had pinned his arms and was latched on to him like a locked coat. He bit and snarled and jerked, but could not break free. He cried out in panic.

"Get off!" Ernst screamed, "You're mad! Sergeant. Alarm. Get her off me. Sergeant shoot her! She is mad. Get her off!"

There was a sound of boots running down the stairs.

"For all eternity, Ernst."

A sun-bright lightning bolt exploded the air and a thunderous, raging storm of black, shrapnel-frenzied smoke blasted the world to an oblivion.

THIRTY SEVEN

The blast wave threw Jack back against the wall and he lost consciousness for a few moments. Hildy was hurled flat back against the blankets and lay there trying not to cough on the black, acrid smoke that deluged and swirled the hole. She could hear hard drops of fierce monsoon rain clattering the floorboards above and it took a moment to realise it was the patter of shattered crockery and glass and cutlery. Her head felt dull and cracked and everything sounded like it was happening far away at the bottom of a deep well. The black dusts dimmed and a grey light filtered back into the world.

Hildy slid over to Jack and covered his face with a blanket. He began to come round and Hildy cupped a gentle hand over his mouth to prevent him crying out. Jack blinked back into the world of dark grey and dust. He felt the back of his head. It was bleeding from a small but deep cut. Hildy warned him to silence. They listened to the chaos charging about in the room above them.

Soldiers were shouting and running. One could be heard retching. The swirling clouds of black smoke and smells of cordite began to fade, replaced by the smells of eviscerated flesh and scorched blood. The soldiers gradually began to calm to some order and down in the hole they could hear a frantic field-telephone conversation with the rest of the troop. The truck and other troops were called back to the farm.

Down in the hole they heard bodies being dragged out over them and soldiers came in with farm shovels to collect the rest of the body parts. Jack and Hildy listened to the scrape of the blades across the floorboards and just felt numbed. Hildy was trying to understand what Georgia had done, to come to terms with the fact that she had sacrificed herself, that her friend was no longer alive. All she could think of was the feel of Georgia's hand cradling hers on the fence rail at the farm. Hildy could not measure or shape the level of selfless courage that her friend had shown. Hildy felt the tears trickle her cheeks. She let them run.

Jack was surprised how unsurprised he was by Georgia's sacrifice. Somehow it had seemed like it was always going to be that way, to end that way. Ordained almost. There had been the devil in Georgia as well as the divine. Opposites that kept her apart from herself and perhaps a little distant from others. The beauty and the beast, always primed and dangerous, ready to detonate. A beautiful blond bomb. And such ultimate selfless courage and sacrifice as Jack could hardly fathom. He raised the brandy to the trapdoor and saluted his noble, fallen friend, and supped deep from the bottle.

From listening to the talk they understood that the major, his sergeant and the major's wife had all been killed. Another soldier had bad chest wounds that looked mortal. It was two hours before the soldiers had finished clearing up and regained some semblance of order. A corporal had taken charge of the platoon.

"Right," the corporal said, "we torch this farm and teach that bastard Clerque what it is to be playing with fire. We owe it to the major. Frankel and Brandorf, you stand guard out front until this pigsty is burnt to the dirt, then make your way back to the barracks. Rest of you, pack up and in the truck. Let's go."

Jack and Hildy heard the truck rumble away and the kitchen above them was silent for a long time. Then they heard the crackle of flame on wood and the faint woosh of curtains catching alight. Thin smoke hazes began to eddy in the hole. Jack put his back to the trap door and pushed up with all his strength. Hildy joined him, but the bolt and planks held. They tried again. And again. The trap door held. After all they had been through, and all the dangers they had faced, they were going to burn to death, trapped in a hole. Jack couldn't help but laugh at the idea.

"I told you it wouldn't be over till it's over," he said. "Not quite the end I had imagined though. Gregor did a fine job."

"Maybe the fire will burn over us," said Hildy, "and I don't think the smoke will get down in this hole much. It will rise. Won't it?"

Jack took a long draught of the brandy, and passed it to Hildy. She too drank deep.

"We can go flambé," said Jack. He grinned at Hildy. "Been quite a ride hasn't it?"

Hildy smiled.

"I wouldn't have missed it for anything," she said. "Mind you I would like to have been around long enough to see those bastards pay. To go out like Georgia. Dying with courage and taking a few with me. Not cowering and roasted in a rat hole. You still have the gun. You remember what we said Jack. What we agreed."

"It won't come to that, Hildy, there's always hope."

"It's getting warmer," Hildy said. She tried the trapdoor again. It held. "Maybe we can wait until the floorboards burn through, and then get out."

"The roof will have collapsed by then," Jack said. "And I will have shot you."

"That's all right then. As long as we understand each other."

They listened to crackling flames. Light from the fires began to brighten their hole. They sat gazing at each other.

"You look quite a sight," said Jack.

"I wouldn't rush to look in a mirror yourself, Jack."

The hole was now getting very hot, the haze thicker and more pungent. Jack ripped his shirt and made face masks for them both.

"If I don't make it," Hildy said, "I want you to know that I told Captain Townsend that Dora and Ma are to stay and live at the farm. Permanently I mean. Merchant has drawn up the paperwork and everything. All legal like. And you of course. If you make it. Just thought you'd like to know."

Jack leaned across, took Hildy's head in his hands and kissed her. It was a long, hot, brandy-scented kiss that Hildy would remember and cherish forever, because forever was now only a heartbeat away. Hildy took Jack's hand and placed the gun in it.

"Pretty much ready now, Jack. Just make it quick and clean. It has been my joy to know you." She turned her face to the wall and sought Georgia's courage.

Jack lifted the gun in his fist. It felt so light, so deadly. The sound of the fire was now beginning to roar. He checked the gun chamber and released the safety catch.

There was the distant sound of a crack. It sounded odd amongst the flames, a sound more remote. Then there was another crack. It was the sound of a gun. Or guns. Jack looked down at his pistol wondering if it had gone off by accident. But there it was and there was Hildy looking at him and listening, her eyes wide with curiosity and doubt. Then they heard the sound of wood crashing, and feet, small feet, running across the floor. A loud shotgun blast sounded so close to their ears that they gasped and recoiled. And when they looked up they saw the trap door rising slowly to a narrow gap and two pairs of young legs come to view. Then the face of young Georges peered down at them.

"Yvette says can you hurry out as she can't hold it much longer."

Jack rolled sideways out of the hole and lifted the trapdoor clear. Hildy followed. The kitchen was furnace hot and alive with flame, the windows, curtains and sideboard all afire. Hot gasses whined and hissed and black smoke was billowing in the roof spaces.

Hildy plucked a blanket from the hole and wrapped it around Georges, who was blackened by smoke and his jacket was smouldering. Jack pulled a blanket to enwrap Yvette, Her nose was bleeding hard and her legs scratched and blackened by soot, her coat was smouldering.

Jack and Hildy picked up their parcels and made for the flaming doorway and burst through it. They tripped over a prone body lying in the yard and tumbled down into the dirt. They dragged themselves across the yard to the hen house and sat against its wall, watching the fire devouring the front of the farm house.

"Is everyone Ok?" Jack asked. "Yvette? Georges?"

"Is the Marianne alright?" Georges asked. "Is she safe?"

"I am now, Georges, thanks to you and Yvette," Hildy said. "We owe you our lives."

"I think it is we who owe you a lot more," Yvette said. "We thought you might have died in Gregor's hole. We tried to unbolt the table but the metal was so hot. So we blasted it free with a shotgun."

"We thought we might be too late because we couldn't move because of the guards," Gregor said.

"What guards?" Jack said.

Yvette nodded toward two German soldiers who lay dead in the yard. One sat propped against a wooden post. Most of his face was missing. The other lay in the dirt outside the front door, the body they had tripped over. He had a hole in the side of his head.

Yvette pulled a pistol out from under her coat and held it out to Jack.

"You had better take this now, we are not supposed to have guns. Our father will be angry. But sometimes the anger is a smaller price to pay. Georges, give him yours."

"But Yv…."

"Do it, Georges. We are in enough trouble as it is."

Reluctantly Georges pulled out his pistol from under his jumper. It was an old pistol from the First War and looked like a cannon in his small hands.

"You killed the guards?" Hildy said. "The two of you?"

Yvette studied her shoes.

"Yes. But we had to. I was going to kill both of them but Georges said we had to do it together or they would be able to kill us. Or one of them would."

"But we didn't shoot them in the uniform. My father says it best to keep the uniform un-shot then they can be used again by us when we fight the Germans."

"Someone is coming," Jack said. Yvette and Georges hid their guns in their clothes.

On the brow of the rise a farm cart and horse team was being whipped along the lane towards the farm at great speed. The cart was followed by a dozen or so villagers who ran along in its wake. Other carts followed them. They could see Gregor on his bike pedalling hard.

"It is my father and the others," Yvette said. "I sent word to them. They have come to put the fire out and try to save M Clerque's farm."

The village firefighters poured into the yard and bucket lines quickly formed from the large water barrels in the cart to the fire. Others were dousing maverick flames with beating spades and flailing blankets. Gregor and others herded the cows and pigs from out of the barns and several women were stripping the dead soldiers of their uniforms, weapons, boots and underwear. The naked corpses were taken away in a cart.

A burly man in a leather jerkin and smoke blackened face presented himself to the small group who sat by the hen house, watching the firefighters gradually beat down the flames to smoke. The two children stood as the man approached. Jack raised himself to a lean against the house, his limbs stiff and aching. The man removed his hat and nodded curtly to Jack and Hildy. He looked down at Yvette and Georges who studied the dirt on their boots.

"It was timely," said the man. "We were almost too late, but I think it is well now. We can save the farm house now. Some repairs, but it is not lost. I am Georges. We will have to get you away from here, The Germans will come back. Get you somewhere safe. Henri knows about this. It will be fine."

Georges looked down the children. Yvette and Georges had moved closer together but still found fascination in their shoes.

"Little Michel came running to me," the older Georges said, "found me at work in the bakery. He had a message, from Yvette. I said this cannot be because Yvette is in school. Studying her lessons. But Michel was insistent. Our Marianne was burning in Clerque's farm and we must come and save her. With the fire carts. To the Clerque farm. To save our Marianne."

The father waited for his children to speak, but they said

nothing. Jack opened his mouth but Georges senior beckoned him to silence with a raised palm.

"So I run home. To get my guns. But my pistol is gone. And so is Grandpa Jean's old pistol. So I rush to save Clerque's farm. And here are my children. Blackened in smoke."

He reached out and took Yvette's hand and inspected it,

"And with burnt hands and legs. Not in lessons at all. Do you have my guns?"

Yvette nudged her brother and they both, slowly, removed the guns from the hides in their clothes. Their father took the guns. He smelt them.

"These have both been fired," he said.

Little Georges could take it no longer. He tried to stand tall and to look direct at his father.

"We had to papa! They were burning the farm and Marianne and the Englishman were inside. They would die. We had to."

"It was my idea," Yvette said, "I made Georges do it."

"No, you didn't," said her brother, indignantly, "We did it together. It would not have worked if we didn't do it together."

"We had no time," Yvette said. "When they set the farm alight we knew we had to do something."

"So you shot the two guards," said their father.

His children found diversion again in their boots.

"We had to," Yvette said.

"But we didn't spoil the uniforms!" her brother said.

"But how did you get so close to them?"

"Oh, I said we were looking for our dog. And I showed them my pictures of Max with his bone. "

"And I showed the other my catapult and he tried it with a pebble. And when Yvette shouted out Max, we both shot. Together. Only I was a bit late because the gun was so heavy and I had to use two hands to hold it."

"Then we ran into the farm and opened up Gregor's hole," Yvette said. "I had to use a shotgun because the bolt was stiff and too hot to touch."

Georges senior studied his children for some time.

"Yvette, Georges. Look at me when I am speaking to you."

Two young heads lifted and looked anxiously into their father's face.

"Never could a father be more proud of his children that I am of you both right now. Never have I known such courage and selfless disregard and bravery in ones so young. You do honour to me, our family and to Belgium. But you are also sneaky thieves playing truant. So you will now get yourselves back home where your frantic mother can tend to your burns and scratches and you can await my return. Then we can explore the merits and penance of extra lessons, and we can also discuss at length matters of moral guidance in respect of thieving and lying. Now go, and quickly."

Yvette turned to Jack and Hildy.

"We're glad that you are not dead."

"Our Marianne lives," said little Georges

Hildy stood up on shaky legs. She pulled little Georges and Yvette to her and enwrapped them.

"We owe you our lives," she said. "Such bravery! But you must now do as your father says and get on home. We will always remember you in our hearts. Now go!"

The children turned and walked away. As they reached the rise in the lane they began to run and jump imaginary mounds and ditches

The elder Georges turned to Jack and Hildy.

"This war is a hard school," he said. "What a world we pass our children, eh?"

"Yvette and Georges seem like very able pupils to me," Jack said, "They saved our lives. And the new world will have great need of their bravery and courage."

"And I dare say a little of their sneakiness also," Georges said. "For who are we to teach them our moralities, eh? Look where they have landed us." He laughed. "Now one of my men will take you in the cart up to Mafron's hut in the hills. Quickly, before the Germans come back. Mafron is a strange old goat but you will be safe until it is time for you to leave. Now hurry, the Germans might be back any time."

THIRTY EIGHT

Mafron's hut was a rambling collection of stone walls, iron-sheet roofs and tumble-down outhouses knotted together high on the slopes of grassland and forests above the valley.

Jack and Hildy were dropped off at the door of the remote hut and the cart had left abruptly, as if not wishing to linger any longer than necessary. There was no sign of Mafron. Three cows stood in the straw of a large shed which had a hay loft above. A kitchen area containing a large open fire pit, a large pig skin of water and sparse crockery, chairs and tables. Outside the back door a ramshackle sty of three huge pigs grunted in the yard and chickens pecked and skitted about the grounds. A large, scorched and empty oil drum served as some kind of brazier and a covered stone well stood in one corner of the yard. On the grassed hills above, below and about them sheep idly grazed.

Mafron did not appear until late afternoon. Jack saw him striding down the hill through the shin-high grasses with his rifle shouldered and leading an old mule and with two large, wolf dogs padding at his heels. Mafron entered his house and didn't appear to be surprised or at all curious at seeing two strangers standing awkward and on edge in his kitchen. His skin was leathered and weather-tanned, his frame stick-thin and he moved with surprising agility for one so old. Mafron studied Jack and Hildy for a moment through deep set, pale blue eyes and then hefted a dead rabbit and pheasant from his shoulder bag onto the table and placed his rifle in its hooks above the door.

"Eats," Mafron said, "needs gutting. See to the pigs." He went out in the yard and busied himself feeding the dogs, cows and pigs.

"Know how to skin those things?" Jack asked, "because I have no idea."

"Of course, I'm a farmer's daughter. Are we expected to make supper with this?"

"It would appear so. I'd better find something to start the

fire. Not exactly the Ritz is it?

"No, but it isn't a burning pit in the ground either."

"Very true. It suddenly has all the charms. I'll look for vegetables."

They passed the days at Mafron's hut and the routines and ambience did not change. Mafron uttered barely a dozen words a day and was content to keep the nights to silent rocking in his chair by the fire, or long dusk hours in his work shed where he banged and welded the farm machinery and tools back to shape or repair, or cleaning his knives and guns at the table by the light of an oil lamp with his dogs asleep at his boots. He would disappear every dawn with his rifle, dogs and old mule to shepherd his sheep on the hills and to hunt food in the upper forests. He returned in the late afternoon with his kill and a mule net of full water skins filled from some distant spring. Jack and Hildy prepared the meals from whatever he brought back. They slept in the hay loft above the cow shed. It was the warmest and most comfortable night's bed they had slept in since arriving in Belgium. They slept as logs.

In the late afternoon of the fourth day Hildy saw someone coming up the lower valley slopes towards the hut. The figure was steering a slow horse and cart. She called out to Jack. They watched the cart and distant figure make its slow way up the slopes and it was only when it had breasted the final rise that they saw it was Gregor. The cart carried two bicycles, two oil drums and a pile of turnips.

Gregor hitched the cart by the well and jumped down to accept the warm embraces and greetings of Jack and Hildy. Gregor fed his cart horses from two oat bags and then unloaded a skin of wine. They raised goblets to the reunion and shared the news.

"Monique says you are to go out tomorrow. I have come to take you. You must leave tonight. It is a landing place five kilometres away. A plane will come for you. It will be maybe two hours or three to get to the field. We have to go tonight. London has arranged it all."

"Do we go in the cart?"

"Yes. You will hide under a canvas of turnips. It is safer than walking or cycling. The Germans are everywhere. They are going crazy trying to find you. Many beatings and burnings. But they must not find you. It cannot happen."

"It can happen," Jack said. "It only takes someone to talk or to bend or to make a mistake. It can happen,"

"Not to our Marianne," Gregor said. "We will not let this ever happen. The Belgian Marianne must live. Or at least the spirit of Marianne has to live, to give us all hope and inspiration. That is why I have to ask for two favours from you. It is Monique, Cesar, Jerome and the others, they have asked me. To ask you."

"What favours?"

Gregor looked a little sheepish.

"It is difficult. You understand? But they are important. To us and to Mons and to Belgium. It is important that you live on, that Marianne lives on, even if you are not here. Important for the people here, in Belgium, fighting for our freedom. The idea of Marianne must carry on. You understand?"

"When we have returned to England, you mean?" Hildy asked.

"Or if we die in the attempt," Jack said.

"I said it is difficult," Gregor said, "I would not ask if it was not important."

"What favours?"

Gregor looked up and fixed them with a determined gaze. He seemed to steel himself to ask.

"To know your real names and to have a lock of the Marianne's hair. These are the two favours. Just tell me the names and we will remember. And we can honour you when we are finally free and this war is over. Mons can honour you. Is it too much?"

The small group was silent for some time.

Hildy reached into her coat and pulled out her knife. She took a fist of her hair, pulled it tight and cut through it. She handed the locks to a smiling and relieved Gregor, who pulled a metal tin from inside his jerkin and placed the locks inside the tin with careful reverence. He returned the tin to its jerkin pocket hide.

"M Martin, the stonemason, is repairing the cross in the Grand Square and we will put the locks of the Marianne inside a foundation stone. The Germans will not know, but all in Mons will know. It will be there forever and all the people of Mons will know it and they will be given courage and hope."

"I am to be a shrine?" Hildy said.

"It is important Giselle. Saints and martyrs have great power in times of war. These symbols help fight the Germans as much as any rifle." Gregor said.

"Jack Summers and Hildy Potts," Jack said.

"Thank you," said Gregor, "I have been so worried about asking these favours. All the way up the hill. I hoped the cart would never arrive."

"Put your hands up or we will shoot you dead!"

The voice barked at them. The group turned to see two German soldiers in soft-capped, ranger uniforms advancing through the rear of the yard, sighting their Mauser semi-automatic Karabiner rifles over the stunned group, and scanning the outbuildings for more.

"Do it, or die. The choice is yours."

Jack slowly raised his arms. He felt stupid and helpless. How could he have let this ambush happen? How had he been so crass and foolish? Now of all times. Just a day away from home. They must have followed Gregor, or perhaps they were just sweeping the hills and just happened to come upon them. Either way, Jack had dropped his guard and they had simply strolled up through the back yard and taken him by total surprise and with untroubled ease. He had failed. Maybe if they came close enough he might be able to overpower one. Hildy and Gregor could take the other. If they still lived.

Hildy felt herself melt in disappointment and anger. They had never seen the Germans coming, even on the open hillside. It was all going to end in this dismal place with the smell of England and home so tantalisingly close. She

313

raised her hands. At least she would go out with Jack. But poor, brave Gregor's end was weighing in her like a boulder.

"Who are you? What are you doing here? Answer quickly."

One soldier halted at a distance but kept his rifle on the group, the other advanced towards them. He was young, tall and athletic. He stood before Gregor and lifted his rifle butt as if to strike Gregor in the face. Gregor didn't move. The soldier raised his rifle higher.

"Answer boy, or I will stove in your head!"

The crack echoed across the hill and the soldier at the rear with the aimed rifle flipped up and backwards off the ground as if flung back by an unseen catapult. He fell on his back amid the yard muds and lay still, his hand still clutching his rifle. The young soldier, his arms and rifle still held aloft ready to strike Gregor, turned to check on his colleague and a second crack sounded. The young soldier jerked, grunted and fell onto his knees and slid slowly to the yard cobbles, one side of his head a bloody mass.

Jack and Hildy dived down and crouched behind the cart and dragged Gregor with them. They saw Mafron loping fast down the hill slopes towards the yard with his dogs at his heels and his rifle to hand. The rifle had a telescopic sight. A sniper's rifle. Mafron ignored Jack and Hildy and made for the soldiers. He cocked his rifle and shot each body in the chest and set about stripping them of their weapons, money, belts, boots and anything else that might be useful.

He threw straw into the oil drum brazier, doused it with some petrol and set it alight with a whoomph. He fed the uniforms and caps to the fire, then stripped the bodies of their underwear.

"Good rags," he grunted.

Jack moved forward as if to remonstrate with Mafron, but Gregor stepped in his way.

"It is best not to interfere," he whispered, "Mafron would not welcome it. And he can be very…" he seemed to search

314

for a word, "vengeful."

"Why?" Hildy asked

"My father tells me that Mafron was a fine hunter when he was young. Best shot in all of Hainaut. Then he went to the war. Something changed him in the war. No one knows what. He came home angry and a little crazy. He took to the hills to live alone. He does not like people. But he hates Germans. He really hates Germans. Best not interfere."

They watched Mafron hoist up each dead, naked soldier across his shoulder and then heft each of them down the stone well as if unloading corn sacks into a chute. He took the leather belts, boots and weapons to his workshop and returned with a grenade, which he unpinned and dropped down the well. There was a sound of distant booming thunder, and a billow of grey smoke and dusts belched up into the blue skies before drifting away on the breeze.

"Bastard Germans," said Mafron and strode to his workshop to begin working the newly acquired leather.

"When I was coming up here my father told me not to drink the water from Mafron's well," Gregor said. "Now I understand why."

THIRTY NINE

It was a slow, bone-shaking ride in the back of the cart. Jack and Hildy lay under a canvas smelling of wet straw and oil. On top of the canvas the turnips had been piled along with the bicycles. Two large oil drums had been loaded on from Mafron's store. The ride down the sheep-furrowed hill slopes was slow, precarious and painful but once they reached the levels of the metalled road in the valley floor the ride and going became a little more comfortable. In between geeing up and soothing the horses Gregor kept up a narrative of what was happening.

"Steady there, Bess. We are on the road to Quevy-le Petit. It is quiet. It is getting dusk now. Keep quiet and still. It will all be fine. Walk on Jenny."

Jack and Hildy lay facing one another under the canvas and turnips, each gazing at the other as if content to look nowhere else. The light was sepia-dim but offered enough to shape and image a cheek, an ear or nose, or give shine to lambent eyes locked on each other.

"German patrol coming. Two soldiers. Waving me down. Stay still. Whoa there girls!"

"Where are you going boy?"

"To my uncle in Blaregnies. To take him the turnips."

Under the canvas breaths were stilled and they followed the sound of footsteps as they circled the cart. The bicycles were shaken, a few turnips tossed.

"Late to be delivering turnips boy. Got your papers?"

"Yes, here,"

"Your uncle expecting you is he?"

"Yes. I bring the turnips and he trades me some flour and wire. We need to repair the power at the farm. The electricity went off. It blew our box. But we have no wire. So we trade turnips for wire."

"And the oil drums and bicycles?"

"I am to leave the oil and the cart and cycle back with the flour and wire. The other bicycle is part of the trade. Not

316

much trade value in turnips. But it is all we have."

"Not seen any strangers around? On the road?"

"No. Except you. And a soldier on a motorbike passed me about half an hour ago. That is all"

"Ok, on your way son. And be quick about it."

The cart moved on.

"It is all fine," Gregor whispered. "On Jenny, Good girl. They are behind us. Guarding the road. They are not moving. We have about three kilometres to go. I can see across to the Mons road and there is a lot of troop trucks and motor bikes. Gee Bess, get on. This is a quiet road and maybe they don't come here."

A half an hour later the cart stopped.

"OK, I think you can get out now," Gregor said.

Jack was surprised how far night had settled in. He checked his watch. It was getting on for nine. His bones ached from the ride and his blanket of turnips and he had to hold on to the side of the cart to get the feeling back in his legs. Hildy was undergoing similar exercise.

They had stopped some way below the brow of a long hill that stretched back down into the valley and showed the long, winding way they had come.

"Why have we stopped here/" Jack asked.

Gregor was staring intently back along the road.

"I think there is a truck coming this way," he said. "See there?"

He pointed to a dim set of twin lights away in the distance.

"Yes," Hildy said, "I see it. Troop truck?"

"I think so, yes," Gregor said. "See how the lights are set. It is not a farm truck or tractor. It is moving too fast."

Jack looked about them. Woods lined the road on each side. The brow of the hill was a few hundred metres above them.

"How far are we from the landing strip?" he asked.

"Over the hill and past these woods the land will become fields on that side. The landing strip is half a kilometre or so along after the woods stop. You will know the field because there will be a blue tractor in the gateway. The plane is landing in that field at midnight."

"Midnight?" Jack said, "I thought just before dawn."

"London brought it forward I understand. Monique knows. And L'Araignee. It is all arranged."

"But they can't land in the dark!" Hildy said. "In a field? It will be suicidal."

Gregor shrugged.

"As I say, it has been arranged. It will be fine I'm sure. I think you now have to go on by bicycle. It is not far."

"Why not just take the cart?" Hildy asked.

Gregor stared back down the road.

"The truck is following us and it will soon catch us. The cart is too slow. So we have to slow the truck down so you can carry on to the plane."

"How are we going to slow it down?" Jack asked.

"This hill will help. And the trees on each side of the road. Take the bicycles please."

Jack and Hildy lifted the bicycles from the cart. Gregor picked up the reins and moved the cart into the centre of the road. Then he climbed onto the cart and unscrewed the caps of the large oil drums and rim-rolled the drums towards the rear of the cart. He kicked them over so they lay at the back of the cart. A gush of dark, viscous oils splurged out onto the road, sluicing and spreading down the slope. Gregor walked the horses forward and applied the cart brake. Unhitching Bess and Jenny from their harness he led Jenny into the trees and tied her to a branch. Bess was led down the edge of the road and a rope tied to the side of the cart.

"Hey up, Bess, walk on!" The rope became taut and the horse pulled the cart over onto its side with ease, a small avalanche of turnips cascaded onto the roadway. The cart now lay on its side across the road, above a sheen of oil now bouldered by turnips

Gregor led Bess back up the hill to join Jack and Hildy. Back down the road they could see the lights of the truck now closer and winding the road on the lower slopes.

"You must go," Gregor said. "Now. You have to catch

318

your plane. We must say goodbye,"

"What about you?" Hildy asked, "You're not going to do anything stupid are you? You are getting away too?"

Gregor grinned.

"Yes, I ride the horses back to the farm through the woods. Like a cowboy, eh? It is night they will not see or find us. But you have to go. Please I beg you to leave."

Jack stepped forward and embraced Gregor.

"You are a true friend, Gregor. But be safe. We will only leave when we see you go."

Hildy hugged Gregor,

"Albert is right. You go now. And take our hearts and thanks with you. And look after my hair!"

Gregor swung up onto Bess's back. He walked her to Jess and unhitched her tie.

"It has been my honour to know you," he said, "I hope when Belgium is free once more I will see you both again. Until that day let us all be brave."

He turned with the horses and led them into the gloom of trees, and was gone.

Jack and Hildy looked back down the road. The night was now settling hard and the lights of the truck were closing in.

"Time to get pedalling," Hildy said.

The hill was too steep to ride, so they pushed their bikes to the top of the hill. It was a longer journey than it first appeared. Panting at the brow of the hill they looked back down the road to find the truck now speeding fast up the road towards them. Its engine was roaring against the effort of the climb but it was making good progress and its headlight beams were eating up the road before it.

"We might have to abandon the bikes and take to the woods," Jack said. "I don't think we can outride it."

Even as he spoke the truck engine changed from a roar to a sudden, high whine and the headlights weaved across the road. The truck was skidding on Gregor's oil slick. The truck lurched left and right and then skated sideways before coming to a crashing halt into a ditch at the road side.

Shouting and swearing soldiers jumped down from the back of the truck and an officer leapt from the cab barking orders.

Hildy and Jack didn't wait to witness the chaos but pedalled on and away into the night.

The going was easier along the flatter road and a shrouded moon gave enough light to travel by. Each field they past seemed vast and they were soon sweating with the effort.

The noise of the motorbike sounded clear in the still of the night and Jack could hear it coming up fast behind them. Looking back he saw the thin beam of headlamp, strobing its light fast against the trees. The motorbike was going to catch them. But it didn't have to catch Hildy.

Jack skidded his bike to a stop and let it fall in the road. He took out his pistol, checked the chamber and stood braced in the middle of the road, facing the oncoming motorbike. The motorbike leapt out of the dark behind a dazzle of headlights and high revving engine, speeding along the road towards him. With a sinking heart Jack saw their pursuers were a motorbike and sidecar. In the sidecar a soldier sat hunched behind a swivel-mounted machine gun.

The machine gun spat and screamed into life, tracer bullets slicing the night and exploding in fireworks about him. Jack stood steady and took aim on the driver, trying to ignore the machine gun as the road and airs sparked like fireworks all about him. Jack fired off two quick shots. The motorbike swerved momentarily but came on, the machine gun still clattering out its deadly spray.

Jack was aware of someone at his side. It was Hildy. Her pistol held double-fisted, her arms outstretched, her eyes fixed on the target screaming towards them. She gave a sudden cry of pain and her left hand dropped. She turned sideways, adjusted her stance and fired three one-handed shots that sounded almost as one.

The motorbike and sidecar jerked hard to one side, then to the other, and the front wheel seemed to turn in on and under itself and hurled the driver upwards from his seat. The motorbike and sidecar flipped up into the air, its wheels spinning at the heavens, and then fell back to the road with a crash of tearing metal and screaming engine. The machine gunner lay still under the wreckage, the driver lay dead in the road, his body bent back at a grotesque angle. The sudden silence was broken by a sound of hissing. A moment later there was a woomph, and the woods and road were illuminated by a sudden roar of bright flame that engulfed the wreck of the motorbike.

Jack turned to Hildy.

"You were supposed to get away,"

"I know. But alone away didn't seem that great a deal. Besides, you're a lousy shot. Brave, but lousy."

"Your hand, are you hurt?"

They inspected Hildy's hand in the dying light of the motorbike inferno. It looked like a bullet had gone clean through her hand, leaving a mess and a lot of blood behind. Jack ripped his shirt tail to a cloth and wrapped in around the hand.

"You OK to move?" Jack asked.

"Of course, But I won't be able to hold the handles to ride."

"Ever bike-hitched?" Jack asked.

Jack pedalled as steadily as the weight of Hildy on his handlebars would allow. Hildy perched awkwardly on the bar and held on to Jack's shoulder, trying to ignore the pain in her hand and watching back over Jack's shoulder at the road just travelled.

Hildy returned to a memory of the bike-hitch she had given Captain Rockingham. How long ago was that? It was more than a lifetime. How innocent she had been. And now here she was hitch riding in the dead of night with Jack in the middle of Belgium and the whole German army after them and looking to hunt them down and kill them. It was just all too crazy. She began to laugh.

"I don't see what's so funny," Jack wheezed, "I'm doing all the work here. Are you feeling OK? Not going to faint or anything?"

"No, don't think so. Can you hear that?"

The sound a distant engine rumbled through the night.

"I can see lights coming up behind," Hildy said.

"They must have got the truck past the oil." Jack said, "God, this damn field has got to be here somewhere."

"They're coming up behind us again Jack. I can see the truck lights." Hildy reached down and pulled Jack's pistol from his coat. "Keep pedalling. I can try to shoot the tyres, or something"

The truck now growled loud from the dark behind them. Only one set of headlights shone to the road ahead, the other had obviously succumbed when the truck crashed.

"I think our luck might have run out this time, Jack" said Hildy. She checked the chamber and settled the gun in her hand.

"It was bound to sooner or later. Enjoyed the ride though. Hitched with you. Seems a fine way to go."

"Wouldn't want to go out with anyone else," Hildy said.

She leant down, cupped Jack's chin in her good hand.

"Just keep pedalling", she said, and kissed Jack long and hard. "Now keep me steady and we'll go down like Georgia, eh? By the way. I love you."

Hildy rested her arm on Jack's shoulder and held the pistol as steady as she could. The truck loomed fast into view and the cab seemed to swell before her.

"Now you tell me!" Jack said.

Hildy leant down and kissed Jack again.

"Now be quiet," she said, "this girl's got work to do,"

Hildy sighted along her arm and fist to the cab now roaring just a hundred meters from them. It was going to ram them down. Hildy could see the driver and an officer through the windscreen, their faces relishing the hunt and anticipation of the moment of kill. Hildy moved her aim to the front tyre and re-sighted along her arm.

The truck exploded.

It simply exploded. It was there, and then it was just inferno. It seemed to disintegrate in a bright blossoming ball of flame that boomed from inside the truck and lifted it up off the road and enveloped it and sent it careering sideways into the ditch at the side of the road. The canvas roof was instantly alight and the night air full of grey smoke and screams and shrapnel and the pungent smell of cordite. Ghosted human torches danced wildly within the flames and tumbled into the road. Almost immediately the woods on either side of the truck erupted into a cacophonous clatter of machine gun and rifle fire and figures emerged from out of the trees to encircle the wreckage, killing the surviving soldiers staggering among the debris.

Jack and Hildy were hurled forward by the force of the blast, Jack instinctively wrapping his arms around Hildy and taking the weight of her and the bike's fall on top of him. He felt his head crack as they hit and then rolled to the side of the road, They lay in the ditch and looked back dazed to see the ambush erupt in its storm of gunfire and exploding grenades.

Jack and Hildy looked at each other. They both began to laugh. Jack took Hildy in his arms.

"That was one damn impressive shot!" he said.

"But I didn't fire a shot" Hildy said, laughing. "It must have been a grenade or mine"

Jack kissed her on the forehead and pulled her tighter to him. "I thought our luck was really done that time, Hildy. Maybe you are the Marianne after all. I should have more faith. By the way," he said, "I love you too. How's the hand?"

"Throbbing beautifully. Your head. It's bleeding."

"Just a bang from the fall in the road."

A figure emerged out of the woods. A familiar burly frame in a leather jerkin.

"I think you can catch your plane now, eh," said Henri. He sat down beside them and pulled out a bottle of brandy.

"I tell you I come to say goodbye if I can. And Henri is as good as his word, eh? I brought a few friend along to make sure you leave safely. Cesar, Fabrice and the others. They are all here. All say farewell. We give a good leaving party no?"

Henri drank from the bottle and passed it on. Hildy and Jack both drank deep.

"You are wounded Giselle?" said Henri, "It is bad? I have Jean with me, from Cesar's group, he is a doctor, or a vet maybe, he can see. Maybe help."

"It's nothing, Henri, really," Hildy said. "Fine, really." She poured a little brandy over her wound and refused to acknowledge the pain. She ripped a strip from her skirt, doused it in brandy and held it to Jack's head wound.

"We can't thank you enough, you know that don't you Henri?" Jack said. "We are only here because of you and Cesar and all the others. And Gregor deserves a medal all of his own. He has done you proud."

"The oil was his idea, and the hill. He worked it out. " said Henri, "He knew they would come looking for you. And Monique helped me with the ambush and landing. We all make what contribution we can. And one day Belgium will be free of the Germans and you and the Marianne will come visit us at the farm and we can have a proper feast with plenty of wine and brandy, eh? But now you have to catch the plane or it is all for nothing. So come, we go."

Henri walked with Jack and Hildy along the moonlit road. Behind them Henri's men were dousing the flames and clearing the ambush debris into the woods.

The field with the blue tractor in its gateway was just a short walk away. The field looked like any other, but figures ghosted at its hedges and sporadic lights of cigarettes danced the darkness like fireflies.

Henri smoked his pipe and waited calmly by the tractor. Hildy was beginning to feel a little faint and pressed into Jack for comfort and support. She took more brandy.

"I hear about Agnes," said Henri. "It is so sad. She was a very brave woman. A true patriot. That we could all be as brave and as true. We will not forget her. We will have a plaque at the farm. And in the Grand Square. Agnes will not be forgotten."

"Georgia Melrose," Hildy said. "That was her name. Georgia"

Henri nodded and continued to suck on his pipe.

"Georgia Melrose," he nodded," It will be done,"

They heard the low drone of a distant engine in a far sky and listened intently as its engine grew louder. Henri was watching the skies to the north-west and a far light flared briefly on a distant hill.

"The plane is coming in," said Henri, "We have no time for goodbyes. You must not look back or worry about us. We are fine. We are alive and we fight. As do you, eh?"

Hildy hugged Henri and kissed him on the cheek.

"And one for Gregor," she said and kissed him again.

Jack shook his hand and they embraced.

"Courage, Henri, we will be back. We will see the Germans dead and gone."

"It is all I live for my friend," said Henri, "That and the thought of seeing you again when the war is done. Now go. Do not look back. The plane comes in over there. Hear it? Yes."

Henri put fingers to his lips and gave a piercing whistle to the night. Almost immediately a runway of burning hay bales lit up a landing channel through the field. The drone of the plane engine changed as it banked in the sky to come in on its approach glide. The plane appeared over a far hedge as a dark silhouette against the flaming bales.

"It will keep its engine's running but it can only stay for a minute, no more."

The sound of gunfire sounded back down the road. Soon the night was alive with it.

"It is fine," said Henri, "my men are just dealing with a patrol checking on the fires. It is nothing. Now go. Go. And tell London we need more guns eh?""

Jack took Hildy be the arm and they began running across the field. They saw the plane come in low over the hedge and make a soft glide and gentle landing in the field and taxiing to an idling rest.

As they ran for the plane the gunfire still sounded. It seemed closer. The door of the small plane swung open

"All aboard for the Skylark!" bellowed a cheery voice.

"And make it fucking quick fellas. Long way home, the natives seem hostile and my dear old mother's waiting!"

Jack shoved Hildy in and tumbled in after her.

"Only two? I was to pick up three." The pilot sounded Australian. He wore a wide brimmed hat. An unlit roll-up dropped from his lip,

"No, only two." Jack said.

"Looks like you had quite a party," said the pilot. "You might need this," He flung over a first aid box."

"Now head down 'cos we aint't holding back the horses."

Jack pulled the door to. He fell back as the plane revved engines and began bouncing fast along the grass field. He felt his stomach lurch as the engines whined and the plane lifted to the air, gathered speed and banked away up into the night skies.

Hildy lay on the floor on her side, the cramped plane allowing little room for comfort. Jack got some bandages and lotion from the first-aid box and dressed Hildy's hand as best he could. Then he lay down beside her, swaddled her in his arms and joined her in deep sleep,

FORTY

From the balcony of the control tower Captain Townsend scanned the pre-dawn skies through his binoculars and, again, saw nothing but charcoal grey clouds. He had been searching the skies for half an hour and the airs were chill and the breeze stiffening. Merchant emerged up the stairs with a coffee. He handed it to Townsend.

"No contact yet?" said Townsend. The coffee was hot and welcome.

"Nothing since the location call. They'll be here soon. Probably got delayed by weather or something."

"The pilot definitely said only two?"

"That's how the radio girl heard it. Line was full of interference."

Merchant offered a cigarette which Townsend took. Merchant lit them both in a cupped hand. Out on the airfield the fuel trucks and mechanics were already about their work, A warm yellow glow lit from the far all-night workshops like a Santa's cave.

"God I hate this waiting," Townsend aid. "Worst part of the whole job. Waiting. Idling. I should be doing something."

"You are, sir. You are seeing your soldiers home. Reckon they deserve a bit of waiting."

Townsend grinned.

"You are quite right Merchant, damn selfish of me. And too damn moody to boot."

He lifted the binoculars again and failed to find the plane. It was another half hour before they heard the unmistakeable sound of a small plane engine, like a bee in an unseen and distant jar. It was a few minutes more of scanning binoculars before Merchant found it.

"There sir! Coming in over the water tower."

They ran down the steps and into the two waiting cars. The plane came in slow and steady on an even glide and touched down lightly at the far end of the runway. The two cars drove out to where the plane taxied to a stop.

Townsend ran to the plane as the pilot jumped down out of his cockpit. Merchant hobbled up to join Townsend.

"Two packages duly delivered," said the pilot breezily. "Sorry for the delay but we ran into a bunch of bastards over Cherbourg and had to dodge and hightail. Point me at the dunny mate, I'm in danger of camouflaging my pants."

Merchant pointed him to the latrine block and the pilot hurried away.

Townsend pulled the plane door open.

Jack and Hildy lay coiled together on the floor. Hildy's chest was covered in blood and Townsend felt himself ice at the thought that she was dead. But he soon saw that it was just Hildy's hand, it had bled and spread as she slept. Jack had an equally bloody cloth on the back of his head and his hair and shoulders were matted with blood.

Merchant leaned in and gently and deftly checked the wounds.

"They'll be fine, sir. Looks worse than it is. Soon have them to rights."

"It would seem that Georgia didn't make it." Townsend said.

"So it would seem, sir. Unless she was delayed. Shall I wake them?"

Merchant shook Hildy gently awake. She sat up slowly, blinked in the world about her and didn't seem to be making many connections.

"What is....where am I?" She gazed at Merchant. "I know you. Merchant isn't it? Am I dead? Where am I?"

"You are back in England, miss, Safe and sound now. This is England"

"Then I am in heaven," Hildy said. A pain in her hand made her look down at the bloody mess and it all seemed to come back to her and click into place.

"Jack!" she said. She turned to touch him, to try and pull him up, "Jack, come on we're home. Is Jack alright? He's alive isn't he?"

"Yes miss, he's fine, Really. Just a cut on the back of his

head. It's all alright."

Jack groaned and slowly opened his eyes. It took a moment to focus and to stop the world spinning but he found Townsend and Merchant, but most of all he found Hildy.

"We made it then," he said "I told you we would."

Hildy laughed and then winced as the pain in her hand shot like electricity up her arm.

Merchant reached in and helped guide Hildy to her feet.

"Come on miss, I am taking you to the medics and get your hand seen to. That's an order. Dare say a nice cup of tea might be welcome too."

"With two sugars," Hildy said.

"We might even stretch to three, miss, seeing as it's you."

Merchant escorted Hildy to his car, She sat in the passenger seat watching Jack slowly emerge from the plane and stand beside Townsend on unsteady legs, She watched Jack stretch upright and arch his back. He looked over at her, nodded and his face cracked open in a huge smile. He gave a thumbs up. Hildy blew him a kiss as Merchant whisked her away in the car.

Townsend gave Jack a cigarette. Jack lit it and drew in a deep lungful that he let jet to the dawn airs.

"You've had quite a trip Jack. Lots of fun I'm sure. The brass hats are purring in the section. You did a fine job. And Miss Potts."

"I wouldn't be here if it weren't for Hildy. And Georgia."

"Georgia, er, didn't come back with you," Townsend said.

Jack watched a Halifax bomber leave its hangar and make a slow crawl to the runway skirts where fuel trucks and mechanics saw to fuelling it and loading its bombs.

"No. She didn't make it. She had a family row to settle. I'll tell you about after I've slept for about a week."

"Of course, plenty of time for debriefing later. Let's get you to the medics and have that head seen to."

Jack sat beside Townsend in his car as they drove slowly over the airfield towards the welcoming lights of the mess and medical rooms.

"Colonel Amies is delighted with the Belgian project. Wants to meet you and Hildy as soon as. Thank you personally. He'll need to know your measurements. I'll see to that."

"Measurements?" Jack said.

"Yes, for a suit. Colonel Amies doesn't give medals or promotions. Not that you can get those anyway. But he does gives suits. Made to measure. From his tailor. You'll need one."

"Why?" asked Jack.

"Well you'll be doing the rounds with all the top brass over the next few weeks, they'll want to know all about your exploits. And it's best to be well dressed for these occasions, particularly for the one at Chartwell next week. You and Miss Potts are invited to tea, Winston will want all the details. He is quite thrilled with it all. Says we've finally lit the fire before the inferno comes. So you'll need a suit. I warn you it might come with yellow socks though."

"A suit will be useful,"

"That's fine,"

"Useful to get married in,"

Townsend turned to Jack.

"Anyone I know?"

"Giselle. I believe you know her."

"Indeed I believe I do. Quite a catch."

"I know so,"

"Do you have a date settled?"

"No,"

"Church?"

"No."

"Have you actually proposed?"

"It's an understanding."

"Based on what?"

"Making it back to England alive."

Townsend was silent for a while.

"Have you got a best man?"

"Not until you say yes,"

"Me? But I'm a bastard Jack, you said so yourself."

"True, but you're the only bastard I know. And you are responsible for introducing us. So you owe me. Well?"

"Well, it just so happens that I too have a smart new uniform. It needs an airing, So yes."

"Good," said Jack then let's go and tell my fiancé the good news and then we can find the biggest breakfast and sweetest mug of tea that's going."

THE END